HIGHSHIELD

BOOK I

RANDOLPH LALONDE

EBook ISBN: 978-1-988175-08-9

Print ISBN: 978-1-988175-09-6

This novel was originally published in serial format on www.patreon.com/randolphlalonde

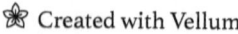 Created with Vellum

For everyone who sat at my table and rolled dice.

PROLOGUE

Brightwill and Highshield

Brightwill, the continent that carries the largest city in creation on its back boasts only a few forests, and too little farmland. Everyone, whether they are aware of where their food comes from or not, depends on colonies from the provinces across the Narrow Seas to the south and east. Most aren't aware of where the grain and meat come from, the city-continent of Brightwill is a busy place with many things to be concerned about.

Every King and Queen in Brightwill has colonies in other lands. Most of them rely on religious orders to rule in their stead when new lands are settled in their name. Every month ships carry new the poor, the unwelcome, the displaced, and the desperate to the New Provinces. They are put to work in the ports, the cities or more distant lands, where the Wild Woods are still being cleared and new farms are rising up past the Highshield Wall.

Highshield was founded nearly nine hundred eighty-nine years before the beginning of our story. It is the name given to the first large city on the Western Coast facing Brightwill across the Narrow Sea. Dragon Kind still ruled the new land where colonies were being established then, and Ava-Ondi, a smaller race that mastered magic, were in league with them in those days. Using magic, the efforts of dragons, and countless human slaves, a wall was built inland, called Highshield. The land between it and the shoreline would be enough to provide Brightwill with all its food and materials for a thousand years, and true to that prediction, it did just that.

Since the culling and taming of Dragons in Brightwill and the overthrow of Ondi rule during the Liberation War, the cities on the new shores have grown past the safety of the great wall protecting the early colonies, and new cities fight to exist in the wild green lands past it. The Pantheon Houses still serve the Monarchy, sending seven tenths of everything produced in the New Provinces to Brightwill, while hoping to be freed from their Kings and Queens by bringing their Gods back into the world. They use shrines to accomplish this, where followers are encouraged to leave offerings to their household deities.

The most prosperous Pantheon House is that of Miradu, boasting the largest following, the guardianship of the city named after the great wall, Highshield, and the greatest temples. It is said that their Gods have become so powerful that miracles happen, and that they have taken control of ancient sacred places far inland from the protected New Provinces. The Goddess, represented by a long, powerful black dragon coiled on a white flag with a shield to the right side, a sword to the left, and a staff below her, is rising and many believe her return to the mortal world is immanent. The few leaders in her faith who are allowed to read the prophetic tomes, the Mirac Alta, watch for evidence of the fulfillment of prophecy closely, eagerly anticipating the arrival of important figures that will mark the beginning of a new age. An age of justice and peace for the Miradu faith. One that would bring about the separation of the New Provinces from the tyrannical monarchies of Brightwill.

This is the story of the difficult to recognize Prophecy of Three that predicts: *Three warrior spirits will return with Her word. The hidden child will become one with three powers. Three betrayals will break the City.*

1

———

*I*t was a sunny morning in Highshield City. The clamor of carts, merchants and commoners was thick in the streets. Wind from the north brought relief from the suppressive heat as it howled through the many white and towering grey spires above.

A carriage with a carving of a great black dragon was rushing through Shaletown, and drivers were unmindful of the people who hurriedly retreated from the street ahead of it.

The hooves of the four horses drawing the long carriage pounded the street with urgency, their crushing weight clashing against the heavy paving stones. "Damrin! Would you slow down?" shouted a slender faced man as he leaned out of one of the front most windows.

The carriage driver looked over his shoulder. "I thought youse were hurryin?" he called back.

"Look out!" his passenger cried.

As quickly as the warning could be uttered, but much faster than the horses and their burden could be stopped, the beasts trampled a young boy in brown and faded blue clothes. Rendiran rushed from the carriage before it was fully stopped, his narrow face filled with concern.

"Tadrin!" shrieked a woman from one of the tall, narrow row

houses. She rushed down the narrow wooden stairs from the third floor, a tall man with broad shoulders right behind her.

"I'm afraid it's my fault, I distracted my driver here trying to tell him to slow down," Rendiran the priest said, paying no mind to his blue and white vestments as he crawled under the carriage to find the boy. He scraped elbows and knees rushing to the child's side, pulling his long cape off his back. "I surround you with the love of Miradu," he said, gently wrapping the small body in the white cloth he wore over his back. "Might of Irenick and fortitude of Viis maintain you."

The child was twisted in unnatural ways, blood pooled beneath him, and bone protruded from his leg, arm and right side where the trampling had caught him the worst. Somehow his face was untouched, his eyes were closed, but his unconsciousness was only a small mercy. His chest twitched and struggled to draw breath. "Mend him, Miradu, I call on you to heal his wounds."

Hot tears filled Rendiran's eyes as he felt the boy's spirit slip away. It was too late, all his power could do was mend the flesh, he had never successfully recalled a spirit. The sound of the child's weeping mother filled his ears as he wrapped the remains up in his once white cape. He was careful to hide all but the boy's face. Despite the violence of his death, the child's expression was peaceful, his blonde hair was almost completely free of blood. "I am so sorry," he whispered, backing out from under the carriage, dragging the bundle with him.

"Tadrin!" screeched the young woman as she saw her son. Her husband drew her into his arms, trying to shield her from the sight of their boy's body.

"I'm afraid he's..." Rendiran started to say, but he was interrupted by the sight of the commoners clinging to each other in their grief. The boy's mother was a blonde haired innocent with pointed ears, a descendant the Ondi-Ne, who once roamed and ruled the coastline when it was still wild and thickly forested. The boy's father was nearly two heads taller, broad and powerfully built. His calloused hands held his wife gently, and while his weeping may be silent, the tears spoke volumes.

"I felt his spirit pass," came the gentle, elderly voice of Umner the Dawn Shaper. He emerged from the carriage, his pristine black and white robes making him seem much larger than he was. His wrinkled face was surrounded by a mane of well dyed black hair. He peered into the still visage of the boy. "This child was a result of absolute love, I can feel the light he brought to the world fading, but it is not gone entirely."

He looked to the child's parents, gently guiding Rendiran, who still had the child in his arms, closer. A crowd was gathering. "What joy he must have brought to you both," Umner said quietly, touching the bundle and the shoulder of the boy's mother. "What was his name?"

"Tadrin," came the reply from his father in a rumbling voice. "Is there anything you can do?"

"If I told you there wasn't, what would you do?"

Tadrin's mother shuddered as she was overcome with a fresh wave of grief, hiding her face against her husband's chest. His father looked to his boy's face then back to Umner, but didn't offer a reply.

"You wouldn't blame my driver? The carriage? Anyone inside?"

"Horses couldn't stop in time. The fault is mine. He was watching me hang a new door on its hinges and I told him to keep from getting underfoot. He must have gotten bored, saw something across the street."

Everything about the large man was gentle, with the kind of dignity the best of people had. "I will do anything, sacrifice anything to have him back."

"No," Tadrin's mother said, looking up at her husband gripping his tunic. "Not anything. I want him to breathe again, but not if you sacrifice yourself. Sacrifice me, but I won't see you die."

"Don't worry," Umner said. "My Order would not accept the sacrifice of a father or mother for a son, we are not Lucents, there are no followers of the Bright One here." He looked at the child again. "I can only offer the arms of our Matron. She is near enough to this world to find his spirit if we draw her attention to it, but there will be a cost."

"We have no money or livestock. I'm an apprentice mason, we still depend on charity bread."

"Who do you worship?"

"Irenick, the Just," Tadrin's father said. "But we have not been to a shrine in weeks. We haven't had anything to offer."

"Do you think this is punishment?" Tadrin's mother asked.

"No, dear woman, he does not punish the faithful, even if your offerings are few. You are lucky, he's in Our Lady Miradu's Celestial House, Her first son, sitting to Her left side. Come to the temple, attend Her shrine. Rendiran's guilt will turn Her eye in your boy's direction. We will attempt a resurrection, though you must know that they are very rare."

"Anything to get him back," Tadrin's mother said, her lips quivering.

2

---

*J*adrin had never seen so many white and blue flowers in his short life. He recognized shrines, the arched wooden and stone fixtures set into stands throughout the garden. Gold, silver, blue and white flowers of all kinds were piled on most of them. On one of the shrines for Irenick, the patron spirit of his house, he could see the smooth blue and white river stones he had offered weeks before. It confused him, that shrine was in Amerano Square, near his home, not in a garden.

He shrugged his questions off after a moment and kept looking around. On one of the biggest shrines he saw a bird roasting on a spit, it was larger than he was. Much larger than any pigeon he'd seen on his family's dinner table.

The sounds of laughter and rhythmic clapping drifted up from somewhere down the path, and he rushed towards it. At a large shrine to Miradu that featured a fine statue of the black haired Goddess under the arch, he could see through to another place as though he were looking through a window. Behind the statue he could see revelers in white and dull red clothing, an old laughing Priestess who led the crowd in clapping for a newlywed couple who danced joyously. Flower petals were kicked up as a blonde woman and a crowned black haired man whirled and stepped to the rhythm. "He must be a King," Tadrin said as he beheld the rings on the clapping hands of the audience, and the grandeur of the blue and white painted hall they were in.

"Tadrin," he heard a deep voice beckon in a gentle tone from somewhere down the path. He had a feeling that he knew who it belonged to. Irenick, a God for knights and everyone who believed in justice and goodness, it could only be him.

There was a path leading up a hillock, and his mouth dropped open at the sight of a long dragon with dark blue and black scales. White and gold stripes ran from its powerful looking head and down its length. It moved so gracefully, curling into a coil at the top. "Please come and see me, I have heard spirits from the other side sing loving melodies for you. Their mourning is powerful."

A tall, heavily muscled man in blue and white plate armour joined him on the path and offered his hand. He had a shield on his left arm.

"Irenick!" Tadrin cried with excitement. "My father tells me stories about you every night at bedtime."

"I'm honoured to be so quickly recognized." He said, gently taking Tadrin's hand.

It felt as calloused and strong as his father's. "Is it true that you killed Ubnacron and all his dead things in the caves of Chirana?"

"It is," the paladin said with a smile. "Someone had to clear a path for the dwarves. It's important to remember that I didn't do it alone. My sister was there, and we had some good friends who risked just as much as I did."

"The Bear and Doro the Dwarf? Are they here too?" Tadrin asked.

"They take their ease just there, by the river until the next battle," he nodded in the direction of a great, winding river that led into a thick forest. Along it were several fine houses, a few were two stories tall, and on the porch of one he could see several people taking their ease in the gentle afternoon sun. One was sharpening a sword, while another was drinking from a tall mug, moving a game piece from one place to another on a table between them. He squinted enough to see

Doro, the beardless Dwarf as he nodded his satisfaction at his move before taking a long drink from his mug. "Deal with that while I get a refill."

"We should leave them to their relaxation," Irenick said. "We'll be off to battle again soon."

"There are battles here?" Tadrin asked.

"The Celestial Houses are at war, yes."

"Why?"

"Some Houses are envious of the peaceful realm our Goddess has made here, and we must defend it. Other Houses are led by dark gods, and they want to take the power we've been given by our followers."

Tadrin looked to the west and saw dark clouds in the distance over a shadowy forest that he felt was anything but empty. "Look away from that, Tadrin," Irenick said, gently guiding him. "I shouldn't have mentioned it. You won't have to worry about that unless you decide to join our ranks, and even then, it will be some time before you ride with us here."

"I wish my Dad were seeing this," Tadrin said. "He's been worshipping you all my life."

"I know, and you've been making offerings to me for a long time too, I have known you since your name day, when your father presented you in front of my shrine. I have been proud to call your family my people, and I would like to introduce you to my mother, Miradu."

He looked up the hill where he'd seen the dragon to find that the top was covered in dark glass, a long padded red seat adorned the middle and a beautiful woman lounged there. Her long black hair was her only adornment, and she was looking at a well-crafted but small shrine at the left side of the seat. "Your mother? I would be honoured," Tadrin said, trying to make the words sound as important as the paladin had moments before. Irenick chuckled softly and smiled down at him.

They made their way up the path and stopped to kneel at Miradu's feet. Irenick placed his shield on the ground, then carefully drew his long sword and laid it down on top of it. Tadrin lowered himself to one knee as well, bowing his head exactly as Irenick did. "I present Tadrin of Highshield City to you, mother. He has been a true believer of mine all his life, and celebrates our Pantheon every day."

"I have heard his mother, his father, and even one of my Priests," Miradu said, turning her attention to Tadrin. He wasn't looking up at her, but he could feel her eyes on him, warming him from the inside, it was a strange but comforting sensation. "You are truly young, a new soul that is pure and handsome. Rise and be heard, Tadrin of Highshield."

Tadrin got to his feet slowly and looked at Miradu, whose light gray eyes watched him closely. He didn't think he'd done anything wrong, but under such scrutiny he felt as though he might have. "It's good to meet you, Miradu, I love hearing about your son, he's a great House God."

She smiled a little, her blue lips stretching across sharp features. "He is a great warrior and still pure of heart. Your family has given their devotion to him even though he has never granted you a boon, do you know how important that is to a Spirit's House?"

"My mother taught me that if a Shrine Spirit is given enough offerings, and you live your life the way they'd want, they might come back and help the world. Sometimes they give boons, but that's not a good reason to make offerings," Tadrin said, hoping he was answering the question properly. "We want Irenick back in the world so he can help the weak and make the shadows safe. I live a life of honour because it's right though, not because he's watching." Tadrin looked to Irenick, who was still down on one knee. "Sorry, I don't do it just because you say it's good."

"You are an honest person, a trait my son admires," Miradu said. "I am indebted to him for bringing you to me. As his House rises, so does mine. Perhaps we'll both rise so high that we can return to your realm. Do you understand why you are here?"

Tadrin took a moment to look around at the endless garden and saw people there for the first time. How he could have missed the people clad in dark blue and bright white, he couldn't have guessed, but there were dozens of them around. Some of them watched shrines, others were taking precious stones and other offerings from them, while a few more wandered between the flowers. His eye was drawn to a woman who emerged from a stream, walking towards young ladies waiting to help her take her heavy white and blue plate armour off. "Viis," Tadrin said under his breath.

The armour was taken from her in layers, revealing minor wounds that some ladies laid their hands on. Strands of light looped from their fingertips through Viis' flesh, and her wounds were healed. Her muscular form glistened as several girls carefully dried her blonde hair and others approached to pat her skin with cloth. She was almost as powerfully built as his father, but still pretty like his mother was. Muscular men and women began emerging from the river behind her, their heavy armour was taken from them as healers got to work, starting with soldiers who had to be carried back. If he was seeing the heroes return from war with other shrine spirits and their followers, there could only be one answer to Miradu's question.

In a flash he remembered running across the street to visit Paulo, his best friend. "I forgot to look and listen," Tadrin said, realizing with quickly sinking spirits that something happened to him in the middle of the road. "I'm sorry."

"How it happened is not important now, but you are in the next realm, yes," Miradu said. "In my part of the realm, where we can keep you safe." She patted the seat beside her.

Tadrin joined her, hopping up and accepting her caring arm as it passed over his shoulders and drew him to her hip. "Dad's always telling me to look and listen before crossing the street."

"I know, he's a good father, but sometimes we forget, and at your age, that's nothing to feel too upset about," Miradu said. "Forget that for a moment. There's something more important to talk about. You know, people like your parents and you built this place for me, with their worship and their offerings. As more people follow the ways of my Celestial House, as more people offer what we need at our shrines, our power in this realm grows. We also get closer to where your family lives, and someday we may get so close that Irenick, Viis and some of their friends can start rejoining your world, to lead a crusade for peace and order. Someday I may even be able to go back, to roam the land and make it more fertile than ever. That means no one goes hungry, people happier and safer than ever. Until then, I can only do little things, grant small boons, occasionally give a Priest or Priestess the power to bring someone back from death. Do you understand?"

"I think so," Tadrin replied. He couldn't help but notice that she was cool to the touch, not like stone, but like he was sitting in a comfortingly chill breeze.

"All right, that is important for you to understand since you have a decision in front of you that will change the rest of your life. How old are you, Tadrin?"

"Seven harvests," he said proudly.

Miradu laughed lightly and nodded. "Very good. Would you believe that there are people here who are thousands of harvests old? They have lived many lives, and when they come here they remember everything that happened to them – both good and bad – but when they are alive they can only remember the life they are living? I can see you don't really understand, someday you will. Suffice it to say that you are only seven harvests old, your spirit, your light is very new, and that makes it much easier for me to send you back to your life, back into your body so you can be alive again."

"You can?" he asked, hopeful. The thought of never seeing his parents or friends again was starting to creep into his mind. That brought with it a kind of distress that was so powerful that it threatened to overtake him.

Miradu directed his attention to the grand shrine arch at the side of the long padded seat and he saw his mother, crying and kneeling there beside his father. A priest with a long face had his arms upraised, tears in his eyes, he spoke swiftly and passionately but the words were unclear. "Your parents miss you very much. Your mother didn't think she could have children. I heard her weeping one night when she thought your father was asleep, and I made certain that you began to grow inside her. When it came time for you to enter the world, and the Priestess feared that your mother would not survive, I guided you myself, and ensured that she survived and healed quickly. Irenick, Viis, and I have all celebrated how well you have grown, how your parents have raised you, and we don't want to see your life come to an end."

"I want to go back," Tadrin said, a tear rolling down his cheek, his head started to feel hot.

"I know you do, but understand, it will cost me more than you can imagine to send you back and mend your body. It's a cost someone will have to pay, and my son does not want me to take it from your mother and father. His shield raises against even me when he disapproves of an act, and I would not strike him down to have my way. No, you will have to pay the price. You'd have to become one of His Paladins and a paragon of justice if you were to be given life in that world again. You would serve him for the rest of your life, live his way, obey the leaders of the Eventide, the order started by Irenick and Viis, the greatest Paladins of all time. You won't be alone. There will be two more like you. One will bear Viis' shield, the other will be an example to you both. You will bring the Eventide's justice, guardianship, and champion their cause to protect the weak against dark forces. I'm afraid the Miradu Order in Highshield will remove you from your parents. They have practices that began after my death, so they will think it's the right thing to do. Rendiran will make sure that you aren't too far from them though, look to him for protection and guidance. He may be young, but his heart is good, and he will always want what is best for you and the pair you will come to know well. He will make sure that your parents don't go hungry, they will want for nothing thanks to the Miradu Temple."

"But I'll see my Mom?" he asked. "And my Dad?"

"Yes, you will."

"I would be honoured if you carried Irenick's banner back with you into the living world, Tadrin. Will you serve me?"

"Yes!" Tadrin cried out.

"There is something else you must hear," Miradu said, guiding him to look at her by putting her finger under his chin. "You can remain here. An innocent soul like yours in my garden will only make it more beautiful. Eventually you may even grow up, and join my children in their fight against the other Pantheon Houses. My son would be honoured to have you amongst his warriors and would train you himself. Think on it, training from Irenick the Hero himself."

"I want to go back," Tadrin said, wiping tears away. He didn't care that he might offend Irenick.

"You will serve Irenick and my House for the rest of your life and return here when you have given your life in that service. This is a choice you only get to make once."

3

"We lowly petitioners have made these offerings with the hope that your faithful son will be returned to us in good health. We pledge our living service to you, oh the holiest of House Spirits, Miradu. Miradu the wise, the just and the ruthless. We beg Irenick, your son, The Paladin of the Dawn to defend him on his journey and to draw your eye to judge Tadrin's plight. Tadrin of Shaletown, only just beginning this life," Rendiran stopped as he saw the body wrapped in his stained cape at the foot of the great shrine stir. "I thank and praise you for heeding us, please return him in good health."

"Oh my Goddess!" cried Lesta, Tadrin's mother. She reached towards the bundle containing her son. The blood stained cape was a harsh contrast against the bed of blue and white tulips. Harsh white light filled the large temple hall for a moment, and when they could see again, Tadrin was standing where he once lay, the flowers and copper pennies stacked beside the shrine were gone. Rendiran's cape was wrapped around him; the bloodstains were gone. The boy's hair had turned white. "I'm back, mommy," he said to her.

Lesta snatched him into her arms, and Nebrin, his father,

wrapped his arms around them both. Their son was alive and completely healed.

Rendiran noticed something strange about his cape as he finished offering his thanks. He picked up the cape and held it out in front of him. It was perfectly white again, and the fine cotton cloth had become a perfectly smooth material that was light and shimmery. The bloodstain had been drawn into the centre of the garment, reshaped into the detailed print of a man's hand. "Your son has been made an apprentice paladin, and he's been given his own sigil: the Crimson Hand. He will follow Irenick in praise of Miradu for the rest of his life." It was a statement that filled Rendiran with awe, but at the same time sadness. He knew there would be sorrow for the young family, and he couldn't help but feel responsible.

4

*R*endiran, the first priest Tadrin saw after he was reborn had been very kind to him. He watched on that first day of new life as the tall, narrow faced priest of Miradu argued in whispers with others who were covered in fine robes and bedecked with jewelry. Tadrin's parents tried to hide it from him, but he could see how busy the awkward looking priest was, and eventually he heard enough of the arguing to learn that Rendiran was fighting to keep Tadrin and his parents together.

"He is too young to be on his own, and too young to be shuffled off to train in arms or be tutored from the altar," Rindiran was overheard saying. "I agree that he shouldn't be sent back to Shaletown, but there must be a compromise that doesn't involve separating this family."

"He is a servant like any of us now, all of his time must be spent either learning our ways or holding a shield, no matter how small that shield may be," Tadrin heard a man with a gold ring around his head say. "He is Her first miracle, and other Pantheons will be looking to capture him so they can sacrifice him to their own Gods."

He was drawn away by his mother then, but he'd heard enough to know that he might be in danger, and hearing that Rendiran was fighting to keep him and his parents together was encouraging, but he was certain it would fail. Miradu herself had told him it would be so, it was a part of the payment he owed her for being able to see them at all, for being alive.

The day was glorious regardless of the fighting in the background. In the middle of the white and black stone temple was a great garden, so large that Tadrin couldn't see the walls around it through the trees. He played hide and seek with his father, picked fruit from his shoulders for his family's lunch, and when he was filled with peaches and apples, he accompanied his mother on a walk as his father took some time to give thanks at the shrine of his God, Irenick and the Goddess that ruled his Pantheon, Miradu.

The sun shone through the high branches, a little cool drizzle falling on them as he quietly walked with his mother, hand in hand. "You had fun this afternoon?" she asked him.

"I don't think I've ever had this much fun," Tadrin replied, looking up at her for a moment. He could see she was sad, but she tried to hide it, flashing a smile at him. "Did you?" he asked.

"Watching your father and you? Of course," she laughed. "I spoke to Priest Rendiran. I think he'll make a wonderful guardian for you, and a great teacher."

Without warning, tears filled Tadrin's eyes. "I want you and father..." he couldn't finish, it felt as though his throat were closing.

His mother knelt down and took him into her arms. In her tight embrace he could feel her crying softly, but her tears didn't flow for long. "We must be strong," she told him, gently wiping his tears, then hers away with the hem of the soft white robe the priests had given her. "We will see each other again, I know it. These people, they'll teach you things you'd never know if you stayed with us. They'll teach you to be strong, and how to use that strength for the good of the people. That is Irenick's way, he is the Guardian, and that's what you'll be."

"I know, I just wish you could stay," he replied with a sniffle.

"You're going to go on a marvelous journey far from this smelly city. You'll see things your father and I never will, and when you return we'll be waiting. Don't worry about us in the meantime, the Miradu Temple keeps its promises, and they've promised to take care of us. We are fortunate to have been in Highshield, it's ruled by a good Celestial House, I'm lucky I found your father and learned to believe in Irenick."

"I know, Miradu promised me they would help you, and that I wouldn't be alone," Tadrin said.

"There will be servants and guardians around you all the time," his mother agreed.

"No, they're sending two more guardians like me. One is my age, and I know her. I can't explain how, but I already know what she looks like, and that she's Viis' champion here, but somehow getting her to us is harder."

"Are these things Irenick told you?"

"No, I just know them. Like how I can see her face, she had black hair, like Miradu, but she's only seven, like me, and she's very nice. So are her parents, but they all died in a fire when Miradu's enemies attacked her village. She's the only one coming back, though. Her hair will be white like mine."

"That sounds almost like something from the old legends, the kind of thing your Grandfather would tell stories about. I'm glad you won't be alone," Lesta said. "Are you sure this other guardian isn't from a dream?"

"No," Tadrin said, shaking his head. "I know all about it."

"Then I'm glad. I hope I get to meet your friend soon."

"You will," Tadrin said. "I can't wait." The cool drizzle had stopped, and a shaft of sunlight blinded him for a moment. "Did you always pray to Irenick and Miradu?"

His mother smiled at him in a way that she never had before, as though she had a secret, and a good one. He'd seen that smile before on his friend, Ilsa's face, when she stole a whole plum pie from her aunt and wanted to share it with him and Lannerin, a friend. Both of the children were older than he was by a few years, and he didn't realize the pie was stolen until his belly was full, his hands were caked with its innards and evidence was on his cheeks. Thanks to his tender youth, he was absolved from blame, but Ilsa and Lannerin weren't allowed to play for a week. He hoped the secret his mother was hiding was as good as that pie.

"I wanted to wait until you were older before I told you. Your grandfather was a wonderful Ondi-Ne man, a Man Who Wandered. He lived nowhere and everywhere. He brought me and your grandmother everywhere as he traded anything he could make money on, and for a while I saw things my mother's way; I wanted to settle down in one place and call it home. Now, as I remember him before he went away, I recall seeing so much of the world, and he'd have such stories to tell me about every place. He knew the world and, well, he was very charming. I see some of him in you, especially when you think you're getting away with something." Lesta sat down with her back against a large ash tree – everything seemed large compared to her – and he took a seat in her lap. "I used to ask him to tell me the same story over and over again, and it's a good thing too, because I'll never forget it. Would you like to hear?"

"Yes," he replied. Tadrin loved to hear Grandpa's stories.

"Well, he was a young man when all this happened, so try to imagine that. He was a man not much taller than me with golden-silver hair and much pointier ears. The Ondi were vanishing from the world, some settling here in these lands, while others used their magic to escape to places that I'll probably never know. Many were being hunted down and killed by Kings and Queens who feared them because they thought they may take control of the land again. Do you remember what I told you about the Liberation War?"

"It's why we're here, far from Brightwill where people with pointed ears can be free," Tadrin said. There were other things, he knew, but that was the important part. They were safe in Highshield.

"That's right. Back then, some parts of Brightwill were safe and others weren't. Your Grandfather, Duhin was a sailor who would climb high up to the crow's nest and watch the seas for passing ships, land, foul weather, and anything else that may come. He would swing and run around in the rigging like he was a squirrel in a tree, something I saw with my own eyes more than once when we were travelling as traders. The Lovely Tide, a trading ship he served aboard pulled into harbor the day before the Knights of Amru took control of the city with the blessing of the King. Until then it was safe there, Ondi-Ne were like anyone else, but the Knights of Amru serve Xanis, a God that believes that the Ondi-Ne corrupt the natural order by having too much control over nature, so they were imprisoning them wherever they were found."

"Where were you?"

"I wouldn't be born for a long time, this is when my father was only ten or twelve years older than you are now, during his first wandering days."

"Okay," Tadrin said.

"Your Grandfather realized he had to get out of Hennen Hall, the city the Knights of Amru took control of, so he and a few friends pooled all their money and bought a small sloop, a tiny sailing ship, and slipped away from the dock as the sun was setting. They thought they were safe, but then a patrolling ship spotted them, and even with wind magic, they could not outrun their pursuers. One had a gift for controlling fire and he tried to set the galleon's – a galleon is a large ship with tall masts and big sails – anyway, he tried to set their sails on fire, but he only managed to burn one and the galleon had many more. The Sun Song, that was the galleon's name, chased them for hours, and everyone on the sloop knew that they would be caught. So, using a few bedrolls and sacks they made dummies that looked a little like them, enough to fool someone in the darkness, and got off the boat. They clung to a barrel quietly, using a little magic to conceal themselves."

"Why didn't they just hide their sloop?"

"They didn't have enough magic for that, because even a sloop is still boat sized, much larger than seven Ondi-Ne clinging to a barrel."

"Okay," Tadrin said.

"Okay," Lesta replied, smiling at him and tapping him on the nose gently. "The crew of the Sun Song smashed the boat with heavy stones. Your grandfather and his friends could only watch it sink as the galleon disappeared over the horizon. The water was cold that night, and some of your Grandfather's friends were weak because they hadn't had time or money to find something to eat before they tried to escape. Your Grandfather, Duhin, looked to the sky and was humbled by the sight of so many stars. He could see pools of coloured light behind them, and several streaking overhead as Gods made their journeys from one sky realm to another. He began to pray to the Goddess of his grandmother: Niami. She is the sleeper from who all Ondi came. She lived in the darkness until she found the light of our sun and followed it into our realm. All the while she had twenty-one children in her belly, all of them Ondi, and when she found Brightwill, she saw it was a good place. She had already lived in the darkness as a hopeful young girl for a long time then. Her grown years were spent exploring this world. As she neared her crone age, she finally met humans. They needed the help her children would bring using their magic and knowledge of all the things humans hadn't yet discovered. The Ava-Ondi would teach them about the sky, and the spirit realms. The Ondi-Ne would teach them about the forest, the water, and all the lands. The Ondi-Un would teach them about the mountains the secrets hidden deep inside.

Humans didn't have language then, but Niami would make sure she taught her children to speak, and how to find their own wisdom. The Ondi-Ne were the only ones who remained long after the others left, reluctant to leave their mother, so she taught them to be kind above all else, seeing that not all her children had taken that lesson on. Then, when she knew the Ondi-Ne had truly learned the lesson of kindness, that it always comes first, and that fighting comes last, she took her rest. She was very old by then, and her slumber very deep. Many of her first daughters and sons became Gods themselves, most of whom are forgotten because the dragons and the Gods of men have been fighting them for so long, but your Grandfather remembered Niami and the names of all twenty-one of her children. He named them all in his prayer before breaking a law his Grandmother taught him: to not wake Niami the Sleeper. He prayed; "I feel my fingers slipping, but even still I thank you for all your children, and for bringing us here, where I've had an exciting life. A life so thrilling that I pray that this is not my time to join you in your dreams, but that we can have more adventures here."

"If Niami wakes, everyone in her dreams fall out, Ondi-Ne won't have a place to go when they die," Tadrin said, repeating everything he knew about Niami the Sleeper. "Then again, maybe that's not true anymore? I don't think I was in Niami's dream."

"That may not be where we go when we die, but your Grandfather's friends thought it was. Most of them were angry with him. They believed they were near the end, that their strength would soon fail and they would drown one after another. If his prayer woke the Sleeper, not only would their ancestors be sent out to wander as her dream faded, but their spirits wouldn't have a place to go either. As they were berating him, and arguing amongst themselves, one of them said; 'Oi! I see land!' None of them believed, but after a moment of looking, they did, and it seemed to be getting closer. Before anyone could slip off that barrel and drown, your Grandfather's feet struck something, and the stony ground rose until he and all his friends were out of the water."

"Parono!" Tadrin cried.

"It was," Lesta laughed. "The Great Turtle was there to save them, and they ate from the trees on his back for two days before they found themselves close enough to real land to swim to shore. It brought them to the northern most point of Highshield, where they were able to safely find work and live for several years with the dwarves. Your Grandfather became a trader and began wandering again when things settled down in Brightwill. Whenever he told me this story he would say; 'We can trust very few people in this life, and the sharper our minds are the better off we'll be, so don't trust a God, no matter how old or how great, to save you. But, there's no shame in reaching skyward for a little help, or thanking the Gods for all the things they've done, even if you don't know exactly what that is.' My mother never believed that story, but I did."

"How did Grandpa and Grandma meet?"

"I'll tell you that story when you're a little older."

"Aw," Tadrin said.

"Sooner than you think," Lesta said. "For now, I want you to remember to be like your Grandfather. He was curious, and he always watched and learned from everything around him. He was the first to tell me to be wary of humans, not all of them are like your Grandmother, or your Father. Many of them tend to be greedy, or bent towards a purpose so much that they forget everything else. Follow the way of Irenick and Viis, the commandments of their house are a good code to live by, but remember to learn everything you can. Learn who to trust by their actions, and not by what you're told. You are very young for these lessons, but they're important. Do you understand?"

"I do," Tadrin told his mother before hugging her tightly. She embraced him until his father returned with five priests. It was time for his parents to leave.

5

*T*adrin picked at his plate that evening. He dined beside Rendiran at a short table in rooms set only just above most buildings in Highshield. As he began to get used to the polished white stone ceilings, walls and floors and the gold scrollwork on them, he realized that there was something strange about the sounds drifting up from the market below. It took him half the meal to realize that the clangs, the calling of booth minders and buzz of people were at a great distance from where he sat. Through the open window he could see more sky that city, and the air felt clearer, cleaner.

"Boy, I asked you a question," Gomal, a slightly portly man who always wore thick, rough looking blue and brown robes asked him from across the table. "Did your God, Irenick, tell you anything about atonement while you were there?"

"I don't think so," Tadrin answered, looking to Rendiran first. He didn't feel hungry, but shoved a baked peach slice into his mouth. The food was better than he'd ever had, but his appetite wasn't rising to the occasion.

"I'm surprised, considering where you come from. Did you know that we rescue more discarded children and beaten wives from the district where you were born than anywhere else in the city?"

"That's simply not true," Rendiran replied as though Gomal had said something funny. "There are a few places worse than the Shaletown. There are many good people there, most of them are struggling. We need to establish them in the country, where our lands are expanding and there's plenty of work, even more food. It's that simple. Get them to a place filled with opportunity."

"This, again," Gomal said, throwing his hands up. "We can control the inner city, at least track how many are coming and going, but the country is too open. Someone could leave for Shavi and we wouldn't know for years."

"We should concentrate on spreading the bounty of Miradu so people don't feel they need to leave for more prosperous lands rather than track their comings and goings. You know my mind on this, there are more people coming to Highshield every day. Even more will come now, the congestion will only get worse."

Gomal looked to Tadrin then back to Rendiran. "They come already. An audience of mourners and petitioners gather on our temple steps with the bodies of dead children in boxes and rags. If this keeps up, they'll start calling it the Wailing Stair."

"Are you finished eating?" Rendiran asked Tadrin.

Tadrin pushed his plate away, most of the lamb and greens still on it. "Yes."

"Then let's take a walk," Rendiran said, taking his hand gently and leading him out of the room. The causeway was raised above the city as well, and large openings along the sides let a breeze through.

"People are coming to the temple so you can bring their children back," Tadrin said. "Why is Gomal angry about it?"

"Gomal is the kind of man who weighs everyone based on how much they can offer Miradu and Her House." He picked Tadrin up and sat him up on a ledge where he could see the city below and feel the breeze. He was at Rendiran's eye level. "He is a good man, but he puts a lot of importance on where people come from and how many coins they have in their purse. What does Irenick tell us about that?"

Tadrin had heard that lesson so many times from his mother and father that he didn't have to think about it. "All are equal, life is sacred."

"What does that mean to you?"

"We should treat people right, be good to them, and if they're not good to us, we should leave them alone," Tadrin replied, recalling the lessons from many stories and discussions he had with his parents.

"What if we can't leave them alone? What if we have to work with someone who isn't being good to us, or is making us do things we don't think are right?" Rendiran asked.

Tadrin thought for a long moment, but he wasn't sure he had the answer his new guardian was looking for.

"I only want to know what your heart tells you," Rendiran said quietly. He touched his chest and smiled. "Answer without thinking, but try to tell me how you would feel if another boy or girl was being cruel to you, and you were cornered."

"I don't know," Tadrin said.

Rendiran smiled at him, it was a warm, approving expression. "These questions are complicated, even for people my age sometimes. I can only tell you that your God, Irenick, would have you fight only until you were free and no more. His Matron, Miradu, our Goddess, would suggest the same, but would be more pleased with you if you tricked your suppressor. She does not look down on violence, but appreciates cunning more than Irenick does."

"Okay," Tadrin said. "I'll try to remember. What about Wydu?"

Rendiran seemed surprised at the question, but not displeased. "Why, he's the greatest trickster of them all. He would probably turn the bullies against each other so he could teach them a lesson, which is wise in a way. It's important to remember that Wydu's ways are rarely our best first option. Irenick and Viis' ways are good for someone your age, resorting to reason, people's better instincts, and running away because you're too young to be a guardian, or to enforce justice. I'm wondering, did you see Wydu at all during your visit?"

"No," Tadrin said.

"Not so much as a man in the shadows? A boy with an old book in his hands? He's been known to make himself look like that, you know."

"He does?" Tadrin thought and couldn't recall seeing either. "No boys with old or new books."

"All right," Rendiran said. "I'll share that with a few people I know, they'll be interested to hear it. Thank you, Tadrin."

"Why wouldn't Wydu be there?" Tadrin asked. "He's Miradu's son too."

"They say Wydu doesn't always get along with his Mother because they are so alike, only he is sometimes cruel in his trickery, and She doesn't like that."

"How do you know? Did you die too?"

"No, we know from when they were alive. They were both great black dragons, but Wydu never grew as large as his mother and he envied her power. I'll teach you the history sometime, it's a good story with many lessons. Some of which I'm still learning."

"What's going to happen to me?"

"We haven't decided, but I would expect you'll be sent to the Citadel on Mount Nule."

"With the Paladins?" Tadrin asked, so excited that he almost couldn't stand it.

"That's right. The High Matron of my Order would like you to train as a knight and a paladin. It's going to be a lot of work, but I think you'll be a great paladin someday."

"I'll try," Tadrin said.

Rendiran took the boy on a tour of some of the innermost areas of the temple, which seemed to go on forever. It was a blur of rooms, fine sconces and smiling faces. Everyone he met wanted to smile at him, or gently touch the top of his head and render a blessing. Some were joyous, like; "Miradu be praised. The Guardian Irenick be praised. You are such a gift to us, child." Every dwarf he met said; "Three blessings to you!" before anything else. He didn't know what the blessings were, but they were all very pleased to offer them.

Some of the things people said to him were a little more ominous. "Protect the chosen one from our enemies, grant him the light he needs to see in this dark realm." But the one that Tadrin enjoyed came from three wrinkly old women who were delighted to see him more than anyone else. "Oh bless this boy, Goddess and her House. Viis give him strength, Irenick the will to protect the innocent, Wydu cunning and the ability to know when a little mischief is called for. Miradu guide his teachers so this boy becomes a man with all those things, but also a sense of humour, because he's going to need it."

Everyone around thought the blessing was hilarious, but Tadrin was sure he was missing something. "You'll understand soon enough," the shortest of the women said, gently patting his cheek before she shuffled off.

Of all the things in the temple, Tadrin liked the paintings the most. There was a story for each one, and when it was time for bed and he was shown to a room with five small feather beds inside, he asked to hear the story behind one that featured a tall knight in blackened plate armour. The image of that man holding his gleaming sword up by the hilt so it pointed down, climbing the last step to top a stony hill as though it were a great victory, was burned into his mind.

"That was Irenick's lost brother, Ire Kirk," Rendiran said from his bedside as he tucked him in. "I noticed that painting caught your eye. Miradu actually had many children while she was alive in this world. She enjoyed the company of humans and Ondi of all kinds when she took her smaller, two legged form."

"I saw her do that, change from a dragon into a woman."

"That must have been amazing," Rendiran said.

Tadrin shrugged. "So, why didn't all her children become Gods? Why didn't she take them all with her?"

"Irekirk and several of her children were called to other adventures. Irekirk was the one who founded this temple. He marked off a large area with roughhewn rope and began cutting stone. He was part Ondi, like you, and he attracted many of his own kind. Your father didn't tell you about Irekirk?"

"No," Tadrin said, yawning.

"He was a great knight, Irenick's older brother, in fact. He and Irenick served Miradu while she was alive in this world, defending her followers and ensuring that the lands she watched over were safe from things that shrink away from the light."

Tadrin's eyes grew heavy and he kicked his feet to stay awake.

"You've had a long day," Rendiran said.

"No, tell me what was happening in the painting," Tadrin said. "Please?"

"All right," Rendiran said. "Long ago there was a great dragon who was envious of Miradu. Her name was Odilexa, a green beast of the wild. Miradu's kingdom and her talent for getting along with people made Odilexa very jealous, and one day a follower of hers – a large bear – crept into her cave to tell her that Miradu had a brood. It was true, Miradu had laid eleven dragon eggs, her first brood after mating with a dragon of the deep. They would be powerful offspring, but so many baby dragons would need more food than Miradu normally had at hand, so she would have to hunt in other territories, Odilexa's included. Odilexa wasted no time, but ordered all the creatures in her wood to attack Miradu's villages so her guardians would have to defend them, leaving Miradu and her brood alone. It worked, and Odilexa gathered her children – six dragon kind of her own – and attacked Miradu's lair. She lost two of her own children in the fighting, grown dragons in their own right, but she managed to run Miradu off and shatter her eggs. Irekirk heard of this days later, and gathered his knights to set out on a crusade to slay Odilexa and her entire family of green dragons. Seeing Miradu's sadness, Irenick decided to remain behind to console and defend his mother. Miradu did not give Irekirk's crusade her blessing, because she was afraid to lose another son to the green dragons of the east. He pushed on anyway, and in four months killed all of Odilexa's children, but in the end he only had two companions left to face her with. They travelled through the thickest of the eastern forests, where light hadn't touched the ground in centuries, and tracked Odilexa to her lair. It is said that on the very day that our Goddess was poisoned and killed, Irekirk slew Odilexa, our worst enemy. The painting is a portrait of Irekirk on the day he learned that, despite his victory he'd lost everything. It was then that he decided to build this temple."

That was the last part of the story Tadrin heard before drifting off into a restful sleep in the softest bed he'd ever had.

TADRIN DREAMT. Irekirk finished adjusting the padding under the left forearm plate. His armour, though fine it was, had been a hindrance in the swamps of the far-east. The place had no name, no one knew these woods, so his people had started calling them the Creeping Woods. Moss, water, and life of all kinds surrounded them as much as the ancient trees in the thick marsh.

The bottoms of the trees hung over the water, creating the illusion that the thick trunks above were twisted arms with root fingers that dug into the water and soil beneath. "We press on, we're close," Irekirk said, making sure that the bag on his back with the lower half of his armour and the jerked deer meat they'd made the week before was secure.

"I'm done hunting once we finish in this place," said Doro, a stocky half dwarven knight who Irekirk had come to know during the crusade. "This searching about in marshes and lowlands is for foolish explorers, it's taken the taste for adventure right out of my mouth." He was a complainer, but a good man. "I'll find me a wife – any woman will do if she can cook and doesn't sound like a shrill bird when she's yellin' at me – and buy some land on a mountain where I can plough over here, and dig a hole for some iron over there," he said, sectioning off his imaginary settlement with his calloused hands.

"I'm sure you'll have a dozen children and build a great mining empire," said Challen, a woman of undetermined age who was half Ava-Ondi and Ondi-Ne. She was Irekirk's oldest friend, and the woman he loved more than any other. Her hair was brown and she was short, traits from her Ondi-Ne side. Her features were thin and delicate, showing her

Ava-Ondi half. Sometimes she seemed ancient, with a vast wealth of knowledge, but at others she was aloof and youthful. "I'll help you dig your first tunnel and harvest your first crop, but past that, who can say?"

"Maybe you'll put Irekirk out of his misery and join him in whatever castle he hangs the skull of our quarry on."

Irekirk couldn't help but shake his head. The time for that discussion was long past. He knew Challen would never accept a marriage proposal, she'd never share his bed either. "I won't be building any castles," Irekirk replied. "Not when there is so much left to build for Miradu's followers." He looked through the branches of the trees and caught a glimpse of open sky. "Are we still on her trail?"

"She was here recently," Challen said. "The essence trace is strong, Odilexa's den is close." She looked across the water, seeing traces of the dragon that was beyond her companion's sight. "This way." With a flick of her fingers, the three of them could walk on the water as though it were rippling sand.

"Today is the day we find that bitch and end her, at last," Doro said.

"Try not to become overconfident," Challen said with a sigh.

They made their way through the dark wood and Irekirk's unease grew as they made progress. By the time they arrived at the base of a large hill, he was sure there were eyes on him. "Something is wrong," he said, drawing his long sword. The keen blade glinted in the scant light.

"Her den is just here, it must be, but I sense magic is muted. I can wield it, but I can't sense any power but my own," Challen said.

"Follow me then," Doro said. "I'll read this mound of dirt like any dwarf can read any mountain. Except my cousin Kirden, he's shite at reading the stone. Couldn't find his way out of a pothole."

"Good thing he's not here, then," Challen replied. "Do you see an entrance?"

"Feel, more like," he replied, crashing through brush so loudly that Irekirk cringed. "Wait, the stone tells me there was something..." he stopped, gently pushing a few brambles aside. "Something unnatural here!" he retreated so quickly that he fell onto his back, but continued to scramble away from the mound as the old skeletal remains of three humans in heavy plate armour ripped free of the growth. Black moss and swamp sludge clung to their bones and the rusting armour. Gemstones shone red in their eye sockets as they closed in on Doro with spears in hand.

Irekirk wordlessly gathered the life energy around him, bending it to his purpose. With speed that would normally be beyond what his body could accomplish, and weight that was many times his own, he crashed into the nearest foe, sending the undead dragon hunter sideways into the one beside him. It was enough to save Doro, who managed to get to his feet and drop his pack on the ground. He hurriedly took his working hammer from where it hung on a loop then turned to face the skeletons. "The eyes, their eyes keep their spirits imprisoned in those corpses," he said.

A jet of flame descended on the one that had avoided being pushed over by Irekirk, but the fire barely scorched him. "They're too water logged for fire to do anything," Challen said.

Irekirk stepped away from the pair of undead that he'd knocked down, slashing at the slit in one of their helmets with his sword, his blade clashed against the old steel instead of hitting its mark. "Doro's right, the souls of these hunters are trapped in the gemstones, probably revenge for their attempt to hunt her."

"They got close," Doro said as he squared off with one of the armoured dead. "Poor lads."

"We should do what we did in Treston," Irekirk said.

"What?" Challen asked. "Well, if you think it'll work."

"Like Treston, right," Doro said. "What did we do there again?"

"You'll remember," Irekirk said. "Do it."

Challen raised her hands high in the air and closed her eyes. The sounds of rushing water filled Irekirk's ears as he deflected several of the dead dragon hunter's spear thrusts. The heads of the spears were in perfect condition, and he was so busy noticing that they were enchanted that he almost didn't get out of the way when a wave of water as tall as he was crashed into the three dragon hunters and Doro.

Before the undead hunters could recover, Irekirk leapt onto one and dug his dagger into its eye socket. For a moment he thought the thing's helmet would keep the gemstones secure, but then the first ruby dislodged and fell to the side, and the second came out even more easily. Doro, spitting a mouthful of swamp water and moss out as he recovered, was quick to bash the one skeleton without a helmet in the back of the head.

It was a good idea, thinking that a hard enough whack would knock at least one of the gemstones free of its eye sockets, but the head of the hammer crushed through the back of the thing's skull. Instead of relenting and changing his plan, Doro leapt onto the skeletal warrior's back and grabbed at the gemstones with one hand, while his other gripped the edge of the hunter's armour. "By Krezzt, he stinks!"

Irekirk was about to tell Doro to get off the warrior, who was turning and writhing, trying to dislodge the dwarf, when he managed to poke a gemstone loose from the thing's eye. It fell backwards onto him, the rotten contents of its skull spilling out along with his hammer, mostly into the dwarf's face.

Irekirk didn't have more than a fleeting moment to laugh, there was one more rotting dragon hunter to defeat, and he was already on his feet. Irekirk pushed the point of the thing's spear aside with his forearm plate and wove the forces of wind and stone into his free hand. The punch he landed bent the rotting hunter's helmet inward. A second powerful blow cracked his face shield in half, and he dug his fingers into the thing's eyes, scooping the gems free. "Now, to free them." He gathered all the rough ruby gemstones together and piled them on a bare rock. "Challen?"

She put her hand over them and immediately stepped back. "I can't dismiss these souls, the one who crafted these prisons was too powerful. They'll have to be broken."

"Doro, you'll have to use your hammer," Irekirk said.

"Can I finish washing old skull-innards from my face first?" he said, coughing.

"We don't know what'll happen if these gems are left unattached for long," Challen said.

"Fine," he said, gripping his hammer and smashing the first red stone to dust with a hard swing. "Shame these can't be purified, though. They'd buy three farms each once they were properly cut."

"I can feel their souls drifting free, moving on to the next realm, they have ancestors who have been waiting for a long time," Challen said.

"If nothing else is accomplished here, that was worth the whole journey," Irekirk added.

They entered the hill through a mossy opening barely large enough for Irekirk and found no further opposition or traps on their way through the rough tunnels. "The stone tells of a large cavern up ahead," Doro said. "Older than the moss and muck that this beast used to bury this place. It has a shaft that leads straight up, large enough for her to come and go from. Why couldn't we have come down through there?"

"Odilexa would have sensed us the moment we peeked over the edge," Irekirk replied.

"Like she doesn't already know we're coming? Don't get me wrong, the beast needs to be put down, but I think she'll be harder to take out than her whelps, even though they were the size of houses."

"I've been shielding us from her, she won't know we're on our way," Challen said.

"End of the tunnel," Doro said in a near inaudible whisper as he pointed to an overgrown opening ahead.

Irekirk carefully parted the curtain of moss and old vines. A large cavern was beyond, light from a large opening far above illuminated it just enough for him to see a large shape resting on a bed of green. He stared silently, unmoving until he eyes adjusted and then he saw that the shape had scales. It was massive, with claws half as long as he was tall, only there was something wrong.

"What d'you see?" Doro asked in his ear.

"Something isn't right," he whispered.

"What? That we're about to try to kill an ancient dragon, a living Goddess with just the three of us? What could be wrong with that?"

Irekirk gently pushed his friend back and continued watching. Something was definitely wrong, the cave was too still. Where were the host of Ondi that he expected? Why were the doors dug into the sides of the large cavern darkened? Why couldn't he hear the dragon breathing in her slumber? It struck him then: there was no movement at all, and only the sound of water trickling through a part of the cave in the distance. He searched the cave with his more mystical senses and found that the dragon, or the shape of it, was surrounded by a deceptive lattice of magic, one that could trick some people into thinking that whatever that was could be a sleeping dragon. "This is an old den," he said, pushing through the overgrowth into the cavern. He walked, unafraid of attack. He drew his sword and poked the side of the dragon with it. The tip cracked through the brittle, old skin and touched nothing on the other side. Irekirk took a quick step back and cast light above him. The followers of Odilexa had fused together large sections of their master's shed skin into the shape of three quarters of her body then enchanted it so anyone looking for her would find that instead. The head and right shoulder were missing, but the magic and shape would be enough to fool people far more powerful than he was as long as they didn't enter the den. But it shouldn't have fooled Challen, who was a traveler and seer with nearly unparalleled skill.

"All this work and we've come to a fake den?" Doro asked, throwing his hands up.

Irekirk turned just in time to see Challen step behind Doro and slash through the air using a clawing motion. It was a gesture that directed threads of magic that passed through the dwarf's skin and bones. Irekirk wasn't quick enough to counter it, and he wasn't powerful enough to save his longtime friend before his body slid apart into six pieces. He had no magic that could heal such dire injuries.

"He was the last true believer, barring you," Challen said coldly.

"I'm supposed to kill you here, but I know I'd only invite my own defeat. I'm not powerful enough to end you."

Irekirk slashed at her with his sword, unthinking, and it flashed through her insubstantial image. She was somewhere else entirely, it could have been so for hours. "Why are you doing this?"

"Miradu is breaking the natural order, growing the human, Ondi-Ne and Ondi-Un populations by keeping them safe and leading them towards the ancient places. I can't let the woodlands fall, so I joined Odilexa years ago. She didn't want to see Miradu or her followers destroyed, but she is defending her territory, after years of encroachment there's no other way."

Irekirk reached out with his consciousness, using his second sight to search for Challen.

"You won't find me, and you won't find Odilexa or her followers. She is dead, she made the ultimate sacrifice to save her land – the Kraxa-Kraxa is complete."

Irekirk's heart sank. "She surrendered her own life to destroy her enemies? It isn't done, not anymore." Legend told of a dragon who sacrificed their own heart to destroy an enemy brood, an act that no one alive had ever witnessed.

"Not for centuries, but Odilexa did it. When you return to your people, you'll find that Miradu, all her high priests and priestesses as well as your beloved brother and sister – Irenick and Viis - are dead. You were the only one who could stop it, that is why I helped you on your quest for vengeance. You have been distracted, Irekirk, and it wounds me, but Miradu could not be allowed to continue."

"Don't let me leave, Challen!" Irekirk bellowed. "If you do, I will build a temple for Miradu and my family. I will call Wydu, and we will raise enough power to bring my Mother back as a Goddess!"

"Wydu is barely an adolescent, he has no power in the world," Challen retorted.

"He already has his mother's charm. We will gather followers and your forest will never be safe again. I will make it a prime order to tame your wilderness, turn your woods into farmlands. Then my shrines will bring them back for a final reckoning!"

"You will fail," Challen said. "Temples and shrines built on vengeance are haunted by corruption and darkness. Goodbye, Irekirk. Because you are a good man, and you've always been kind to me, I'll give you one last piece of advice: Never forget that your infatuation with me was what led you here. Your lust is your greatest weakness."

6

*R*endiran listened to Tadrin describe his dream as they walked to the Mierisember Dining Hall. It had a great view of the city the priest thought his new charge may enjoy. Instead of a wall along the outer side of the room, there were large arches that let everyone at the tables see far into the distance. "From here, you can even see the eastern city wall, see over there?" he pointed. It was true, the tall wall that kept their massive coastal city safe was there, he'd never seen it before.

"Now, have you ever remembered a dream that clearly before?" Rendiran asked as he sat down beside him on a bench.

Tadrin thought a moment then shook his head. "I could smell in this dream, that's never happened before either. I don't think, anyhow. Everything was rotten."

"All right, I have to go speak with someone, and I need you to stay here. I have a friend, Crista, she spends most of her time in the wild woods, and she smells of cook fires and burning leaves."

"She doesn't live in the woods, there's nothing but outlaws, wolves, bears and monsters there," Tadrin replied.

"You think I would exaggerate about her?" he asked, feigning insult. "I do so have a friend from the deep woods, and she's no outlaw, beast or worse. You'll see, but only if you stay here for a while so I can speak to someone, all right?"

"Okay, I'll stay here."

"That's a good boy," Rendiran said before he walked down a causeway that ran along the outside of the building and took a left through a door which was shut hastily.

Tadrin watched the farmers maneuver their poor carts through the streets, even watched a pair of older people make a delivery to the rear of a great house. The cooks inside had a whole cartload of vegetables and fruits unloaded and sent inside through the kitchen door in a hurry, while an older cook with an apron dotted by gravy stains dropped coins onto one of the farmer's hands.

Not far from there, a small woman hung a large carpet and thumped it with a broom with such ferocity that her feet nearly came off the ground with each swing. He watched until dust stopped puffing from the fibers and she struggled to take the rug down.

Bored, a little hungry and restless, Tadrin decided to see if he could find out what Rendiran was doing, and he was barely ten paces from his seat when he heard a woman's voice shout. "There are warnings in the Mirac Alta about this kind of thing, we must be cautious." From the sound, he could tell that she was struggling to speak around something in her mouth, or through malformed lips. He'd heard something like it before when Barli Stow was given two fat lips by his older brother, Tannerin.

He peeked up through a window and caught a glimpse of Rendiran walking across the room. Tadrin dropped down and put his back to the wall so he faced the city below. He'd wait for his new master there, he decided, looking down the causeway to his empty bench.

"First he's given to us by Irenick, so you say, then he's having Ondi ancestor dreams? You know what this means, don't you? Irekirk or someone else who was there, maybe even Challen, is close to him in spirit. They could be sending these moments to him in his sleep as a prelude to a haunting, or to distract him with suspicions and doubt."

"It's the time of the return," Rendiran said more calmly. "If Irenick sent him to us – and there is no reason why we should suspect he didn't – then he is a guardian. We must train him to be one of our best, and raise him properly. If these dreams become a problem, we could protect him from them, and combat any doubt with education. We know the guardians who rise during the Time of the Return would face challenges, so we deal with them while raising the boy well."

"We don't know that he is one of the guardians promised for certain. The prophecies telling of the Return are clear; there will be three guardians. There will be the one that is given, the one that is found and the one that is restored. I see the one that is given, perhaps, and you want to be the one to oversee his upbringing. Even at your age, you're barely old enough to be a parent."

"Men my age have children a year or two older than Tadrin. I may be young for a priest, but I feel I already have a rapport with him, and I am known to his parents. I'm sure I'll need help, but there are many people I trust here."

"Raise him here? Oh, no, not if he's having dreams about the very origin of our religion. Not if some unseen hand is guiding him to dream of the forbidden histories."

"How and why our religion was founded is immaterial to his upbringing."

"How can you be blind to the change that is already taking place?" she asked. "The great steps leading to this temple are filled with parents who have dug up their lost children's bodies."

"I know, every priest has been pressed into service trying to resurrect the recently dead," Rendiran said. "The offerings they bring must be mountainous. We've had four successful resurrections so far. You must be pleased."

"The good work is being done, offerings are being given, that is true, and for the first time this decade some of our priests have the gift of resurrection as it once was, but only for the recently dead and only in familiar ways, not in the miraculous fashion that you brought

Tadrin back to life with, not with the blessing of a Goddess or any memory of where they'd been."

"That can only serve us, bring more people to our Temple. I've already heard of three Lucents abandoning the Bright One, this is the kind of thing that makes history and defeats dark religions without the use of violence."

"Don't you see? While our power rising is good, you have to realize that, in the eyes of the people, we are writing a new chapter in the history of our holy order. If it comes out that our founder had vengeance in his heart when he laid the foundation and performed the first rites, then that will become a part of that history with such indelibility that it will do irreparable harm. Irekirk must be forever seen as the brother who erected a temple and started this order out of love for his Goddess and all her children. Our guiding principle must remain intact: love calls us, love guides us and in love we serve. Now is the time to be careful, to limit risks and control everything that is revealed. Everything anyone from our order says will be repeated and twisted by envious Celestial Houses, so I have ordered the construction of a gate at the base of our temple steps. I'll let anyone who is building a shrine along the edges of our steps to finish, but starting at dusk, the hours we will allow our followers to visit them will be restricted. This will enforce the control we need over the people and limit risk to the priesthood."

"Our doors have always been open, even during times of conflict," Rindiran said.

"You question my order? You forget your place," the woman warned.

"My apologies Grand Matron. I'm sure our followers will adjust."

"They will, and we must deliver the message that we can't resurrect a pile of dust and bones while we offer our sympathies for their losses. We also have to limit how many petitioners we see in a day, which would normally fall to you, but I can't depend on you for that while this boy is here."

"I would normally redouble my efforts to fulfill my duties, but I feel responsible for the boy, and hope you can see that he needs a constant guardian. I humbly beg that you allow me to be that guardian, even if you decide that he requires more than one."

"Do you doubt that you can handle him alone?"

"No, but I will require assistance in his education and training. I'm sure you understand I want the best for him."

"I do, so I'll consider you as his interim guardian and render my final decision on the matter soon. Even still, I must ask if you believe that everything he described from his dream last night is accurate."

"He recounted it like a memory. At first he was sincerely moved, even though some of what he was describing was beyond his understanding. I believe he had an ancestral dream, that he experienced a memory from Irekirk, yes."

"So you believe the forbidden scriptures? That this temple was erected by Irekirk while he had vengeance in his heart?"

Rendiran hesitated. "You know I've never read them. A Priest of my station would never have the holy privilege. I've never even been to Saserin Temple. I believe the story as the boy tells it, every part of it makes sense to me. My faith in Miradu and her Pantheon remains unshaken because I've seen the good they bring. I am unshaken."

"You'll make sure what you've learned won't be repeated, that the boy who is listening outside won't speak of it. Furthermore, neither of you be allowed to remain here if you accept custodial duties over him."

Tadrin was immediately alarmed at being discovered, and ran back to where Rindiran had sat him down earlier. "There you are," a woman in dark leathers said. She was as short as his mother, but had dark brown hair. In her hands were two large, steaming bowls. She set them onto the table. "I'm Crista Vasto, Rendiran wanted me to meet you because there aren't many Ondi-Ne in the city."

"I'm Tadrin," he said, trying to act as though what he overheard didn't make his head spin, and as if he hadn't been caught.

"Here, eat up, it's good."

In front of him was a bowl filled with completely unfamiliar food.

The cook had poured hot fruit sauce with pieces of strawberry, apple, orange and raspberries over bite sized pieces of bread. "This is amazing? I always have it when I come back to the temple," Crista said, digging in with her fork. "Be careful, it's hot, and made to be eaten slowly."

A baked orange slice burst in his mouth and he couldn't help but giggle a little as his breakfast companion helped him wipe his chin. "That's going to get sticky," she said with a chuckle.

"Do people eat this all the time here?" Tadrin asked.

She nodded. "They are so rich that most people have it all the time. This temple serves the best breakfast pudding."

"My mom said that most people in the temple have porridge in the morning."

"Well, when the crop isn't so good, they go back to porridge, but that hasn't happened for a while. Even if things weren't so good at the moment, I'm sure they'd feed you as well as the Grand Matron."

"Why?"

"You've seen their Goddess's Glade, that doesn't happen more than a few times in a lifetime."

"I don't remember much now," Tadrin said, shrugging then stuffing a large piece of strawberry in his mouth.

"You remember the dream you had last night though," she said. "I have ancestor dreams too, I bet that's what it was. Without knowing the details, Rindiran had a feeling you'd have one, probably from knowing me for so long."

"What's an ancestor dream?" Tadrin asked.

"Ondi-Ne are always very close to the spirits of their ancestors, so sometimes we remember things that happened to them while we're sleeping," Crista replied. She lifted a lock of her hair to reveal a pointed ear. "There are times when my ancestors just won't leave me alone, sending me on their adventures night after night."

"Why?"

The question seemed to take her off guard, and she thought for a moment before answering. "I always thought that they gave us the dreams to prepare us for something. It's like they are teaching us by showing us lessons they learned. No one really knows why though. I use them to find secrets, hidden places that everyone else has forgotten."

"I saw Irekirk see the weave and change it. Maybe he wanted to teach me that," Tadrin offered, a little proud of himself for finding something in the dream that he was sure he learned something about. He'd never heard of or seen what he experienced through Irekirk's eyes the previous night, but he knew what it was somehow.

"There's nothing wrong with what you're saying, except we're not supposed to talk about any of that here in the temple, okay?" Crista asked quietly. "A lot of the people here don't like the Weaving Way."

"That's right," Rendiran said from behind.

Tadrin jumped at the sound of his voice, and his spoon spun across the table. "There will be a time to speak about the Weaving Way, but people don't use that kind of thing here," he said gently. "It's important that you stop talking about your dream or anything you might have overheard right away. I promise we'll be able to talk about everything soon, just not right now, okay, Tadrin?"

"Am I in trouble?" he asked.

"No, but you shouldn't have wandered. You have to listen to me and to Crista."

"Okay," Tadrin replied, still worried.

"Now, finish your breakfast, we have a long day ahead of us. Later this week we're going to go on a long journey all the way to Ironmaw."

The change in Crista's expression didn't escape Tadrin's notice. At the mention of Ironmaw she looked startled, then she did her best to hide it with an awkward smile then a spoon full of fruit that didn't get entirely into her mouth. "You have something just there," Tadrin said, offering her the napkin she'd used to wipe his chin.

"Before that I'm sure there will be people who want to meet you. I hear the Captain of the Eventide Paladins is on his way. Have you heard of Captain Haffor?"

Tadrin couldn't hide his excitement, he was a real hero, everyone knew stories about him. "He was a prince but gave his rights away to become leader of the Paladins. He fought a dead dragon."

"Well, not alone, and it was an undead dragon, but yes, he did," Rendiran replied. "You should get used to the idea that you will meet important people so they aren't too distracting."

"Do you know Captain Haffor?"

"No, I can't say that I do, he's much more important than I am, not to mention a very busy man," Rendiran replied, amused. "Speaking of which, there is a lot for me to do today, so please stay with Crista, all right."

"Okay," Tadrin agreed.

Rendiran recovered Tadrin's spoon from where it teetered on the edge of the table and handed it to him. "Enjoy your breakfast," he said before departing.

When they finished eating Crista took him on a tour of the massive bakery behind the main temple. More cooks than he could count manned ovens. Priests blessed loaves as they were set out to cool on large stone tables.

To Tadrin's delight, he was invited to help knead dough – a more taxing task than he expected – then put his loaf in a special oven that was marked with a red hand and symbols he'd seen at Irenick's shrine. The short, bald baker who helped him knelt down to speak to him while the bread was rising. "This loaf is going directly to Prince Norrich, do you know who he is?"

"He watches over Woodside and Gachin Province with the Miradu Order for his father, King Ormet," Tadrin replied. His father was careful to teach him who they paid taxes to. "King Ormet the Second."

"That's right," the baker said, a little surprised. "He'll be very happy to be presented with a loaf prepared by Irenick's own servant. This oven is dedicated to his followers, the guardians of Gachin Province. The bread baked in there goes to some of the most important people in the land."

"So my mom and dad would get bread from here?" he asked.

The baker's smile faded as he looked to Crista and a few of the other bakers. "We could make them bread in another oven while we wait for this loaf to rise," he offered.

Tadrin looked past the baker and saw a table with bread that he recognized. Those loaves were heavier, not so pure and white, and they had nuts, sometimes a little cheese and always a little meat mixed in so it was like a meal for a small family. "That's the kind of bread I used to get with my mom and dad."

"They don't eat that anymore, dear boy," another baker said. She was tall, with big dusty hands. "Your parents have the best food and wine from today on, I saw the order myself. There was not only good food and wine, but fine cloth, beeswax candles, orders for a shoe-maker and thatcher to visit their house today. You've got them in the church's good graces."

"We always liked that bread," he said, remembering riding on his father's shoulders to the temple steps where callers shouted news and bread was handed out. Every day his father didn't have work they went, and when his father was working, he'd go hand in hand with his mother.

"That's not for the likes of you," the taller baker said, dusting her hands. "We've got better loaves over here."

"We'll have one of those with dinner," Crista said, pointing at the pile of brown, lumpy shaped loaves Tadrin knew.

"Can we?" Tadrin asked, looking up at Crista, who only nodded as the bakers wrapped a loaf in cloth and handed it to her.

"Send one to his parents as well," she added. "Still warm, please. They should know it's from their son."

"Yes, Ma'am," replied the tall baker.

"Would you like to see the loaf we've prepared in your name for the Prince?" asked the shorter, bald baker. "It's ready now."

"Okay," he replied.

The baker carefully pulled it from the oven with his wooden paddle and presented it as he slipped it onto the table. "There it is, perfect."

Tadrin looked at the smooth surfaced, blonde loaf, remembering the big, brown, nutty loaves he'd have with his parents. "It looks boring,' he said quietly, and Crista laughed softly, patting him on the back. "Let's go see the upper gardens. I hear they're picking apples today."

Tadrin nodded and they took their leave. "Have you ever been outside the wall?" Crista asked him.

"No, this is as far as I've been from home," Tadrin replied.

"Well, what if I told you that it was my job to explore out there, past the wall," she said as they topped a stair leading to one of the highest walkways in the temple. He could see the thick green forested mountains in the distance.

"It's dangerous there," he said, remembering his dream from the night before.

"Sometimes," Crista said. "But the forests hide secrets, like the remains of whole cities that are so old that no one knows their names anymore. There are people there too, people who don't depend on charity bread every day to stay fed. They live on what grows on the ground, on the branches and they hunt for the rest. Every day is an adventure once you enter the forest, and if you know someone like me, a guide, you will learn how to avoid the dangerous places."

"Like old swamps," Tadrin said.

"Especially old swamps. Why would you want to go there anyway? You can smell them miles away, and it's not a good scent, either," Crista said, fanning her nose.

"You've been to one?"

"I had to go deep into one to help find what I'm about to show you," she said. "There, look into that case."

He ran to the edge of a case decorated in white and blue cloth and under glass was an old lantern. The rough glass had been broken, but it looked like any old oil lantern he'd seen before. "You had to go into the swamp for that?"

"Yes, it was the first lantern lit in this temple, and it uses Quick-amber oil, one of the most valuable things in this world. It was on display here for a long time, then someone from Odilexa's Order stole it. It happened even before I was born, but then I was sent out to bring it back, and I did."

"How did you find it?"

"When I was young, not much younger than you, I learned to track things through the forest. I learned to hide, to survive better than most people I've met, and to follow people who I think may do harm. This world is larger than anyone knows, and most of it is wild, like the forest you see out there. I've been looking for someone like you to teach, would you like that?"

"Because I saw Irenick and Miradu," Tadrin said, already growing tired of being treated like he was some kind of prize or curiosity.

"No, someone young and smart and brave," Crista said as she knelt down and gently grasped his shoulder. "I think you qualify, unless you're older than you look. Hold still while I check for wrinkles." She pinched his cheeks, turned his head, and tugged at his ear, stopping when he chuckled at her. "Looks like you're really as young as you look. What do you think? Can I teach you about the world out there, Tadrin?"

The dream and the dangers he saw in it were still fresh in Tadrin's mind. Remembering the swamp, how dark and endless it seemed, he could only say; "Yes, please. There are more like me coming, well, at least one like me. You'll have to teach her too."

She hesitated for a moment before nodding. It was as though she wanted to ask him another question, but decided not to. "Definitely, I'll tell Rendiran that I'll be teaching you and one more. But, until he finds us, let's go steal some apples. C'mon," she said, running down through an open archway onto the high causeway beyond. High above the city, and just beneath the upper spires of the temple was a large garden. Fruit trees of every kind were grown there, and they spent the afternoon playing hide and seek – Tadrin suspected that Crista let him win a few times – and eating delicious, perfect apples from the east grove.

Rendiran joined them for dinner, where he told them that the first three floors of the temple were filled all day with worshippers and petitioners. There were so many, in fact that the Priest suspected they may have to leave for Ironmaw earlier than expected.

Tadrin wanted to ask if he could see his parents again first, but held the request in, remembering his promise to the Goddess Miradu. He went to bed with a heavy heart, wishing he could creep into his parents bed as he'd done countless times. He would have taken that over the comfortable featherbed in a heartbeat.

7

*T*adrin didn't know when exactly he woke, only that he could see one of the moons high in the sky, its crescent sliver shed little light on the outer causeway as he idly walked down the ramp leading to the front of the temple. "Ho, there, little man," said a guard with a polished breastplate and a pair of swords on his belt. He smiled at Tadrin, who met his gaze with confidence he didn't know he had. "Shouldn't you be in bed?"

"I have somewhere important to go," he said, realizing that it was true as he said the words aloud. "You can come with me if you want."

The guard seemed a little surprised. "This midnight errand doesn't take you out of the temple, does it?"

"Not out of the temple," Tadrin replied. "I need to see Viis."

"No harm in visiting Our Lady's shrine before I walk you back to bed," he said, rubbing his broad chin.

The guard walked at his side as they descended several staircases. "I'm Marjay, my friends call me Mar," he said, offering his hand.

"Tadrin," he replied.

"Everyone knows who you are, no worry there. I'll have a good story for the morning when I tell people how I found you sleep walking. My grandmother once told me that you should never wake someone when they're walking asleep though, so as long as you aren't about to walk off the edge of a dock, or into the street, I'll just just be your shadow."

"I'm not sleep walking," Tadrin said.

"You sure look like you are," Marjay said with a soft chuckle. "It's all right, just lead the way and we'll get back to your bed eventually I'm sure."

They finally arrived at the shrine of Viis. It was in its own large alcove that smelled of rich rose and earthy incense. A small pool was built into a dais, and around it were fresh white roses and blue iris. The last offerings of the day were still there, bars of glittering silver and several bolts of pure white silk. Above the shrine a long sword hung with three gemstones in its hilt, there was a place for a fourth but it was missing. The leather had long rotted off the hilt, but the blade still glinted in the dim lantern light. A small pot of Quickamber hung above the pool on chains, where its yellow flame burned low. A beautiful, clean but slightly sweet fragrance wafted from it as a breeze stirred the air around the polished bronze pot, and it swung on the chains slightly.

"I've never seen Her shrine at this hour," Mar said quietly. "It's as though She's here watching over us." He knelt, looking up at the portrait of the blue eyed, blonde haired woman for a moment before bowing his head. "I pray she does."

Tadrin knew there was a secret shrine below the grand spectacle the temple built for her. He could see Irekirk placing a bowl on a standing square of granite centuries before. Tadrin crawled to the foot of the grandiose shrine. He pushed a tile with both hands hard, and it fell inward to reveal the original offering bowl. "This is the real shrine," he said, looking over his shoulder at Marjay, who was stunned.

"You're desecrating her shrine!" he exclaimed in a hoarse whisper.

"Look," Tadrin said, moving out of the way and touching the brass bowl in the compartment he'd just revealed. "It's time, put an offering in the bowl." He pulled a shoe off his foot and put it in the bowl, he was surprised at how small it looked there.

Tadrin sat on the polished stone bench in front of the shrine and watched Mar gently place a few coins inside the bowl. "That looks old, all right," he said quietly. "I'll probably still catch a lashing for letting this happen." The wisps of incense smoke and the pot stirred as though caught in a sudden gust. A woman emerged from the arch, ghostly and bright at first, then solidifying as she stepped down onto the dais.

She was tall, muscular and was dressed in heavy armor that glinted like the rainbow scales of a fish. A fine sword with a silvered hilt was hanging on a thick belt. She knelt down and tilted Marjay's chin up so she could smile down at him. "My Goddess," he said in hushed amazement. "You've returned to us."

Viis got him to his feet and laid her hand on his cheek. "Not yet," she said with a smirk. "But your calling has come, you don't have any more time to devote to me."

Viis looked to Tadrin, who stood up and accepted her outstretched hand. The tall Goddess took a bolt of silk from her shrine before leading him through the hall. There were many guards between her shrine and the temple steps, and each of them knelt in deep reverence as the three of them made their way to the main doors of the temple. Light emanated from her in all directions, bright enough to see by, but not so brilliant that it was too harsh for the late hour.

A young priest saw them as he emerged from one of the side rooms and nearly tumbled as he dropped to his knees. "My Goddess! Please, pardon my departure, but I must fetch our High Matron so she can witness your return."

"You're dismissed," Viis said, rolling her eyes. "I knew someone would think I was here to see *her*."

They followed Viis down the main stairs. At the bottom of the grand steps, easily large enough for hundreds to pass with ease, there was a new gate. Beyond that, more people than Tadrin could count were sleeping, waiting until the gates opened again in the morning.

Dozens of shrines had been hastily built along the sides of the stairway, and Viis led them half way down where she stopped and looked at one poor display. Raspberry branches and thin reeds had been woven together and bent into an arch that decorated a burnt plank. The freshly carved heads of a woman, a man and a young girl stood on the plank with a few copper coins and several smooth river stones. Tadrin knew that beneath the burnt plank was a box with remains inside.

"This is who I've come to see," Viis said. "Oria and her family died in a fire in Surwood. Followers of Challen and her dead dragon attacked in too great a number. The surviving elders left this here, because the Ofshea family were a bright light amongst them." Viis looked to Tadrin. "She is your counterpart. You will carry your shield on your right arm, she will carry hers on her left. Someday, when you've both grown, the two of you will be Paladins for Irenick and I. I trust you to welcome her." She handed Tadrin the bolt of silk from her shrine then turned to Marjay. "I cannot bring your daughter back to you, she has gone on to live again, but I know you will care for Oria and raise her."

"I will, my Goddess, on my honor and on my life, I will."

"I know," Viis said with a warm smile. She turned to the shrine, carefully removed the statuettes and handed them to Marjay for safe-keeping. The rest of the offerings were set aside before she knocked on the box below. "Time to return to the world, little one." She didn't wait for a response before turning towards the tall iron gate. Most of the people there had woken up, and were staring up at Viis from their knees. "Respect my Grand Matron's house, and do not interfere with what happens inside. An era of justice approaches." She drew her sword, raised it high over her head and brought it down with a thunderous clang on the latch holding the gates closed. Shattered pieces of metal clattered to the bricks. Viis looked over her shoulder with a satisfied expression and then faded away.

Tadrin watched as the plank of wood was pushed upward and a pair of small hands gripped the side of the box underneath. He helped a girl his age out of the rough coffin as she emerged and wrapped her in silk. "I'm Oria," she said as she embraced him. "You're Tadrin, Viis and Irenick told me about you."

"They didn't tell me much about you," Tadrin replied. He felt as though a weight had been lifted from him, though he wouldn't be able to explain his relief at her arrival if he was asked to.

He held her tightly in his arms, it was as though he'd found his other half. Marjay fussed to make sure she was well covered for a moment before embracing both of them. "Life's about to get interesting," he said.

Priests came rushing down the steps as people came up the stairs to see the girl a Goddess came to resurrect. The two groups met peacefully, all forming a semicircle around the trio.

Rendiran emerged after a moment, looking the three over. "Are you all right?" he asked, kneeling down and patting Tadrin on the back.

"Viis came to bring Oria to help us," Tadrin said.

"I'm to become Viis' paragon in this world, just like he's Irenick's. I have a message for you from Miradu. She wants me to tell you that one more is coming soon, but not to wait. There are people who may not celebrate the arrival of the third guardian, so where they will come from and who they are has to remain a secret, even from me. She told me Tadrin and I would be enough to keep you busy."

"I always knew the Gods had a sense of humor," Marjay said, shaking his head.

8

"Wydu, your teachings will guide me in the darkness," Lena said, feeling the effects of the Gold Wine begin to take hold. In the flickering light of a torch held by one of her hirelings, she knelt before a statuette of Wydu. It was only one finger tall, but as her concentration focused more sharply, it seemed to fill her vision. The effects of Gold Wine were familiar to her, and welcome. Lena felt warm, giddy and as though the whole world was slowing down. The light of the torch behind her made the shadows shift and twitch, she could feel the edges of them around her, as though that darkness was substantial, like curtains she could slip behind.

Wydu didn't demand that his followers kneel on most occasions, but she was about his most important work. "You are the master of shadow, where secrets are kept, all is known, power over the unwary is yours, all is known." She shrugged into her heavy silk robe, making sure it was closed all the way up the front. "Tonight I am not only your eyes and ears, I am your hand, and I personify you as I enter the den of your unknowing servants. Watch my journey, and welcome me home if I'm bested."

"Never heard that prayer before," Storo whispered.

"Quiet," Gamm replied.

"Few have," Lena said, chuckling to herself. "Few who still live, but the wandering dead remember it well." She took her idol from the stone she'd perched it on in the rough cave passage and stood. "I'm finished with prayer. Wydu is either watching or he is not."

"So, can you actually feel some kind of power? Did he give you something?" Gamm asked.

She looked the two men who she hired only fourteen days before over briefly. They were both a little road worn, but their clothes and weapons were still new. They wore metal breastplates over heavy cloth tunics and blackened codpieces affixed to thick belts. The armour and the thick bladed swords they carried were gifts from her, of a quality that they would never have seen in their lifetimes if they hadn't agreed to be her armed men. Gamm was ready to become her blind follower the moment she showed him his first day's pay. He had been a mercenary for so long that he'd fought for more Lords and Pantheons than most could name. Any trust the world of men ever had in him was long gone, he had killed while in the service of too many masters. Lena's visions guided her to him, a man who would slaughter for the right money and she was surprised to find him, grizzled, with his hair retreating from the top of his head. It took the shake of a small bag of gold to win him to her cause, a bag of gold that would have bought three houses in the town he was drinking dry.

A purpose revealed him for what he really was in a very short time, a heavily muscled, experienced killer. Wydu's Way had led her to him, and at first she had doubt that he could become a devout of Wydu, her follower, but that doubt had been allayed. Whether it was his approaching old age, a life with too much death, or her own charms, or Wydu's will, he showed a deep interest in her God. He shadowed her during every prayer, and made efforts to learn Wydu's Way. If he made it back to Nightbreak Castle, she would make sure that he saw the delights and wonder of her master. He would make a powerful Acolyte.

Her other hireling, Storo, was a knight for the Imartine Pantheon before his Goddess' temples were destroyed, the leaders were disemboweled and burned in the streets. He hated the same Pantheon that all Miradu followers did: the Odilexa Pantheon that dwelt in the forests of the East. They orchestrated the downfall of the Imartine Pantheon in cooperation with the Bright One's followers, the Lucents, or so it was said. Lena knew that it was thanks to some manipulation inspired by Wydu that created the opening necessary for the Imartine's enemies to destroy them.

Storo was easy to find, thanks to her sisters and brothers at Castle Nightbreak, and easier to manipulate. He was in her service for less than three days before she was sure that Storo was deeply in love with her. He bore her affection for her stoically, even though she encouraged his baser appetites regularly. Gamm's jealousy of him would lead to one of the men's death eventually, but she was sure she could use it somehow. He was much less interesting, a paladin whose Goddess was so diminished that the only story anyone knew about her was that her people had been slaughtered.

Storo was a powerful warrior, even without the power of a Goddess behind him, and his guilt at going into hiding while his people were crushed made him easy to manipulate. She turned towards Storo and kissed him briefly, he tasted of jerked pork. "Wydu's Gift approaches, he won't be outdone by his brother and sister."

They followed her down the stony passage, barely keeping up. The stones under her feet were uneven, but she could see all around her with or without the torchlight. The passage was filled with sounds of high pitched chanting, growing more and more frantic as they came to the end of the tunnel. "Up ahead," she said, stopping. "You have to kill the worshippers." She held her hands up and faced her hirelings. "I draw the shadows in and wrap you in them. I recall the silence of the void, and conceal you in its perfection."

Gamm and Storo became blackened as though they were made of shadow, and she could no longer hear them as they set the torches down and moved ahead. Lena resumed her stride towards the end of the tunnel at a casual pace. By the time she arrived, the last of five small, thin limbed creatures were grasping their throats, trying to stop their blood from gushing down their rough cloth tunics. The wide-eyed, grey and red skinned imps who worshipped from the tunnel opening that overlooked the main temple chamber were helpless, dying quickly. "Thank you for your devotion," she whispered to the last as his eyes began to lose focus. "Your new God awaits, be with Wydu."

Her shadowy hirelings crept up to the edge of the tunnel opening beside her. There were hundreds of imps and dwarves who interbred with each other and other creatures in the mountain over the generations all praising in a language that Lena could barely comprehend at all. "They pray to Yut, a Goddess who Wydu chained to his throne centuries ago. Her power is his power. Watch, they are about to sacrifice the Prince of this mountain for her to return." She pointed to a broad, natural pool surrounded by candles. "His royal line is so corrupted by breeding with the creatures they found in and on the mountain that he's barely a dwarf at all. He's a mongrel of high and low species, goblin kind. His blood may as well be mud, save for the fact that he is a leader."

A pair of priests marked by rough gemstone studded armbands guided a young man to the edge and leaned his thick head down towards the water. He shouted his dedication in such a sloppy dialect of Unso that she almost failed to understand him. "I sacrifice myself only to take your place in the heavens, oh Yut the jewel of the Mountain," she translated quietly for her henchmen. "He thinks that he will inherit the celestial kingdom of his Goddess if he trades his life for her emergence into this world. His efforts will be wasted, Wydu will chain him to his cloak, another prideful spirit to howl in dismay. Of all the creatures my master likes to trick, royalty is his favourite."

The chanting in the cave; 'Hooo-na-mor-na Yut-vor-cha,' grew in volume until the din was so overpowering that Lena couldn't help but sway to its rhythm. Then it fell silent, and Lena grinned at the prince far beneath them, wide eyed. One of the nude, emaciated goblin priests drew a blade across the neck of his prince while another slashed down from behind.

The sounds of the prince struggling, his gurgles and the scraping of his nails at the stone lip of the deep pool in front of him continued for much longer than Lena anticipated as the priests worked hard to saw through the muscle and cartilage of his thick neck. A third priest came to hold the prince's body near the end, and pushed the gushing corpse part way into the pool as the water turned red.

The stone around them shook once and a sound like a massive, deep throated bell filled the chamber. "I can feel it, the power of a true God," Lena giggled. "An age ago, a little girl was drowned in that pool as a sacrifice. Her bones were covered by silt and stone. Wydu found her spirit wandering, and has been whispering in her ear for years. Now he brings her back. The time has come, I must catch her, defend me or die."

In one smooth motion she slipped her robes off her shoulder, stepped forward and leapt from the outcropping. Long heartbeats later her pointed toes struck the cool, bloodied water. Her hirelings would follow, only they would slip down the wall as shadows do, and then they would begin to kill the imps and the goblin kind that could no longer claim that they were dwarves, or mountain imps, or earthen men, humans or anything else that had been bred into their jagged ancestral lines. They believed that the Imp Goddess, Yut, was the light in the darkness, and her hirelings would make it seem as though darkness itself had come to slash them to pieces.

The dim light from above did little to illuminate the deep waters of the pool. Red murk surrounded Lena, and she began to stretch her arms and legs out, feeling for Wydu's Gift. A surge of pressure swept her up. As she rose a bright, small body joined her from below. She took the girl in her arms and held on tightly as they surged to the top, breaking the water, gasping.

Lena kicked her legs and swam to the edge of the pool, clutching the coughing child to her so her head was above water. Her shadows were busy, slashing the nude priests open with their finely sharpened blades. The screeching and screaming of the worshippers, the rumble of their fleeing feet was all the reassurance Lena needed. The plan had the blessing of Wydu's wisdom, they would prevail. Her shoulder gently bumped the edge of the pool and Lena forced the water to push her and Wydu's Gift up onto the edge with a gesture of her hand. With a yank, she ripped a hanging flag from the wall and wrapped the girl in it. Deep blue eyes looked through curly white-blonde locks at her, and she cleared hair from the face staring up at her. "You are such a beautiful child," Lena breathed, kissing her on the forehead. "Did he give you a new name?"

"He told me you would have one for me," Wydu's Gift whispered.

"Then you are Shani," Lena replied, tracing the outline of the girl's pointed ear, sharing a smile with her. The shrieks and desperate cries of the retreating followers of Yut didn't interrupt their meeting. When the only sounds in the cave were those of the few who were left to slowly die, Gamm emerged from the shadows with Lena's robes. He carefully put them around her, and then took a bundle from his pack and handed it to her. The garment within was a smaller version of Lena's. Dark silks on the inside, and fine white cloth completely obscuring the darker garment by fitting over top.

When the pair were dressed, Shani took Lena's hand. "Wydu told me no one can survive, these goblins and their imp allies cannot spread the story of what happened here."

Lena nodded and descended the stairs to the floor of the main chamber. There was an imp to her left clutching his side. He regarded her with fearful wide eyes as she knelt down and put her hand over his slashed belly. "Your Goddess will see you healed and well," she said, mending his seeping wound. "Go and help everyone who has a chance to survive here, then spread her word, Yut's miracle is coming." It was the kind of lie that would spread. Lena kissed him reassuringly. As her lips touched his, she conjured a disease that would spread to everyone he breathed near until he would die, no more than two weeks later. She knew the disease of rotting chest and gut would most likely pass beyond the mountain, but it would definitely ensure that there would be no survivors. The small Kingdom of Munixen would disappear.

9

*E*ven the foothills of the Onhin Mountains were dangerous and craggy. Lena, Grenn, and Storo were settling in on a shelf set against a tall flat face of green and grey stone as daylight began to wane. "Do you think that moss up there is any good? It looks thin, like I'd have to scrape it off, but I bet it's rare, maybe something an apothecary would want?" Storo asked, looking up at the sheer rock face.

"That's copper, there's no moss on that stone, not on the western face, at least," Lena replied.

"Oh, tricked my eye."

"Be careful near the edge," Lena told Shani, who approached the lip of their path gingerly. Past the edge was a straight drop down to stone and brush.

Storo turned towards the girl and smiled, kneeling down behind her. "Look, out there, the crown of Brightwill – Samlen in Highshield." He pointed. His finger led Shani's gaze past the thick green forest at the foot of the mountain, over a sea of farmlands laid out like a patchwork quilt of land parcels, to a tall white wall protecting more farmland and a city beyond. "When I was a boy there were almost no farms past the wall, but Lords and Kings cut down the forest for leagues and leagues, and now these fields are planted."

He looked to Shani and shook his head with a smile. "You're probably more interested in the city proper, in Samlen." He pointed at the tall spires and whitewashed buildings beyond the wall, a thick belt of civilization between a wall and a seemingly endless ocean. "I haven't been there for years, but it's a marvel."

"A crowded, dangerous marvel," Grenn said.

Storo looked over his shoulder at him, and to Lena's horror, Shani broke into a run. In an instant she crossed the five steps it took her to leap from the high ledge where they rested and was in mid-air. For a frozen moment it seemed the girl was suspended in the sky. In a motion so quick, Lena could barely see it, Storo leapt forward and caught the girl's ankle, his momentum carrying him over the edge.

Lena and Grenn were on their feet and at the edge of the stone ledge in an instant. "Got her!" Storo called up from where he hung from a jutting rock by one hand. Even hanging upside down with the forest hundreds of feet below, Shani struggled, flailing and screaming. "Let me go! Let me die!"

Storo's grip on her ankle was firm, but his other hand strained to keep them both up. "I can't reach you," Grenn said after laying on his belly and stretching as far as he could. "Just hold a moment longer, I'll get a rope around you."

"No, I'm goin'," Storo said. Lena could see his grip on the stone slipping. She tried to reach him through the stone his fingers clung to, tried to focus enough to force the rock to close around his wrist, but failed. "Catch her," he warned through a grimace before swinging the girl up and letting her go. The effort didn't dislodge him, but it shook his grip enough so he slipped after Grenn caught Shani in his arms and fell back onto the ledge.

Lena watched as Storo fell through the open air, wishing she could do something, but she was no wind weaver. He braced himself long seconds into his fall, and was struck by an outcropping, sent spinning through the air until he landed on a stony clifftop far, far below. "Wydu and Miradu, take his spirit into your protection."

"Why did you do that?" Grenn shouted at Shani, who squirmed and writhed in the vice of his arms. "What's wrong with you?"

Lena turned towards the girl and her hireling. "Shani!" she shouted, wishing she hadn't given the girl the name.

The girl stopped squirming and her blue eyes locked with Lena's, she was furious. "I don't want to be here, I want to go back to Wydu! I hate this place!"

"Little girl," Lena said as she held her anger in check. She strode towards Shani, whose struggle began anew at her approach. She caught the girl's jaw in an iron grip and stared into the child's eyes. "You are here now, servant of Wydu. Why did he send you here?"

A tear rolled down Shani's cheek, her defiance replaced with fear and regret.

"No, you don't get to weep," Lena said. "Not after what you just tried to do, not after what it cost. Now, answer my question; why did Wydu send you to us?"

"To elevate His glory," she replied through more tears. "To bring the kingdoms of the west to heel, to bring Him more power in the world in preparation for His return."

The first part, elevating Wydu's glory, didn't surprise Lena, but the rest was dangerous knowledge, the kind of thing that could damage relations between the Temple and the kingdoms it was attached to. "You must never tell anyone else about your whole purpose. Only tell them that you are here to elevate Wydu and Miradu's glory."

"But I don't want..." she started to whine.

"I won't hear it!" Lena shouted into the child's face. She pointed her chin towards the city in the distance. "Do you see that? It is what Storo was trying to show you, an entire city with all its riches and luxuries that will bow and scrape to you but only if we manage to turn it away from an ancient, evil God. The Bright One would bathe us in his horrible light, making mindless servants out of all of us and they are the neighbors to our people, good people like the man you wasted. If you don't serve your purpose, the Lucent will end us before we can defeat them. You could be their liberator, and they will worship you with such devotion that queens will envy you.

That city, that whole province could be yours when we reveal you to our followers, when we show everyone the power of Wydu. This," Lena said, gesturing to the mountain ledge. "This rough passage is only the small cost of your return to this world, a return that thousands of people would wish for their dead. You have the entire Order of Wydu, tens of thousands of followers and teachers to give you an enviable life and raise you into such a woman that people will praise you as a Goddess yourself by the time you're finished growing."

"I was the companion to a God," Shani replied, much calmer.

Lena released her and threw up her hands. It was time for another tact. "I wonder, have you ever seen what Wydu does to those who fail him? A God with a cloak of chains tied to lesser deities that he has bested? A great God who sits upon a throne built from the bones of the ancients."

"He doesn't torture them all," Shani said. "Isema the Wise took care of me, he was kind to him even though he was chained to Wydu's throne."

"What about the ones that Wydu was angry at? Did you see what happened to them? Imagine if you returned to him as a failure? Do you truly think he'd want you back after you wasted your life? Wasted all the effort and power it took him to bring you into the world? What would he do? How horrible do you think it would be to return to him as someone who wasted a gift more precious than anything?"

New tears, and real fear filled Shani. The girl hadn't thought of that at all in her efforts to return to the afterlife. As her weeping deepened, Lena gestured for Grenn to release her and took the girl into her arms. She was shaking. "I only want to protect you," she told the girl who clung to her. "Wydu is wise, witty, but he can be wrathful. I would have you spared from that. Let me care for you. Promise me that you'll make the best of this life and all it offers."

"I promise, I'm sorry," Shani said, her weeping already beginning to ease.

"Wydu will welcome you back someday, after you've done his will and had your fill of this world, but only if he knows you've lived in a way he sees as admirable." Shani's quakes and her tears came to a slow stop. "Do you understand?"

"Yes," Shani replied. "Can you be my mother?"

Lena was awed by the request, surprised by the quick turn. "You'll mind what I say? No more attempts to rejoin Wydu before your time?" she asked.

Shani shook her head, blonde curls ringing her head like a halo. "I'll keep my life and listen to you."

"Then I'd be proud to call you daughter," Lena said.

10

*R*endiran looked down from the high window into the Upper Spire Garden to where Tadrin and Oria chased an eleven week old pup in the perfectly trimmed green grass. Their white trousers and tunics already showed green scuffs from an activity that only started minutes earlier. The puppy, brought by Haffor Entin, the Captain of the Eventide Guard, was already wound up and ready to play the simple game of chase in the garden.

The Compassionate Sisters and a special visitor watched, letting the children do as they liked as long as they stayed away from the pond and the railed edges of the broad tower top. Dark stone statues decorated the circular yard, all icons of the Order's early formation. Rendiran momentarily wondered how many hidden truths there were about those times, when the first followers of Miradu were gathered.

There were living icons to consider, like the tall, dark haired woman who watched the children with an amused smile. She was a visitor of importance, and made haste to see Tadrin and Oria as soon as she heard the story of their origin. Rendiran was glad to see her. Not only was she a voice of reason that he could count on, but she was the one who decided that he would be schooled by the

Mystics when he was a young orphan. Donatella Of The Writ was the High Master, the one who decided which masters of craft would visit the Miradu Orphanages and schools to choose their young apprentices.

Crista noticed that he was looking down and smiled up at him for a moment before disappearing into the hall beneath. "You're already here, Captain," Umner said as he entered hurriedly. Both men were in stations so high above Rendiran that it was unusual to see them address each other casually. Haffor was a thickly muscled dwarf who sat one seat over from the head of the oval table. "I thought you'd be with the children, watching them play with your gift," Umner said.

"Haven't seen the wee ones yet, want to save that for later, when some things have been decided. Is our Matron going to join us?"

"I'm afraid not, her old injuries are acting up again, we must pray to Miradu for an ease to her suffering, for she refuses to pray for herself," Umner sat at the side of the table then ran his hand across the smooth, white marble top. It was free of inscription or feature, meant to foster open-minded thinking.

"I'll dedicate a duel to her," Haffor said.

"When was the last time you had to duel anyone?" Umner laughed.

"A sparring duel," Haffor retorted, waving the comment off.

Rendiran took one last look at the children below, then turned his full attention to the table. He stepped to a seat across from Umner and stood behind it. Crista, flushed and catching her breath, entered the room and stood behind the lowest seat at the table.

"Crista, the Wildling of Lower Timber," Haffor said. "You recovered my brother's favourite hammer, I remember you. Please, sit."

"I did, and no thank you, sitting at this table is above my station," Crista said with a smile. "I hope your brother is enjoying the Hammer of Dolumna."

"It's been used in the making of every Paladin's sword since you put it in his hands, I would say he does. You should visit him if you find yourself near Forge Hin, he'd dote on you more than all his daughters combined," Haffor said with a wink. He turned his gaze to

Rendiran, who could feel his palms begin to sweat at the attention, looked him up and down and shrugged at Umner.

"I'm sorry, I thought you'd know Rendiran, he's a Mystic of some note, and the Priest who resurrected Tadrin."

"Are you a powerful Mystic?" Haffor asked with an upraised eyebrow.

"Well read, perhaps, though I tend to get distracted by the histories. I've had success at healing, and I know my community, but powerful?" Rendiran found that he was out of words.

"He is quite talented, and modest," Umner The Dawn Shaper said. "Both the children like him a great deal and more importantly, they mind what he says. Please, take a seat, Rendiran. Oh, and Crista, be at ease here, half the halls have something you've dug up, recaptured or tracked down, you've earned a cushion."

The pair of them took their seats, it was the first time either of them had sat with their betters at an official table in the temple. It still didn't alleviate Rendiran's nervousness at being in the same room as one of the most important Paladins in the world. The more than one-century old dwarf still had a black hair, a braided black beard, and only wrinkles around his eyes. He was a legend, a Prince of his people who would not take the throne, leaving a Regent Council to rule, and the end of his days didn't seem apparent in any sense.

"Meetings and long discussions aren't something I excel at, so I'd have you lead us, Umner, judging from how you've grown in the middle since I last saw you, it's probably all you do."

Umner laughed quietly and shook his head. "There's truth to that. Very well: we're here to decide who will be the long term caretakers and where Tadrin and Oria will be raised, among other things."

"Other things, like the Eventide Guard's claim on these children. Twice the halls of Forge Hin have been filled with the sound of tolling bells. Irenick and Viis's banners changed on the same day. They were tattered, stained things, now they're pristine once again. A red hand and a sword with wings for a cross guard appeared to either side of their device." Haffor pulled Tadrin's cape from a bag beside his seat and spread it out so everyone could see the red hand. "The left hand," he said before hurriedly pulling Oria's cape from the bag, spreading it out and exclaiming; "The right hand. We are eager to train them as Paladins."

"I thought I was hosting this meeting?" Umner asked.

"I've had enough time in this realm to know not to waste it," Haffor said.

"Well, then I must state that our Matron would have them train up the wall, in Ironmaw."

"Ironmaw?" Haffor asked, near outrage. "I would train oxen in Ironmaw, or a full grown man if strength was the only measure that mattered, but not a paladin. These young ones could have the best training from the perfect age, Ironmaw is a quarry, barely a mine, and half the paladin pledges that train there have stony brains by the time they get to us, difficult to teach on finer points and often stubborn past usefulness. No, we train them properly, with knowledge of the world, of our order, as well as the hammer for the undead and the sword for the living. We can make sure they're plenty strong in the meantime, if that's what concerns our Matron."

"Her concern is that it will be difficult for us to hide them anywhere else. No one would suspect that we'd send them to Ironmaw."

"Because it's a dung-headed plan," Haffor replied. "It's too late to hide them anyhow, there are celebrations under way spreading for hundreds of leagues up and down the coast and the wall. I'm here only a day ahead of the Prince and his party, who come with useless trinkets and promises for the children, no doubt. I'd say the concern is to get them to a place where they can be separated from such useless doting and kept safe behind a thick mountain gate. Forge Hin is the greatest vault protecting the most precious jewels in the world; my people. The Bright One's followers and who knows who else are already aware of their coming, and I guarantee that assassins sharpen their blades for them now."

"Our rivals may plan a kidnapping, but assassination? I doubt it," Umner scoffed.

"You spend too much time in the temple and the isolated homes of our patrons. We are not the only ones with Gods who rise in power, whose priests have been able to raise the dead for a price just in the last three years. The Bright One's followers have Chosen Ones now, members of their temple that swear they have glimpsed the face of their God and they have begun preaching about a Final War, where all other Gods and their followers will be brought low, slaughtered on their altars. There are others who are less vocal about their plans to contest Miradu's grip on Highshield, and even more mysterious things beyond the wall. These children are an easy target for everyone who wants to hinder the return of Miradu and her children. They are the subject of envy and hate for so many who follow other Gods, the dark intentions of our rivals would haunt you."

"I'll have my people near the temple watch more vigilantly," Umner said.

"They won't have to for long if I put those children behind proper fortress walls and surround them with paladins who have taken oaths to Miradu's cause. Tadrin and Oria will be buried so deep in my mountain that they won't know anything about the dangers outside until they're good and ready to face them themselves. Add the teachers, culture and hospitality of Forge Hin to that, and I can't see how any other place could be an option."

"Your proposal has merit," Umner said.

"What do you think, Mystic?" Haffor asked Rendiran.

Rendiran cleared his throat and measured his words carefully. "Prisoners serve in the lower quarries and mines of Ironmaw, and the fort isn't as well defended as yours. I only know from their reputations, I've never seen either place, to be honest. If I had to choose, they'd go where they would be best protected, and possibly where they should have a childhood, filled with education and training, yes, but they have to have a chance to play, know other children. I'd also look to accommodate Tadrin's parents, I believe they'd be good to Oria as well." Rendiran's mouth was dry, and he was aware that he was spilling his thoughts out without much thought to which order they were presented. "We also have to think of the third one, who is yet unknown to us."

"The Order of Wydu claim that the third will be a Gift from Him," Umner said. "They expect a child to be presented here any day now."

"Do they, now? I don't imagine Wydu sent us a young paladin ready for shaping, who knows what he has brought forth or where it will come from. Was there any indication as to what kind of Gift we should expect?"

"No, it was only revealed that Wydu's servant should have the Gift in hand by now," Umner replied. "They call it the Stolen One, because Wydu is using the power of one of the Gods he's imprisoned to bring her forth."

Rendiran expected trickery, especially from Wydu. The darker side of the Miradu Church had been drifting apart from the rest for centuries. The gap only widened faster after humans overthrew the Ava-Ondi kings and queens of Brightwill, and he always hoped the rift could be closed. Even still, he knew enough to question anything that came from Wydu. He was wise, but a famous trickster.

"My people don't worship Wydu for a reason," Haffor said.

Umner smiled at Haffor. "If you truly want the two who should train as Paladins, then you'll eventually be tasked with the Third One's education and care as well."

"Just what Forge Hin needs, a Gift from a trickster God."

"You have Wydu's Emissaries in your city, yes?" Umner asked.

"Three of them, and we know what they're doing, where they are at all times. They are not only meddlesome and skilled mystics, but they are political – a perfect combination for trouble," Haffor said.

"I've always found Wydu's followers to be great entertainers," Crista added. Haffor fixed her with a withering glance and her smile faded. "Not trustworthy, though, that's true." Haffor was about to say something to Umner but was interrupted by Crista. "But if you don't take the Third One in, you'll be missing an opportunity, don't you think? So far Tadrin and Oria are both seven harvests old, we may be able to assume that the Third One will at least be close in age. You can make sure that not only Wydu's Order is involved with their train-ing, but other Mystics who you can trust have a hand in it. If nothing else, perhaps the influence of Tadrin and Oria could help the Third One find a good path."

"Or she could corrupt both of them," Haffor replied.

"Why are you assuming Wydu's Gift is a girl?" Crista asked.

"Five wives," Haffor said, holding up one hand with his digits splayed. "Just a habit."

"Dark minded thoughts," Umner said. "We must have faith in the wisdom of Miradu and Her children. I feel that these Gifts should be brought together, schooled together. I also believe that Rendiran and Crista should be their primary teachers."

"A Mystic and a Wildling training two Paladins and whatever Wydu has for us?" Haffor asked. "What about him?" he asked, standing and pointing through the doorway and down the hall at Marjay, who paced the width of the passage. "Do you hear me? Guardsman?" he shouted.

Marjay regarded the dwarf, surprised, then nodded.

"Don't just stand there, bobbing your head, come here," Haffor said. "What are you to the children?"

"Good Captain, Sir," Marjay said, bowing deeply on the threshold.

"What are you in this situation? What is your place, man?"

"Oh, uh, pardon, Sir. When Our Lady Viis appeared, she declared that I was to be Oria's guardian. I have sworn to protect Tadrin as well. My Lord, Captain Paladin, Sir."

Haffor looked the guard over before sitting back in his seat. He appeared as weary as Rendiran felt but was in perfect order. "You will, then. I'll measure your wit and might first, but I wager you will."

"Pardon, Sir, but may I ask?"

"How you will be measured? In a duel." Haffor said, finding the entire situation more humorous than Rendiran thought it was. "In a duel with me right down there when we're finished here. Go and prepare yourself."

"That's not terribly sporting," Umner said as Marjay retreated down the hall. "I hear he's a good fighter, but you have advantages too numerous to mention."

"I'll keep magic out of it, and I'll keep from permanently injuring the man, don't worry," Haffor said. "Now, back to the matter at hand: this Mystic," he gestured towards Rendiran, "I promise to learn your name in time. Crista, and you will help me train Tadrin and Oria. You'll see to the quality of their upbringing and I'll make them paladins of the highest order. While you're caring for the children, Umner will watch over you."

"Hold a moment," Umner said, alarmed. "I never volunteered."

"But what an honour, to be responsible for the very Gifts our Gods have given us. Crista and this one here are experienced, and good people, I'm sure, but you have an education that absolutely outstrips theirs. What say you, Master of Masters?"

With a swirl of cold steam, Donatella Writ appeared beside Crista. She looked to each person there, giving them a few seconds observation before answering. "The people and tools to educate them are in Forge Hin, and they could be guarded well enough from capture or interference. I would have your pledge to take the Third One in as well, Haffor. That is if you have the Lord of Forge Hin's proxy in this."

"I do," Haffor said, running his calloused hand over his thick braided beard. "I do have his proxy." He thought for a moment before regarding Donatella again. "I pledge to take her in until she's a woman grown unless her order threatens to spill blood over her guardianship. I will not be responsible for a war within the church. If they allow us to be guardians, we will treat her like one of our own, fair enough?"

"Absolutely," she replied.

"High Master, what do you think of Tadrin and Oria?"

"They're remarkably good-natured children with a great capacity for learning," she replied. "I would like to offer whatever time I can to assist in their education."

"I welcome that," Haffor said.

"Then you don't need me," Umner said.

"Afraid to be parted from all the luxuries here?" Haffor asked, amused. "This city has made you soft."

"That may be true, but I also have countless responsibilities, and as much as I'd like to be a part of this, I can't just pass them off to someone who isn't as skilled or well known. Besides, how many favours do I owe you? What good would those unspent deeds be to you if I were in your own stronghold?"

"He has a point," Donatella said. "Whoever I send will be a better teacher, I already have candidates in mind."

"In that case, I release you, but only if you convince the Grand Matron to concede to my plan."

Umner looked to Rendiran with a smile. "I hope you don't have much packing to do. I expect you'll be setting out for Forge Hin as soon as Captain Haffor decides it's time to leave."

11

It was not customary to have sparring or matches anywhere but the rough lot at the rear of the temple grounds. So, it surprised Rendiran to see a crowd begin to gather on the grassy tower top where the children were playing. Several priests, ushers and temple minders were already in attendance. Off duty guards had heard that there would be a match between one of their own and a paladin, so there were a dozens of them. Their Sergeant, Manda Cullen was nowhere in sight, she may not have approved of any kind of contest between a Paladin and a guard, no matter who the Paladin was.

Tadrin and Oria were all smiles when they rushed to meet Rendiran and Crista at the upper entrance to the tower. It was one of the oldest buildings in the temple, a round, broad tower that once held the most sacred relics in its middle floor, but it had long since been turned over to serve as quarters for lower ranking people of the Order. Rendiran never had to stay in the tower, being of higher education and station than any servant or usher, but he heard it was cold and drafty in the winter, overly hot with thick air in the summer.

"Are we going to see the Paladins?" asked Oria, rosy cheeked and breathless from running around with the blonde pup.

"Yes, they're on their way up now," Rendiran said. He knelt down. "It turns out that they want you to live with them more than anything in the world. They'll help take care of you and train you in Forge Hin, the oldest and greatest Dwarven city in this land."

"You're coming too? And Crista?" Tadrin asked, worry beginning to show.

"Of course," Rendiran replied, glancing at Crista.

"There are lost treasures in the mountains," Crista said conspiratorially, "We'll find them together."

Rendiran could hear the marching feet of the paladins approaching. "All right, let's settle in somewhere, the Captain of the Eventide Guard and Marjay are going to put a show on."

"What kind of show?" Oria asked as the dog bumped her then Tadrin behind the leg with his nose.

Rendiran and Crista led the children to a nearby bench, the pup followed. "A fighting demonstration."

"Captain Haffor has challenged Marjay to a bloodless duel," Crista explained.

Rendiran was surprised to see that both children seemed to understand, and take the news with quiet excitement. They settled on the bench between Crista and Rendiran without saying a word. The pup laid down at their feet after coming to the realization that playtime was over for the moment. The children looked to Marjay, who winked at them while he took a few practice swings with what Rendiran would guess was a medium sized wooden sword and a short blade with deep teeth on one side. When the sounds of approaching feet grew louder, their attention was drawn to the large entrance, where the top of the tower joined with the larger main temple building.

The Paladins marched through the broad doors, their armor covered with thin white cloth bearing the device of Miradu on their chests, a coiled black dragon in the middle with a shield to one side, a sword on the other and a staff beneath. Their plate armour had a milky white tint. On the foreheads of each of their helms was the device of the Eventide Order, a red sun over a black field against a white background. The banner carried at the front of the group carried the same devices.

They marched in perfect synchronization, silencing everyone in the upper yard with the chink-chink of their muffled armour plates. Rendiran took more delight in the awe the children had, he could see excitement building in them as the Paladins double line formation broke and they formed a half-circle that determined the size of the dueling space. Marjay stepped into the middle as his fellow guards quickly formed the other side of the circle along with the few combat priests that were visiting the temple.

There was enough room between them for the spectators to see, but it was clear that no one but the duelists were allowed in. "This is a bloodless duel," announced a Paladin who pulled her helmet off and tucked it under her arm. She was as broad and powerful looking as the rest, and spoke with the confidence of a seasoned battle leader. "A demonstration of skill and an exhibition for the benefit of the witnesses. Honour and personal property are not at stake, nor will wagering be permitted. Rules: no blood is to be spilled intentionally. No divine power may be used. The combatants will only use blunted blades. A call for pause from either side must be obeyed immediately. Violation of any of these rules will end this match in disgrace to he who breaks them. Once a strike is landed, you will part and a new round will begin. There will be a total of three rounds. Come to the centre. Gentlemen, good luck." She put her helmet back on and drew her long sword, holding it out in front of her.

Marjay accepted a pair of blunted blades from a fellow guard. One was two thirds as long as a Paladin's longsword, the other, shorter blade had deep jagged teeth on one side. He strode to the centre of the circle with the most serious disposition.

Haffor accepted his shield – a wall of metal with the device of the Eventide Guard on it – and a blunted long sword from one of his Paladins and met Marjay in the middle, grinning at him. The officiating Paladin's sword was all that divided them, and when it was raised the pair began circling each other slowly.

Haffor was a head and a half shorter than Marjay, who was short for a human but thickly muscled. "Where did you train, guardsman?"

"On red fields and in darkened alleys," Marjay said with confidence that surprised Rendiran.

"Vague, lad,"

"I hunted Nux Assassins for three years before joining the Temple Guard," Marjay added. With shockingly quick movement, he charged at Haffor, who planted the bottom of his shield in the ground as he ducked behind it. Marjay kicked the middle hard enough to slant the heavy metal defense, then he leapt up, stepped on the top edge of the shield, deflecting Haffor's longsword with his toothed blade and slicing at him with his short sword. The showy maneuver ended as Marjay summersaulted over the dwarf and landed behind him, turning quickly to continue his attack.

To his surprise, Haffor was already turning, his longsword slashing through the air inches from his nose. The dwarf pressed on, his footing sure, his shield blocking his left side from his attack, and his longsword lashing out with quick but measured attacks. Marjay deflected many strikes with his offhand weapon, trying to catch the longsword in its teeth, and dodged the rest. Every time he attempted to counterattack, he found Haffor's longsword deflecting his slice or that the dwarf had pivoted, putting his shield in the way.

The slow, sure walking assault of Captain Haffor lasted until he'd driven Marjay to the edge of the circle, and the guardsman had to break away, running to the other side. "No hits," he shouted, shaking his head.

"No hits," Haffor announced, laughing as he adjusted his shield and rolled his shoulders. "I can't count the number of times he came within a hair of landing one."

The guards and paladins applauded briefly, clanging metal on metal instead of clapping hands.

Tadrin looked to Rendiran, a little confused. Crista answered the unspoken question instead, and he was grateful, duels weren't exactly within his expertise. "Normally two warriors would have scored at least one point in that exchange, which is touching one of their blades to the chest, legs, arms, or head. The neck and back are not allowed, since they both seem to be playing by the paladin's rules."

"But if Haffor hit Mar in the face, it would have really hurt him bloody," Tadrin said.

"That's against the rules," Oria added.

"Yes, but they can forgive a strike that draws blood, and the match will go on," Crista said. "Haffor and Marjay are so good at fighting that they can't beat each other unless they fight as fast as they normally would, but they don't hit as hard, that's the only way they seem to be changing their style."

"But someone could die?" Tadrin asked.

"No, don't worry, you see those people in red and black armour? They're War Menders, they can heal almost anything, so it's safe, don't worry."

"Marjay could get hurt," Oria said, crossing her arms.

"Just watch, they're both experts, so it's safe," Crista said, rubbing the girl's back.

"You've got more skill than I would have wagered, Guardsman," Haffor said as he slowly approached the middle of the ring. "You're wasted here, lad."

"It's an honour to defend Her most sacred temple," Marjay said. He looked relaxed as he approached the centre, casually holding his blades at his sides. "Do any of your Paladins have Deri-Sen training?"

"Ondi-Ne two-blade fighting?" Haffor asked. "Not for two genera-tions. You about to show me something I haven't seen in a while, lad?"

The pair circled each other again, exchanging tentative strikes, each one easily deflected. Rendiran knew just enough about fighting to see that they were testing each other's defences, looking for weak points in their styles. It seemed that Marjay had completely caught his breath, and it was impossible to tell what state Haffor was in, but from the tone of his comments, he seemed to be enjoying the contest a great deal.

Tadrin began to yawn after several minutes passed, and as he gaped widely, Haffor lunged with his long sword, attracting a counter from his opponent. As Marjay attempted to disarm Haffor, the dwarf turned his shield into the guardsman's sword and rushed him, bashing the man to the ground so hard that his shoulder caught a thick chunk of dirt and flung it into the air behind him. "Point, Haffor!" shouted the officiating Paladin.

"Agreed," Marjay said as he rolled to his feet and walked back to the centre with his opponent. "Never seen anyone that quick with a shield."

"I missed it!" Tadrin shouted, disappointed.

The crowd laughed at the boy's exclamation just as much as they cheered and applauded for the exchange.

"I thank you," Haffor said to his opponent.

They stood across from each other and settled into their stances – Haffor with his shield half raised and sword at the ready, Marjay relaxed with his blades raised – and the officiator shouted. "Begin!"

To Rendiran what happened next was a blur of blades, with Haffor's long sword lashing out from behind his shield and Marjay working both his blades into the fight, trying to create an opening. The exchange kept up until Haffor's sword was momentarily caught by Marjay's toothed blade and he only kept his weapon in hand by turning and attempting to bash the guardsman with his shield.

The pair parted, Marjay looking frustrated for a moment before he shook his head and took a breath. He returned his full attention to the dwarf, who stood with his shield up, looking like a squat fortress near the middle of the circle.

"Come on, you're better than that," Haffor called out.

"Aye," Marjay said, switching his toothed blade to the other hand, so his longer blade was in his left hand instead. He charged at a full run, weapons raised.

Haffor braced himself behind his shield and brought his long sword up, readying his defence and a counterstrike. To everyone's surprise, Marjay stopped short, just out of striking distance, tricking the dwarf into raising his shield just a little.

It wasn't much of a mistake, and Rendiran couldn't see what advantage Marjay had gained until the guardsman used his toothed sword to catch the edge of Haffor's shield firmly. He pulled it aside, deflecting the dwarf's longsword then striking him on top of the helmet hard. Haffor's foot came up and he kicked the guardsman's thigh hard enough to send him to the ground.

"Point, Marjay!" announced the Paladin officiator. There was polite applause – in the form of hilts tapping on shields - from the Paladins, but the guardsman greeted the point with high applause and loud cheers.

Haffor helped Marjay to his feet. "Good strike, there," he told him. "You really do know a thing or two about taking a Paladin down."

"If you were allowed to use magic, I'd be taken care of already," Marjay said.

"Only if I saw you coming," Haffor retorted as they reached the centre.

Tadrin and Oria were fidgeting, they were so eager to see the fighting resume. The Paladin and the Guardsman truly were experts, Rendiran had to admit. He would have expected anyone fighting with such ferocity and speed to have incurred severe injuries. The bloodlessness of their contest had to be a result of their skill.

"So far, Marjay hasn't taken any strikes or nicks on the wrist," Crista said. "I'm surprised, he's very good."

"That normally happens?" Rendiran asked.

"Constantly, that's why most warriors have good protection there, and they get it enchanted if they can afford it."

"Final round! Begin!" the Paladin officiator shouted.

"Hold!" shouted another woman as she broke through the semicircle of guards. "This is over. I have five empty posts and the Main Temple Hall is busy. Whatever honour you've gained on this field will have to suffice."

"But it's a tie!" Oria shouted, throwing her hands up.

"Over, I said," shouted the High Guardian of the Temple, resting her hand on the hilt of her sword. "Get back to your posts, and every guardsman here has just earned an extra shift."

"I apologize, High Guardian, I was sure someone had gotten your approval," Captain Haffor said.

"You would have made sure I was here before this started if that were the case. You and your Paladins don't get the run of the place whenever you visit, and you still owe me two of your best in trade for Marjay. I'll make sure that happens before you leave."

"One of our best," Haffor countered, "We agreed on one."

"Now that you've disrupted our day here, and you've seen Marjay fight, you know two is more than fair compensation. It's two, two of your best Paladins."

"One of my best initiates, a squire and my most heartfelt apology," Haffor said.

Rendiran didn't know the High Guardian, but the tall, blonde haired woman was well respected, and he knew why; under her watch, the Temple had never suffered a severe attack and any incident was resolved very quickly. She worked with Umner constantly, and Rendiran suspected that she most likely knew what was going on in the entire city at all times, so he imagined that a duel on a tower top happening without her approval would deeply wound her pride.

"Haffor is in trouble," Oria said as Tadrin whistled mournfully and shook his head.

"It can happen to anyone if you don't think things through first," Rendiran said.

"It's still a tie," Tadrin said. "They can't leave it that way."

"Some things never get resolved," Rendiran told him with a sigh.

12

———

*C*rista was sound asleep when something roused her. First, there was a cold nose, then the enthusiastic licking of a young dog, he started with her ear. "Hello, Ander," she said, stroking the pup's smooth fur. "How'd you get away from the little ones?" Her question was answered as soon as she looked past the dog. Tadrin and Oria were standing at the foot of her bed, looking uncertain. "What are you two doing out of bed?"

"Bad dreams," Oria said as Tadrin nodded.

"Both of you?" Crista asked.

They looked at each other, then back to her and nodded. "Can we sleep here tonight?" Tadrin asked sheepishly.

A guardsman walked past the half open door, obviously trying not to look but keeping abreast of events just the same. "You followed them, guardsman?"

"Yes, Ma'am, I did," he replied, still not looking into the room.

"You can look this way, I'm decent," Crista said, checking the neckline of her nightgown. It wasn't something she'd wear in her own home, but much more modesty was expected with so many people who had taken oaths of celibacy about. "Can you make sure that everyone knows that they're staying with me tonight? I don't want to cause a panic when they're not found in their rooms in the morning."

"Yes, Ma'am," he replied.

"And close the door please," she added.

"Have a restful night," he said before quietly closing the door.

The children were already climbing into bed, and their pup, only recently named Ander, tried to climb on top of her. She guided him down to the foot of the bed, pushed his haunches down then pulled his front paws out from under him. "You sleep at the foot, Ander." He whined at her as she laid back and she stabbed the air in his direction with her finger. "Stay."

By the time he laid his head down on his paws, she had Tadrin snuggled into bed on her right side, and Oria on her left. "You realize this can't be a regular thing," she said. "You're both supposed to be in separate rooms."

"I know," Oria said. "But we had a bad dream."

"The same dream?" Crista asked, hoping it wasn't the case.

"Yes," Tadrin said, yawning. "Wydu is angry."

"Well, he was," Oria said. "Look." She touched Crista's forehead then, and it felt as though she fell through her bed into a darkness so deep that she immediately felt lost. Just as panic began to take hold, she felt as though a pair of eyes she'd never used opened, and landscape choked with old trees filled her vision. Angry, red skies shed ruddy light on a forest unlike any she'd seen. The leaves on the plants along the path were large, thick and leathery, and vines choked the twisted grey and brown trunks.

She was dressed as she was when she went to bed, in a light but long night gown, and the cold, clammy ground under foot immediately made her wish she was wearing boots. The sound of armoured soldiers drew her attention to her right, and she peered through a round break in the woods. Irenick and Viis walked towards a granite dais under a canopy of thick, dead tree trunks. The space inside seemed darker than it should have been, and much larger than its surroundings would suggest. Her feet had a mind of their own, and she found herself running down the narrow path, branches and dead brambles pricking her until she arrived at the end of the trail, where she was less than twenty feet from the side of the dais.

There were women, men, and half-animal, half humanoid things chained to the dais, and the man who stood atop it wore a heavy cloak made of chains. Behind him, in the darkness of the interwoven dead tree trunks were even more gaunt captives who were chained with irons to their master. Wydu, she knew she was looking upon the face of one of the most feared Gods in all the lands. Many put him up beside his mother, Miradu, in her pantheon so he wouldn't be displeased with them.

The face of Wydu was handsome, with dark eyes, unnaturally broad features, framed by curled red and black hair. The few scars on his pale cheeks and chin didn't diminish from his appeal. "Brother, sister, have you come to celebrate with me?" he said, his voice was smooth and beguiling. "My Gift is almost in our mother's holiest temple."

"There were only to be three gifts to our followers, now you've put everything we've worked to accomplish into question," Viis said, pulling her heavy helmet off.

"The balance may be ruined," Irenick said.

"What? The quest to bring peace to all of Highshield and unite three of the celestial realms is ruined? If it was so delicate, then it would have failed eventually anyway. Besides, I felt neglected, without a representative. You should have invited me into such a grand plan."

"Invited you?"

"I have methods and resources that are starkly different than yours, how could that not be helpful?"

"I don't see any resources of worth."

"My realm! All you see here!" Wydu said, waving his arms at the thick jungle surrounding them. "How can it be so quickly discounted? I've been growing it, protecting it for hundreds of years now, does it not look like the very kind of forest where our mother was hatched thousands of years ago? Well, a little less than three thousand, to say simply; 'thousands' sounds more grand, but still so long ago that the story of her birth has passed out of knowledge and myth into the unknown."

"No one is impressed, not even our Mother," Irenick said.

"She should be," Wydu said, his expression fierce. Wind shook the trees and caused a mournful howl as it pushed through the branches. "The size of this realm rivals the one you work so hard to defend, and most of the Gods know well enough to stay clear of my borders. It is defended, and not by some self-important order of paladins."

"You imprison souls and line your borders with them, create walls with the lesser Gods you've managed to best, and weave the jungle like a maze," Viis said. "There is no honour in that, you've created a hell that few Gods want."

"A hell," Wydu said it quietly as though it was a curse. He tipped the head of a blonde woman with a fine beak who was chained to his cloak up and looked into her face. "You've had luxuries and I've created incredible experiences for you in past years. Would you call this 'a hell?'" She stared at him wordlessly, gaunt and nearly limp. "See?" Wydu said, releasing her. "The pleasures of my realm exhaust her."

"Yut is drained of all the power her followers have given her, and she has watched as their souls are drawn to your realm and chained along its border."

"I unite her with her people," Wydu said. "Finally, they can look upon the face of the woman who rose to become the one they worship and realize that she looks nothing like them, that they are only that: followers who empower her." He shook her chain violently, sending her to her knees. "Deceiver, you never deserved your power."

"She was always a friend to us," said a strong, beautiful female voice from somewhere above. The wind changed, pressing down from above, and Crista saw a black shadow descend. A long bodied, great dragon with a pointed jaw set down above the dais, resting one foot on the overhang above it. She looked down at her son with blazing eyes and a great, sneering maw. "Yut's people were once inno-cent, imps and dwarves and men and other things that lived in the mountains and wild forests. While chained to you her guidance couldn't reach them, and they interbred with each other and forbidden things that shrink from the light of day. It only took fourteen generations for them to become the worst sort of goblin kind, of diseased blood and short lived lives. Their corruption has spread into the deeper wilds, sowing tribes of goblinoid cannibals and raiders that will threaten civilization now that the power of the Ondi is diminished. This would have never happened if you accepted my guidance."

"Yut was a lesser Goddess, with less power than I who threatened my realm. If I took your advice, I would have appealed to her, given her an opening through which she could have gained a foothold in my house. I would have been sent straight back to you, as a dependent, a refugee."

"I will never stop offering you a place at my side, Son," Miradu said.

"Not if I have to dwell in the shadow of your loss. Have you found Irekirk yet? Or have you finally given up on him. Is that why you seek to raise two paladins and a king?"

Miradu's massive head looked to Irenick and Viis before returning her attention to Wydu. "You seek to injure me when I only offer open arms."

"You didn't think I knew about your plan to awaken the King in Forge Hin, did you?"

"It doesn't matter, it is done," Miradu replied. "There will be three, and your Gift will fall aside."

"But she is only a child, a one-time sacrifice to a weak God who I rescued and healed myself. Much like your other children did. Save the lost, the literally trod upon so people would rally around them. It's cheap, and it's brilliant, bringing even more followers, more power to you by introducing your instruments at a tender age. I emulate the ultimate trickster, I imitate you, dear Mother."

"We have our reasons for sending our Banner Bearers into the world at such a young age. By giving them to our followers they have a chance in making them their own, of learning from the best of them. That way they represent us as well as the mortals below. You assume trickery and malice where there is none. I weep for what kind of mother I must have been to inspire such venom."

"Spare me!" Wydu said, his ferocity only diminished by the fact that he was shouting at a creature hundreds of times his size. "I am your only true son, and if that weren't horrific enough for you, I am now as powerful as you are."

"If only that were true," Miradu said, slashing savagely at Wydu. A single claw scarred the granite dais, and thunder clapped as Yut's chains were broken. Wydu, was flung against the side of a dark wood wall. He watched as Irenick and Viis mounted the stairs. Viis drew her sword and put herself between Yut and Wydu as Irenick picked Yut up.

"No! You can't have her!" Wydu said, rising to his feet and drawing a sharp, serrated long blade. He surged towards Viis and swung it with both hands, the blade was covered in fitful spectral fire as it came down on Viis' shield.

Her blade burned with white light as she counter attacked, catching him on the shoulder, where it broke several chains before biting into his flesh. As she pressed her assault, her shield clattered to the black granite. Wydu countered each quick, heavy strike, sometimes barely.

Miradu brought her clawed forefoot down between them and Wydu slashed at the scaly skin savagely before backing away. Several scales the size of wagon wheels were flung free, and they melted into the ground along with Viis' shield. It was then that Viis sheathed her sword and clutched her shield arm.

Two weakened Gods who she'd struck free when she landed her blow against Wydu came to her aid, one with the head of an eagle but the body of a starved man, and an Ondi-Ne God who had hair and a beard made of leaves. Wydu had cut through Viis' shield and her arm.

"I could transform into a dragon rivalling even you, Mother. All the Gods here would bear witness from my flesh as I strike you down," Wydu spat. "But I'd rather see how all of you suffer on, knowing that my Gift is in the world, and she will be more impressive, do more for my Order than any of yours. Punishment is due, and it will be administered in the mortal world."

"Our people will take her into our care, just as we will absorb your Order," Miradu said as Viis, Irenick and the lesser Gods they saved retreated. "You will join us, or you will watch your realm shrink until you are left to wander. I am sorry, my Son."

"You'll have a place in my realm when your Gifts fail," Wydu said. "I'll even let you depart in peace today. How is that for unconditional love?" He looked across the opening in front of the dais to where Crista was watching and met her gaze. It was as though he was nose to nose with her. "I see you, little wanderer girl," he growled.

CRISTA WOKE WITH A START. Only Ander raised his head, looking at her from where he lay at her feet and thumping his tail against the covers. Both the children were sound asleep. She gave herself a moment to catch her breath. "Ever feel like you walk in terrain built for much bigger folk?" she asked Ander. She could sense that he didn't understand a single word, his young brain was trying to decide whether or not to try to climb up the bed to lick her face, or to put his head back down and get some sleep. "Sleep, young one," Crista soothed, and he put his head down. She did the same, but didn't sleep until the first sign of morning light was coming through the window.

13

"High Priestess Tyshon and her Honor Guard should be here, waiting for us, I don't understand," Lena explained to Grenn quietly so she didn't wake Shani, who slept beside her in the room's only bed. There was nothing special about the Rhymer's Inn, it was just another average inn with an overlarge, busy taproom at the bottom and normal rooms throughout two broad floors above.

The sun was setting, the middle of the city was under the shadows of taller buildings and towers. It seemed as though the night's revelry was already reaching a higher pitch downstairs. The noise didn't bother Lena, it was good to be back in civilization even though she was used to better accommodations.

Grenn was impressed, however, he hadn't been in a place like it for years, and his comfort annoyed her. He lounged in a large chair that, to her, needed re-upholstering, but he had his pipe in his teeth and was puffing away happily as soon as he was sure they were alone and the door was locked. "Couldn't we make it to Miradu's Temple? I can see the spires from here," he said, nodding at the open window.

"I was told to come here, to get instructions from one of the leaders of my order," she replied. "I don't know if we're taking her there or if we take her to the nearest Hidden House."

"I've heard of those places, supposed to be a place for special rituals and such, right?"

"They're sanctuaries, little more, but yes, they all have shrines, some have altars with long histories, but special things don't happen there."

"I've heard they are haven to spies and secret Miradu warriors," Grenn whispered. "Shady stuff that I've tried to get close to for years, the pay's better when what you're doing is a secret."

"Their reputations are inflated, trust me. Besides, I'm one of the closest things you'll see to a secret warrior to Miradu, or Wydu. We don't hide our people unless we must, there are few mysteries."

"Whatever you say," Grenn said, a little amused. "The first thing someone with secrets says is that they have nothing to hide."

"Greatness attracts followers, and greatness earned in secret doesn't draw any attention."

"But for the appreciation of your Goddess and her children," Grenn said. "I'm sure I'll be able to find my way to the underside of your Order, and I bet I'll be right at home."

A gentle knock at the door gave Lena hope, and she started getting to her feet but Grenn motioned for her to stay seated. "I'll see who this is, it's what you're paying me for. Besides, I want to introduce myself so I can get a start on joining the Order's guards."

"Now is not the time," Lena warned, sitting back down on the edge of the bed.

He drew the latch aside and started to open the heavy wooden door. Grenn was bashed off his feet as the door burst open. A tall figure in a hooded yellow robe came through. By the time Grenn had a chance to draw his sword, the robed man had a short, thin, sharp blade at his throat. The grinning red mask made the newcomer seem gleefully malicious.

Lena threw herself onto Shani and brought her into the shadows with her. "They're still in the room!" cried the shortest of the cloaked figures as she pressed through the door with another robed figure behind her. She drew a long scissor from a side slit in her robes and pointed it at Grenn. Her red mask was frozen in an expression of joy. "We will start taking pieces off this one if you don't step out of the shadows now."

Grenn flinched and the tip of the scissor lashed out, cutting across his cheek. Lena felt Shani begin to struggle, trying to get free of her arms, and she almost did for a moment.

"In a moment, this man will be missing an ear, then another, then I think we'll take his nose," the shortest of the robed figures, obviously a woman, said. "That is unless you reveal yourselves and hand the girl over. We will raise her in our Order, she will receive the best treatment the Bright One's Temple can provide, which is better than yours."

Shani struggled again, trying to get free, and Lena clutched at her harshly, gripping her arm and shaking her once hard to keep her from slipping into the light. The open window across the room seemed like the only way out, Shani didn't seem to understand what would happen to her if she gave up. The Bright One's followers would sacrifice her to their God after days of sacramental torture, Lena was certain.

"Your people don't care about you," the shortest of the robed people said. One of her companions closed the door and dropped the latch in place. "No one will come to your aid, we paid well for privacy." She glanced at the tallest of the robed figures and said; "Hold him."

Two of the robed figures, men, from what Lena could tell, held Grenn as the shortest slowly cut the top of his ear superficially. "Scream for them, beg for them to reveal themselves. Only their mercy will save you."

"I'm only a hired blade! I haven't even joined their Order! I'm no one, they won't save me!" he plead. "I'll tell you everything I know, about all the things I witnessed."

"You will," the short robed figure in the glad red mask said as she began closing the scissors on his right ear, slowly beginning a two sided cut that would separate it from his head. Lena had never heard a man scream so high, or so desperately.

Shani began to struggle again, but Lena forced her through the room, sheltered in shadow, she pushed her through the the open window and down the wall outside, the screams of Grenn following them out into the street. As horrible as what was happening in that room was, Lena was relieved that they didn't send someone with real magical power. To her knowledge, the Bright One only had a few, but most of them would have been able to see her and Shani with ease, and they would have never reached the Miradu Temple.

Several blocks away, half way to the Miradu Order Temple, Lena finally allowed Shani and herself to slip out from under the shadows in an alley that reeked of old fish. "You're hurting me!" Shani said, trying to pry her arm out of Lena's grip.

"Where do you think you're going?" Lena asked, relaxing her grip a little and turning the child towards her with her free hand.

"You let them do that to Grenn! You just let them cut him!"

"There's nothing we can do for him now. They'll realize we're gone in a moment and stop cutting him."

"You're lying! You're a liar! They're going to kill him!"

"Listen!" Lena said, shaking the little one briefly but harder than she intended. "We'll get to the Temple and tell the guards what happened, then they'll rescue him, don't worry. Until then, we have to go back into the shadows, you can't fight me this time. If I lose my hold on you, you could fall from the side of a building, or end up right where Grenn is if there are more Bright One followers around."

"There won't be anything left of him!" Shani said, big tears running down her face.

"Since when do you care about him? You didn't weep for a moment when Storo was killed."

"He was nice to me, even when he told me not to talk about who I was, he gave me honey drops while you weren't looking."

"Who did you tell?" Lena asked. "What did you say?"

Shani tried to step away, but couldn't get more than one pace's distance. Lena raised her free hand and immediately felt guilty, but her gesture brought a torrent of tears and answers. "The barman asked if I was a little princess when you were paying for the room, so I told him I was Wydu's Gift, and even more important than a princess. Grenn gave me a honey drop and said that I shouldn't tell people that. He was nice!"

The barroom was full when they paid for their room, Lena remembered, at least half a dozen people would have heard her. She should have never allowed Grenn to order their meal while Lena paid for their accommodations; Grenn wasn't exactly quick-witted. They should have been safe there, but they were ruined by Shani's need to boast. "You killed him because you were too proud and stupid to keep your little mouth shut. Grenn is paying for your lesson, so you'd best learn it well. We're going to the temple. Don't struggle."

"You're worse than those cutters! I hope Wydu punishes you!"

Lena's hand came down on Shani's cheek before she even realized she intended to slap her, and she felt like the worst person to ever live, but it quieted the girl, so she took the opportunity to slip into the shadows with her and move as quickly as they could to the Temple. Lena knew she would pay for every injury she visited upon Wydu's Gift, but she would rather face that than another minute with the child. As they passed through the darkness, Lena silently swore she'd refuse to deal with any child for any length or time for any reason again.

*R*endiran was itching to get out of the temple, to begin the journey to Forge Hin. For the first time since he arrived three years before, he wanted to move on. The halls of Forge Hin were legendary, a city that was built inside a great mountain that expanded outwards and inwards. Inner Hin was what many dwarves called Forge Hin Proper, and it was entirely inside the mountain, but when the humans joined them and built a city outside the mountain leaning against the sheer stone face, Outer Hin was founded, and the human kings called it the Dim Fort, because it spent so much time in the shadow of the mountains.

Hundreds of years had passed, and Rendiran knew that there were almost as many humans as there were dwarves living there. Most of the humans there had embraced dwarven culture, a thing he wanted to see for himself, and some families intermarried, reinforcing the bond the people shared there. It was a proud fortress with legendary hospitality, but the politics were complicated. The Lords of Forge Hin had threatened to separate from the Order of Miradu many times, and Rendiran knew that he could be called upon to help mediate if tensions rose while he was there. It was another reason for the Grand Matron, the leader of his Order, to be hesitant to move the children there.

"You've got a weight on your mind," Haffor said, putting a mug of hot tea on the ledge in front of him. "Maybe I can lighten the load?"

Rendiran nodded his thanks at the dwarf, who stepped up onto the bench so he could be the same height. The pair looked over the busy city as the setting sun turned the landscape rose red. The light grey brick, dark wooden buildings and cobblestone were painted in the hue as people travelled through the streets. "I'm going to miss the Temple, but at the same time, I can't wait to get underway." In only a few more moments the sunlight would be entirely gone.

"I've enjoyed my time here, it's been six easy days," Haffor said. "But I feel like we've enjoyed the temple's hospitality too long. That's why I'm happy to tell you that we've had a pigeon arrive with a message from Forge Hin. My father sits the throne again, he's awakened from the stone sleep. He has awakened, and he is displeased with the work of his Regent Council."

The stone sleep, something Rendiran had read about with fascination when he was only a few years older than Tadrin. Some dwarves who master the art of manipulating the earth with magical power could enter a sleep so deep that they turn to stone. Haffor's father, King Nyder, suffered a deep magical wound from an Ava-Ondi Queen named Vishen. He nearly defeated her, but that wasn't the purpose. The purpose of his direct assault on her was to distract her from her armies while the Battle for Great Carn, the neighboring mountain to Hin, was under way. The King fell, and the wound that Vishen inflicted on him was corrupted, spreading disease through the rest of his body. His army victorious, and the Queen nowhere to be found, he entered the stone sleep, leaving his brother to rule as Regent and raise his young son. "He's been asleep for ninety-one years," Rendiran said. "You must be beside yourself."

"Haven't seen that man since I was a boy on his knee," Haffor said, wiping a tear from his eye. "Hearing his voice come off that little scroll was like being wee again. He says Miradu came to him, coiled herself around his body and purified his wound, made him whole again. He is the third Gift from Miradu's House, and what a Gift it is. Umner is in with the Grand Matron now, deciding whether or not to heed his instruction; to get the children to the mountain quickly."

"It's happy news, to be sure, but this could get complicated," Rendiran said, taking a sip of the hot tea. It was ginseng with sweet root and cinnamon. "King Ormet owns Gachin Province, his line backed the Miradu Order," Rendiran said. "The children, the prize of the Temple being outside this province will cause tension now that your father is sitting on his throne."

"You know your history well," Haffor said. "Most have forgotten that my mother was killed during the Liberation War. They swore up and down that they didn't do it on purpose, and I believe them, but you have to expect a few visiting royals to get crushed when you bash the wall of a keep down. I'm sure he's wounded at her not being there to welcome him back, and having a Regent Council cede control of his Kingdom to humans to prevent a war will only rub salt into it. I fully expect him to separate from King Ormet, maybe this temple. I wonder what our Goddess' plan truly is. I know she was friend to Ondi, maybe this is a backlash for the millions who were killed."

"Miradu's oldest teachings tell us to find a way to peace whenever possible. Revenge would not be her motivation. I suspect something good will come thanks to Her Gifts, perhaps a great change for the better, but it's too early to tell. Rendiran said. "We must do our utmost to keep Miradu's Gifts from used as political pieces."

"Imagine how wealthy your Order would be if it didn't have to send seven tenths of all its product to Brightwill, to King Ormet and his rotting cities? Your Order has all the power, and my father would treat it with reverence. Unlike the Lords of the Mountain, my father isn't afraid to march with the Paladins of Forge Hin, especially if he's waging war with humans from across the sea."

"We're far from that, aren't we? Separating from kingdom would disrupt everything, countless people in Brightwill would starve, and King Ormet's enemies may close in to finish him off. He has always been a stabilizing factor, even though many of his alliances are forced, Brightwill needs him."

"Umner was right," Haffor said, looking back to the cityscape. "You are much wiser than your years. I was hoping you'd pass this little test."

Rendiran was at once irritated and relieved. "You were putting me on?"

"Aye, you said all the right things," the Dwarf said. "If you argued for anything but peace, I'd have doubts about you, but I think you're wise enough to handle yourself."

"So, your father hasn't risen?" Rendiran asked.

"He has!" Haffor said joyously. "It is Miradu's miracle, one of Her very own. Instead of bringing us a child, she returns our most beloved King. He sits his throne for the first time in nearly a century today."

"And the Council of Lords?"

"I suppose I'll find out how happy or unhappy they are with his return when I arrive in Forge Hin, but I'd wager it's mixed. He's the first King since my Uncle surrendered the Regency to the Council forty years ago. I expect my people are rejoicing."

"I'd imagine," Rendiran said.

"You'll see it first hand, though it will take us some time to get there. Have you ever been up the wall?"

"As far as Forge Hin? No, I'm afraid I haven't. I've only been outside the wall twice," he replied. "The first time I visited Mozib, a village not far from here with a buried Ava-Ondi temple, so I only spent a day out there. The second time was more memorable, I was in the Urfen Forest for a little over a week." He remembered the trip fondly, especially since he met Crista on his third day there. Before he knew it, she'd pulled him into one of her treasure hunts. A mere glimpse into her world changed how he saw nearly everything, and he always looked forward to her visits to the Miradu Temple.

"Not far from the wall at all. Urfen is gone, cut down and tilled," Haffor said. "It'll do you and the young ones good to get past the wall, to travel into the wild north east. Even from the safest roads you'll see things, meet people that you would not have imagined. Why, I'll show you," Haffor hesitated for a moment, "things that will make this city look modest in spectacle." His hand went to the hilt of his sword slowly.

Rendiran felt it then, a chill up his spine. The room was darkening more than it should have, and then it was cast entirely in shadow. "I call on Your protection," he said as he waved his hand in front of himself and Haffor. Golden light illuminated them. The shadow passed up the stairs behind them.

"The children, the Matron," Rendiran said, rushing up the steps with Haffor close behind. "This is her tower."

"How could something cloaked in shadow get past the Wards below?" Haffor asked, running up the steps.

"Some of the windows aren't warded this high up," he replied. "It would take a master to enter from this height."

They came to the top of the stairs and Rendiran could feel the presence in the room. He stepped towards the only doorway on that floor with his hands raised, trying to get closer to the chilling edge of the unnatural shadow, but the room was already darkening, and no one had come to light the candles yet. "Tadrin and Oria are in that room," he whispered, nodding at the only door in the small curved wall. Writing around the edge of the wood in ancient Ondi-Ne script provided protection from most of their enemies. "We leave it closed," Rendiran said. "They're protected while it's closed."

"I call thee forth from the dark shroud that conceals you!" Haffor said, holding his free hand up, sending shafts of light in all directions. A wailing girl in white robes, no older than Tadrin or Oria ran towards him, her cheeks covered in tears.

A dark haired woman was revealed next as she reached forward and tried to catch the girl. She stopped at the tip of Haffor's sword. He touched the top of the young girl's head as she clung to him. "This girl isn't here to harm us," he said.

Rendiran could sense it as well, a feeling of goodness that emanated from the curly haired little blonde girl. The woman who had her bore an aura of death, as though she'd recently been among the wounded and dying, and she had drawn power from it.

"Help me," the little girl said, holding to Haffor for dear life. "She uses dark magic. She killed hundreds of people, and her man tried to throw me off a mountain."

"Who are you?" Rendiran asked the dark haired woman. He immediately recognized the robes of Wydu's Priests. Haffor seemed convinced that the little one needed protecting, but the expression of shock and dismay on the woman's face made it clear to Rendiran that there was more to the story.

"I'm Lena of Castle Nightbreak. I followed a path Wydu set for me to find his Gift, Shani." She gestured to the little girl.

"She keeps calling me that, but I told her my name is Nella!"

"She's never told me that, even said that Wydu wanted me to name her. She's playing games again, something she's done before, you must believe me," Lena said.

"The stench of death is on you, woman. We'll chain you first, then decide what we'll believe," Haffor said, reaching out and closing his hand in her direction.

Her forearms were pressed together as though someone had suddenly tied them. Shackles made of light surrounded her wrists, and she sneered at the Paladin, then at Rendiran. "I only came this way because we are being pursued by Lucents, and I had a vision of presenting Wydu's gift directly to Umner the Dawn Shaper, who I sense is in a room above."

"She hits me! She probably wants to sell me!" the little girl wailed. "All she cares about is gold!"

"A pox on you, little bitch," Lena said as the restraints of made of light were overcome with darkness and she pulled free. "You'll see," she nodded at Nella. "This creature looks sweet, but she's poison, the worst of Wydu is in her. She is his creature, and I've had enough." In four quick steps she made it to the window and dove through it.

Rendiran followed to the edge and watched as her cloaks became black wings, her body took the form of a giant raven and she disappeared into the night. He'd met Wydu's followers before, and while many of them seemed to speak in riddles, they were all clear that they felt like they were part of the Order of Miradu, even if they were the darker side of the faith. Most of them were known for doing good, especially amongst the ranks of the Order's defenders. Most of the combat priests came from that side of the order, even a few notable paladins, though they had their own style. The magic he witnessed - breaking the bonds of a senior paladin, transforming into a great bird while falling – they were things that a well-practiced mystic could do, and her pointed ears indicated that she was at least part Ondi. "She's away, escaped as a giant raven," Rendiran said, turning towards Haffor and the girl, who clutched at him and wept. "You're safe here now."

"What's going on?" Crista asked as she emerged. "The door seemed stuck."

"The wards kept you inside and protected," Rendiran said as he walked to her side. "Wydu's Gift may have just arrived," he whispered as he watched Haffor comfort the young one. "I think we should be cautious."

15

"There's something about this one," Crista said in a low whisper to Rendiran. "Look at how Umner and Haffor are around her."

It was true, Nella, Wydu's Gift, sat between the men on a window seat and they doted on her as though she was their own daughter. He didn't know Haffor very well, but Umner normally didn't get along with children. He used sweets and little bribes to win their silence on the rare occasion that he had to handle them. It worked as long as he didn't run out, but with Nella, he hung on her every word as she smiled at he and Haffor, telling them a long story about how she travelled to the Temple.

"Do you remember what I tried to teach you about the Weaving Way?" Crista asked as Ander the dog hid behind her and Rendiran's legs. The pup didn't want to go anywhere near Nella. "Try to see past what your eyes are telling you, look at the space around her, expect that you'll find something there."

Rendiran tried, even though his order didn't condone the use of weaving magic, he saw its usefulness. It was much more difficult for humans to learn it, making human practitioners an extreme rarity. Even the ones that could use the Weaving Way could only perform the most basic tasks. He'd only had a few fleeting moments of success at even seeing the strands of energy that connected everything. "I haven't tried in a while," he told her. "What are you trying to show me?"

Crista was about to answer when Nella stood and began leading the two men towards the stairs to the Grand Matron's audience chamber near the top of the main Temple spire. They were only one floor down. Nella flashed Rendiran a smile. "I have a gift from Wydu to the Matron, we're going to see her now."

That's when Rendiran felt it, the urge to serve and protect her. Crista gently placed her hand on the back of his neck, a comforting gesture, and then turned his face so he was looking at her. The sensation was gone as soon as he met her dark green eyes. Rendiran took a deep breath as though gasping for air after a long swim under water. "That's what she's doing?" he whispered with alarm.

"Look at her again," Crista said, pointing at the trio walking towards the steps. "You'll probably be able to see it now that I've broken you out of it, now that I'm helping you."

Rendiran looked and saw thin chains of light wrapped around Umner and Haffor. Their eyes, feet and hands were bound most tightly. Other chains were reaching out around Nella, as though feeling for other beings to control. "She's powerful, I've never seen that before," he whispered as they disappeared around the stairs. "We can't let her near the Matron."

"Wait, we know Wydu was powerful in life, a weaver that made most Ava-Ondi master weavers look like amateurs. His magic was focused on manipulation. We should follow them until we discover Nella's purpose. I'll keep her enchantment from taking you." Crista's slender hand took his. "I've been trained to resist that kind of enchantment."

"I forget who raised you sometimes," Rendiran said.

"You're the only one," she replied with a little smile. "If she tries to harm The Matron, I'm the only one who can get in her way."

The pair moved up the stairs, catching up with Nella and her escorts as they opened the audience chamber door. The guards were all smiles, grinning at Nella as though her arrival was an event worthy of celebration. Fine chains of light gripped them, forcing their faces into glad expressions. "Will the Matron be able to resist?"

"Unless she has been trained in the Weaving Way, or has new protections drawn on her skin, definitely not."

"What if the Matron draws on her divine connection with Miradu while she's trying to resist?" Rendiran asked.

"I doubt She's favouring the Matron after everything I've seen so far. I wonder how strong that link is."

Rendiran couldn't' help but agree. Viis actually appeared in the flesh and had no interest in seeing the Grand Matron, and neither Tadrin nor Oria were given messages for her. Miradu herself brought a Dwarven King back into the world instead of healing the Grand Matron or appearing to her. It was as if Miradu had turned away from the woman who was supposed to represent her in the mortal word. The Grand Matron must have realized that at some point, but she made no indication of it to Rendiran.

"I requested solitude," came the muffled voice of the Grand Matron from the audience chamber. The black floor was polished to a mirror shine. Constellations were inset with gold across its circular surface. Around the edges were thick padded seats made for lounging and laying, with the most padded, comfortable space being that of the Matron's. She lounged there with books piled high, some looked freshly bound. Arched windows let cool evening air in, and the light of several bright yellow Quickamber lanterns hanging overhead illuminated a great statue of a black dragon with scales that shimmered in rainbow colours when it shifted in the light.

The Grand Matron hurried to put her black veil in place, trying to hide her twisted and deformed face. The first time Rendiran saw her she was one of the most beautiful women he'd ever seen, with long but appealing features and a smile that few could resist returning if they were lucky enough to see it.

Years ago she was a social creature, with a reputation for frustrating her guards by pressing past them to embrace followers and lay her hands on the ill when she had the energy to help them. Her charm, wit and divine gifts were legendary. Only nine years past, she was holding audience in the audience chamber and the last petitioner of the night before the evening merriments were about to begin knelt before her, announcing that the greatest of green serpents, Odilexa, the Goddess of the East, had a missive for her. Before anyone could react, he leapt forward and laid his hands on her face, his fingers pressed into her flesh like they were red hot metal melting into wax. He twisted her flesh, muscle and bone until the Paladin who was tasked with staying at her side at all times, Ulleyo, beheaded the man.

For months healers and even flesh crafters tried to help the Grand Matron, whose reshaped face made breathing a labour, sight a challenge and public appearances an impossibility to her. None of them could do anything to restore her beauty or health.

Finally, the greatest of flesh crafters, Dathanga, tended to her and after several days announced that what had been done to her could only be undone by the practitioner who attacked her. Ulleyo, her own Paladin and favourite Consort, took leave of her several nights later. In the short quest to find him, priests discovered his armour and all the markings of Miradu buried with his sword in the Low Garden of the temple. By the order of the Grand Matron, the search for Ulleyo ceased.

Rendiran was one of the few people she would meet with when she needed to spread new ideas throughout the priesthood. Why she liked meeting with him instead of Umner, who she almost never called on, no one knew, especially not Rendiran himself. He was aware that he had a privileged position in her court, whether he understood it or not, whether it came with a title or not, was not important. He always had the deepest sympathy for her, and knew that she suffered. It was plain to him from the sound of her labored breathing, and occasional sight of her using a kerchief to tend to herself under the veil without revealing what was underneath. Those white cloths always came back yellow and red.

"Grand Matron, I am Wydu's Gift to you, and I have a poor but much desired trick to show you," Nella said.

"What of Our Goddess? What of Miradu?" the Grand Matron asked as she pulled her veil down. Rendiran was only able to see her ruined chin and the living flesh that hung from it before it was in place.

"Miradu pities you, and would have you supplanted before your time. May I approach?"

Rendiran saw that the bright spectral chains stopped short of the Grand Matron. It was as though she was surrounded by an invisible protective shell that Nella's magical chains and light could not get past. He would have gotten between the girl and his Grand Matron if he didn't see that his Great Lady was protected.

"You may approach," the Grand Matron said.

With grace beyond her years, Nella walked to the edge of the thickly padded seat and knelt before the Grand Matron. "I am sorry that the tidings I bring are mixed. From Wydu's side I have been able to see the changes in Miradu's otherworldly realm, and I say that they embrace light to the exclusion of all else. Imperfect things, all beings who exist in the gray and are even slightly sullied by this world are sent wandering from her side. Her children, the lesser Gods, are little better, save Wydu, who embraces all the things his mother refuses. In his warm, dark realm there is room for all, sustenance for every being, even the beasts and night creatures have a place. He looks to you and sees a beautiful being who he accepts with open arms just as you are."

"How am I to know that these are his words?"

"Search your heart, you'll feel his love within you and know that I truly am his messenger." The words coming from the girl, along with the confident tone gave her a strange, otherworldly quality. A suspicion began to grow in Rendiran's mind so he whispered it. "She is possessed."

"By something more powerful than I've ever heard of," Crista whispered back. "I can't do anything. This is beyond any magic I know."

The chains that bound Haffor and Umner were slowly retracting back into her shoulders and arms, releasing them. "As I extend my hand in friendship, you should know that it is His." She reached up towards the Grand Matron.

The Matron touched the girls' fingers gingerly, and for a moment the two were motionless. Nella's hand gripped two of the Matron's fingers hard then, joined by her other hand grabbing her thumb. "Feel the power of Wydu, embrace the change he brings!" Nella shouted, her voice joined by another, impossibly deep one that shook Rendiran's core. It was Wydu's voice, he could not say how he knew it for certain, but the girl was channeling Wydu more completely than he'd ever seen anyone channel anything in his life. "My gifts to you; beauty restored, sight beyond sight, and divine power beyond imagining." It was as though Wydu himself was in his dragon form, filling the room with the sound of his proclamations. "Miradu restored a King, but I restore you, and will see you become an Empress and a Master of Sorcery."

Rendiran tried to step forward but was held in place as his Grand Matron convulsed violently, screaming in her anguish. A glance at Crista revealed that she was straining against an invisible restraint as well.

When the Grand Matron finally fell limp, Haffor rushed to her as though breaking their invisible bonds first. Rendiran wasn't far behind, and Crista caught Nella as she slumped to the floor. "The possession is over," she said. "This girl is free of Wydu's spirit."

Rendiran and Haffor carefully turned their Grand Matron over onto her back as Umner looked on from a few paces away. "What have they done to her, Rendiran?" he asked, half panicked.

"I am well," the Matron said, pulling her veil aside. "I feel that I'm restored, what do you see?"

The face of his Matron had indeed changed, she was more beautiful than he remembered, so much so that he felt a strange pang of guilt while he gazed upon her. Crista came to mind, and the first time she saw her – he thought he'd never see anything more comely in his life, and he still enjoyed taking the sight of her in when he was sure she wasn't aware of him looking. It was strange, but even as he returned his Matron's smile, staring at her in awe, he felt guilt for looking at someone so beautiful when his heart belonged to someone else. "You should tell her," the Grand Matron said in a whisper so quiet that it was little more than a light breath.

"Your beauty is such that it could stop a heart from beating with shock one moment, and restore its rhythm in the next," Haffor said. "Bah, my tongue is square for poetry, a mirror would do you more justice."

"I can feel it," The Grand Matron said as she sat up, gently caressing her re-sculpted flesh. "Is she all right?" she asked, looking to Nella, who was cradled in Crista's arms.

"She's resting," Crista replied, not looking up. "Channeling a God must be exhausting."

The sound of pikes clattering to the floor drew Rendiran's attention to the entrance, where both of the Grand Matron's personal guards were removing their helms and dropping to their knees. He looked to Crista and realized that she was averting her eyes from the Matron, looking anywhere but at leader of their Order, and though it was difficult, he decided to do the same.

"Bring Wydu's Gift to me, I'll care for her while she sleeps so I am the first person she sees when she wakes," the Matron said, patting the deep lounging seat beside her.

"Yes, Grand Matron," Crista said. She laid Nella down at her side as instructed then stepped back and bowed. "May I take your leave?"

"Why do you avert your eyes? Is your Ondi-Ne sight revealing something that our human vision can't see?"

"Only beauty," Crista said. She looked at the Grand Matron fully then. "I fear that it may draw me away from purpose and reason."

"Do not fear," the Grand Matron said, her expression growing more serious as though she had just received unfortunate news. "This is the last time you will see me for a very long time."

16

The Grand Matron was moving about the Temple the next day for the first time in nearly a decade. She was surrounded by human paladins from Haffor's Company and several priests who had the seniority to accompany her. The veil was gone, and Rendiran heard that new robes were being fashioned. He couldn't help but be alarmed at what she wore in the interim – robes from Wydu's Order – white silk overtop a black under layer. Word spread faster than she could tour the temple. That wasn't all. In the middle of the grand foyer of the main floor artisans were marking the marble floor with chalk, drawing the plans for a new shrine to Wydu. It would be the first shrine anyone saw when they entered, even before Miradu's.

Rendiran wasn't surprised when he was pressed into the corner of the room as the Grand Matron visited Tadrin and Oria. They were just waking when she arrived in the bedroom with fourteen little beds made for orphans abandoned in the city. They were moved there after Nella was delivered to them by the Wydu Order priestess. There were no orphans in the Temple's care just then, they had all been moved to the real orphanages, where they would be cared for, educated, and eventually chosen by masters for trades or dedication to the Order.

It was a strange sight, the Grand Matron sitting down on one little bed across from Tadrin and Oria while eighteen paladins looked on. The priests were told to wait outside, with the exception of Rendiran and Umner. Umner stared at the Grand Matron, as though trying to anticipate her moods, or perhaps her needs, Rendiran couldn't say, but when he said; "good morning," to his superior, Umner had no reaction for him.

"It is good to finally meet you," the Matron said after awkwardly embracing each of the children in turn. "How has your time been here?"

"Boring," Oria said, stifling a yawn.

"But nice, the pudding is the best," Tadrin added, smiling and nodding. He elbowed Oria.

"I like the gardens," Oria said, her yawn interrupted.

The Matron's smile faded a little as Crista slipped through the door so quietly that Rendiran didn't realize she was in the room until she sat down behind the children. At a tilt of the Matron's head, one of the Paladins said; "Crista the Wildling, she has retrieved many of our most precious artifacts from the inner country."

"Ah, and what about the Guardsman who Viis chose? Where is he?"

"Marjay is waking now," Crista replied. "He was on watch in this room half the night."

"Ah, I would like to speak to him, but for now, I would ask you both some questions," the Matron said to Tadrin and Oria. "I'm wondering if you carry any messages or gifts from our Goddess or her children?"

Tadrin and Oria looked at each other for a moment, then Oria spoke. "Viis didn't say anything about you."

"I'm sorry," Tadrin said, shrugging. "Neither did Irenick."

Rendiran could see worry on the pair's young faces, and made eye contact with Crista, who nodded her acknowledgement. "I don't think their time with the Gods was long," she said.

The Grand Matron ignored her. "Why are you both half Ondi?"

The young pair thought for a moment, Tadrin shaking his head and joining hands with Oria.

"Is it a secret? You can tell me."

"We don't know," Oria said.

"What about your age? Why are you both so young? Why is Nella so young?"

"I only know that we were chosen," Tadrin replied. "We have young souls, maybe that's got something to do with our age?"

"Young souls can inhabit any age of person in this world," the Grand Matron said. "But the soul of an Ondi joined with that of a human is not common. Why not sent such a mixed spirit back in an adult? A paladin, duchess or adventurer coming to us to be risen?"

"I didn't see a difference between any of the souls I met when I was with Viis. The ondi looked like ondi, human like human, dwarf like dwarf, but maybe they could be different?" Oria said.

"They were all the same, except for looks, but some did seem old," Tadrin added, Oria nodded her agreement.

"Years of study in spirituality says differently," the Grand Matron said, the remainder of her good humour eroding.

"Some spirits were human one moment, then ondi another, and again something else I didn't even recognize," Crista said.

"They've spoken to you about this?" the Grand Matron asked.

"They share dreams and memories with me, it's a gift some special Ondi-Ne children have. I've seen much of what they experienced and helped them understand their experiences."

"Could you share some of it with me?" asked the Matron.

"You're not Ondi," Oria said, shaking her head.

The Grand Matron leaned back. "I wonder, what mysteries could you explain into knowledge simply by telling me your stories more thoroughly?"

"I'm afraid most of what they have seen doesn't explain the workings of the other world past what we already know," Crista said. "Except that Wydu's realm is now fully separate from Miradu's, and it's grown dark, guarded by countless imprisoned souls. The tales of him chaining Gods to his throne are true, and their followers fall into thralldom when they die instead of gathering in the territory of those they worship. He seems more like a kind of warlord rather than a trickster God, or champion of wisdom."

"But he rules wisely, there must be a reason behind his methods," the Grand Matron said. "You should take care when speaking of Him, it almost sounds as though you offer criticism instead of praise."

Crista smiled a little, it was a placating gesture that Rendiran had seen her make when she was confronting someone who was more interested in hearing something they could agree with instead of the stark truth. "I apologize. I'm sure he has a plan. I couldn't pretend to decode the deep mysteries of Wydu and his methods."

"Is there truly nothing I can learn?"

"These two are the miracles we've been entrusted with," Crista said, putting a hand on each of their shoulders. "I believe that we have something to show our Goddess in how we raise them."

Rendiran couldn't have said it better himself, in fact he was sure that Crista's skills at diplomacy outstripped his own despite his training. An abrupt knock at the door preceded it's opening by a brief moment. "Matron, Wydu's Gift is awake and she's calling for you. No one else can console her."

The Grand Matron stood and started for the door, then stopped and looked over her shoulder. "I wonder, could you tell me what happened to your people?" she asked Crista. "How did so many of them escape persecution? Where have they gone? Are they still in this world at all?"

"I would have joined them long ago if I knew how to follow," Crista replied.

As the human paladins retreated with their Lady, Haffor and Marjay entered. "Shane Oakstand," Haffor said to a paladin at the rear, gripping the edge of the tall woman's breastplate. "You abandon my company?"

"I guard our Holy Matron," she replied.

"Has she ordered you to do so?"

"She doesn't have to, my heart tells me that I must be at her side," Shane replied.

Haffor released her with a nod and watched them leave. "All but eleven of my company have reduced regard for me. They follow her as though they're under a spell. Only dwarves and Ondi descendants remain."

"All of the Temple guard commanders are the same," Marjay said, accepting a warm hug from Oria and picking her up.

"You don't feel drawn to the Matron?" Rendiran asked, feeling her pull on him release. He wasn't aware that he was under her influence at all.

"I don't," Marjay said.

"Viis protects you," Oria said. "She told me she saw something special in your spirit, that's why she chose you as my guardian. She gave you her blessing before I came back."

"Well, I've never felt so privileged in my life," Marjay said. A grumble from one of the children's stomachs prompted a little laughter in the room. "Time for breakfast?" Tadrin and Oria both nodded.

"So, it is," Marjay said. "Come with me, then. Hot bread and baked apple with honey should fill those bellies."

"I've ordered three of my best to follow you," Haffor said. "They're just outside, experienced dwarves, every one."

"Thank you," Marjay said.

"Have they had breakfast? Do real paladins eat the same thing we do?" Tadrin asked.

"They will once they get a nose full of it," Marjay replied, putting Oria down and leading the children out.

"Everything is shifting in this Temple, I have to go," Crista told Rendiran as soon as the door was closed. "The children should go as well, especially Nella."

"Aye," Haffor said. "You're right, but only two of them will be leaving with us, and if we don't depart soon, they'll be trapped here."

"Wydu's girl," the fact that Crista didn't call Nella Wydu's Gift didn't escape Rendiran, "is already enchanting the Matron, and even if she is innocent from this moment on, Wydu could seize direct control of her whenever he likes. Beyond that, I'm sure he didn't choose her blindly. I'm sure she's a like-minded representative and he is absolutely opposed to Miradu and her other children. I feel he wants to take the heart of Miradu's following for himself."

"So a split in the Order is coming?" Rendiran asked. "Are you certain Wydu is orchestrating it?" He drew a shape in the air in front of his face; a line that went from left ear to right, crossing his eyes, then back to the middle to come down over his mouth. It was an old gesture that his teachers told him would spare him from Wydu's sight when he was a boy, more a reflex.

"I'm absolutely certain," Crista said. "I'll show you the evidence when we have more time, but I ask for your trust."

"You have it, and that'll have to be enough, I don't think I'll be able to share in that."

"You have Ondi-Ne blood in you, I wasn't sure until last night," Crista said. "You will have to learn how to break through whatever magic they used to conceal it. My Great Aunt can reverse it if you like."

"You aren't the tallest human I've ever met by far, so I'd say that's likely," Haffor said. "I think we should all leave today. Nella will remain with our Matron, I can find no way to counter the hold the girl has on her. It's well beyond anything magical, Nella brought her salvation from years of suffering, an opportunity to outlive her regret and grief."

"Regret?" Rendiran asked. A light, rhythmic knock at the door told him that he would most likely have to wait for an answer to his question. It was the tat-tatta-tatta that Yimere, one of Rendiran's teacher's guards was known for. He answered the door, knowing who would greet him. "Yes?"

The old, yellow eyed, thin-faced Ava-Ondi looked up at him soberly. "My master wishes to have some parting words with you." The thin blades at his side were decorated with silvered cross guards, and his leather armour was adorned with fine metal pieces as though they were finely woven and not hammered. No one knew how old the warrior was exactly, but he'd guarded Hidel Lightcliff, Rendiran's most recent teacher, for the better part of two centuries.

"I must answer his call," Rendiran said over his shoulder to Crista and Haffor.

"We'll begin preparations," Crista said.

17

*R*endiran followed Yimere down a narrow hallway and through a secret door he'd never seen before. His eyes wouldn't have noticed the seams marking the portal if he had all day and all the light he wanted to stare at it. As he followed the short, thin, angular featured Ava-Ondi down a long, winding stair and through several darkened halls that were marked with covered eyeholes, he tried to track his location. "She is right, you know," Yimere said. "As someone who has seen many of mixed blood in my many years, I can tell you; there is Ondi-Ne in you, and any Ondi-Ne blood gives you the potential to become as connected to the universe as any great Ondi. How someone with your potential has missed it is beyond me."

"Mixed blood?"

"Somewhere along the way my ancestors thought it would be amusing to lay with different species. Once a dwarf, and even further back someone had a part imp child. Just imagine." Yimere shuddered. "I do have a remarkable aptitude for channeling though, thanks to my one sixty fourth part imp, but we'll keep that between the two of us, yes?"

"My lips are sealed. How much Ondi is in my blood? What kind?"

"You are one quarter Ondi-Ne, of excellent pedigree from what I see."

"Did you know my parents?" Rendiran was seldom hopeful where finding his parents was concerned. He'd tried several scrying methods, but none of them led anywhere.

"I read your blood, as did my master. We don't know anything more about your lineage because who your parents were isn't important to us. What they were is more pertinent to what you learn from my master."

"How could I not have known?"

"It was hidden from you," Master Hidel said as the pair emerged from behind a book case into his private section of the library. One wall was covered in a tall scroll case stuffed to capacity with records and accounts of divine encounters. Throughout the middle of the room were piles of books as tall as he was, taller than Hidel or his guardian, and in the middle was an old oaken table. It was the centerpiece of the room, with stairs leading up one side and a small chair for Master Hidel in the middle. Normally the old half Ondi-Ne, half Ava-Ondi was surrounded by books, but today he seemed focused on several maps and scrolls. From what he could see, none of the land masses on the maps floating in the air were recognizable. "Our Rendiran's blood carries secrets that no one dared tell. Your lineage is locked. Someone decided that you should live, but be perfectly separated from your parents."

The Master's blue eyes looked to him, they were always bright and youthful looking. An old horn hovered in front of his face and tipped onto his lips enough for him to get a sip of hot tea. When he'd had his fill, it righted itself and kept drifting in its slow orbit around the magician's head. He was never without his tea horn.

"So, I won't know anything until someone has the power to reveal my lineage to me," Rendiran said. "Most likely whoever hid it."

"True, but only a student of reality magic, a master weaver who has accomplished a high skill in healing can hide someone's bloodline like this. Such a practitioner could undo the work, whether they cast it or not. I found it amusing that your area of interest is in healing, and that you excel at it. You have everything to learn about weaving, however."

"The Order looks down on the Weaving Way," Rendiran said.

"Yes, the Order fears it, a sad fact that comes from its mostly human congregation. Humans can learn divine channeling many times easier than reality mastery, the methods humans must use to truly use the Weaving Way are still hidden, and if their keeper has their way, no human will ever find them. There has been enough bloodshed thanks to the human's need for revenge, and the fight for control of Brightwill is still fresh. All of that's political, useless to people like us. Miradu, Irekirk, and Viis were all adept at weaving. Miradu was a true Master of Reality, all of her miracles are the result of High Weaving Magic. She taught her children all they wanted to know about mastering reality through weaving and divine magic, and that is how the Pantheon was created. Irekirk only built the temple in this world, his mother created something much more impressive. I follow Miradu's teachings because I believe they are the correct way to move through this world, and because I admire her. The Miradu Temple Order in Highshield has added so many rules, political mechanisms and such that I would rather not play their games. They even try to convince young priestlings that vows of celibacy and poverty are Miradu's will. Balderdash! Lust in the absence of care and greed with the absence of sense are the things Miradu warns us against, not the absence of lovers and coin. In my time here I've watched humans replace most of the temple officials, and new laws fall into place, creating a political system that stands to work against people like me, and now that you know you are Ondi, you too." Master Hidel took a sip of tea and sent the horn drifting around further out from him with a tap of his finger. It joined the other objects in his orbit: a fine feathered quill, two books, the maps, and an old pipe.

"I apologize for wasting your time with my whining, while I detest politics, I have difficulty ignoring them. You have been brought here because I received word this morning that I am no longer your teacher, Rendiran. A surprise to me, since three years is a very short time to be in my tutelage. If I had known, I would have hurried things along a little more."

"I'm sorry to hear that," Rendiran said, feeling a pang of loss so deep that it surprised him. He looked forward to his assignments from the old magician, even though every one of them was challenging. He finished them as quickly as he was able so he could visit again. Sometimes he would finish an assignment in a few days, other times it took him weeks.

"I know, I'm a charming old elf," Master Hidel Lightcliff said with a chuckle. "It wasn't my decision. Five of my students are moving on today. Drastic changes in this Order are taking place, and I feel even my time will end here before long, and I'll have to find another library to plunder. Perhaps it's time for me to return to Brightwill. What do you think, Yimere?"

"The fires that drove the Ondi out of these lands have grown cold, but I would still not return to that country. I've visited that place, going looking here-and-there while you sleep."

"What have you seen, here-and-there in Brightwill that would keep me from the country of my birth?"

"Jealousy. For most it is for money or political power, but the desire of a Thanga or two might be alarming to you. They are jealous of anyone with your kind of connection to the divine or mastery of reality."

"Thangas," Master Hidel scoffed. "If Coriath could have prevented them from appearing, then I may not mourn the purging of my kin as much. The masters of their practices are a blight in the universe."

To Rendiran, a Thanga was as much myth as flying horses or white dragons. When Coriath began teaching magic to humans, several of them began to mix divine and Ondi magic with it. Most of the experiments didn't work, but Lisar of House Thanga, a powerful disciple of Coriath, found a way to twist his teachings in order to command the flesh and minds of humans as well as some Ondi. Before long, she learned how to apply the new style of magic to other things, especially the recently dead.

Before he could discover the corruption, or because of it, Coriath left Brightwill never to be seen again. Her household was eventually stripped of all titles and lands, and the bloodline was hunted down and killed, but Rendiran had heard that it left an order of powerful magicians behind – the Thangas. He knew there had been people who claimed to be Thangas, but he never found evidence that they were in some dark order, or practiced in any particular tradition. It was the first time he'd heard any indication that they were real, and the very idea that some of the stories he'd heard could be true, that greedy, powerful magicians practiced that line of conjuring and control sent a chill through him.

"So, we won't be going to Brightwill, then," Master Hidel said. "Perhaps we should go see the dunes of Old Sharr"

"That desert is called Ember Scar now," Yimere corrected quietly. "It is watched by a living dragon-god."

"Zirex, that's right. Surely he doesn't actually see everything that happens in that land? It's the size of an ocean."

"You're right, it wouldn't be too difficult to hide from him."

"Are there still any large cities with old libraries?"

"Three, two swallowed by the sands."

"Then perhaps we'll go digging for something everyone else has forgotten. I love old books. Well, perhaps not books, what I'm looking for was probably written on slats, or scrolls so old that air's caress would turn them to dust. Do you think we should go on an adventure? It's been some time."

"I'll begin packing, Master," Yimere said.

"Just the prizes of my collection this time, no need to bring anything after the Second Age."

Rendiran drank in every word, memorizing the names of places he'd never heard in his life. He'd never heard of the Ember Scar, didn't know there was more than two Ages – the Old before Coriath and the New – and he'd only seen one ancient scroll written on slats of wood held together with string, it was older than anyone could estimate accurately. He'd only seen one such candid conversation between the Master and his Guard before, and he ended up delving into countless tomes, learning unbelievable things about the world thanks to it.

"Oh, Rendiran, I forgot you were here in all the excitement. Yes, I wanted to tell you personally. You have been assigned to Worton. It seems this Order wants to bring your days of study to an end so you can administer to the needs of that fine city instead. You will be a street healer, drawing people to Miradu as you mend wounds and cure ails. I was surprised to hear your new assignment, since Warton is almost entirely in the Order's pocket already, I even told them you'd grow bored, but the Matron's man didn't seem very interested in my objections."

"So I'll travel to Worton," Rendiran said, thinking of Tadrin. It was half way to Forge Hin. He'd heard it was a great, bustling city that attracted as many pioneers looking to expand past the wall as well as soldiers who wanted to train for the Order of Miradu's army. It was also a producer of the finest ale he'd ever tasted, though he rarely imbibed. The fate of Tadrin, his parents and Oria weighed more heavily on his mind.

"I wonder, would you like to come with us on our adventure, Rendiran?" the Master asked. He observed his student as he snatched the pipe from where it drifted by in the air then lit it with his forefinger. "No, I see you wouldn't. You feel responsible for Tadrin, and you should. It is an old law of magic: 'what you bring into the world does not belong to you, but you are answerable for it.'" He puffed on his pipe.

"Irenick The Just brought him into this world, I was only his instrument," Rendiran replied. "His humble instrument."

"Humble you are, but you must know that the Gods require someone competent and dedicated to perform a resurrection. It is an act of love that requires a partnership, one that leaves an indelible mark."

"Where do you think I should go? If you were in my place, where would your wisdom take you?" Rendiran asked.

"You flatter me," the Master said with a puff of smoke. A little ember escaped his pipe and he patted it out on his thick, tea stained silken robe. "What would you learn if I made this decision for you?"

"He doesn't always give the best advice, anyway," Yimere muttered as he passed by with an armful of well-worn leather bound books.

"You know what choices you have. To leave the cloth and find your own way, or follow Haffor to Forge Hin, me to a still uncertain adventure, or to take your place in Worton. Tell me what you would do, I know you've already decided."

"To Worton," Rindiran said, but it wasn't the answer in his mind.

"The Order you owe much to for your upbringing is fading, changing by the moment in this Temple," Master Hidel said. "You can see it, and feel it more so. I've never known you to lie to me, why lie to yourself? What is your true answer?"

"I'll fetch Tadrin's parents and make sure that he and his family reach Forge Hin safely," Rendiran said with more certainty.

"The truth of your heart's desire," the old Master said. "Let me give you some actual advice, just as a parting gift from a master who barely had a chance to teach you anything. I'll send my most trusted messenger, Onila Splitfoot, to fetch Tadrin's parents and lead them to Forge Hin. I've looked ahead a few chapters and see that Tadrin's father would die protecting him if he and his mother accompanied their boy on their journey. It would be a valiant death at the end of a melee that takes place in an unforgiving grey realm of dust and hunger. I would rather see them survive, if only to prevent horrible grief. Tadrin's parents will be safe."

"Then I'll stay at Tadrin's side," Rendiran said with a bow.

"You should take your leave, then, though a sorrowful parting it is," Master Hidel said. "Oh, but there's a book!" he said, gesturing to Yimere.

"Here, it's a book of tables for translating ancient languages," his guard said, handing him a book only a little longer than his hand that was bound in thick, stiffened leather. The metal latch keeping it closed seemed new, but there was some wear on the leather. "Oh, and don't take up smoking of any kind," Yimere said. "I've been trying to get him to quit for a century."

It was then that Rendiran noticed that there was a pipe jammed into the spine of the volume. "Thank you," he said. He turned to Master Hidel then. "Thank you for your help, and for being a truly great teacher," he said, feeling that it wasn't enough.

"Read the book, skip the preface if you must," the Master said. "I'll see you again if luck is kind."

18

*R*endiran was more saddened to see his most recent mentor, the greatest he'd ever known, leave the Temple and the Order. He was known as a wandering scholar, any temple or institution of learning should be happy to have him. His students were few, but he always left valuable knowledge behind. He certainly left Rendiran with a great deal to ponder. If he was a quarter Ondi-Ne, then he should have pointed ears, and his hair should be blonde or brown, not black.

There was only one conclusion: someone used magic to change his ears and the colour of his hair when he was very young, most likely an infant. He was leaving the province, so he wouldn't be able to start digging for the truth behind his lineage. He crossed the large central hall in the third floor of the Temple proper and continued down to Ferriere Hall. It was adorned with busts of great former members of the priesthood. He could only name three. Denvi the Resurrector, Monder the Redeemer, and Albia the Luminescent. They were some of the first priests of the order, bringing people to the flock by telling stories of Miradu and her children spreading kindness, and in the case of Albia, preventing three wars in her lifetime.

They all had legacies that, to Rendiran, epitomized the love and kindness that made the Miradu Order the great cause that it was. He never enjoyed hearing about the politics and inner workings of the Order, The stories he'd heard of those great Priests made it seem like politics were either cast aside or used as a tool they manipulated like a master strategist to help the people of Highshield and shape the future.

Monder the Redeemer was more than a bust, he was the statue at the end of the hall. It was old, chipped here and there, but it still made everyone who cared to notice it smile. Rendiran always believed Monder must have been a good man to know. His hands rested on his round belly, he wore baggy robes and looked as though the statue was carved as the Redeemer was about to break into a great belly laugh. Around his eyes were wrinkles that only formed for people who spent a great deal of their time being mirthful.

Monder was named The Redeemer because he converted so many members of royal families to the Order of Miradu. Most knew him for telling stories from across Highshield, the best of them were of Miradu and her children. Many of his stories were still in the record, and a few were read from the common gospel. He wasn't seen as a political creature, mostly because the vast amounts of coin he raised were used to feed, relocate and settle the poor. There were three towns named Monder outside the wall, all of them settled by farmers who were once beggars in the city. Upper, Middle and Lower Monder were the greatest testimonies to that man, even though Rendiran enjoyed the three books of stories that survived him. Only one was gospel, however, the other two were often humorous, and sometimes raunchy, so they weren't officially recognized as part of the Order's history.

Rendiran reached the balcony overlooking the Lower Garden where all three children played with their pup. Nella, Wydu's Gift, stood atop a pile of old stones with a crown made from a circled branch pretending to be in distress at the sight of the dog, while Tadrin and Oria chased Ander off, or lured him away from her. Ander didn't know what was going on, but was happy to chase or face off with Tadrin or Oria. His high, excited barks pierced the air, sending a sound seldom heard through the lower levels of the temple. He occasionally checked in on Nella whenever she shrieked or feigned a cry that was convincing enough, but the other children would tap him on the back when he stopped and he'd be after them once more.

Paladins and guards were nearby, but they gave the children plenty of room to play on the grass between some of the oldest oak and apple trees in the temple. It looked like the children were having a great deal of fun, except for Nella, who occasionally seemed like she was becoming frustrated with competing with a dog for attention.

Rendiran was half way down the stairs to the garden when Umner rushed up to meet him, the portly man was more excited than he'd ever seen him. "Rendiran, I have to congratulate you on your mission to Worton. The Grand Matron herself put your name forward for this assignment. I can't tell you what an exciting time you'll have there, Worton is filled with important people from Brightwill and the Order. The connections and power you can culti-vate there, with your charisma as a preacher and your new title will lead to a power base that may rival even my own."

"I should thank the Grand Matron," Rendiran said, secretly hoping that he didn't have to see her. The effect she had on most people was frightening to him.

"She's out of the Temple, visiting the Prince for the first time in a decade. I would have gone with her, but someone had to make sure that the orders she issued this morning were executed. Speaking of which, I am placing an important responsibility on your shoulders. Tadrin and Oria will not be going to Forge Hin. Instead a contingent of our paladins will meet you at Worton, where you will stay with the children. They will be raised and trained there, outside of the influ-ence of the Dwarves and King Nyder. Marjay may remain with you and the children, but the rest will move on. They won't have a hand in raising Tadrin or Oria."

"Crista?"

"She has already gone, beginning her quest for some artifact, you'd have to ask the Keeper of Relics. I suppose she could visit the children in Worton, come and go, but she's not what we see as a stable influence, so keeping that to a minimum would most likely be best."

"I see," Rendiran said.

"This is how it will be, Rendiran, they are the orders directly from the Matron, who has seen a future for our Temple greater than even I would have dared dream."

"I'll see it done," Rendiran said, placing a hand on Umner's shoulder and looking him directly in the eye. "You've left this in exactly the right hands."

"I knew you'd be our man. Good things will befall you. You know they're starting to call you Rendiran the Resurrector," Umner said. "Your name rises."

"All in the service of Irenick, Viis and Miradu," Rendiran said. It was time for him to completely commit to his role as a healer and instrument of the Temple. If he gave Umner any suspicion that he had doubts about his new orders, the entire matter would be taken out of his hands. "I've come across some new information about my birth parents, by the way. I'm wondering if you'd know anything about that."

"I'm sorry, Rendiran, everything I know about you has come from your lips. I've seen no reason to look into your past, you've always been a perfectly good man of the church."

"I appreciate your trust, Dawn Shaper," Rendiran said. Umner always brightened at the sound of his title. "I hope..."

A piercing whine came from the garden. Rendiran had heard the pup give a yelp when he was surprised or faced with something new, but the sound coming from the garden was certainly an indication of injury or real fear. Rendiran was running down the stairs by the time he heard a third yelp, arriving at the bottom in time to see Tadrin and Oria shove Nella down onto the grass. The temple guards were approaching the scene, alarmed.

The children were fine, and it didn't look like Tadrin and Oria were going to attack Nella further, it seemed they were saving their dog, which Rendiran couldn't see. "Out of the way, please," Rendiran told a pair of guards who stepped into his path. One of them looked to him with his hand on his hilt but didn't move. "Let me through or I'll have you stripped and tossed out of the Temple." Rendiran told him in a tone so menacing that it surprised him.

The guards parted and Rendiran moved across the lawn to the stone pile and the children so quickly that he was winded by the time he was between them. "Stop what you're doing right now!" he said, something he'd heard more times than he could count when he was in the orphanage.

"She kept kicking Ander against the rocks," Tadrin said, near tears.

"No I didn't! He kept trying to trip me!" Nella retorted.

Ladies in white robes with red hoods and aprons were rushing to attend to the children. "Are you three all right?" Rendiran asked. Tadrin and Oria were deeply upset, but nodded. Nella looked unharmed, only filled with worry that she would take the blame for what the priest would find.

He looked to the stones and saw Ander then, on his side at the base of the old, short stone pile that Nella was standing on. He was trying to roll onto his paws to greet Rendiran, but whined as he failed to do so. "It's all right, boy," Rendiran said, offering his hand to the dog's lips so he would stop trying to get up to greet him. The pup licked his hand, but he wasn't as enthusiastic as he normally was, the dog was in pain. "Looks like you've lost your first real battle," he whispered in a comforting tone. "Good thing you have a healer on hand."

Tadrin and Oria were approaching slowly, tears running down their cheeks, watching with worry. "Is he going to be okay?" Oria asked, lip quivering.

"Our little warrior's going to be fine," Rendiran said. "He just needs some care." With a glance to his right he saw that the Matron's personal servants were standing between Nella and everyone else, creating a buffer for her as she wailed and cried. "He shouldn't have tried to pull me down! It wasn't my fault!"

"I see," Rendiran muttered under his breath, keenly aware that the Matron must have left instructions to keep Nella safe and comfortable above all others. "Let's mend our friend," he said, turning his full attention to Ander.

He grazed the dog's fur with his free hand and closed his eyes. "Irenick, I pray that you empower me with the gift, so I may heal our fallen friend," the prayer was mostly for the benefit of the children, who watched and listened to everything he was doing. Even though most of his experience was with humans, he'd healed several pets for donations. He would have healed any animal without asking for coin, but temple law stated that he and the priesthood could not restore the health of beasts without being paid unless they belonged to the temple itself.

There were two broken ribs, one had punctured Ander's lung shallowly, and there was a surprising amount of deep bruising. One of his legs was dislocated from his hip, the kind of injury that only a firm, heavy kick would have inflicted. If that wasn't alarming enough, he could feel that one of the dog's eyes had been squarely kicked while the dog was pushed up against the rock, most likely by Nella's heel. They were all simple wounds to Rendiran. He could even correct a defect in the dog's hind quarters that would cause discomfort in his sunset years. "I'm going to put him to sleep for a few moments now. It will seem sudden, and he will be very still, but don't worry." He touched the side of Ander's head and the pup slipped into a deep slumber with a rattling sigh.

He gently straightened the dog's small body on the grass and felt his way across the wounds, healing bruises and mending bones. The children gasped when Rendiran closed the dog's internal wounds and Ander coughed up an alarming amount of blood at his urging, clearing his lungs. "Don't worry, our little warrior is almost restored." He told them. It took little effort to finish the task, moving the leg back into its socket correctly with a pop that made the children jump, then finally correcting the damage done to the pup's eye. He caressed Ander's soft fur and spoke to him in a soothing tone; "It's time to wake up, Ander."

The pup blinked slowly as he roused from his deep slumber, then

Ander was on his feet, eagerly licking Rendiran from chin to fore-head and jumping against him as though he couldn't express his happiness at seeing the priest urgently enough. Tadrin and Oria were beside themselves as well, petting Ander and allowing him to jump onto them to give a good tongue-bath.

It was then that Rendiran noticed that Haffor and Marjay had arrived. The dwarf had a tear in his eye at the sight of the restored pup and his reunion with the children. "You three play here, but gently, understand? No more accidents." Rendiran said once Ander was focusing on the children, trying to get them to follow him into a game of chase.

"It wasn't our fault," Oria said, determined to make her point.

"I know, it's all right now," Rendiran said, kneeling down. "We'll be leaving soon, don't worry."

Oria's determination to make sure fault was properly assigned faded and she nodded. "Okay."

"He's all right though?" Tadrin asked as Ander nearly knocked him over.

"Better than ever," Rendiran said. "Just take care of each other."

Nella was already being led away by the Matron's servants. They circled her protectively, and as they moved towards the edge of the lawn, most of the guards and paladins took a formation around them, leaving only a few guardians behind for Tadrin and Oria.

"Got your heart strings pulled, old man?" Marjay asked Haffor.

Haffor wiped his eye. "It's a little dustier this low in the Temple," he replied.

"What kind of dog is that?" Rendiran asked. "Because he's going to be huge, at least three feet at the hip, maybe four."

"It's an old breed, an Ondi Riding Hound. It might not carry them when they're grown, but he'll train with them at Forge Hin," Haffor said. "And they keep children busy."

"Four feet at the hip?" Marjay asked, astounded.

"Aye, rare breed now, most of them were killed when the first Ava-Ondi were overthrown. They can take down a horse in a heartbeat, and they'll guard their masters to their last breath. Why do you ask?"

"Just curiosity," Rendiran replied. His manner became serious as he stepped into whispering range with the pair. "Did you see Crista leave earlier today?"

"Aye, left this morning, said she'd meet up with us on the road," Marjay said. "She looked like someone pissed in her oats."

"All right," Rendiran said. "Things are changing, and not in a way that will be favourable to Tadrin or Oria. Can we leave within the hour?"

"Aye," Haffor replied. "Is there anything I need to know before we go?"

"Only that I need some of your most trusted people to guide Tadrin's parents to Forge Hin. They must be well taken care of and safe, but above all, they cannot make the journey with us. I'm making this request based on predictions from a most trusted oracle, who is sending a friend along to guide them."

"Who?"

"Hidel Lightcliff," Rendiran breathed.

"He's here?" Haffor asked in surprise. "I'm surprised he's still alive, I last saw him when I was a young boy."

"He was, most likely already gone," Rendiran said. "Can you get Tadrin's parents out today? Do you have enough trustworthy paladins to protect them?"

"Aye, I'll tell them to move them in secret, it's something they've done before. I'm assuming it would be best if we moved secretly as well?"

"Definitely," Rendiran replied.

Haffor looked to Tadrin and Oria, who were once again chasing Ander around the broad lawn of the lower garden. His expression remained serious. "I'll have one of my men get common clothing and everything else we'll need."

"I'll secure our exit," Marjay said. "We'll use the tunnel running to East Shale. Tell your men to meet us at the Hungry Nag in plain clothing with the supplies. We'll be able to change at the Inn, no one will talk. I know everyone there."

"It would be best if we could be out of the province early tomorrow," Rendiran said. "We'll be avoiding Worton, so we'll either have to go the long way over land or hire a ship to take us directly to the dwarven provinces."

"Now I know there's more to this than you're telling me, young priest," Haffor said. "You're not just reacting to the mood in the temple and a few changes."

"It can keep until we're on the road, if you feel you can trust me," Rendiran said.

"You have my trust," Haffor replied. "Let's put this Temple behind us."

19

The Hungry Nag wasn't the kind of establishment that Rendiran was accustomed to, but he found it welcoming nonetheless. The sign over the door was well kept, repainted a short time ago, and it featured a stout nosed horsehead eating carrots and what may have been a pile of grains off a plate. The first floor featured a taproom that was partially divided off from a larger dining room with tables and booths. It served as a neighborhood pub and as a place for people who had business in the city of Highshield but couldn't afford to stay in an establishment too close to the temple.

There were only a few people in the taproom that afternoon, and only the young bartender looked up from pouring a tall horn of ale, everyone else minded their business. Behind the bar were large barrels in an iron rack, the kind of supply that only a busy taproom would have, and a stand with long, curly horns on it. Each horn hook had a tag on it with a name, something Rendiran had never seen before.

"Dwarven tradition," Haffor said, gesturing at the rack. "Those horns belong to the regulars, I have one of my own hanging at the Brewing Bear. I expect this might be a fine place."

Marjay descended the main stairway with a maid and a much

older man with a long grey beard behind him. "We have the third floor," he said. "Lunch will be brought up to us after we're settled in. I have clothes for you and the children coming," he said to Rendiran.

The group, Rendiran, Tadrin, Oria, Marjay, Haffor and two of his paladins made their way to the second highest floor in the building and took the largest room. Tadrin and Oria looked inside every cupboard and closet within the large room to make sure there were no spies about. Where they got the idea that there may be spies lurking around, he had no idea, but helping them search was a good distraction for everyone, even if it was a short one.

By the time they were finished the search, plates of fruit, cheese, bread and cold ham were brought up by two young ladies who each gave piece of toffee wrapped in paper to Tadrin and Oria. "You must promise you'll have a good mouthful of veg and cheese before you have this, all right?" the slightly older of the two asked as Tadrin and Oria stared at the candies.

"I will," Oria said.

"Big bites," Tadrin added.

Rendiran closed his eyes a moment, facing away from the servers, and reached out with his mind, looking for anything that may be poisonous in the room and found nothing.

"What do we say?" Marjay asked both children.

"Thank you," both Tadrin and Oria said at the same time.

"They're precious," the younger of the servers said as they retreated from the room.

"Lunch," Marjay said, "Wash your hands, then we eat," waving the children to a side table with two basins of clean water set on it.

Ander got his front paws up onto a seat at the table and Oria laughed at him. "Ander wants to eat with us."

"No dogs in chairs, if he thinks he's a person at this age, imagine what that'll be like when he's full grown," Haffor said, gently pushing the pup down then pulling the bone from the pork plate then tossing it to the floor. It was sloppy with shreds of meat, and Ander attacked it happily.

When he was finished rubbing his hands together in the water,

Tadrin went to Rendiran's side and took his hand. "Am I going to see my mom and dad?"

Oria was taking her seat at the table, but watching the exchange closely as Rendiran knelt down and put and arm around Tadrin's shoulders. "Yes, but not for a week or two. Haffor and I have made sure that they are safe and well taken care of. They're going all the way to Forge Hin so you can be together." His reassurances weren't working as well as he expected, the boy still looked worried, verging on upset. "Haffor has sent his best paladins and all their minders to guard them, to take care of them for the whole journey. It's going to be much safer for them, and for you that way."

"Why can't I go with them?" Tadrin asked. "We're all going to the same place."

It was a good question, and Rendiran didn't have an answer that felt sturdy enough to stand up to the boy's scrutiny. Haffor answered instead, and he did so in a way that made Rendiran grateful. "This journey we're on is for priests and warriors of Irekirk and Miradu. What we'll see, the things we'll do, the people we'll meet will be worth remembering for the rest of our lives. Your parents, the good folk they are, need protection, and aren't made for our kind of adventure, except for your father, but he has to use all his strength and attention to care for your mother," Haffor knelt down and looked Tadrin in the eye. "We're paladins, fledgling or old, that's what you, Oria and me are, and the adventures we'll have will be legendary. You'll have so many stories to tell them when we arrive in Forge Hin, it'll take days, and they'll be so proud of you for being brave, for making this journey."

"What about Rendiran? He's not a paladin," Tadrin said.

"Oh, priests need stories to tell even more than paladins, it seems most of their job is talking, and by Miradu, does he ever chatter," Haffor said, mimicking a talking mouth with his calloused hand. That had Tadrin and Oria smiling. "But we're always glad to have a priest and a guardsman as companions. They both watch for dangers, and those dangers are as different as night and day."

"Viis told me to be brave, that we'd be in danger sometimes," Oria said, slipping from her seat and joining the impromptu circle.

"She's wise," Rendiran said. "She made sure you had a guardian who could take care of you, and now we have no shortage of guardians with paladins along."

"And you," Tadrin said to Rendiran.

"And me," he replied. "Now, time to eat."

Marjay answered a knock at the door, receiving a large cloth bundle and a few heavy bags. He handed Rendiran a pile of clothing. "A big change for you," he said. Rendiran took it and an apple into the next room, where he changed into the tunic and trousers. The cloth wasn't poor, but it didn't compare to the fine robes he normally wore. Seeing his holy garb on the bed made him uneasy, it was as though it protected him from his increasing uncertainty. "Have you spent all your power in this world on raising two children and a king?" he asked Miradu quietly.

Haffor entered the room with a pile of clothing and one of the sacks, followed by Rijen, a taller dwarf with pointed ears who hadn't taken his helmet off in front of Rendiran until then. It was strange to see a dwarf with sharply pointed Ava-Ondi ears and white hair. His eyes were so dark they were nearly black. It was as though traits of dwarf and ava-ondi fought during his conception, and no clear winner was determined.

"Rendiran," Haffor said as the pair worked on unbuckling each other's armour with practiced hands. "I wonder if you can help me with a prayer, a powerful one."

"I'd be honoured to," he replied.

"I can't leave my company in mindless thrall, but nothing I tried last night broke them free of Wydu's influence, or got them clear of the Matron," he said. "In all my years, I've never seen so many paladins turn away from their commander, I've never seen such enchantment."

"I believe that Wydu possessed Nella, but he left after the Matron was healed. Whatever enchantment is on your people is most likely the Matron's doing. She's more powerful than anyone ever gave her credit for."

"You'd know? No offense, but you rank somewhere in the middle of the priesthood, as I understand it," Haffor said.

Rijen seemed to ignore the conversation, concentrating on undoing buckles in the strange turn and bend and turn routine they had. Rendiran returned his attention to Haffor. "She took me into her confidence more than once, and I spent some time with her before I was assigned to a master in the Temple. I don't know why, but she seemed to have trust in me."

"That must make this break with the temple that much harder."

"I've been trying not to think about it," Rendiran said. "The Matron I knew was not so vein, she was patient and kind. She was deeply devout, a follower of Miradu, I'm saddened to say I could see how she may feel ignored, and how Wydu may have turned her without enchantment. She is not fickle, her suffering was constant and deep, and if Wydu could cure her, I don't blame her for asking her Goddess why she didn't do so instead."

Rijen lifted Haffor's chest plate off. When his head was clear he said; "But you do blame her. If you believe she's become Wydu's follower, that she's turning the Temple into Wydu's house. I feel that she's betrayed me, and I came to terms with the duality of our pantheon long ago, so if you don't feel a sting, you're dead inside."

"I feel," Rendiran hesitated, looking to his robes. "Saddened, lost. Our Goddess set a plan in motion, and, if events are what they appear, her own son interfered. We have to deal with the results, and my superiors aren't supporting Miradu's plan. I can't believe they turned away."

"Stop thinking about the whole landscape, Rendiran," Haffor said. "What about this room, those robes, and the situation that's left you with no appetite and that lost look on your face?"

"Lost?" he asked as he caught sight of himself in a polished metal mirror above an old chest of drawers. His reflection looked like he'd suffered an emotional wound, and, yes, looked more than a little lost. His master, wisest amongst any he'd known, was probably already gone, urged by the change he felt in the temple. The greatest of living Paladins was in the same room, and he had been lessened, stripped of most of his command. Crista was gone who knew where, but only after telling him that he wasn't purely human, that he had Ondi blood. He couldn't even look to his Goddess, or her son, Irenick, they had most likely spent much of their power bringing their chosen ones into the world. He couldn't return to the Temple, and he was sure of his choice to disobey orders, to deliver Tadrin and Oria to Forge Hin instead of Worton. Most of these things added up to him being far from the Temple and the home he'd come to know. "They'll excommunicate me," he said under his breath. "The Temple itself, and the highest members of my order will not take me back after this."

"A King in Forge Hin will embrace you," Haffor said. "If you wish to remain there after we arrive, you will find our hospitality second to none. You'll find no end of subjects to study in our halls, and I hope you remain. From the moment I met you I could feel the intention of your heart, and it is too good for a place like that Temple, with its layered politics and practices that take us away from the Goddess. No, that's not the place for someone with a heart as good as yours, a heart that has been waiting for a cause like this."

"You give me too much credit," Rendiran said, his spirit lifting. The dwarf had a gift for speaking; that was for certain. "But you know I'll stay with Tadrin and Oria, I feel that's my highest cause now. I only wonder if my disobedience will someday separate me from them."

"Not in Forge Hin," Rijen said. "King Nyder will not be pleased that Wydu is now the prime God in Highshield City. He has always been a creature of Miradu, and his rule was made better for her guidance."

"I suspected," Haffor said. "Rijen here knew my father for over twenty years before he entered the stone sleep," he explained. "He's older than he looks."

"But still marching," Rijen said. "The world makes me feel young. I love how it changes, and how some things are always the same."

"Every time you say something that makes sense, you make sure to confound everyone in the room with whatever you say next," Haffor told him.

"Age complicates some people," Rijen said with a shrug.

Rendiran found comfort in Haffor's reassurances, but also in seeing the pair of century and more old dwarves getting along after knowing each other for so long. It was like watching brothers, the pair could not have seemed more at ease. It was then that he spotted three rune stones knotted into Haffor's belt. He knew two of them were powerful protection charms, the other he wasn't certain of. It led him to an idea. "I can't say that I know a prayer that may shake your human paladins from the Matron's influence, but I do know a spell."

"Now what's a priest like you doing studying spells that touch the mind?" Haffor asked, amused.

"I'm always looking for ways to help people, even if it's human magic," he replied. "I can use the power locked in one of those runes, or some other enchanted item of equal power to enhance their senses, like an awakening spell, only much more powerful. They'll be aware of everything that's being done to them, and if we do this my way, they will have the opportunity to choose who they want to follow. That's the best I can do, give them an opportunity to exercise their free will."

"That's enough," Haffor said.

"I warn you, some of them may leave both the Matron and your leadership, striking out on their own."

"If they make those choices, I don't want them in my company," Haffor said. "What do we have to do?"

"Oria!" Rendiran heard Kena, the only female dwarf paladin with them shout from the next room. "Come down from the table, please!" she sounded too alarmed for the outcry to be ignored.

Rendiran was out the door of their room and through the main room's entry in an instant, and what he saw was at the same time confusing and alarming. Oria was standing on the table, holding her new dress bunched up in one hand, and preparing to assault it with scissors with the other. Tadrin was in his smallclothes, offering his new trousers to Oria, and Kena, the only female dwarf paladin who remained with their small company, was holding two bows and a lock of Oria's hair in her hands with a look of despair on her face.

"Put the scissors down and come off the table, Oria," Rendiran said.

As she did so, Oria began to cry. "I want to wear trousers too, I don't want the dress."

"I'll give her mine, I don't care," Tadrin said.

"That's all right, you put those back on," Haffor told Tadrin patiently, trying to suppress a smirk and failing.

"We'll buy you some trousers," Rendiran said to Oria. "Did you cut your hair?"

"I just cut the ribbon off," Oria said. "I told her I didn't want it, but she wouldn't listen."

"All right," Rendiran said, sitting her on the edge of the table. "We'll get you some trousers, and I can cut your hair if you like, but we listen to what our minders tell us, all right? Everyone here is only doing what's best for you, so even if you don't like it at the time, you have to go along so we can keep you safe. Do you understand, Oria?"

Oria nodded grumpily, her arms crossed. "I want shorter hair than Tadrin, like Marjay's."

"All right, I'll do my best, but no promises. I only know how to cut hair one way," Rendiran said, pulling a tuft of his hair.

"Okay," she said, already starting to brighten.

"One more set of trousers and tunic, I'll have someone come up and make them for you right away," Marjay said from the door.

To Rendiran's relief, the Innkeeper's three daughters were happy to not only make new clothes for a few coins, but were delighted at the idea of cutting Oria's hair. Tadrin's hair was cut as well, and the children seemed happy to match each other. That left Rendiran with time to write the details of his awakening spell down, and he was soon satisfied with the results when he finished scribing it in his practitioner's book.

Haffor met him in the next room with an object in both hands. "This should do, it's more powerful than the runes you were eying by far." He pulled the thing out of its cloth bag and Rendiran was quietly surprised. It was the head of some old staff. Large rubies were set beneath a cloudy white stone in bronze, and he could feel old power emanating from it. Luminescent smoke swirled slowly inside the crystal, glowing white. "A necromancer past the wall named Kriladun owned it, and we cleansed the power within after he was defeated. Can you use it?"

Rendiran cleared his mind and steeled himself, then placed his hand above the staff head. The paladin was right, there was no master to the power stored inside, and the energy was so clean that he couldn't tell what it was captured from. He opened his eyes and looked at the markings in the setting. "This was used to store a wizard's energy, it wasn't made by a necromancer."

"You truly are well educated," Haffor said. "Kriladun stored his own energy within so it could be used later, like the wizard who owned it before."

"A staff this powerful, this easy to use must have a name, anything like this does," Rendiran said, accepting the staff head. "It is older than the conflict between human and ondi."

"If there's a name for it, I don't know it," Haffor said. "We only made sure it was cleansed completely. As far as it being easy to use, no one in my company found that it was a simple thing. Even priests said it was burdensome, and required a great deal of concentration to master. That's why we cut it from the wood shaft and put it with the relics we're bringing to Forge Hin."

"I'm sure they were exaggerating, this staff head is as easy to control as I've ever seen, easier," Rendiran said. "It's more than powerful enough, and it could be recharged afterwards."

"I know," he replied. "Do you know how to recharge it?"

"I've never done that before, but I know how it's done. I've just never seen such a deep well stone."

"How long before we're ready to unshackle my paladins from the Matron, and how close do we have to be?"

"That's up to you," Rendiran said. "I'll be channeling an order from your mind as an option for your paladins. The clearer your mind is, the clearer the option you offer is, the easier it will be for them to choose. You may provide an option, or even give an order, but it must be clear and free of subterfuge."

"I can do that, now where do we go?"

"I have to be able to see the temple, so that balcony will be fine. We'll be quick, so as few people on the street see us."

"Aye, I'll begin clearing my mind," Haffor said.

The Paladin knelt before the paired doors leading out to the balcony and Rendiran stood behind him. He looked through his notes one more time and began concentrating on clearing his own thoughts. He found it easier to do than normal, and he was a practiced hand. It only took him a few moments to realize that the staff head was helping him. The object, while clear of any intention, was a perfect focus, passively inviting him to work magic and use the power stored within.

As a priest he'd never felt anything like it. His power came from intent – usually the intent to heal – and he always believed, no, he felt, it came from belief. The power inside the staff head was naked, pure, and with perfect focus he could feel a similar power growing within him, as though the seed of potential was always there, and he was finding that there was a deep well of energy waiting to be tapped within him. He'd read about the theory, but never felt it, and the sensation of knowing he had his own power separate from any goddess or demigod was intoxicating. A glance at the bed where he had left his robes spread out reminded him that there were runes there that assisted him when he was trying to focus on healing. There were also wards of protection against evil and unwelcome influences. Before he could explore the idea that they may have guided his power in the past, he purged his mind of all questions and distractions.

"I'm ready, I'm holding my order firmly in mind," Haffor said calmly.

Rendiran took a deep breath and opened the doors with a gesture. He could see how he manipulated reality to do so, like a weave of power emanating from his hand to turn the knobs and push the doors open. He strode onto the balcony and let his words of power flow. "I call Forge Hin Paladins; be free of doubt, free of illusion, free of your bonds. I take you to the crossroads; One road leads back to your oath. One leads to a new master. One road abandons duty. Your minds are clear, hearts unburdened, so make your choice, Choose, your mind, heart, body free."

THE LIGHT inside the gemstones dimmed, Rendiran felt the power move from them towards the Temple, then directly into all the Paladins from Forge Hin and any other Paladin who trained there. Hundreds instead of dozens. It was thanks to a slight miscalculation in wording, but not in intent. He realized that he wanted to punish that place for betraying him, and if his spell worked, he would. Anyone who trained as a Paladin in Forge Hin would be free of any supernatural influence, and forced to choose whom to follow, if anyone.

Haffor pulled him inside and closed the door. Marjay was rushing into the room, wide-eyed. "What was that? Your voice filled the streets like thunder!"

"He was discovering that he's not just a priest," Haffor said.

"I'm a sorcerer," Rendiran said. He was surprised that he was saddened by the realization. He never felt further from Miradu or Irenick, the Gods he'd known all his life. The power was incredible, the sensation of wielding it was better than anything he'd known, but it left him feeling cold.

---

20

*P*rince Norrich flexed his left hand, the leather glove he wore creaked as he marveled at how perfect his arm was. After an assassination attempt that shattered the bones in his left arm from elbow to palm, his healer spent an entire day rebuilding it. The limb felt different, only partially his own, but it was whole, and it worked as well, perhaps better, than the one he was born with.

He regretted the affect the assassination attempt had. He missed his opportunity to meet Irenick and Viis' gifts to the world. He suspected those two children would be more important to his time in Highshield than anything else. The deep slumber that he was in while his arm was being put back together lasted a day, and it felt like it was one of the more important days in recent history. A new Gift had arrived at the High Temple of Miradu, but this one was Wydu's making, and news of the greatest Dwarf King the modern world had ever known waking came as well. The shape of Highshield, not just the city, but all of the settled shore, was about to change.

"Does she know I was incapacitated?" he asked Ofeur, his oldest and most trusted advisor. He was only two years his senior, but they had seen seventeen years of adventures and throne rooms together.

"Word of the attempt on your life has been contained. None but your inner circle know of it."

"Any progress on identifying my attacker?"

"The skull and axe head brand hasn't matched anything yet, Sir. I expect it has more to do with your father the King's reign in Brightwill than anything in Highshield."

"I was afraid of that," the Prince said, flexing his hand. "I still think we should have gotten someone from the temple to do this work."

"Perhaps the Grand Matron will know of a healer who can finesse the work that's already done?" Ofeur offered.

"This is fine, really. I'm just restless, I have too much time to think about it," Norrich said, taking to his feet. He wore a simple but fine dark brown tunic with the sigil of the Miradu Pantheon on its left side and the sigil of his father's Kingdom over his heart – a black ram and a horse head facing right, as though the two beasts were running together. "If it were my sword arm, I'd have it cut off and remade by the best healer I could find. Perhaps the Resurrector, what was his name?"

"Rendiran, Sir," Ofeur replied. "Our ears in the Temple reported that he went with the children."

"What do our ears tell us about the Grand Matron?" Prince Norrich asked. He tugged the high waist of his high black trousers straight. He lost weight on their last journey past the wall. He decided to keep quiet about it, otherwise tailors would create a fuss over measuring him and updating his wardrobe. He didn't love such trouble, and he wore as little adornment as possible. He'd rather feel light and free in simple clothes than be weighted down in all the devices and garb that indicated his station, various titles and holdings. Once a year he was allowed an excursion, and for the last eleven years he went past the wall, following old maps from early deep wood delvers. It would be another nine months before he could go again, and he was already restless.

"The report on the Grand Matron is not very detailed. She has been seen without her veil, and by all accounts she is quite beautiful, but not a delicate creature. I would add that the Grand Matron is widely known for being extremely well read, whether it be books, old scrolls, or messages from Brightwill and across our fair coast. It is worth noting. As for the events today, after personally blessing a breakfast and eating with her High Priests, she had a private audience with all the messengers and avian keepers in Highshield City, with the exception of our own, and sent them all on a mission that we have not been able to find details of. After spending some time with Wydu's Gift, a girl named Nella, she began her journey here. Rendiran, the Paladin Captain Haffor along with a few others and the blessed children departed shortly after that."

"Leaving Wydu's Gift behind," Norrich said as he sat back down on the room's high seat. "I would fear Wydu if my father wasn't a devout follower. His ways don't guarantee that you keep many friends, but I've watched as our House's power doubled then doubled again. Wydu encourages cunning, but doesn't counsel against betrayal." The Prince was a follower of Viis, steadfast in his loyalty, ready to rise to a good cause, and eager to explore. The public believed he was a follower of Miradu, and that was no mistake. Where the province was concerned, he wanted to be seen as a faithful servant of the people and provider, even though seven tenths of everything produced on his land and in the dwarven provinces went to the King in Brightwill. "What do we know about Elise?"

"Sacrilege, Sir," Ofeur said with a smirk.

Referring to the Grand Matron by any title or name besides Illustrious – an old honorific used when announcing a great dragon who is a friend to lesser life forms – was forbidden. "Set that aside and get on with it, she's most likely already walking up the stairs."

"The church has done a remarkably good job at hiding all but the Grand Matron's first name. We suspect that she was lower ranking royalty, but haven't been able to narrow it down. Five ladies disappeared near the time we suspect she took her first vows as a Priestess of the White."

"What is it with the Miradu Pantheon and mystery? Even the

founding is obscured by misinformation. I've read four books on Irekirk and those early days..."

"Five books, Sir," Ofeur interjected.

"Five! Five books on those early days, each tells a different story about the laying of the first stones, the lighting of the first lamp. One even tells a tale about Irekirk facing Wydu after his mother and siblings were murdered. Perhaps I can learn something while she's here. Why do you think she's coming in the first place?"

"Perhaps she wants to announce that she's recovered and is joyous in returning to public life?"

"I bet she's run out of things to read and wants to borrow a few books from our library," Norrich countered. "I've never heard of anyone who's read as much."

The double doors leading into the stylish but small audience chamber parted, and the visitor Prince Norrich was waiting for was announced; "The Illustrious Grand Matron of the Miradu Pantheon."

Prince Norrich was astounded by the woman he beheld as she strode into the room, she was many times the beauty he remembered meeting before the Grand Matron went into hiding. She was not wearing the normal robes of her office, but one of the dress designs that Miradu wore long ago with a few additions. Fine silver jewelry chains held the front together, still revealing a great deal from her neck to her navel. Her collar and sleeves were made of small black dragon scales, shimmering and jutting in sharp layers. The way they reacted to the light, picking up colours from the room like a black mirror, made it clear that they were real scales.

The cloth section flowed from under those layers to the floor in silken panels, teasing a bare knee, or a high buckled boot shin here or there as she walked but never truly revealing. More important than the garment by far was the Grand Matron's new face. Her skin was pale for the most part except for her dark lips and healthy flushed cheeks. Blue eyes peered out from under dark lashes, and her comely guise was framed by a thick mane of black hair woven through a silver frame to make her entire head look like that of a black dragon. He recognized the intended look, and after a moment he realized that the broad features that frame and her hair were made to remind people of wasn't the paintings of Miradu, but of Wydu, her draconian pure blood son.

"Are all my wards in place?" Prince Norrich asked in a hushed whisper.

"Checked this morning," Ofeur replied. "Her bewitchment is real, but not magical."

"What a generous introduction, thank you," the Matron remarked, giving her introducer a few coins. Whether they were gold or silver, Norrich couldn't see. She looked around the small audience chamber, taking in the round room with its lushly padded window seats, the domed ceiling and thickly carpeted floor. Her eyes finally came to rest on the flat seats at the foot of the throne, the second most comfortable places to sit in the room, or so he was told. "I expected to be shown to the Provincial Audience Chamber," she said, looking up at him.

"I find this is a better setting for meeting with trusted allies and friends," Prince Norrich said, stepping down from his throne and approaching her. He held his hand out and she laid her fingers across his palm, curtseying gracefully.

"I apologize for not visiting for so long," she said. "I last saw you in Brightwill, before you took this post."

"There were circumstances beyond your control, I understand," he replied. "You've made an impressive recovery. Congratulations."

"I am restored by Wydu's wisdom and kindness through His Gift to the world," she replied. "I humbly present myself to you, the highest power in these lands, hoping you will hear my proposal."

"I am humbled, and you are magnificent," Prince Norrich said, touching his lips to the back of her hand. She smiled warmly at him. As a prince of his vigor, he'd known many beautiful women from all corners of the world, but he'd never seen a creature like her. He gently led her to the seat nearest to his throne, it was only inches shorter than his. "That dress is familiar, but I've never seen it worn so well before."

"The dragon scale fringes and frame are antiques, you have a keen eye," she replied. "Do you like it?"

"Very much," he replied.

"I'll be sure to tell the seamstresses, they worked on it during the entire journey, finishing in only one day. Work was started on it years ago, before the attack, but they made a few alterations to suit my new purpose."

Norrich made himself comfortable on his throne, and was surprised to see that she had no trouble making herself at home on the side seat, leaning towards him so she was almost so close that an observer might think they were in the middle of an intimate conversation. Her confidence was overwhelming and enticing. "New purpose?"

"I intend to make the Kingdom of Hullen the wealthiest in the world, and my Temple the most powerful."

"You and my father would get along famously, I've heard him say almost the same thing more times than I can count," the Prince said. He made a conscious effort to ignore her charms and focus on the questions burning in his mind. "I must ask, is the Miradu Order turning to Wydu? I understand that you may be grateful to Him, but Miradu has been the Prime Matron in the High Heavens for nearly half an age."

"Miradu will always be the Prime Matron, but I have seen her son, Wydu, rise to her greatness. Her followers betray her in the north. The dwarves of Forge Hin claim their King is risen, and though that may be true, it wasn't Miradu who restored him. He was restored by Odilexa, the ancient enemy to our good Pantheon."

"This is the first I've heard of that deception," Prince Norrich said.

"Wydu warned me that Odilexa's trick should be kept secret until he's established at the head of the Miradu Order, taking his mother's place in the Temple. Miradu, Irenick and Viis are all diminished, they used too much of their heavenly power to raise their champions. Wydu has been raising his Gift for much longer, fortifying her and preparing, using a lost Goddess' power to smite corruption in the mountains while bringing his Gift forward. Your men will find Onhin

Mountain is emptying, a disease is wiping out all the corrupt goblin kind there."

Prince Norrich tilted his head towards Ofeur, and he started for the door. "Have Irogen use his far-sight," he called after him. "I want to verify this within the hour."

"Yes, Sir," Ofeur replied.

"We have to verify, you understand," the Prince explained.

"I would not make the allegation if I were uncertain," the Grand Matron said with a knowing smile. "Odilexa has the dwarves believing her lies in the north, but it is Wydu's time, and unlike his mother, he controls the High Realms and power of many Gods and Goddesses, especially the old ones that the Ondi left behind. He has the power to fight her. I'm thankful that he looks upon this world and likes the followers of Miradu. He sees the potential for peace and prosperity to win through love and harmony. I see that potential too, Norrich."

"Pardon me if I speak plainly, I must know more about Forge Hin and their King. If they plan on following a man who is under the control of an enemy Goddess, there is every chance that they will follow her direction and withdraw from their agreement to provide supplies to my father's Kingdom."

"They will," the Grand Matron replied. "The Hullen Kingdom will have to do without the dwarves' metals, grain and lumber before the year is finished. They will tell you that they still follow Miradu, but they are no longer willing to pay their tithe. Their promise to exist as a province in your father's kingdom will be broken as King Nyder reclaims the land."

"Is there nothing you can do?"

"Their beloved King has been restored after spending nearly a century in a stone sleep, and he will make false claims about me before this season ends. I will fight it, I'll teach the followers of Miradu about the delicate state their Goddess is in, but I doubt I can convince his subjects. Dwarves have never seen humans as their equals despite their tendency to welcome them into their lands.

Belief in my Temple, in my Order will not falter here in the capitol, but for it to spread I need your best gesture of confidence."

"There's little I cannot do," he said.

"I was sorry to hear about the death of your betrothed during the troubles at Cinderhold last year," she told him. Her hand landed on his gently, a comforting gesture, but her fingers caressed his wrist lightly after it laid there for a moment, and she didn't withdraw it.

"Cinderhold represents a grave loss to most of the Kingdoms, my father will take it back," Prince Norrich said.

"I've seen only a few moments in your father's future, but I can tell you with certainty that he should abandon his efforts in Urshyme. That country will not suffer anyone who threatens its borders for revenge, conquest or profiteering. Not for centuries."

"How? No one sits on the Ember Throne, there's nothing but brutal civil war across those lands, and my father has won two battles already."

"You will receive an urgent message on the wind," the Grand Matron said consolingly. "Your uncle Olarren has been defeated in Redfield, and Morrini of Highcrest has taken the Ember Throne. They will call her the Obsidian Queen, the first human sorceress to become royalty. Wydu has given me sight beyond sight, and this was one of the first things he put before my eyes. A field turned to black glass by white flames and an army fallen to the one who wields the white fire. She has disciples who follow her, who learn from her, and they are already indomitable."

"Is it too late for me to send word home?"

"I'm sorry, if I had the vision earlier, you would have had time, but this has already happened. Word of it will arrive tomorrow. What awaits in the future for your father if he seeks revenge will be much worse. I beg that you tell him."

"If everything you say has come to pass, then I will," Prince Norrich said.

"There is something you can do to lessen the sting of these dark times," she said with quiet encouragement.

"Please pardon this interruption, Sir," Ofeur said, entering the chamber with a tall, thin man with grey hair at his side. "Please, tell him what you told me, Irogen."

"The Onhin Mountains have been struck with plague. The temples are abandoned, as are the old dwarf holds. The few goblins that remain inside are near death. Everything I saw outside, imps, goblin kind, and strange dwarves are all ailing, trying to escape the cursed halls. I've never seen or heard of a plague that is so thorough."

"Is there any chance that they may come down the mountain and spread their disease to our countrymen?"

"I don't expect any of them would survive the journey, they haven't managed to wander far from their home in the mountain, less than a league. I'll continue investigating to ensure that the water there is uncorrupted, but those old dwarf holds are far from the water supplies we depend on in that area, I doubt I'll find a problem. The people of that mountain were excised like corruption from a body."

"Thank you, Irogen," the Prince said. "You may go."

He bowed and left, only Ofeur and a servant remained, standing beside the door. "Will there be anything else, Sir?"

"Wine, a vintage befitting our Grand Matron's triumphant re-emergence," he said. "You should remain here, Ofeur. I expect I'll want a witness to stave off rumours."

"I'm sure it's well known that I've never taken an oath of celibacy," the Grand Matron added, lightly running the tips of her fingers over the back of his hand. "Anything could happen."

"Should I remain standing, or?" Ofeur asked with a cocked brow.

The Prince nodded at a seat piled high with cushions and his longtime friend made himself comfortable, looking away from them to the view outside from the high window beside him.

"Those old dwarf halls on the Onhin Mountain will be ready for your men to claim and plunder in less than a week. It's only one gift Wydu put in my hands to give to you."

"I'll have prisoners moved from the wall to go investigate and clean the place first, thank you. I'll be sure to leave something substantial at Wydu's shrine next time I visit the temple."

"While an entire country in Brightwill burns, your holdings in

Highshield grow. You'll find you won't need your contract with the dwarves of Forge Hin."

"There will be a cost to them breaking their contract, if that does happen," the Prince said. "I know my father will want me to pull Forge Hin back in line, regardless of their returned King."

Two servants entered with silvered trays and decanters with red and white wines. Prince Norrich was served his favourite Chatten Red first, then the Grand Matron selected the white, and Ofeur took a brimming goblet of red.

"I have brought you predictions, information that will assist your rulership here, and I have one more thing for you before you invite me to a feast in my honor."

"You foresaw my invitation?" Prince Norrich asked, amused.

"After my proposal, you'd be rude not to. The power of my Order is rising by the day, and there will be a new heir in Worton before both moons rise high in the sky. It's time for us to consolidate power and quell any doubt in your subjects with regard to their ruler or their religion. I offer myself as your bride."

Ofeur sputtered and coughed. "Apologies," he croaked as he fought to recover.

"My blood is from a royal line, it's a requirement of all women who become Grand Matrons," she said.

"Which family? I can't consider it unless you are of the right royal blood," the Prince replied with a teasing smile.

"Wirin, my father still lives, he is Yovril, Duke of Crowrest on Brigthwill's eastern shore," she replied.

"Friend to my father," he said more seriously. "An Ava-Ondi sorcerer slayer in his day."

"An offer worth considering, especially knowing what a wife so well favoured by a God can be."

"It is worth considering," Prince Norrich said as he watched her intertwine her fingers with his. "I find your company..." The Grand Matron smiled as though she knew what he was about to say, that he found her exciting and alluring. "Interesting," he finished.

"Consider it," she said, putting her goblet down and slipping off her seat. "I must prepare for the feast."

"I haven't announced one or invited you just yet," the Prince teased.

"What are you waiting for?" she asked, looking over her shoulder for a moment.

Ofeur and his Prince watched her depart before he sat beside his Lord, who was pensive. "If you ask me..."

"I didn't," Prince Norrich said. They sat quietly for a moment. "But now I am. What do you think?"

"That is a powerful woman. She will either raise you up, or she will be your downfall."

"Find me a seer who can tell me which, and I'll know what to do with her."

"You'll probably *have* to marry her," Ofeur said. "As Grand Matron she could become more powerful than you are on these shores. If her family re-acknowledges her as part of their royal line, she could be a Duchess within a month, perhaps rise even higher. Your father may match you to her regardless of what you decide."

"I was afraid you'd say that. For now, you know what we have to do," Prince Norrich said.

"Prepare a feast with half a day's notice," Ofeur said before draining the rest of his goblet. "I'll see it done, you put your head out a window. Some cool air will do you good."

"I'll need more than that," the Prince said, reaching for the decanter of red.

Ofeur intercepted, snatching the crystal vessel off the tray. "If I could make a suggestion to his Grace; perhaps you should keep your wits about you tonight."

"Good advice," the Prince replied. "Keep eyes on her, I want to know everything said and done while she's here. I'll want daily reports from everyone we trust in the temple when she goes back."

"Yes, your majesty."

he children were made comfortable in the middle of the wagon that Marjay had been able to acquire, wrapped in blankets and a few pillows that the innkeeper volunteered. They laid atop a bed of hay, surrounded by boxes secured to their left and right, a rough wood top overhead. Their pup, Ander, settled in between them, absolutely unwilling to let either one of them out of his sight.

"These aren't normal little ones," Haffor said as he peeked in on them. "They're fast asleep while everyone else is on edge and in a bumping wagon on top of that," he said to Rendiran as he rode alongside the wagon on his horse.

"I prayed to Irenick and Viis that they would remain at ease for the journey, so they could rest the entire way. It looks like they answered," Rendiran replied. The streets of Highshield City were as quiet as any normal night, but to Rendiran they seemed abandoned with the occasional distant clamor of a pub, or light in a window. He could feel some kind of tension all around him, but he couldn't name its cause exactly. The need for them to travel through the night was thanks to his heavy handed spell, a guilty point for him. They were already a few blocks from the inn, so he supposed it could be worse.

Haffor moved up to the lead position, leaving his other paladins:

the young Kena to ride alongside the wagon and Rijen at the rear. They were back in armor, but they left their tabards in the back of the wagon and covered their shields with burlap so they looked more like well armoured mercenaries at a glance. Anyone who took a closer look would know they were paladins, but most knew better than to look at armoured men and women too closely after nightfall.

Rendiran was grateful that the pair of horses drawing the covered wagon were of a gentle sort. He had very little practice at handling any beast, though he liked animals a great deal. The wagon team was a pair of thick bodied, spotted mares who seemed content to move at a relaxed trot. He wished they could move faster, but even he knew that a few moments of speed would cost them in the long run, and they planned to keep going until they were at the docks.

Marjay hopped up the step and onto the seat beside Rendiran, surprising him so badly that he flinched and cried out a little. "Sorry, you just seemed to come out of the shadows there."

"I wish I had that kind of magic," Marjay said, patting him on the shoulder. "You all right, young priest?"

"Just fine," Rendiran watched as five crows flew across the highest moon's circle of silver light. One was clearly leading the rest, who were perfectly spaced behind it. "Crows don't fly in that kind of pattern," he muttered to himself.

"Hold a moment," Marjay called, and everyone halted, crowding around the front of the wagon. "The docks are being watched," he said. "Not three blocks away I saw followers of the Bright One, even got a souvenir off one." He pulled a mask with a surprised expression on it. The former owner was definitely a Lucent. "Saw one of them wearing this, and had to get it. This is about how he looked when I knocked him out while he was taking a piss."

Haffor shook his head a little but chuckled just the same. "How many?"

"At least eight guards that I saw outside, and I heard chanting in a house just down the lane from them. 'Rin la nar-ri tha' were the words I made out."

Rendiran recognized a few of the words and he spoke the partial translation aloud; "'Free air,' that's all I recognize, the translation for 'nar-ri,' it's formal Ava-Ondi, no one speaks it."

"I know what it is," Rijin said. "We have to start for Samford Bridge, outside of the city, right away. Those Lucent priests are trying to break the wards that keep dark magic out of the city. They won't be able to take the wards down on that bridge, but we could be in trouble here."

"Do Lucent use ravens?" Rendiran asked.

"No, but Zherchen do. They use them as spies, why?"

"I just saw a murder of them overhead, I thought it was strange because they were flying in formation."

"Strict formation? One then two then two more?" Haffor asked.

"Exactly."

"That's two orders who would like nothing more than to take our cargo to their altars. I hope you trained in combat healing," Haffor said. "The last of the healers in my command are with Tadrin's parents."

"I've had training, but no practice," Rendiran said.

Haffor looked to the wagon, then to Rijen. "We go as far as we can with the wagon, get them moving. By the way, are you sure you couldn't find a better one? Something with suspension so we could move faster than a leisurely walk?" Haffor asked Marjay. "Perhaps if I gave you some coin, you could do better?"

"This was the best we could get on short notice. Besides, this is exactly the kind of wagon a priest would use to journey from one major city to another. It is practical and modest, anything more would cause questions to be raised."

"Well, we'll take the whole night to get to the gatehouse at this rate."

Marjay took the reins for the wagon team, to Rendiran's relief, and expertly led them down the street and around two corners, sending them towards the edge of the city. It made sense to him then, why he was so on edge. He helped reinforce the city's wards against dark magic for years.

"I can feel the wards," Rendiran said, drawing a quick sideways glance from Marjay as he goaded the horses a little. He let his eyes close to slits and concentrated on them, picturing their locations in his mind, and reached out. "Rijen was right, they are being attacked right now, I can feel dark energy straining against them." The house Marjay described appeared in his minds' eye; dozens of shadowy arms stretched from every window and door onto the street, into the sky, pressing against the bonds of light that were supposed to keep the city safe.

Then another house, this one smaller and poorer in a different part of the city came to mind. Another ceremony was under way there, the main room filled with priests and priestesses in masks. Four sheep were in the middle of the space, all crying out as knives were pressed against their throats. "Sacrifices," Rendiran muttered to himself. An idea occurred to him then, and he bent his entire will to one purpose. "Innocent souls, I take you in my arms for Miradu, my generous mistress who will grant you safe passage to her heavenly realm."

Rendiran could feel the blade of the Lucent Priestess as she dragged it across the sheep's throat as though it were cutting his own. "This pain will end, and your journey to light and peace begins," he prayed. As he felt the animals begin to die, he reached out and sheltered their spirits. "I call Miradu! Dragon of peace! Dragon Queen of justice and light!" In that instant he was there, in the room as a spirit. He could barely feel the sensations of his body.

"Rendiran! What are you doing?" he faintly heard Haffor ask.

"They sacrifice sheep to their Gods, to bring the wards down. I'm calling Miradu to protect their spirits."

"You're doing it yourself! I can see it, it's your power that's being used here! You're putting yourself in too much danger," Haffor said.

Rendiran felt a chill run through is body. He was surrounded by blazing light. His skin felt as though it could catch fire any moment, and the air he drew into his chest threatened to burn him from the inside. "The Bright One is here!" he cried out.

"He's attacking you with illusions, the wards are not broken yet," Haffor said.

All he could see was violently shifting yellow light. "Miradu, I humbly call for your aid," he said through a mouthful of ash.

"He assails your spirit, your mind," Haffor said. "And if there's one thing I know about you, it's that you command your wits better than anything else. Fight, boy."

Terror, he could feel the fright from the four sheep spirits he was protecting as the Bright One reached for them, and Rendiran forgot the physical world entirely. He existed as a spirit above the poor house, corralling the four sheep behind him while he fended the harsh flames off with the other. "I am true light, the leading flame that guides the lost, and I oppose you!"

He could see the wards beneath him strengthen, glow brightly across the vast city of Highshield, and knew that the work he was doing was pure. His power would have done nothing at all if there was so much as a selfish urge. The harsh heat of the Bright One had been pushed back, if only for a moment.

He wrapped his spirit around the innocent souls and recalled the signs they used to protect the city and flung them in all directions. "I channel the power of the ancients into these holy symbols. By my will and the will of Miradu I protect this space, and call it a sanctuary for goodness." A barrier of gentle light surrounded the four innocent souls, and he could see the city below growing smaller. The Bright One was unseen, but Rendiran could feel that he was furious, seething just beyond the barrier he'd reinforced.

He knew what he had to do next, and was sure it would make the Bright One even angrier. Miradu's spirit was near, as was Irenick's and Viis', but they were too weak to cross the astral plane where the battle for their Gifts threatened to break out. "I send these innocent souls to my Heavenly Matron. Miradu, take them into your realm where they may be at peace." He felt the flames close in on his spirit again as the four sheep spirits were taken away by the globe of protection he'd made, the Bright One didn't follow it. Instead he focused his attention on another sacrifice that was taking place in the city. He had protected one offering, but there were at least three more. Rendiran withdrew his spirit from the astral realm quickly, before the Bright One changed his mind.

He opened his eyes and was surprised to discover that he was on the roof of the wagon. He was out of breath and sweating profusely. "How did I get up here?"

"You arched your back and pushed yourself from the seat to the middle of the roof," Rijen said. "Very amusing."

"Sometimes when your spirit strains, your body finds a way to show everyone how difficult and dangerous your trial is," Haffor said. "And how completely foolish you are."

"Don't be hard on him," Rijen said. "He bought us time, most likely a lot of it, actually."

"There are other sacrifices happening in the city in at least three places," Rendiran said. "I couldn't stop them, but I fortified the wards."

"Well, perhaps not that much time," Rijen said. "Did you see any sign of other priests trying to fortify the wards?"

Rendiran thought for a moment, the memory of his spiritual journey already fading. "I didn't. The wards seemed to react only to me."

"Then something is either blinding or has corrupted the Temple," Haffor said, his mood darkening further. "All the Temple's worst rivals have come to either destroy it, or take these children and we're down to three paladins, a guard and a priest who doesn't know his limits." He paused a moment then asked; "Was that the first time you sent your spirit to fly free?"

"No, I've practiced it a few times, but always within a protected space," Rendiran said, carefully crawling back down the the wagon's seat. "What I did there was new, but it felt familiar at the same time."

"I was afraid you wouldn't come back," Haffor said. "Don't do it again. There are too many beings watching us."

Rendiran nodded. "I'm afraid I've frustrated the Bright One. Well, frustrated is the wrong word, I'd say irritated."

"You are powerful, there is no doubt," Haffor said, "but you are pushing too far, too quickly. Are you burned anywhere?"

After a scant moment of checking, he found a burn mark on his arm, the size and shape of a large man's hand. "It's deep," he said, focusing his will and healing it. The flesh recovered beneath the skin, but a scar remained, it would take much more attention to remove. After all his ordeals that day, he realized he should be exhausted, but he'd never felt more alert in his life.

"If the city wasn't still warded, you would have brought the Bright One's spirit down on us," Haffor said. "Think about that the next time you take on a new challenge, young priest."

here were things that Prince Norrich liked about Highshield. The routinely plentiful harvests, and constant flow of materials ranging from common to exotic made it easy to make his castle seem richer than many in Brightwill. In Highshield almost everything was fresh, while Brightwill – that crowded, over-populated place – struggled to feed itself. Much of what was shipped there from Highshield had to be preserved, especially the meat.

The Prince normally made sure that his hall was filled with nobles, heroes and the most interesting people in Highshield, but on short notice only the people who were regular members of his court were in attendance. They were the boring ones, nobles from Brightwill who wanted to see the expansion of the new provinces and the wilderness but from the protection of a castle wall, or from within a circle of armed guards. They were excited to meet the Grand Matron, so she never ran out of people to speak to.

Ofeur arranged for her to sit in the middle of one long side of the banquet table, far from the head and the Prince. The simple act proved that Ofeur truly was worthy of the title of Chief Advisor, it was fascinating to watch the Grand Matron from so many seats away as she daintily ate chicken, a fine selection of vegetables and a little glazed pork. It seemed as though she was holding back, he could imagine her eating alone, tearing into the bird flesh and well-seasoned pig as though she was starving. The mental image was delightful.

Her meal was frequently interrupted by courtiers low and high who asked her questions from up, down and across the table. Lord Umblin, whose hearing was cursed into near deafness, asked the loudest question of the evening; "Grand Matron, is it true that your Temple has been planning to empty the city? I've heard that you'll be staking new farm land at the end of the season."

That was a controversial topic, one which Prince Norrich knew the answers to, but he could shirk accountability because the Church was responsible for developing and cultivating the province. He wasn't interested in what she'd tell him, but in how she would answer.

Instead of yelling at poor Lord Umblin, she used magic to raise the volume of her lovely voice, so she sounded like she was speaking normally. "It is the only prudent measure. Highshield City and other major towns along the shore are filling, and they are taxing the product we can send Brightwill. We also promise everyone who comes here a life in nature, which can't be found in a large city like this. So, new lands are being staked according to provincial boundaries past the wall, and families will be able to farm, raise livestock and contribute to the bounty that flows from Highshield's shores instead of reducing it by living in the city. Once Brightwill learns that there are empty homes on the shores of Highshield, more will come, and the cycle will continue."

"What about the wild lands past the wall? Aren't there still dangers?"

"Progress overcomes all obstacles, especially with our Goddess Miradu and her children watching over us," the Matron replied. "The mother country will be astonished with what we send them in quantity, quality and rarity, especially once we begin work in the foothills."

Prince Norrich could see that the old Lord was about to ask another question and interrupted him by raising his goblet. "To the

King, who is responsible for sending everyone here to this land of plenty, long may he reign."

"Goddess save the King, long may he reign," replied the entire room. Everyone who had a cup in their hand made sure to drink.

"I would also like to toast our Grand Matron, who has dazzled us upon her sudden but welcome return. I would raise a glass in her honour every hour if only to see her blush and fluster." The court was surprised and, judging from the tittering laughter, amused by his second toast. He drained his glass and stood. "Now, I invite you to walk the gardens with our guest of honour." He extended his hand to the Grand Matron, who carefully rose and joined him.

"In celebration of the Grand Matron's attendance this evening, and of her Goddess Miradu, we will be serving fresh apple cakes, a selection of wines and fruit throughout the evening." Ofeur announced as servants cleared the trenchers, platters, plates and silverware from the table.

Prince Norrich led the Grand Matron through tall double doors furnished with perfect red glass into the lush garden. The broad walkways were paved with white and blue quartz, and they wound between planters featuring lush berry and fruit bearing plants. It was the largest curated garden in Highshield, and he was more than a little aware that he didn't visit it often enough. He preferred the wild woods beyond the wall, but the gardens were peaceful, a place for play as much as contemplation.

The warm, yellow glow of Quickamber lights hanging along strings throughout the space – a treasure in themselves – gave the night an otherworldly air, as though time was suspended. They walked away from the din of the courtiers leaving the great hall, collecting fresh cups and steaming cakes, and for quite some time Prince Norrich and the Grand Matron made their way up the main avenue arm-in-arm without saying a word.

Coming around a large oval planter of dwarfed chokecherry trees, the main feature of the garden came into view. The sound of running water could be heard before the grand fountain came into view, and when it did the Grand Matron gasped.

Miradu, in the form she took as a woman stood in the middle of the fountain, smiling down at a bountiful harvest piled at her feet. A halo of mist rose around her head from behind, sprayed by hidden nozzles, her marble skin glistened in the gentle light. In front of her nude figure were Irenick and Viis, who knelt with swords in front of them. Behind the matron was Wydu, in his broad headed black dragon form, holding a crooked scale in one hand and several coins in the other. "You had it restored," the Grand Matron said, amazed. "This is beautiful."

"I can see it from my bedchamber, and every morning I would look down at it and shake my head. It took longer to find craftsmen who were worthy of the project than it did to see the work completed, but I'd have nothing less for everything that Miradu has brought to the Kingdom."

"Is it only the service of Our Lady's Temple that inspired it?"

"I'm Lady Viis' creature, even though I love Miradu, Irenick and even Wydu at times, Viis will always be the Goddess I praise first." The Prince took a gold coin from his pocket and laid it on the small tray in front of Viis' kneeling form. "So, yes, there is some faith, and some reverence behind this project. When I was sent here I hoped to meet the kind of people who explored the wilds, had the grit and bravery to settle new lands with little more than their wits and determination. After more than one trek past the wall, I've found that those intrepid folk are few, and the old forests of this land have a more dangerous reputation than they deserve. It's nothing but mountains, trees, and a few craven crossbred creatures that would rather be left alone than attack an explorer. Viis lived a life of great exploration and fought beasts, even demons that make the risks of these days look simple, even boring. I'm afraid the kind of world that made people like her is long gone."

"I'm sorry you didn't find the adventures you were looking for, but you are the most powerful man in Highshield, it must be possible for you to find equally thrilling excitement," the Grand Matron pulled his arm against her gently.

He smiled at her and started a slow walk to the east side of the garden. "The nobles here found me, and with them came an endless stream of petitions, pleas and plans that they'd like to pull me into. Plans that would elevate them and earn them a seat in Brightwill. There's a secret about the continent that I keep, one that would cost me friendships amongst those lesser nobles. I'll share it with you, because, even though your approach with me today was obvious, bordering on salacious, at least it was somewhat honest. I see your lure, and have a good sense in how high you want to rise." He felt her start to pull her arm from his and turned to face her. She retrieved her arm only partially, but he pulled her against him gently. "I've met many women, but few are as enticing despite your obvious desire to trade carnally for a place at my side."

"You embarrass me," the Grand Matron said, looking away.

"In front of who? Your minders aren't close enough to hear anything I say, and all they see is proof that your ruse to attract me is working." He drew her a little closer, his hands crossing her lower back. "Or are you embarrassed now that I see through your superficial approach?"

"It's obvious that I've embarrassed myself," she said, standing stiffly against him.

"What's beneath the pretense?" Prince Norrich asked. "You want to make a union of some kind with me for political gain, I acknowledge that. It's nothing new, but I'd like to know something about you before we take another look at the validity of your proposal." She looked up at him then away. He leaned in and turned his head so he could catch her eye, but she wouldn't meet his gaze. "Nothing? I only ask the simplest of questions; 'who are you?'" the Prince let her go and stood back. For the first time she seemed meek. "Disappointing." He would have to send word of the proposed strategic marriage to his father, it was law, but he didn't like the idea unless he got something out of the match as well. If he was to marry a woman who he had to share with a religion, he wanted to know that there was some substance to her.

Prince Norrich began to turn away and he was taking his first step towards the eastern balcony when she said; "It's true, I've been shut away for years."

Her gaze still avoided him as he turned towards her. "I heard, go on."

"I read what was going on in Highshield, Brightwill and beyond, had people bring me every scrap of news for years."

"I heard that many great libraries in Brightwill know your name well," the Prince said.

"Yes, that's true, word from near and far wasn't enough, so I read books, took lessons from the pages," she replied.

"Lessons on?"

"At first, I tried to discover a way to correct the damage done by my attacker. Years passed, and there was little relief to be found in books or from masters, and I began to read about the Ondi-Ne. You offered me a secret a moment ago, and I wonder if it can compare to the knowledge I uncovered. Forbidden knowledge."

The Prince smiled, genuinely pleased: the night had promise after all. "Forbidden? This conversation won't land us in Shadow Hold, will it?"

"No, but I know things that would shake my own Temple, and parts of your kingdom."

"You have my ear."

"The Ava-Ondi ruled Brightwill because they lived and thrived there for thousands of years, we know this, it's proven history. Meanwhile, the Ondi-Ne were rarer in those ancient histories, not because they were the meeker of the two races, but because they were less involved with The Continent, they had little care for Brightwill until the last age."

"I remember hearing most of this in my lessons as a boy, yes," Prince Norrich agreed.

"I found historical records of Ondi-Ne going back nearly seven thousand years," she said in a whisper. "Proven history of Ondi-Ne and humans living together only a few hundred miles from where we are standing. Out there, past the Great Key."

"Past that mountain?" Prince Norrich said, leaping up three stairs and running to the balcony's edge, pointing at a mountain that he knew he'd be able to see in morning's light. Its jagged top was the inspiration for its name. "Humanity hasn't been here for that long, there's no history that proves otherwise."

"The Ondi-Ne were great travelers," the Grand Matron said, following him to the balcony with less zeal. "They brought humans here from Brightwill to escape the Ava-Ondi, even fought against them north and south of Highshield, but in these lands. They fought them because these were Ondi-Ne lands thousands of years ago. This," she gestured towards the city, "is all built on what were once flood plains. Humans settled here again a thousand years ago because of the flat, fertile land, but even that is only recent history compared to what I've come to know."

"So the Ondi-Ne were here first. If only there was a single one in the castle we could ask," the Prince said.

"Where the Ondi-Ne who were persecuted have gone is a great mystery of our time, and after reading their stories, their poetry, their great romances and the charts they made of the stars, I tell you they are a people worth knowing. The Ava-Ondi ruled Brightwill mercilessly, left scorched scars across the land, but have you ever heard of tyranny or a wounded countryside found in the wilds here?"

"No, but the best of our magicians fail to see far past the Titan Chain, those mountains are filled with stone that hamper their sight," Norrich said.

"The Ondi-Ne are a people guided by kindness, naturally drawn to music, love, and excitement. Miradu knew this, and she loved the Ondi-Ne so much that she found two wonderful men, Rin and Olm, to have a son and a daughter with. Wydu surrounded himself with Ondi-Ne who had the hearts of tricksters, and it is known that few humans spent much time in their company."

"I've never heard the names of Miradu's men, or that humans weren't preferred," he said, enjoying the new knowledge almost as much as he liked seeing a different, genuine side of the Grand Matron. She seemed excited, genuinely interested in telling him about what she'd learned.

"While the church does not forbid the teaching of these truths, they prefer that they were not mentioned. This is a human civilization now, and the temple leaders have pushed for the exclusion of all Ondi, humans have wrested almost all control from the Ondi-Ne founders. They have imposed a whole new set of rules atop those set down by Irekirk and Miradu herself, going as far as to encourage a pledge of chastity wherever they can."

"I always thought that was ridiculous, even I know Miradu had many companions that she loved deeply, and several were of a more intimate sort."

"It is a part of how some humans want to control the Temple of Miradu. I suspect that the next Matron will be completely human, the first ever."

"Not for a very long time, I hope," Prince Norrich said. "I'm just starting to enjoy this Matron's company. Tell me a secret that can only be whispered, something dangerous."

The Grand Matron smiled at him, a spontaneous, true smile as she closed the distance between them and stood on her toes so she could whisper in his ear. "Wydu gave me a vision when he saved me. The Ondi-Ne will return, but the Sage War must begin first. A war that will bring him into this world. My work will be celebrated, my husband will be made emperor, and we will be able to look from this balcony and see Wydu's great black wings carry him towards the shore, towards Brightwill. Before any of that can happen, Highshield City must burn and empty."

"Do not repeat this," Prince Norrich said, stepping away. Predicting the return of a God was one thing, but telling him that Wydu would crown him, and that he would act on the world was dangerous – there were thousands of priests who would decry her prediction, call her mad. The worst of it was the prediction that Highshield City would be in flames. It was the primary port for all things going to Brightwill, he couldn't afford to have a disruption.

"I have seen only moments of your future, and been given a glimpse into your true being," she whispered at him. "I know you are a good man, and that you may have a long life, that it'll be lengthened if I am at your side. Look there, to the harbor districts," she invited. "The magical wards defending the city are about to fall."

"What?" he rushed to the railing. "What have you done?"

"This morning I foresaw many things, including the departure of Viis' and Irenick's gifts from the Temple. Instead of stopping it, I saw it as an opportunity, so I ordered the city guards to withdraw at sundown. I'm obviously not the only one who foresaw that those gifts would be vulnerable, because all the major religions – let's call them cults, since they are so much smaller – saw an opportunity to take them for their own purposes. More importantly, with the absence of the guards, the cults see an opportunity to do what they like here, to bring corruption and flame. When it is done, I'll send my Temple Guards back into the city, and we'll sacrifice them to Wydu. Since sundown rites have been taking place all across this city that will leave it open to dark magic. The Temple and your castle wards remain up, so will the ones on the outer wall, so we are relatively safe. It's time for Highshield City to be purified, the Sage War begins with black fire and a battle that will pit the worst cults in the city against each other." Red and cold white light flashed across the city, and Prince Norrich was shaken by a sudden shiver. "The wards that hold dark magic at bay have failed. I recommend you shut everyone not already here out of your castle and have every magical practitioner within reinforce the seals and wards on every door."

"I won't have a war in this city," Prince Norrich said. "I won't stand idly by as Viis' and Irenick's gifts are taken for slaughter on some black altar."

"It is too late to stop it; any soldier you send will only become a tool for evil practitioners to manipulate. We can watch from here, anyone at my side will be protected from all but the worst they can bring to bear."

Norrich saw another side of her then; a woman who was truly confident, had unshakable belief in a cause that he knew almost nothing about, and someone who could prove to be more dangerous than anyone else on the continent. The responsibility of caring for Highshield belonged to the religious orders. He didn't have to get involved in anything unless it threatened his castle, and he kept that in mind as he decided that wasting his own soldiers on cleaning up a mess that came from foreign religions was a lost cause. "We'll see what remains in the morning," he told her. "I'll order the castle to be sealed for the night, then return so you can tell me about this war."

———————

23

The bump and roll of the wagon wheels over rougher, less used streets along with the creak and squeak of the seat made Rendiran wonder if anyone wasn't aware of their passing. "This is no way to travel quietly," he muttered to Marjay.

"Our original plan required that we could pass as merchants on the road," he replied. "I wonder; do you know much about the woodlands? Do beasts from the wilds come down into the city this far?"

"No, we're firmly in the realm of pets and strays. No wilderness here unless it's in a cage, bound for some Brightwill zoo or private menagerie," Rendiran replied, happy to be asked something that he actually knew about.

"That's what I thought," Marjay said.

"Why do you ask?"

"In the last hour I've seen a fox three times, the same one. It was definitely on the large side, I think," he said.

"Was it wearing anything?" Rendiran asked. He'd read about shapeshifting but it was considered a lost art.

"Now that you mention it, I think I caught a glimpse of some kind of straps, perhaps a harness? The beast is quick, and good at keeping to the shadows."

"Ondi-Ne used to shapeshift, so it says in rumour and old legends. The fox was always associated with messengers, sometimes thievery, but it was never known as a fighting form."

"You learn that from your books?" Marjay asked.

"Yes, I've been reading about the Ondi since I could understand script. Well, when I had time, and when I had instructors who would allow me to."

"You weren't always allowed?"

"Most of my instructors saw Ondi as our former suppressors, especially the Ava-Ondi. Learning about their legends and magic wasn't something they condoned. Two books in my collection are a little singed around the edges, rescued them from a burning when I was a boy."

"Your collection, that chest that took two of us to load?"

"I'm afraid so," Rendiran said sheepishly.

"I thought you only brought the essentials."

"Those are the essentials."

"What's that then? The one you keep tucked into your vest?"

"Ah, the most recent acquisition, a guide to languages written by one of the most well-travelled masters I've ever met. I don't know if it'll help, but it's the only book I own that I haven't read several times. Do you have a favourite?"

"Favourite what?" Marjay asked.

"Book? I've read The Legends of the Shade Gate Volume three at least ten times."

"Ten times? I can't say I do. I can only scribble my name and sound out enough to read orders. I know a little Low Script too, but I can't imagine reading for fun."

"Oh, once you've become practiced at it, your eyes fly across the page. Worlds long gone become as real in your mind as this road. I could help you, I'll be teaching the children to read." Rendiran could tell that something he said irked his companion, and he thought about it for a moment. Perhaps it was the idea of being taught like a child that bothered him. "I bet if you simply stand guard close enough to listen and watch, you'll pick it up."

"I just might," Marjay said. "There it is again," he added, nodding towards an alley to their right.

Rendiran looked just in time to see a large fox watch the wagon pass for a moment before scampering down the alleyway. He cast a simple empathy spell and sensed its intention. There was something familiar about the fox's spirit. "That is a friend, it checks the path ahead and worries, but I can't clearly sense what it's concerned about."

"I know that wasn't in any of your books," Marjay said.

"The spell was. A simple empathy trick – I can reach out and sense someone's basic state of mind and intentions. I've mastered it to the point of gleaning a thing's plan, thanks to the guidance and support of Miradu."

"I've always wondered, where does the power you use come from?" Marjay asked. "I know it's the gift of the Gods, but I've never really understood how that works."

Haffor dropped back to ride his horse alongside the wagon. "Rendiran will give a lecture on the topic just to answer the question, so I'll do it for him."

Rendiran couldn't help but be a little offended for a moment, but finally sighed and nodded. "Perhaps not a whole lecture, but you're right; it's a subject I could go on about," he conceded.

"The short answer is that we learn to draw on power given to us by our Gods. We gain their notice and their blessings by doing their work, gaining their favor. For a paladin, we hope to impress our Gods during training, and some of us gain power before the training is over. We earn more by following the directions given in our oath. For priests it's not much different, only the duties change. There's also a lot more prayer. In any event, Miradu and her children grant power to those who focus on doing Her work. If we practitioners go against her will, performing acts that she does not approve of, we may find ourselves without her blessing. Some of us have the focus and talent to make better use of her gifts than others, and then there is the whole, wider world of magic to consider. Someone like our Rendiran here has the blessing of Miradu as well as the gifts of a sorcerer."

"I don't know about that," Rendiran said. "I've never truly practiced sorcery."

"You did so tonight," Haffor said. "The power you used to wake the paladins' minds in the temple was well beyond the scope of all but the most powerful priests, you have the gift only Ondi carry, the tethers to a more elusive but older kind of magic."

"With no result," Rendiran said quietly. "I haven't seen a paladin, squire, or combat priest. Wouldn't they have found us by now?"

"Those wards you reinforced are still holding," Haffor said. "You can't scry in this city, so they would have trouble finding us until we reach a main gate or cross street, but I know your magic worked, young Rendiran. The only question is if they answered my call, chose to remain in the temple, or to wander away from all responsibility. The Eventide have had a rough go of things, I expect a few men decided that freedom is a better option and left their armour and the temple behind."

"And if those paladins fail to perform their duty, they'll lose favour and their power as well," Marjay said.

"Yes," Haffor said.

"There have been a few who carry the blessing and power of Miradu after abandoning their positions with the paladins, or the priesthood," Rendiran added. "In The Wanderings Of Offenmir, Offenmir the Great gathers a company of men and women together from heroes who toil in obscurity with Viis' blessing. They had powers of healing, protection and stranger gifts in some cases. There are other scattered examples of people who carry the blessings of their Gods long after they abandon their Order. Some who were never members of any order at all."

"They may not seem so rare when you consider the broad scope of history, but I've known fewer than ten men and women who carry a God's blessing outside of a religious order. It seems the Gods like their followers to be organized," Haffor countered.

"It's like looking through a keyhole, trying to understand the workings of gods and magic and such," Marjay said. "You only get to see a little at a time, and it feels like you're trying to get a glimpse of something forbidden."

"Maybe Rendiran could make it clearer," Haffor said. "Some things do require a lecture, I suppose." He rode ahead again to lead the wagon.

"We have plenty of time until sunrise," Rendiran said, hoping the wards around the city would hold until then. He doubted it, but would welcome the opportunity to teach Marjay as a distraction from the dark streets.

"No," Marjay said. "No, thank you. I don't truly need to know the secrets of the faith, not after meeting Viis myself. I've got faith to spare. If you'd like to lecture me at length about something, how about telling me where the Ondi-Ne have gone? Read anything about that?"

"Plenty, but it's a modern mystery. If anyone knows where the ones that weren't burned, drowned, or otherwise killed, are, and there were plenty Ondi-Ne left by all accounts, then they haven't taken the time to speak or write about it. I haven't known many pure Ondi-Ne in my lifetime though, so I can't shed much light on the topic. I'm sure Haffor and Rijen knew more." Rendiran said.

"I hear my name?" Rijen called from the rear, where he had no trouble keeping up with the wagon on his horse.

"Did you know many Ondi-Ne before they began disappearing?" Rendiran asked.

"You mean before the humans began hunting them down? Hundreds, some of them were very good friends. Why do you ask?"

"You wouldn't happen to have a theory about where they went?"

Any good humour the man had drained away at the question. "The Ondi-Ne are a people wronged in so ways, you could scarcely imagine. I visit Aldum whenever I can. Even after decades of human occupation, it is still the most beautiful city in this world, and the last place I saw Velia, the keeper of my heart. She warned that our days together were growing short, and in my youth I didn't listen. I was called away to a stinking hole where an Ava-Ondi named Krikus practiced necromancy. Weeks after his head was burned and his skull was cracked, I heard that King Obart, a human king that died before either of you were born, marched on the city. I expected news of some carnage, another purification of Ondi that was unprovoked, but King Obart's men found the city completely empty. I went to the Ondi-Ne towns, the dens, the burrows, and thickets where I knew they should be, gathering people like me along the way – searchers, questioners – and we discovered that tens of thousands of Ondi-Ne were gone. Almost all those merry places filled where Ondi-Ne families lived were empty, with the exception of three places that took me years to find. Places that have emptied over the years as well. So, do I know where they went? I don't. What land would they love more than this? What refuge would hide them from every magician and explorer? Even Miradu, a champion of love and family, won't tell me where I might find my Velia, and she has been in my prayers morning and night for longer than you've been alive. Perhaps you should ask the fox, when she reveals herself for more than a heartbeat or two."

"I'm sorry, I didn't realize it was such a heavy question," Rendiran said.

"I should apologize as well," Rijen said. "I tell the story whenever I can, and sometimes I forget that the question; 'where did the Ondi-Ne go?' is a simple one to most. It comes up less and less."

"Thank you for sharing your story nonetheless, I'd like to hear it in greater detail some time, if you'd..." A blinding flash of red followed by cold, colourless light interrupted him. When he could see again, Marjay was looking at him as though he didn't notice it.

"Are you all right?"

"The wards are down!" Haffor cried from the lead position. "They'll know where we are any moment. We can't afford to spare the horses any longer." He increased his own pace and Marjay pushed the horses, forcing the wagon down the street faster.

It still didn't seem quick to Rendiran. "I wish we were able to steal a carriage from the temple," he said, looking into the shadows around.

"Told you, they were all gone with the Matron," Marjay said.

That was the last thing the party said for some time. The ease they knew moments before was gone. For several blocks they peered down dark alleys and at quiet houses as they passed. The bumpy street ahead was no more welcoming, but the watch towers of the northern city wall were visible, an encouraging sight.

"Do you hear that?" Marjay asked, and Rendiran heard it a moment later – a scampering, scratching – as though something moved with clawed feet through the nearby alleyways.

Haffor drew his sword and slashed at something in the air. His attack hit its mark again three times before Rendiran realized what he'd struck – a gangly limbed, two-foot-tall, wide eyed and sharp toothed imp.

Before Rendiran could react to a clawed hand on his arm, Marjay had his blade out, and with a deft hand stabbed the imp in the eye. The piercing scream was unlike anything he'd heard, and it continued making its death knell until it was shoved off of Marjay's blade, had fallen to the road and was crushed under the wagon's rear wheel.

"Light! Give us light!" Haffor shouted as the horses, Kena riding alongside the wagon, Haffor and Rijen all came under attack.

It took Rendiran a moment to realize that Haffor was speaking to him, and when he did he clapped his hands over his head. "Light of day, light my way!" he shouted, and the street was illuminated as though it were noon for a quarter mile in each direction. He would have been astonished at the effectiveness of his prayer, which he'd used many times to much, much lesser effect, but he was too busy noticing the small army of imps that were all turning their attention in his direction.

Marjay drew and tossed several small daggers from a bandolier in quick succession at the green skinned imps. He threw the reins in Rendiran's lap and drew two short blades. An imp clutched Rendiran's sleeve, and he grabbed the thing's forehead in his panic, barely able to grip it well enough to pull it loose and kick it, sending the screeching assailant between the horses.

The carriage team whinnied and stomped as they pulled them more roughly down the street. "Don't throw imps at the horses!"

Marjay shouted as he slashed at a pair trying to get to the driver's bench.

"I'm sorry!" Rendiran said as he flailed to fend another imp off. It had a good handhold on the step leading up to his seat, chittering and clawing at him. "It's my first imp attack!" The thing lunged open mouth first and sunk its teeth into Rendiran's calf. He nearly dropped the reigns as he frantically reached down and grabbed the creatures neck. It clawed his arm and clenched its jaw as he tried to pry the biter loose. Two more were coming up the front of the wagon, leering at him with yellow and black eyes.

Marjay was no help, he was fending off twice as many from the top of the wagon's cabin and left side. The teeth dug in and the imp shook his head, causing a higher range of pain, and Rendiran did something his instructors, his mentors and his Order forbade him to do as a Healer of the Temple – he turned his healing art to the purpose of savaging his attacker. The muscles, veins and bone of the imp's shoulders and neck were torn in every direction as he focused a burst of power into the little beast.

When they saw their fellow imp explode into shreds of flesh and bone, the pair coming up from the front of the wagon over the foot rest leapt at Rendiran. He caught one by the chest with both hands, and forced the creature's organs to crush into each other, twist and burst through its belly. The other slashed at Rendiran's head as he prepared to bite his face. Marjay caught that one, taking its head off with a single swing of his short blade.

"Are you all right?" Marjay asked.

Rendiran looked to his right, where a small tribe's worth of imps was running alongside the wagon, getting ready to leap at him. "That remains to be seen. Miradu forgive me," he said under his breath. With no small measure of guilt, he reached towards the nearest imp and, using hand gestures instead of the poetry he sung when he was healing people, he twisted the imp's flesh and bones into a knot of ripped and broken pieces. He crushed another's legs and shoulders together, tore the next one's spine part way out of its body, and broke several thin, green necks before he began attacking two at a time with gestures that directed perverted healing energy into a weapon that could reach ten feet, sometimes more.

He almost slowed down when the thought occurred – it was so easy to mutilate and murder instead of mend and heal – but he kept going, refining his new skill until he could disembowel the small beings two at a time. To his surprise, a troop of at least a dozen men with swords and coal blackened armour rushed into the street. The wagon came to a sudden halt.

Two of them charged at Haffor with spears, and Rendiran gestured towards the nearest. A human's flesh was tougher than a small imp's, but he envisioned his fingers wrapping around the precious flesh inside the belly of Haffor's attacker, and then made a pulling gesture that was so extreme that he smashed his elbow on the edge of his seat.

Haffor defended himself against the spear of the second man, deflecting the spear head and stabbing him in the neck, but the first, the one Rendiran assailed, dropped to his knees clutching his belly. His middle was twisted and ripped so badly that the gore was visible through the chinks in his armour, and he only screamed twice before he fell silent.

"Don't wake the children," Rendiran said as he raised his hands menacingly at the group of soldiers in dark armour and stood on one foot. He could feel a river of power flowing through him. He healed his own wounds with a thought – the mouthful of meat an imp nearly tore off of his calf, an elbow with a chipped bone, and scratches on his scalp – then reached towards the black armoured men.

"Kill the sorcerer!" cried the soldier in the lead. They rushed the wagon, and Haffor cut two down, the last of Marjay's throwing daggers slipped through the eye slit of another, but Rendiran's hands gripped another pair's throats from afar. His hand motions were rough and jagged as he pulled with one hand and a soldier fell to the paving stones, his breastplate covered in blood. He pulled at the second and that soldier kept running several steps, as though he didn't realize that his throat had been torn open, then he fell as well.

He was about to turn his attention to the new group of riders coming from the alley to their right when he saw that they bore the markings of the Eventide Guard and Miradu. The riders, guards, priests and paladins of Miradu killed the last of their enemies and surrounded the wagon. "Rendiran the Resurrector?" one of them said with a pleasantly surprised grin. "More like Rendiran the Ripper. I could see your power from a block away. I'm Drikson, High Combat Priest of Forge Hin," he said, offering his hand as he gracefully guided his horse into position beside the wagon. He was human, and well into middle age – surprising for a priest of Forge Hin.

Finding himself numb to the core, Rendiran shook the man's hand. It was unlike any priest's, calloused and strong. "I only did what was necessary."

---

24

*W*hen the fires started in Highshield City, Prince Norrich watched in disbelief. The first was a three story building on Shalecrop Street in the middle of the slums, then there was another across the way. Trees in Janetin Park, many blocks down became torches that spat flaming leaves and finally one bright red and yellow explosion started on the Gold Road. The Gold Road, one of the main arteries through the city. Bells rung, men and women emerged from the houses with buckets and shovels.

Moments later the true chaos started, the shadows were filled with terrible things. Warriors in darkened colours, priests with sharp sacrificial daggers, opportunists who took their chances in the streets to rob people who were just trying to keep the city from burning. All the while, the High Matron prayed under her breath.

Norrich made out only a few words; 'cleansing,' 'Wydu,' 'fires,' and 'punished,' and he found none of them comforting. "Enough, I won't idly watch the city burn, and I can't leave the Gifts of the Gods to traverse it alone."

"There is a contract, centuries old," the Grand Matron said. "Would you break it?"

"I know, you religious people are tasked with the building, care and expansion of everything here," he replied. "But that is contingent on you providing seven tenths of everything you produce in these lands, and how in all the hells will I explain to my father, the King, why the mechanism of this city has stopped refining metal, grinding grain for flour, and can't ship that or anything else to Silverport? That's why I'm here, his second son, to make sure the goods flow, that Brightwill does not want for anything."

"This city will empty, the survivors who are fleeing right now will settle outside the wall. Taxes will be collected from what they make there, and then the new immigrants who come to the port will rebuild, make the city theirs and when they finish we'll push them further out past the wall, where they can develop more lands, cut more of the woodlands and tame it. This is Wydu's plan, and it is violent but wise and expedient. Would you question the wisdom of a God?"

"Yes," Prince Norrich said. "Guards, see her and her minders to her carriages and have them leave the castle. I'm no worshipper of Wydu, and I won't have this mindless zealot in my castle."

"There will be repercussions for your actions, Prince," the Grand Matron said as she stormed past him.

"Yes, there will be," Prince Norrich said. "If three hundred and fifty ships don't leave that port at the end of the month, heavily laden with cargo, I'll personally strike your head from your shoulders, have all your advisors hung along Gold Street and we'll see if Wydu has the power to resurrect any of them."

"Progress comes at a cost, you will see," the Grand Matron replied on her way out of the garden.

Prince Norrich followed her and the guards who walked by her side to ensure that she at least made it out of the garden. The Matron and her minders went quietly. The guards didn't have to lay a hand on them. He stopped at the fountain, beside the statue of Viis. It was as tall as he was. When the doors closed behind the Matron and her escort of castle guards, he ignored the other retreating revelers and looked to Viis, whose stone face was downturned in reverence to her mother.

The story of Miradu's arrival was long, the scriptures were compelling, but the lesson Norrich took from the hundreds of hours of teaching was simpler than his instructors liked. When Miradu revealed herself to the Ondi-Ne of the Highshield Shore, she came with gifts of food, wine, and saved many.

Miradu was also a hedonist who admired beauty, enjoyed comfort, and used magic to grant wealth to herself and others. Her time in civilization became interesting when lords looked to her for advice, and she was given responsibility by the people who loved her. Her lessons came hard as she found herself tricked into using her power for their ends. After being deceived by nine lords and ladies, she retreated to the wilderness.

Nearly two decades later she emerged with children and a new purpose: to provide justice for the low born and anyone else who would serve the same cause. She still brought a plentiful bounty with her, but she watched for the greedy and careless this time, and anyone who partook too much found their meals rotting in their bellies, and their hands unable to grasp any more of her gifts.

Her half Ondi-Ne children, Viis, Irenick and Irekirk learned the way of the sword and donned armour. Their adventures filled books, and Norrich read everything he could get his hands on more than once, even two of the forbidden tomes. His favourites were always focused on Viis, her cunning, need for adventure and sense of good-ness always gave him faith that the world could be as Miradu and her children wanted it. A place of justice, peace, beauty and happiness.

"What have I done to follow in your footsteps?" he asked as he gently stroked Viis' cold stone cheek. "What have I done to honour you and shape this world as you'd have it?"

"Adventures, and acts of charity for a start, milord," Ofeur said. "The Matron is in the courtyard being loaded into her carriage."

"Good, that woman is deluded," Prince Norrich said.

"I knew a cat like her once," Ofeur said. "A purring, loving crea-ture who would be good company for hours at a time. Then, when you least expected it, the bites and clawing would come, often right after it's been curled up in your lap. I could never guess what the damn thing would do."

"Was this back in Brightwill? I don't remember meeting that cat," Norrich said, not looking away from Viis' statue.

"You never will. I wouldn't leave that thing with my little sisters, not in my absence, so when it was busy purring in my lap one day, I snapped its neck."

"If you have a point, please get to it."

"When you're confronted with the unpredictable and the innocent are at risk, take control, even if force is required," Ofeur said.

"The Blackened Field Chronicle," Norrich said. "Almost word for word. You're telling me what I already know: I shouldn't be idle while the innocent suffer. How? I don't have an army, or even enough protection for a large company of men to go out into the city without falling prey to magic wielders. I was taught that magic was rare, but tonight," he gestured to where he knew the protection cast on his castle ended, high above. "I feel like the darkness threatens this place. As if the wrong door opened would expose us to some hateful wizardry."

"We have thirty-five enchanted suits of armour, let me put one on and lead some of your best out there, where we can mitigate some of the damage to the city, maybe find Viis' Gift and see her to safety."

"Thirty-five men can't make much of a difference in this disaster, the night is dry, the wind is picking up, the fires will spread."

"Then I'll bring Viis' Gift back here, where she will be safe behind the castle walls."

Prince Norrich wished he could lead that expedition, but he knew he'd only meet resistance at every turn if he tried. Everyone around him was charged with his safety and comfort, and they would lose their heads if they failed. The fastest way to save Viis's Gift was to agree. "Take my sword, it'll do you far more good out there than it will here. Bring her here and I'll see you knighted, and I'll carve a good piece of this province out for you. Bring Irenick's Gift if you can as well." It was a good plan, but also an important one. It would prevent the Gifts from being wasted in another city, or killed by an enemy priest. Having them in the castle would also give him power in the Miradu Order and the Grand Matron. "Yes, get them both, bring them here."

"Thank you, my Prince," Ofeur said. "I'll have Irogen scry for their location and we'll have them back here, safe and sound."

25

The smell of the city burning was thick in the air as the double column of mounted paladins, squires, priests and temple servants made great haste towards the North Gate of Highshield City. Nearly all of the Eventide Guard returned to Haffor's side. Any celebration of the reunion was short, they had miles to cross, and the city of Highshield was slowly becoming overwhelmed by destruction and chaos.

Combat healers cast protection spells and healed the people fighting fires as they passed, but they could not stop to help. Rendiran didn't trust his talents enough to do the same. Fires were spreading, and the healers mended several people who were dying bloody in the streets and back alleys as they passed without slowing the double column down.

Families were already gathering their things in sacks and making for the nearest city gate. It seemed that everyone was coming to the same conclusion: the City of Highshield was dying from the inside.

"Pick up the pace!" came a call from Haffor at the front. The pair of horses pulling their wagon had no problems keeping up, thanks to several enchantments the more advanced combat priests cast to keep them energized and to magically reduce the weight of their burden.

"You all right?" Marjay asked.

"I'm fine," Rendiran replied.

"Never did that before? Used healing to defend yourself? To harm?"

"I've only ever used my talents for good," Rendiran said. "It's the only purpose of a Temple Priest, a holy purpose. I cannot do harm."

"Well you're not a Temple Priest anymore, but you did use your power for good," Marjay said.

Rendiran was keenly aware of who was riding alongside the wagon – Drikson, a legendary combat priest, the first human to rise to the position of High Combat Priest of Forge Hin and a well-known battle commander – he was sure that the man was listening to his conversation. Instead of following his training, and asking his superior for advice, Rendiran felt shame at what he'd done, and how he'd done it. "I don't feel anything I did to those imps, or that man was good," he told Marjay.

"If you tear a good number of those bastards apart, then we wouldn't have held out until our reinforcements arrived. I've been on a wall when it was overrun – have three scars from the one battle to prove it – so I know what it looks like. We were on the verge when you started pulling those little bastards apart. You saved those children from some priest's sacrificial knife tonight, I don't care how you did it."

"I am made to draw power from the light so those in need can be mended, and until today I've never strayed from the practice. I trust that Miradu will leave me powerless by morning."

"You frightened yourself," Drikson said. "I give you credit for never imagining that you could use your gifts to do harm, that tells me your intentions have always been pure. You must have been a good Temple Priest. You were never seduced by the incredible power our Gods give us. If we were in Forge Hin, and we had time to sit with some dark leaf tea and discuss the implications of your work tonight, then we could sort your feelings out properly. We're in a burning city, where the Tombs of the Founders are under attack. You'll have to trust my judgement in this – you did nothing wrong."

"The Tombs of the Founders?" Rendiran asked, shocked at the news. Ondi and human alike were interred there. Powerful magicians, great rulers, royalty, and heroes rested under the protection of the wards that kept necromancy at bay in the city. Those wards were gone. Those sacred tombs contained invaluable objects for necromancers, grave robbers and some darker religions. That wasn't all that worried Rendiran about those tombs being opened. Rumour had it that there were caches of artefacts there from the time of Ava-Ondi rulership, even a few prizes from ancient dragon hordes. The breaking of the wards over the graveyard would have long lasting consequences. "We should do something."

"Aye, we should, but the graveyard is already filled with raiders, and our precious cargo would be at great risk. What I need from you, Rendiran, is to realize that even the best men, the holiest of men, must fight for what they believe in from time to time. You don't know how to use a sword, but you can mend a man from twenty yards away, or tear him down. The first time I harmed a man with healing magic, I felt that my hands were stained with blood. I scrubbed them until the soapy water turned red, and then reached for fire to burn my corruption away. My betters stopped me before I did irreparable damage. I wasn't right in my mind again until I learned to read a being's intention as quick as blinking an eye. Since then, I've never felt regret after vanquishing an enemy. I know their hearts before I do so, and if I can't read that person, they are too well warded for me to affect anyhow."

"What if they attack you? Immune to your magic, you'd be helpless," Marjay asked.

"I eventually did learn," Drikson drew a long sword from a sheath hidden in the folds of his long robe, "to wield a sword." The runes etched down the middle were transparent, glowing slightly with white light. "Look at the blade, reach out to it with your mind as though you are about to heal it like a person."

Rendiran did as he was instructed and felt the blessings on the blade. The edge would remain sharp so long as it was never used to harm an innocent. It had defeated many foes, most of whom were undead, corpses animated by the power of necromancers. "I can see the truth forged into it," Rendiran said. "The blade is..." he tried to find the right word to describe the qualities he saw and settled on; "pure."

"There, now break your concentration and turn your attention to your friend there. Read him the same way."

He did so, and immediately sensed that Marjay's only objective was to transport Tadrin and Oria out of the city to safety. He would do anything to see it done. "I see it; he only wants to save the children."

"Priests," Marjay tasked, "No respect for privacy."

"Good, you won't get much deeper with this trick, it's a quick reading, not made for real inspection," Drikson said. "But it's never wrong."

"I've read people before," Rendiran said, "but it normally takes much more concentration. How am I doing it so quickly?"

"You're reading people like objects, just like the sword. In combat a person's immediate intention matters, whether or not they want to strike you, or whoever you're protecting, and you must react. If you have time to simply protect your charge, then do so, but if that is not possible, defeat them utterly. Let them lament their choices and the road that brought them to their end if they can, your duty is to those who you protect."

"I understand," Rendiran said. "I never thought I'd have to harm anyone. I felt them suffer and die. Tried to reach for their minds so I could make their ends quick and painless, but I was never able to touch that part of them."

"Tearing a brain with healing magic is almost impossible. It is shielded by a being's consciousness; the one place every creature can protect from magical harm. Only very powerful magic can break through that defence. You had no choice but to give your foes a painful death, but you must learn to separate yourself from them so you don't feel their pain."

"I don't intend to be a combat priest," Rendiran said.

"Tonight you are one," Drickson said. "Most of our enemies won't attack now that there are over seventy of us here, but I believe we'll be tested eventually. You will assist me."

"Yes, High Priest," Rendiran replied.

The coordinated column moved through most of the night, the rhythmic sound of hooves on cobblestones and the droning of the wheels under him became almost hypnotic as the fires in the city spread, becoming so bright, spewing smoke so dark that the stars disappeared. They had to take many detours, extending their trip to the wall by more than an hour, by Rendiran's estimation. With stunning regularity, there was a short clash at the front of the line, many horses ahead, but they concluded so quickly that Rendiran never got a good idea of what they were fighting.

Less than three blocks from the North Gate, the whole column was ordered to stop. Rendiran reached out with his mind and checked on the welfare of the children to find that they were resting peacefully along with their furry companion. Once they woke they would be so well rested that they would be quite a handful, but he would rather face that than let them watch a city die as horrors threatened to leap at them from the shadow.

The gate was open, city folk were rushing through, and even from where he was, he could see only two city guards in one watch tower. There should have been dozens atop the ramparts just near the gate, the Temple provided over two thousand city guards, and in times of trouble, he expected to see an auxiliary that was ten times that size.

"Do you see any guards up there?" Marjay asked, looking sullen. He remained seated, the reins in his lap.

"Two, as far as I can see, they're watching people progress through the gate, not giving any direction."

"So the temple knows about this and has offered no help," Marjay said. "I can't believe it. They're letting the city burn."

"Sir," said a young temple guard on a horse just ahead. "I'm sorry to say: that was the order. It's why, when I heard the call from Priest Rendiran and Captain Haffor, I abandoned to join this force. I'd rather see the children conducted safely from the city than sit in the barracks. It may be some comfort to know that one of our own, Nora

Wyrick, has led over a hundred into the city. They intended to keep the peace near the docks. Not all hope is lost, Sir."

"I'm no Sir to you, just Marjay. Thank you..."

"Perci Vallen, of the House by the same name,"

"Joined the guard for adventure?"

"I'm afraid so," Perci said sheepishly. "Looks like we're getting it."

"Aye."

A large contingent of paladins, several guardsmen and a few of their Combat Priests left the column, taking their mounts west down a broad street at a quick trot. "Our Captain has ordered forty four of our number to the City Graveyard," Drikson said. "We can't let it fall into enemy hands uncontested."

The warriors and priests on horseback reorganized themselves in a quick, practiced fashion, and when everyone was in place they moved ahead slowly. Haffor rode along one side the wagon while Drikson rode on the other. They were slowly moving into the mob. "We pass through this gate and then ride at speed to the Abbest Docks. I've sent a rider out of uniform with gold who will ensure that there's a ship waiting for us. I only wish I could have sent some people with him to guard it."

"What about the other contingent? Will they be able to protect the tombs?" Rendiran asked.

"I can't tell," Haffor said. "There is so much dark magic assailing that place that the number of enemies waiting for them is difficult to guess. More power is gathering there than I have seen in one place."

"You can't join them, even after we've passed through the gate," Drikson said. "We could find ourselves under attack by masters of darkness who are just as significant at any moment."

"Aye, don't tell me my job, Priest," Haffor replied without looking at Drikson. "I'll keep my own counsel on which cause I'll abandon and when."

They approached the broad gatehouse, its portcullis yawned wide at the end of the block. The passage through was choked with peasants who carried their most precious possessions in their arms, the going was slow, but they were moving to the other side. "Careful! We don't want anyone to get under hoof as we make our way through," Haffor ordered.

The gate was in reach when Rendiran heard a human shout; "Halt!" All the gatehouse's small doors opened. Soldiers in shining breastplates made of blue tinted steel emerged, roughly pressing the peasants aside. The breastplates were etched with symbols of protection, and even Rendiran could recognize that the quality was superb. The value of such armour was equal to the cost of three or four houses near High Street.

"I order this company to halt!" repeated an officer who called from above the gate. "By order of his Royal Highness, Prince Norrich!"

"I'm afraid you'll have to do better than that, boy. That man is not my commander, nor do I kneel for any human lord," Haffor said.

"His Highness wishes to take your wards into his protection. We will escort you to the castle, where they'll be safe. Where you will be safe."

"You have a hearing problem, or has your sight failed you?" Haffor asked. "There are fires spreading throughout your city, not all of it red or yellow. Some of those flames are black, and cold to the touch, they use the dead as their fuel instead of wood. The Tombs of the Founders in the city graveyard, where some of your Prince's kin are at rest are under attack. I'm sure the city food stores and the Gold Road are all assailed, not to mention the docks. Pick your cause, they're all worth your efforts. All but this gate, which won't hold us in. We won't be turning back into this city." Haffor signaled their group forward and they began moving. The commoners did their best to push through the gate faster, and fewer were trying to squeeze in beside their group.

The portcullis gate began to close, lowering like great teeth that would puncture and crush anyone caught below. "Damn this Prince," Drikson said as he raised his arms high over his head. "I can hold the gate for some time, but not indefinitely." He announced as the gate stopped descending many yards ahead.

Rendiran was amazed at the power the Priest was showing,

holding a gate made of thick wood braced with heavy iron with magic alone. "Make way!" Haffor shouted to the citizens on foot around them. "For your own safety, find a place to hide or finish moving through the gatehouse quickly. We'll try to get out of your way as soon as we can."

They reduced their width into a double column of riders with the wagon in the middle. The outer gate doors facing the countryside began to close as they progressed through the gatehouse.

Rendiran looked up as they cleared the portcullis to find that there was a metal grate above, where the Prince's representative and a few of his soldiers looked down on them. "It is my duty to inform you that your man there is now guilty of using magic to impede the will of the Prince, a charge that will cost him his head," he shouted down. "I will advise leniency if you come with us now."

The front of the double column of Paladins and their company along with the wagon and the peasants who were still trying to get through the gatehouse passage crowded the space. The heavy braced doors facing the countryside closed with the creak of heavy iron hinges. The bar was on the inside, meant to hold people out of the city, not inside, so Rendiran supposed they were holding the double doors closed from the outside with manpower.

More soldiers with the Prince's markings on their tabards rushed to four gated doorways inside the gatehouse. Their company was surrounded, along with several peasants who looked for any way out of the predicament. "You are trapped, there's only one choice," the Prince's representative called down from the iron grid above them.

"I can't hold the portcullis forever," Drikson warned. "We will be cut off from our rearguard."

"What's your name, boy?" Haffor asked the man above them.

"Ofeur Nemon, Esquire. I am the official Advisor to His Highness, Prince Norrich."

"You have the opportunity to avert disaster, here, Ofeur," Haffor said as he calmly dismounted. "You let us through and report that we had things well in hand, that the children he's so concerned about are safe. His Highness is invited to Forge Hin, he can see that we're caring for them well with his own eyes. He might even meet the King, who knows?" he moved through the crowd surrounding their company gently. Many of them seemed more at ease as he passed. "But if you somehow manage to capture these children after defeating us, your Prince will look like he didn't care about his own city burning, dedicating all your men to kidnapping instead of saving lives. He'll also start a war with the dwarves who have occupied this land longer than any human," he continued. "All that's unlikely, since I'll be knocking these doors off their hinges and beating you and your boys into the dirt. If you're well loved by the Prince, or he wants these children badly enough, that may start a war as well." He reached the large double doors, they were easily five times his height. The peasants pressed back, giving him room. "I can live with starting that war. We won't have to send anything to King Ormet anymore, we can sharpen our warriors against your human armies, and maybe we'll take Gachin province for ourselves in the bargain. I know a thousand dwarves who would love to begin using your rivers to launch raids across this land, dwarves who haven't forgotten our ancient heritage." Haffor drew his longsword, shifted his shield high up onto his arm, and tapped the doors with the tip of his blade. "I'd like to see us part friends here instead, but that depends on what you do once I get through this door."

"Don't do it, Captain," Ofeur called down as he rushed from the room above into a narrow side passage, his men followed him.

Haffor lowered his head for a moment, then rushed for the few steps between he and the heavy wooden door. Before his sword struck the iron reinforced doorway, he was surrounded by light, it shielded him, and drove him forward with incredible force. Rendiran felt the impact in the air around them, through a shock under foot and inside his chest.

Whatever braced the doors from the other side shattered in shards of wood and stone as they swung open. "Run!" Haffor shouted to the peasants behind him. "Leave the gatehouse and get clear. It looks like the Prince's men want a fight, regardless of who they might trample to have it."

The commoners listened, the company of Paladins surrounding the wagon remained where they were so they could get clear. Drikson was straining, sweat rolling from his forehead into his eyes. Rendiran leaned over and wiped his face with his last kerchief. "Don't know how to do this yet, do you, young priest?" Drikson asked quietly.

"I'm afraid I've never thought of using my gift to hold a door open, sorry, High Priest."

"Remain at my side long enough, and you'll learn all kinds of useful tricks and new ways of using your gift to preserve life. It's amazing how many hides you can save by holding a door open."

The peasants were clear, most of them leaving the road for the field to either side so they could avoid the Prince's men. They were forming up twenty yards up the road from the main gate.

"Riders! Prepare to charge!" Haffor said as he mounted his horse.

"Oh, thank Irenick," Drikson said. "I'd rather heal warriors than hold this gate."

Rendiran recalled his training, combat healing was a challenging, difficult skill to master, and he'd secretly wanted to do it for years. He looked down at his hands, unsure as to whether he could trust his talents after tearing living creatures apart.

"Be ready, Rendiran," Drikson said. "Assist me in keeping our company alive. The Prince's men are protected against magic. You won't be ripping them this morning."

Rendiran looked through the gate and down the road. The Prince's men had formed up to block them, they were several rows deep. The front line was set in a shield wall, and their commander ran to join them with a few more men behind. There were roughly three dozen, and in the rosy morning light, they looked like heroes from some tapestry or painting. He wondered if the ensuing battle was really necessary, but his uncertainty didn't last.

"This is your final warning, Captain!" Ofeur cried from behind the Prince's soldiers. "My orders are clear: I am to take Viss' gift back to the castle. I only need the one, you can have Irenick's gift. I'll make that concession if it avoids bloodshed."

"No," Marjay said.

"Don't worry, separating them is not something I'm considering." Haffor turned towards Rendiran. "Ever meet this Prince?"

"I've seen him, never met him," Rendiran replied.

"Would you trust him? Speak honestly, I am a servant of peace and if I can find any reason to avoid this bloodshed, then I would."

"I would not trust him," Marjay said. "Speaking as Oria's guardian, I want her in the protection of your family and Forge Hin."

The wagon and the company surrounding them moved ahead far enough so Drikson could lower the gate behind. Rendiran took those few moments to think about everything he knew of the Prince. Most of it didn't pertain to their situation or the children, but he knew one thing for certain: the man let his city burn. The greatest city in Highshield, the city bearing the same name as the wall and all the country, was in chaos, and hundreds, perhaps thousands of lives would be lost. "Could he have stopped all this?"

"The Prince has control of at least two thousand men in and outside of the city," Marjay said. "But these are the only ones we've seen. The rest must be guarding his own castle walls, or ranging outside the city."

"He is the highest power in the province," Haffor said. "If anyone could have helped Highshield City, it would have been him."

"The Grand Matron was in the Prince's company, and the guards under her command were absent, ordered to retreat to the temple barracks while chaos took hold," Drikson said. "He could have convinced the Grand Matron to signal the guards to act. He should have."

"Anyone who would let this happen should not be charged with protecting these children. Even so, I would prefer not to have bloodshed here. It seems pointless," Rendiran said.

"It is," Haffor said. "But these men will not allow us to pass. They obey the orders of their Prince." He sighed and looked to the shield wall blocking the road. The stony, rough terrain of the fields to either side made passage by wagon impossible. Taking the children from the wagon and going by horse or foot would be too slow to get around thirty five soldiers. "You've inspired a compromise, but we'll need healing, will the two of you be able to do it?"

"You're going to charge on foot, aren't you?" Drikson asked witheringly.

"Aye," Haffor replied. "We'll be able to control how badly we beat them, and save the horses."

"I believe Rendiran and I can keep you paladins alive, but use the rest to guard the wagon, please."

"That's how it will be, then," Haffor said. "Paladins! On foot!"

"I can help break their line," Marjay offered.

"No, you stay with the wagon, if we lose, you make sure you stay with the children, no matter what you have to do."

"Aye," Marjay replied, nodding despite his disappointment.

Rendiran watched, worried, as the paladins in their company, only fourteen, formed up in a wall only four men wide and began marching forward. Everyone else formed up around the wagons.

26

Fourteen paladins expanded into a wedge two lines deep with Haffor in the lead. They marched down the street methodically, smashing the bottoms of their tall shields against the ground every second step. The sound their heavy metal shields made was thunderous, and Rendiran could see a few of the castle guards at the back of the enemy line waver.

Ofeur ordered his men into a tighter group to form a shield wall using their smaller, round shields. Even though there were less than half as many paladins, they seemed more substantial, as though they were made of much stronger stuff. Ten squires brought pikes and settled into formation behind the paladins in a quick and orderly fashion. The ends of those pikes had a double edged blade with a hook to the side of the head. The four guards who abandoned their posts in the temple remained with the wagon.

The last members of the Paladin's wall were the combat healers. All three looked calm and cool as they followed several steps behind the triple line of paladins and squires. Each drew an ornate sword that looked viciously sharp, even from a distance.

"This is going to be a slaughter," Marjay said.

The Paladins and their support halted ten yards from the enemy shield wall. "Surrender," Haffor said. "There will be no dishonor if you retreat and allow us to pass."

"We're immune to your magic, dwarf," Ofeur shouted from behind his shield. "It's knights and guards against paladins who have had their teeth pulled."

"I do not want to murder you today, Ofeur Hemon, Esquire."

Both groups remained still and silent for a long moment. Rendiran saw what Marjay meant about a slaughter. To his knowledge, the enemy had no healers. Even if they did, there was little chance healing magic would reach the soldiers thanks to the magical protection their breastplates offered. The armour of the paladins offered more physical protection and even though they were nearly completely covered, they didn't seem to have much trouble with mobility. The thing that worried Rendiran the most as a healer were those pikes. They would pull and tear at the castle guards, reaching between shields and catching limbs. A few of the squires carrying them looked young, a few were dwarves – short for that kind of duty perhaps – but none of them looked weak or unsettled. If anything, they looked grim, as though they've used their weapons in battle before and knew what they could do.

As the paladins lifted their shields just high enough to step forward, the fox ran between both sides and stopped in the middle. It looked at the paladins first, yapping loudly, then at the castle guards. Haffor signaled for his paladins to move back, and everyone took eight steps backward then formed into a shield wall that covered their front flatly, and with another layer of shields atop those at an angle.

"Do you hear that?" asked one of the temple guards watching the wagon. As Rendiran was about to ask what the man was hearing, he noticed it too – the hum of thousands of insects from a distance – and then he watched as a cloud of hornets descended upon the castle guards. The fox broke into a dead run around the paladins and their support, then into the gatehouse and out of sight.

The castle guards screamed, recoiled and scrambled to fend the stinging swarm off. Their line had not only broken, it was in shambles, several running down the road, and even more rolling on the rough ground in the field alongside. The cries of Ofeur could be heard; "Form up! For your lives and your honour, form up on me!" Rendiran could not believe the man was on his feet, wiping hornets off his arms, face and neck as though they were only flies. He drew his sword and strode ahead, a few of his most steadfast men following.

Haffor charged with only the paladins, faster than Rendiran would have believed possible in so much plate armour. They crushed into nine castle guards, bashing them to the ground with a wall of steel. "Yield!" Haffor shouted, and most of the soldiers remained on their backs.

Ofeur stood, a sword in this right hand, his shield on his left arm. "My orders were clear."

"You can't win like this," Haffor retorted.

A well-aimed but slow slash at Haffor's face was the only response. The sound of a sword clashing against a metal shield drowned out everything else. "Roll ahead," Marjay said as he urged the wagon team forward. The guards watching them followed.

"Surrender or flee and keep your head!" Haffor shouted as he blocked attack after attack with his shield alone.

Two castle guards tried to stand to assist their leader, but were each dissuaded of the notion as they earned a kick to the head from a paladin's iron toed boot. In a motion that was as surprising as it was skillful, Ofeur feigned an attack then struck from another direction, catching Haffor on the wrist. The strike must have caught a chink in the dwarf's armour, since Drikson had to raise a hand and heal him.

Haffor bashed his foe with his shield, sending him wheeling back. Ofeur sprang forward in an instant, but his guard was easily knocked down with two quick counters from the Paladin Captain. "He's ending it," Marjay said, lowering his gaze.

In one powerful swing, Haffor took Ofeur's head off his shoulders. The hornets were gone, the field outside the gate seemed quiet, and for long moments, no one moved. "Return to the city," Haffor ordered, looking around at the castle guards who remained. "Help who you can, but stay out of our way."

When they finished rolling through the outer doors of the gate-house, Rendiran heard someone shuffling inside the wagon and pulled the small hatch between him and Marjay open. The rectangular slit was only large enough to see some of what was going on in the darkness, it was only there so passengers could speak to their drivers. "The fox went inside during the duel," Marjay said. "Would have said something, but I'm pretty sure it's a friend."

Rendiran looked through the small opening. There was just enough light to determine that someone inside was changing, then he caught sight of what he was sure was the shape of a shoulder, then shapes that indicated that whoever was changing in there was a woman before he hurriedly closed the sliding door. "It's not a fox anymore," he said, wide-eyed.

"So it isn't," Marjay replied with a chuckle. "Why'd you close the door?"

"Seemed the decent thing to do?"

He suspected it was Crista from the second time he saw the fox, but he still wasn't sure from the scant glimpse he caught in near dark-ness. Rendiran was relieved when the rear doors opened and she climbed on top of the wagon to sit behind him and Marjay. She was in smaller leathers than normal, and her hair had turned red-brown. "I didn't know if the Temple Guards would be looking for me after I was told not to return. I made off with a few things on my way out."

"So you ran around as a fox?" Marjay asked. "You have to teach me that sometime."

"They dismissed you?" Rendiran asked, surprised.

"Aye, but there's something more important. There's something coming," Crista said.

"Our scout returns," Haffor said as he approached the wagon. "What say you?"

"The company of paladins you sent to the Tombs of the Founders are holding a large force of risen dead at bay and closing on the tombs. I didn't see any casualties when I left, but I tracked three fiery dead things to this street, several blocks back. It's as though whoever raised them infused their armour and swords with a flame spirt, and they set everything they touch ablaze."

"Describe them, what did they look like exactly?"

"They wore armour with the emblem of downturned swords on them, but now they're not painted on, they glow like fire. The gaps in the armour and eyes of their helms are filled with black smoke, and they carry two long swords that are thick with embers except for their edges. I could smell rot, fire, and burnt bone."

"It takes master necromancers and elementalists months to create an Immortal Ember, and these have King Derron's sigil, they must have been the guards that were entombed with him."

"So they have been planning this for some time, and they have the bones of a king," Drikson said. "It's as though Wydu let the word slip to all the wrong oracles months ago."

"There were two in the city graveyard, your paladins are fighting them, I worry about the other three," Crista said.

"Form up! I need volunteers from the castle guards!" Haffor ordered. "Volunteers will be healed, everyone else can sod off down the road or back into the city!"

"I'll have the volunteers take their breastplates off for a moment so we can heal the fox's handiwork," Drikson said. "Those hornets were your doing?"

"They were," Crista said sheepishly. "They might be immune to magic in that armour, but they weren't protected from insects."

"Very nice work," Drikson told her before retreating to treat the group of nearly twenty castle guards who were volunteering. Many of them were already taking their breastplates off, begging for healing.

"Can you stay with the wagon?" Haffor asked Crista.

"That was my plan," she replied.

"Thank you, I'll assign an escort and you'll keep going." He looked back the way they came. From where they were it looked as though half the city was on fire, and it was spreading quickly. With the wagon out of the way, and the threat of a serious melee just outside the gates gone, peasants were evacuating the city as quickly and in as large a number as they could manage. "We're going to have to put those Immortal Embers down. I'll meet you after that's done." For the first time in his life, Rendiran saw a paladin appear hesitant to do their duty.

he number of people coming through Highshield City's North Gate was simply astonishing, Rendiran had never seen that many people in one place. He could feel the desperation and fear rolling off them. Many looked to the paladins and castle soldiers as they hurried to ready themselves for a fight on the other side of the gates.

There was something there with pure malevolent intent, he could feel it, and it was getting closer, coming for them. When he saw the first people screaming, escaping through the gatehouse more frantically than anyone so far, he knew whatever was spurring them on with such recklessness that he feared some people would be trampled was worse than he thought. When some people emerged, flailing and falling as they burned, he stood and reached out to the flames with his mind. It was something he read about but never tried, and when the flames dissipated and he healed the charred flesh of three people, he was relieved and encouraged to see that the theories he'd learned were easy enough for him to put into practice. Again, he felt a power all his own, it kept him from feeling fatigued, helped him focus, and worked alongside his healing gifts.

A hard tug on his pant leg pulled him back down to the wagon seat. "You're drawing too much attention to yourself," Drikson said. "It's not the time, there are more important things coming to save your energy for. You'll know it when it happens, or, if we're lucky, you won't be needed at all and you'll make it to the boat while Haffor and I lead our company back into the city to buy you time."

"Something is setting people on fire as it moves through the gates, I won't watch them burn when I can save them," Rendiran said, turning back towards the gate.

That's when he and Drikson felt it, a surge of power from their right, fire and the force of a thousand hammers focusing. A tall man with dark hair grinned from the crowd with his hands held high. Peasants did their best to get clear of him as a rolling ball of fire as bright as the sun erupted from the space between his hands and crossed the distance between him and Drikson in an instant. The world around Rendiran exploded. Heat and unbelievable pressure pushed him off his seat, into the air, and commoners caught in the direct blast were blown to pieces as easily as a harsh gust scatters a pile of leaves. His ears rang, his leg and arm were in shreds, and he could feel a sharp stabbing pain in his side.

Rendiran closed his eyes, the lesson of his teachers surfacing from memory as loudly as a bell – a healer is worthless if he cannot maintain himself - and he focused all his will on rebuilding his arm and leg, screaming as pieces of shrapnel were forced from his wounds. He intentionally neglected to regenerate three fingers on his right hand and most of the toes on his right foot, that could wait, as long as the wounds were closed and he was out of pain.

Then, he focused on his side, where he found a spoke from the wagon's wheel jutting out from under his ribs. He opened his eyes long enough to see Crista kneeling down over him. She cringed as he yanked the spoke from his side. "The children," he told her before focusing on mending his own internal injuries. It was easy to restore himself, he knew his own body better than anyone's and blocking pain was something he'd practiced, but he didn't bother, he still wasn't feeling the full extent of his own injuries yet. He was mended and on his feet before it set in. He was unsteady without toes on his right foot, a strange feeling.

Haffor and the paladins were rushing the magician who had caused the explosion. The magician was joined by two more who savagely slashed at the shields of metal and divine power that sheltered the nine paladins who were in fighting condition. The wagon was on its side, the wheels facing the fireball were shattered, one of the horses was dead, and the other struggled under the corpse of its companion, screaming.

People who were caught in the blast were all around, there was no room for them to avoid the bodies of the dead as many struggled, stunned and fearful as they were, to get away from the site of the explosion and the city walls.

"Broken leg, I think," Marjay said behind Rendiran. "I think you landed on me. You're heavy for a priest."

It took Rendiran only a moment to find the fracture and mend it. His other injuries were superficial. He reached out, mentally surveying for the children inside the wagon and found them panicked but in good condition. "Tadrin and Oria are awake, we have to get them out of here."

New screams from the gatehouse drew his attention in time to see two figures in plate armour emerge. They were in darkened plate armour, wearing tall helmets. Dirty orange flames spat embers from chinks between the steel plates as black smoke rose from their forms. They slashed at anyone in their path, a touch of their swords setting people ablaze. "I'll get the children, then find us a horse to get away on," Marjay said.

Rendiran limped back towards the wagon, extinguishing people who were set alight by the Immoral Embers, that must have been what they were, from how Crista described them. She emerged with Oria clinging to her and the dog circling at the rear of the wagon. Tadrin was right behind.

"Good morning, little ones," Marjay said with some cheer. He took Tadrin onto his back. "Hold on tight and close your eyes, don't open them for anything."

A shard made of light and heat split the air, rushing towards him and the children behind him, and without thinking, Rendiran lashed out with a barrier spell. The deadly shard of focused heat exploded harmlessly overhead, but he felt as though something bashed him from the inside and he fell backwards.

He glanced to Haffor in time to see that he and his remaining paladins were cutting down the last magician. "Help!" Rendiran shouted as he felt another shard of heat and light coming towards them from the armoured assailants that were marching ever closer. He blocked that as well, and felt the impact of the power he was countering inside himself, pushing him flat onto his back. The magic he was fighting was powerful, and he was aware that he wasn't properly shielded, he wasn't prepared for the kind of fight he was already in.

"Rendiran! Use a divine shield!" Haffor cried out as he rushed towards them.

"I call Viis and Irenick to my defence, protect your faithful servants as they guard the innocent," Rendiran prayed with loud conviction, focusing as best he could on visualizing a shield made of crystal and light around them. He focused all his will on it as well, the act of a sorcerer, and felt the leading Immortal Ember Knight's sword slash against it and bounce off harmlessly. He'd done it, brought his own power as a sorcerer and that which was gifted to him by his Gods together in one effort. He remembered his lessons on combatting the undead, though they were a long time ago, and he never thought he'd use the teaching. "I am the light, the paragon of my Goddess' goodness, Her power resides in me, and I will see this place cleansed of evil."

He repeated the prayer as he reached towards the nearest Ember Knight, and watched it stagger back into the pair behind him. He was only able to hold one there, still and braced as though it was tightly chained, reaching out to the other two, who slashed at his divine shield sending sparks and embers flying, would have broken his hold. "This won't last!" Marjay warned.

"You two, run!" Haffor said to Crista and Marjay. He whistled and

Rendiran heard the approaching of heavy hooves behind him. "Take Do'lii, she'll bear the weight of all four of you." Haffor sheathed his sword on a scabbard strapped to the right of the saddle and took a heavy hammer from its loop. He rushed past Rendiran then, shouting; "My company will take these whoresons apart!" He lashed out with his hammer, white sparks burst forth as it struck the nearest Ember Knight's helmet, bashing it part way open and exposing black bone beneath. One of them turned towards him, landing a heavy blow against his shield and loosing embers from its sword. Haffor's next strike landed on the Ember Knight that Rendiran was holding, driving it to its knees. Half its helm was crushed inward, and Haffor struck once more, shattering the skull within the steel. The fire and smoke dissipated from the Ember Knight. The rest of the paladins joined Haffor, circling the last two undead warriors.

One of them was struck in the neck right away, their flesh sizzling and catching fire as the Ember Knight's sword wedged in a small chink in their armour. Rendiran focused on healing Kena, the young paladin as she struggled to survive, and when the blade was knocked loose by the paladin beside her, Rendiran was able to heal her completely.

"Go! Rendiran!" Haffor shouted. "We'll kill these and catch up."

With hesitation, Rendiran let go of the divine shield and felt a wave of fatigue fall on him like a heavy yoke on his shoulders. As he limped as quickly as he could away from the city, commoners all around him who were doing the same, he noticed a scrap of a combat healer's robe and realized that it could be all that remained of Drikson. Beside it was the staff head he used earlier, and he took a moment to pick it up before hobbling on.

28

*L*imping away from the Northern Gates of Highshield City felt like the most cowardly act he'd ever taken. Haffor wanted him to run, it was an order from the Captain, but every instinct told him to turn around and do his duty as a healer.

He was surrounded by the low born, people who had no business fighting, and every reason to flee, but he had power; a new, wondrous and terrifying well of power. He could feel the book he'd been given in the pocket of his tunic, and laughed about how it managed to survive there unscathed. It felt like a wildly inappropriate thing to do, but he couldn't help himself. He tucked the staff head into his tunic then, who knew when it might come in handy?

He started looking over his shoulder when a strong hand wedged under his arm to aid his progress. "No looking back there, fella," said his helper in a gruff voice. He looked at the man, it was a stout half dwarf wearing a heavy leather apron. In his other hand he carried a smith's hammer that had seen a fair bit of use. "Me and mine are going north. The further we go, the more likely I'll find kin. You're welcome to come with us, but I don't know anyone with a boat, so we'll be crossing the river and walking the rest of the way."

There were two boys running alongside him, obviously his sons, and his wife – a dwarf with uncommonly fair hair – had a young half dwarf girl on her shoulders. "Thank you," Rendiran said as he kept up with the crowd thanks to the half-dwarf's assistance.

"Saw what you did back there," he replied. "You're a hero."

They reached the Kirk Wall, a barrier made of massive boulders and jagged foothills that ran the length of the city's north wall two hundred yards away from its face. The town of Nebore lay just past it, and past that farmland and the Hurien River. A clamor from the city, like thousands of bone feet running, drew Rendiran's attention back over his shoulder.

Seven paladins stood in a circle of light at the gate as an army of ragged undead warriors rushed along the outer wall. The gatehouse was consumed by flame, people were climbing over the wall behind them to escape the city using ropes, blankets tied together and makeshift ladders. There was nowhere for Haffor and his six paladins to run. Rendiran leaned down and whispered into the smithy's ear. "Hurry to the Abbest Docks. The paladins have a man there, tell him Haffor and Rendiran sent you, they'll take you and your family up river." He gently pried himself loose from the smith's helping hand and started for the high stone at the edge of the north road.

"I will, thank you," the smithy called after him. "Don't be too much of a hero!"

The spells and theories in Rendiran's books were coming to life in his mind with new purpose, becoming methods and practices. He climbed on top of a stone and looked to the North Gate. He did his best to shake his weariness off. "Through mist and over distance, I now see friend and foe without resistance," he announced. A moment later he could see any part of the distant battlefield as though he was standing only a few feet away.

The army he thought he saw were hundreds instead of thousands. Most of them were skeletal, wearing bits of ornate armour. "Those are from the Inner City Graveyard," Rendiran said to himself. "The paladins Haffor sent there are defeated." The volunteers from the Castle Guard were the first to fall, bravely standing in their way despite being stung and just recently defeated, they crushed the bones of many foes before hard fingers and old blades tore them to pieces. To his surprise, Haffor and his six paladins were holding fast against the army of hundreds that rushed to meet them.

In the corner of his vision, Rendiran spotted movement further up the road. There were children and imps in rags amongst the fresh dead and dying commoners nearby. They finished the weak and immobile off with thin daggers. When they bled their last, they stuffed a rough gemstone into their mouths, pushing until it was wedged into their throats. They did the same whenever they found a corpse, and to Rendiran's horror, those bodies rose and joined the attack on the paladins.

He reached out with his mind and gripped the throat of one of the imps, then with what felt like his last strength, he tore it's throat open before it could finish planting another quartz gemstone. "I need more power," Rendiran said to himself, out of breath and falling to one knee.

Fleeing would be the most sensible course of action. The children were depending on him, but they had Marjay and more importantly to him; Crista. They could get them to Forge Hin, where they'd have no end of minders and instructors. He glanced back to Haffor and his circle of paladins. They were frantically fighting the undead, and what they defended – the commoners who were trying to get away – were only growing in number. If Haffor and his people fell, hundreds, perhaps thousands of innocent people would be killed.

Everything Rendiran knew made it clear that if he pushed past his physical limit in helping the Paladins, he could do severe harm to himself. "Raise them well, Crista," he said as he rose unsteadily and closed his eyes. He could feel the staff head he used only a twilight ago. He reached out to the power stored within, there was still more than he knew what to do with, and was interrupted by a presence.

"You'll destroy yourself if you attempt this without guidance," he heard the voice of Drikson tell him from within. "So, let me direct your hands, your mind, and maybe I can save my friends one more time."

Rendiran surrendered his will to the spirit of Drikson, and felt him work through him. Drikson put protections against harm in place in his mind with great alacrity, then directed Rendiran to reach deep into the staff head and become one with the power inside.

Haffor and his paladins were so well surrounded by their ragged bony assailants that Rendiran couldn't see them, but he could feel them. Four were near death, their eyes gouged by bare bone fingers, bodies pierced by rusty blades, choking on their own blood. Haffor was down to one eye, but he fought on with the paladins who were still on their feet, bashing with elbows and helms when their enemies were too close to crush with hammers.

Rendiran felt Drikson's expert instincts and experience wield his power in healing Haffor then the rest of the paladins in only a few heartbeats. "Fight, my brothers! Rise and fight!" he shouted with such thunderous volume that the whole field was filled with the sound. The words were as much a blessing as they were a battle cry. The effect was immediately apparent – Haffor and his six remaining paladins were blessed with holy power, giving them inhuman strength and speed – once again the circle of enemies around them widened as bones shattered and plate armour cracked. A shield of holy energy appeared around Rendiran, it was a gift from Miradu Herself.

Drikson's spirit continued to work through him. "I clear your minds of corruption and fear," he chanted, momentarily directing the spell at the children and imps who did the bidding of their necromancer masters. They dropped their quartz gemstones, stopped recruiting fresh corpses for the army of the dead and all fled from the grisly field.

The shield around Rendiran deflected several arrows and small shards of fire flung by sorcerers behind the undead. With surprisingly little effort, Drikson flung a pile of fist sized stones at the origin point of several fire slivers, pounding the sorcerers there mercilessly before they could jump behind cover. One of them was struck down with a split skull, the others managed to get away with only a few bruises. His concentration turned back to Haffor and his paladins for a few moments, long enough to heal them completely again.

"By Miradu's grace, Viis' might, and Irenick's conviction, I open the heavens, calling the enduring fire." Rendiran was overwhelmed by a feeling of bliss as the sky above the ragged dead opened, and a shaft of warm, golden light shone down on them. "I free the souls empowering these corrupt things, and call them to their rest in the next realm," Drikson said.

Most of the undead army crumbled, lifeless once more, and Rendiran watched as Drikson's spirit separated from his body and drifted up to join the hundreds he'd freed from their corpse prisons. "You are a great healer, Rendiran," he said over his shoulder. "I wonder if you can be a wise sorcerer?"

Drained of all vigor, Rendiran fell to his knees as he watched the freed spirits disappear into the heavenly gate above. His heart sank as he looked back to Haffor and saw that four columns of living soldiers were emerging from the burning gatehouse. They were undaunted by fire, protected by sorcery, and wore the sigil of the Bright One over their armour. "May Irenick come to your aid, Haffor," Rendiran managed to say as he collapsed under the weight of his weariness.

29

There was a school of perch nearby, so many that he wondered if they'd impede the broad riverboat's passage as it moved through them. He could feel the life around him in the river as the boat moved on, from the bottom feeders, and crabs to the ancient sturgeon that gave the boat a wide berth.

He was faintly aware that he was waking up – slowly, hesitantly – and his senses were more open than ever. He merely thought of the children and he could sense Tadrin and Oria above. They were healthy, happy, watching crewmen lower a net into the water. The moaning of a man next to him woke him completely. He couldn't help but ask himself if it really was a dream – being so well connected with nature was something some Ondi were known well for – and he tried to reconnect with the creatures he'd sensed before he roused from sleep completely.

Just as he thought he was about to manage it, he heard another person nearby groan, and he opened his eyes. He was in a pile of furs in the dimly lit hold of what must have been a large river boat. "That's why I must have felt the fish, we must be under the waterline," he muttered to himself as he looked around. There were dozens of refugees, many of whom were injured.

He was still dressed, the toes on his right foot were still missing, as were all but his index finger and thumb on his right hand, well, he had a knuckle left on his middle finger, but that barely counted as half a digit. The nubs were healed over, there was no pain, so he crawled out of the furs and stumbled to his feet. He moved to the nearest moaning commoner, he was leaning against an older woman. It was surprisingly difficult to keep his balance with no toes on his right foot, but he managed a little grace as he knelt down in front of them.

His energy had returned, and other than a dry throat, he felt better than ever. Even with missing pieces, he'd never felt so alive, and there was something else, something new that he couldn't name just yet, but he didn't want to lay around any longer. "I'm a healer, and would like to help if you'll let me," he said.

"My Bruun got his leg gashed and burned," the woman said. "They gave him something to make him sleep, but he's still half waking."

"Let's see," Rendiran said as he lifted the rough blanket off the young man's leg. The burns were severe, and the cut was worse. "Tousled with an Ember Knight?"

"Nail on a board as we left our home," the woman corrected. "I would have died in the flames if he didn't pull me out."

Rendiran didn't attempt to heal the boy using his old practices, with song and prayer and ceremony, but tried the practical method of restoration that he learned from Drikson. With only a little energy the wound was closed, the burnt skin was healed, and the corruption coursing through his blood was purified. "He'll wake soon," Rendiran said. He noticed a burn on the back of the woman's hand and healed it as easily as he might have brushed a fly from his arm. "You should get some sun if there's room out there."

"Thank you," she said, astonished. "We don't have much, but..." she attempted to hand her a few iron and copper coins hanging on a string.

Rendiran smiled and pressed the coins back into her hand. "You'll need those."

"Healer? Can I have help, healer?" asked a young man with a thick accent. Rendiran followed him to a man who was doing his best not to cough. The stench of corrupted flesh and a pierced bowel hung around him in the dark, and Rendiran didn't wait for an explanation as to what happened to him, or offer niceties. "Hold him still, and put this back into his mouth," he said, picking up a finger length stick from where it lay with the man in his hammock. Rendiran leaned against a post for stability and closed his eyes. This was a real challenge, but he'd mended worse. All his life he primarily trained as a healer, and with more power, a better understanding of magic than ever, he put his knowledge and experience to work. Rendiran corrected the man's ruined flesh as he felt his way through his body mentally – there was no need for the laying of hands, cutting or any of the other things a Lucent healer might do.

There was a great deal of dead material, and its removal caused incredible pain, but the relief followed only a few breaths later as Rendiran forced new flesh to grow in its place. In only three screams the man was whole and healed. The piece of wood fell from his mouth, and Rendiran found himself drawn into an enthusiastic embrace. "I thought I'd leave my boy alone today," his patient said to him. "Thank you for keeping us together."

Rendiran was thankful that the refuse from healing the fellow had fallen on the other side of the hammock, and returned his smile. "You're welcome," he said. "You should go clean yourselves up and get some air."

After realizing that he didn't feel fatigued in the least, Rendiran went on to hobble his way around the large hold, healing every injury he found. After he'd mended more wounds than he could count, he heard the running of little feet. "Rendiran!" cried Tadrin, who was only a step ahead of Oria. Rendiran tried to kneel gracefully, but ended up half falling to his knee as he lost his balance on the way down, but he managed to catch Tadrin and Oria in his arms as they collided with him at a full run. Crista was behind them, smiling and watching with crossed arms. "We thought you left us," Oria said.

"I had to make sure that trouble didn't follow you," Rendiran said.

"It didn't, we're on a boat!" Tadrin exclaimed cheerily. "They've caught perch with a big net, we're going to have fish for breakfast."

"That sounds wonderful," he croaked, his throat was still dry. "I'm so glad to see you're both safe."

"Do you think you could fetch Rendiran a cup of water?" Crista asked the children. "We'll be up soon."

"Don't leave us again, okay?" Oria asked as the pair set off on their mission.

"Where would I go?" Rendiran asked, gesturing to the cargo hold. He noticed that it was much emptier than it was before he started healing people.

"When I heard a young man missing a few fingers was healing people in the cargo hold, I couldn't believe it," Crista said as she closed the distance between them. "You slept for an entire day then through the night, it was as though all but the very last of your energy was spent. Just enough to keep you alive. Whatever you did, it cost you all most too much. I didn't expect you to wake up and start all over again." With a gentle touch, she lifted Rendiran's right hand and looked at the perfectly healed nubs where his fingers once were. "You'll heal everyone else before completing yourself," she said.

"Other than an itch on my missing little finger that I can't scratch, I feel fine. I'm far from exhausted, don't worry."

"How bad is your foot?" she asked. "You stumbled."

"Toes are a nuisance, they get stubbed all the time, and I've never been very good at keeping my toenails trimmed anyway. How did I get to the boat?"

"Heath, a blacksmith you told about the boat and several of his neighbors went back for you. He saw what you did, opening the heavens."

The memory of that battle was immediately sobering. It was as though the air thickened, and a weight pressed down on his shoulders. "Combat Priest Drikson guided me, no, took control and made that happen. Haffor? What happened to him?"

"The Lucent Guard, the Bright One's paladins got him. When Heath last saw, Haffor and the last of his paladins were in chains," Crista said. "I'm sorry."

"What was it all for?" Rendiran asked, lowering his head.

"You saved thousands of people," Crista said.

"Haffor, his paladins fought without consideration for themselves. Drikson continued to fight even after he was killed. I was only the vessel."

"If you weren't there, if you weren't willing to make the same sacrifice, this boat would be nearly empty. There's a chance – a good one – that Tadrin and Oria wouldn't have made it either. I won't let you believe that you didn't make a difference. If the undead defeated Haffor, they would have been sent down the road and the children would be in enemy hands. I'm sure of it. You gave us the time we needed to get away, gave Haffor a fighting chance, and even if you say Drikson was in control, you still made a miracle happen."

"There was so much death, so many people who never had a chance. I've never seen such disregard for life. You read about war, the number of people who died, and it's all academic. The horror we survived brings all that to life, but it doesn't make any more sense to me than it did before. How could anyone murder so many innocent people? Most of the bodies on the field were just folk who wanted to get away. With all this new power I still couldn't help them."

"You have to let them go," Crista said. "They move on to another life, and you will go on to heal people. Despair will only get in the way."

A prayer recited by servants of Miradu came to him then, and he tried to say it aloud, "When light fades, and darkness descends," he hesitated, remembering the Immortal Ember Knights with their black smoke filled helms and flaming swords.

"I will not give in to despair," Crista continued for him. "For I carry the light. Come to me,"

"And I will shine on you," Rendiran added. "Keep the darkness at bay." His spirits didn't lift, all he could think about were the people he saw killed, whether it was by fire, explosive magic on the field, or at the hands of decaying abominations.

Crista wrapped her arms around him and clutched his head to her chest. "You did more than anyone could have imagined."

"The waste of it," Rendiran said. "People who trusted their church and their Lord were cut down, mutilated, and murdered by the thousand. I can't believe we couldn't have done more."

"This boat is full, thanks to you," Crista said, stroking his hair. "You've healed almost everyone here."

"Just a broken foot here, I can wait," a young man, who was in surprisingly good humour, said.

"I'm sorry, I'm supposed to be the light," Rendiran said, pulling away a little and raising his head.

"You were, you definitely were," Crista said. "We saw the lights in the sky when you defeated the army of the dead."

"More of a large militia of the dead, really," Rendiran corrected with a crooked smile, wiping his eyes.

"All right," she replied. "I didn't know you could do that, even with the direction of a Combat Priest like Drikson."

The fellow with a broken foot was trying to stand, possibly to avoid bothering the pair. Rendiran felt for the injury mentally, located two broken bones and mended them using quick combat healing. The fellow cried out in surprise at the sharp pain of rapidly knitting bone, then stopped and tested his foot. "Like new, thank you, Resurrector," he said. "I feel like dancin'," he took one dance step and bounced his forehead off a beam.

"Outside, perhaps?" Crista said.

"I do feel like a stroll," he replied, rubbing his forehead.

There would be a bruise, but the bump wasn't enough to warrant healing magic, so Rendiran left it alone. "I never thought I'd be able to heal without the ceremonial component supporting it. Combat heal, I mean," he told Crista. "It requires a detachment I didn't think I could accomplish, and more power than I thought I'd have."

"I have a theory about that," Crista said. "If you're interested."

"There are other people in need," he replied.

"No, only people sleeping," she said, gesturing to the quiet cargo hold. "Maybe you should heal yourself?"

Rendiran attempted to focus on his hand, and began to force a new finger to grow. To his surprise, there was no progress at all, he felt as though he was trying to add knuckles to a hand that was already perfect. Instead of taking another approach, he surrendered. "I don't think I could focus enough to do that right now," he told Crista. "I might end up with a claw. What's this theory?"

Rendiran got to his feet, and Crista put his arm across her shoulders. "Well, the Temple, the orphanage you grew up in, even the holy caravans you travelled with were all heavily warded. Not just against what might attack from the outside world, but against all but divine and certain types of human magic on the inside. So, weaving is possible, but very difficult, casting spells of harm or magic made for combat is nearly impossible unless it's divine, and most conjurings don't work either."

"True, but how do you know my orphanage was warded?" Rendiran asked.

"I've seen a few Miradu orphanages," she replied. "I just assumed the one you were in was warded since they were. Anyhow, since you've been under these wards your whole life, you're finding that you can control more than you ever thought possible now that you're free of them."

"Free," Rendiran said as they started up the stairs to the main deck. It seemed like a strange word to use, he never felt like he was a captive, but it was the best word. "Like the staff head. That kind of artefact wouldn't work inside the temple."

"Right. So, you're discovering all this untapped potential. Without knowing it you've been preparing to wield that kind of power all your life, reading about it constantly. Well, whenever you weren't helping people."

"Thank goodness I did the reading before the lesson," Rendiran said. "Sorry, academic humour, not very funny to anyone outside a library. Speaking of surprises and power, you were a fox."

"I was," she replied. "Something I couldn't do in the temple."

"Shape shifting isn't something most people there approve of, especially the priests."

"What about this priest?" Crista asked.

"I think it's amazing," Rendiran said. "I didn't know you had so much talent."

"You'll be amazed at how much you'll learn if you look up from your books for a while, explore a little, starting with what's right in front of you," Crista said, pinching his side.

Tadrin and Oria met him at the top of the cargo hold stairs, each with a cup. He accepted one from Tadrin, drank it, then took a second from Oria. "I'm glad you both brought be a cup, I was very thirsty."

The deck of the ship was broad, it was made for hauling bulk cargo from farms and mines in the north. Most of the people he'd healed and their families were lining up in front of a grill. Crewmen were filleting perch and other fish with expert efficiency. "Maybe you should line up for breakfast," Rendiran told them. They ran the few steps to join the growing line. "No running please," he called after them.

"Awake at last," Heath said. It was the half dwarf that helped him get away from the city. "I didn't know priests slept in this late."

"Thank you for saving me," Rendiran said.

"Figured it was the least I could do, since I invited most of my neighbors to the boat after you told me about it. Speaking of which, we worked on your staff yesterday while you slept through morning, noon and evening," he gestured for three humans with calloused hands to come forward. "This is Berko, Vickin, and Cary from Dower Street. Carpenters, except for Cary who's a jeweler. It's nothing special, but we put your staff back together with a sturdy pole the right height for someone your size." Cary pulled a burlap cover off the staff head with a flourish and presented it to Rendiran.

He accepted it, looking into the gem in the middle of the staff head, where milk-white smoke slowly swirled within. The jewels and metal had been polished to gleaming, and the pole was simply carved with non-descript grooves that made it easy to hold. "Thank you," Rendiran said. "This is good work."

"It's the least we could do for a young hero such as yourself," Berko said.

"I'm no hero," Rendiran said. He could see the mood around him begin to sink. "I'm a survivor who's lucky enough to have a craft and new friends."

$\mathcal{I}$n many chambers of the inner city bathhouse that the Bright Ones' followers used as their temporary temple in Highshield City, the once clean waters ran red. Paladin Lonen Kerd of the Lucent Guard had seen so many sacrifices in His God's name through the last day that screams haunted his dreams.

The Bright One demanded that all heretics be slain in his name. 'You shall gather them into the temples and the fields, draw their blood and collect it in my name. When my enemies' life is spent, the body and blood shall be discarded. Only the living sacrifice has worth.' It was in scripture that Lonen read many times, so many times that he wondered why the High Priests of his order allowed necromancers and freaks from other, lesser religious orders do their work for them. Only at the end did the Lucent Guard come out of hiding, when the fires in the city were in full bloom and their enemies had already been laid low.

He had the opportunity to fight only twice. Once without any real meaning when they captured a small group of city guards who took refuge in the eastern gatehouse, and in a much more meaningful skirmish with what remained of the Eventide Order. There were seven of them, including their legendary Captain, and they killed thirty-five of the Lucent Guard, his own order of Paladins, before two of them were captured. The power and skill those Miradu Paladins was terrifying and amazing. Lonen was the one who caught Captain Haffor with a weighted net, giving his company a chance to restrain him and bring the fight to an end. After that, Lonen and most of the paladins in his company guarded the makeshift temple, dragged living sacrifices from room to room, and watched as the priests drew blood for their God.

"Surely, the Bright One's thirst is slaked by now," Lonen said to himself as he watched a priest begin to skin the young man he just brought into a private bathing room. The young man was a soft looking fellow with reddened blue eyes that Lonen would remember. He was barely a man, but the priests didn't seem to care as they strapped him down and began to cut and peel skin from his chest. The screams were so desperate, so shrill that it was difficult to tell whether they were from a man or a woman. It didn't matter, they were from a sacrifice, a heretic that had to be destroyed, Lonen reminded himself.

He left the room behind, closing the door. "Paladin Lonen," a High Priest in clean white robes said. The man was missing both ears, sacrifices to demonstrate his devotion to the Bright One. "I need you to witness the sacrifice of Captain Haffor. Ensure that he draws on no magics while I perform this holy rite."

"Yes, High Priest Datho," Lonen said, following into step behind him.

"How long have you been with us, Lonen?" the High Priest asked.

"I joined almost two Bounty Days ago," Lonen said, realizing for the first time that it had been almost two years.

"You've made a name for yourself in such a short time, I am truly impressed. That's why I've decided to give you this honour. You will have the opportunity to recount the destruction of one of our greatest enemies first hand."

"Thank you, High Priest Dotho, we clear the way so the Bright One may shine on us."

"May He shine eternal," the High Priest responded.

Lonen followed him through a door that was guarded by four Ladies of the Blade, women who were trained to fight and die for the Bright One. Their order was exclusively women, a place for girls to fight since they weren't allowed to become Paladins for the Bright One. All four of them wore masks that were frozen in expressions of joy. He knew each of them were as significant on the battlefield as he was, to have four of them there said something about the person held inside.

Lonen had to duck so his head didn't bump the doorframe. At a nod from Datho, he closed the door behind him. The room was dimly lit. A stone table that was once padded for massages and oil treatments was stripped bare, so Haffor the dwarf was chained to its hard surface. Several Priests and Ladies of the Blade stood against the walls, their silver, white, gold and green masks bore expressions of pity, sorrow, lust and joy. There was no rhyme or reason behind the variety, just an random array of different worshippers who chose very different ways to express their faith.

The faceplate on Lonen's helm was that of a grim stoic. He worshipped the Bright One by being his direct instrument in battle, not by infusing his life with emotion or expression. He'd killed more armed men and women than he could count or even recall. Seeing Haffor, Captain of the Eventide Order, a Paladin from the Miradu Order should not have affected him in the least.

It should not have affected him, but he could not help but admire Haffor. He laid on the table as stiffly and as straight as he might be if he were standing before his own Gods. The silver plated enchanted chains holding his ankles and wrists prevented the dwarf from using any magic, and they were drawn taught. "He stopped praying only a moment ago," said a High Priest in a mask that was frozen in a jackal like laugh. "All offering praise to Miradu, Viis and Irenick. He has not petitioned them for salvation."

"This man wouldn't," Datho said. "Would you, Haffor?"

Haffor looked the priest up and down. "Finally, someone whose brave enough to show his real face, not hide behind a mask."

"I have transcended the mask of metal or porcelain, and wear one of flesh. My face is the face of my God in this world, for I am Datho Umbra, the Justice, the Diviner for the Bright One."

"Ah, then we can begin the skinning and poking and stabbing," Haffor said. "Good, I wasn't looking forward to spending the night on this table, it's a little soft."

"Of all the characteristics I would have expected from the Captain of the Eventide Paladins, a sense of humour wasn't one of them. Good, we'll see how long that lasts. I'm afraid there won't be much cutting or poking, Haffor. We're trading your body once we're finished with you."

Haffor's expression turned sour and angry. He relaxed his arms and legs for a moment then pulled at all his chains suddenly, with such ferocity that they bit into his wrists and ankles, and the chains ground into the stone table they were wrapped around.

"You don't like that, do you?" Datho said with a snicker. "A week from now, your body will be back in armour, walking without your spirit. They're preparing for your body's arrival with much anticipation."

"How can you work with necromancers?"

"I hear my God, and he tells me to seek godless allies, so they may stand in his light and see that he is the true power. These are new days, dwarf, and all magic, all kinds of power must be His."

The thought of necromancers getting Haffor's body gave Lonen pause. Only a year ago he hunted down and killed several necromancers who were trying to use the corpses of Ava-Ondi to access ancient magic. That was the will of the Bright One then, to destroy the ultimate heretics, the ones that shrank away from all light, not just His.

"You, Paladin!" Haffor called out as he gave up on the chains. "You can't condone this. Worshipping a blood God is one thing, but trading with necromancers to try to bring them into the fold? I know your people hunted their kind down, I've even fought alongside someone from your order once."

"We clear the way so the Bright One may shine on us," Lonen replied.

"May he shine eternal," replied everyone except for Haffor.

"Don't let them use my body for something unnatural," Haffor said.

"That's enough of that," Datho said. "There is one thing I can do to help this trade along. They will have to remove your eyes to do their work, so I think I'll do that for them." He turned to an acolyte who held a wooden tray with a number of savage implements.

Haffor closed his eyes and began to pray. "I am a Guardian of Miradu. I give them my knowledge, my power, my worldly possessions, all the moments of my life and my life itself. As Paladin I will be just, kind, and steadfast in defending those who cannot defend themselves against abuse and despairing times." It was the sacrificial pledge of the Eventide, Lonen recognized it from a book that was read to him about their order, a book that was burned not long after. It was only recited when a servant of Miradu was about to go into battle and was sure they were about to die.

"Into position, please," Datho said. "Hold him steady."

Acolytes and priests held Haffor in place, grabbing legs, arms, his shoulders and his head as the dwarf prayed with the voice of a practiced orator. "For Miradu, Viis, Irenick and all those who serve goodness, I lay my sword down, surrender my shield, and put myself in your care."

The notion was simple, a demonstration of trust in his Gods and anyone who served his cause, which wasn't the cause of Miradu or any of her children, but goodness itself. Lonen was reminded of what he imagined a Paladin was when he was just a boy: a paragon of goodness, justice and a defender of the weak.

With a practiced hand, Datho dug a scoop with sharpened edges into Haffor's right eye socket. The dwarf tensed and clenched his teeth, struggling not to scream. The scoop sliced through one side of his eyelid, into his eye socket and scraped against bone before continuing on. Haffor's hands opened, fingers splaying as his body twitched, then they closed into fists.

Then, the eye was out and Datho dropped it and the flesh that came along with his expert removal into a small jar. "My best yet."

"Send me to your God, you whoreson!" Haffor bellowed. "I will tear him to pieces and bring his kingdom down!"

"That's more like it," Datho said. "That's the dirt eating dwarf I expected. I will end it right now, just as you wish, if you tell me where the dwarves are hiding the Ondi-Ne? We know you have them, we know that's where they went to avoid the rightful justice humanity brings."

Haffor laughed ruefully. "I know, you git. I could tell you everything."

"I'll make your end quick, you only have to tell me."

"I am the light, I am the defender of the weak, I am the beacon calling to all who shiver in the dark. Rikaam, Toriz, and the forbidden darkness between are my battlefields. I heed the call of the secret Knights, Irekirk and his shadow, I will bear the flame." Haffor's response surprised Lonen, it was passionate, and he recognized Toriz, it was one of the hells of his faith. A place where magic was wild, twisting and corrupting everything that entered. The Bright One sent magical practitioners who turned on him there.

"Hurry! Kill him! Kill him!" Shouted one High Priest in a laughing mask.

Haffor continued. "I face the hazard, I challenge our enemies so you may rest," Datho dropped his scoop and drew a dagger from his belt. It was through Haffor's heart in the next instant.

"I go so you may know peace," Haffor finished with his last breath.

As he watched the life drain from the dwarf's body, Lonen's vision was blurred by tears. He felt as though something much greater than himself, it could not have been the Paladin, perhaps one of his Gods, had taken all the burdens of his life from him, washing all his regrets and fears away.

31

Oria and Tadrin were the darlings of the River Gull. Over two hundred refugees, crewmen, and other people aboard the heavy barge seemed to enjoy seeing the pair run about with their dog, Ander, at their heels, discovering new sights as they passed on the shore. They were regaled with stories about the lands they passed through as the seemingly endless ribbon of green and grey shoreline passed to their left and sometimes to their right. The river was so broad at some points that the shore on their right would often grow so distant that it couldn't be seen.

Even with all the excitement, there was one constant question on Tadrin's mind: "Do you know where my mom and dad are?" Every few hours Tadrin would find a way to ask Rendiran, only Rendiran, if he knew.

He didn't know, but he was sure he could find out using fairly simple sorcery. Using his new power gave him pause, because the time he had to rest allowed him to contemplate his new path. A sorcerer and healer walked along very different roads. Humans drew from sources of power outside themselves whenever possible because they could easily drain their own bodies of energy, causing permanent damage. Most humans worshipped Gods, did their bidding, and some of them gained their favour along with the power that came with it. That was Rendiran's road, the healer, the student and the preacher. Sorcerers sought out sources of stored energy so they didn't exhaust themselves by drawing on the power within. He had an energy source already, the unnamed staff. Corrupting that kind of energy source was easy, and it had to be guarded, accessed by a disciplined mind.

He had seen Ondi magic as well. It was a frightening way to interact with the world, using a kind of second sight to understand how all things interacted with each other. That pattern was called 'The Weave' and if one was focused, knowledgeable and powerful enough, an Ondi could change the world, follow patterns woven throughout the lands to other places, even change the shape of a living thing while doing no real harm. Crista must have been a powerful weaver to transform into a fox then return to her Ondi-Ne form. She was even able to use magic to draw a swarm of insects to the Castle Guard while she was still in the form of a fox. That was more impressive to him than anything he'd done. Her magic had a kind of grace, an elegance that made human sorcery look carless, even sloppy.

That reminded him of one of his current problems, his missing digits. He could find no proper way to regenerate them, which left him with few options. He had the options of forcing the replacement of his fingers and toes using pure sorcery that was closer to necromancy or flesh craft, or to accept that losing those fingers and toes permanently was the cost of over-exertion. The latter felt right, and likely.

The shoreline grew nearer. Three Mills, a town named simply because they had three mills at one point. From the looks of things, they were up to five. The gentle breeze that kept them moving up river thanks to large sails also moved the giant arms of the grand mills. The River Gull would most likely stop there on its way back down river to pick up a shipment of flour. Many of the houses further away from the mills looked new, most of them were brick and two stories, a clear sign that the town was doing well. He idly wondered how things would be over the next year as the docks in Highshield City recovered. Several of the refugees saw the warehouses and dockside burning before they made it out of the city. That could be terrible for everyone in the eastern provinces who depended on getting their wares to Brightwill. It would be even worse for Brightwill. King Ormet's people would be short on food for months, and knowing that man's reputation, Rendiran was sure that he would raid neighboring kingdoms for their stores, send his fleet out to capture other ships coming from the eastern provinces, and burn what he couldn't use so enemy kingdoms starved worse than his own.

The gang of children rushed to the port side and looked at the five tall brick and mortar mills. Their arms were painted green, brown and yellow. Oria picked up the shortest dwarf girl – Banna was her name, a small creature with red curls and a giant smile – so she could see over the rail. "Look, Rendiran! It's Five Mills!" Tadrin announced excitedly, pointing to the shore and looking at him over his shoulder.

Rendiran was about to correct him, but smiled and stood instead. "Can you imagine anyone built such incredibly large things?" he said. "Today they grind enough flour to feed everyone here for half a year." He told them.

"So pretty, they're like giant flowers," said one of the dwarf halfling children.

"That too," Rendiran agreed.

Marjay watched the whole scene from several steps back, he was never too far from the children, especially Oria, who had adopted him whole heartedly. Seeing that they had a minder nearby, Rendiran walked to the aft castle section of the massive barge. The staff helped him move about much easier, making up for the balance he lost with the toes on his right foot. He climbed the stair and didn't stop until he was leaning on the railing.

"Three blessings to you, Rendiran," said Captain Ollins. He was a tall human who had the look of a retired warrior, well-muscled with short white hair.

"Three blessings, Captain," Rendiran replied. "I would like to ask your permission to use magic while I'm aboard your ship."

"What spell?" he asked, looking up from a book of charts.

"Spirt sight, it's a far-seeing spell that follows the path of a person I've known before."

"Aye, I know it," Ollins said. "I thought you were about to offer a wind or passage spell, which I never use. A sight spell doesn't worry me, go ahead."

"Thank you, Captain. I'm wondering, do you have any sorcerers aboard?"

"Other than you, no. Last one got off right before you got on. Sorcerers don't find my boat interesting. I only keep them around to defend us against their own kind, I don't allow weather magic or the like on my ship. Always seemed selfish to conjure a wind that only benefits one ship."

"There's wisdom in that," Rendiran said, remembering the lessons of cost where sorcery and weather were concerned. "A small change in one place can cause great change elsewhere."

"Aye," the Captain said. "I'll let you get to it."

Rendiran closed his eyes and concentrated on Tadrin's parents. He pressed all assumptions about where he thought they may be, and what they might be doing out of his mind and once his thoughts were clear, he gently drew on the power in the staff head. An image began to form in his mind, it was murky at first. He concentrated on Tadrin's father specifically, and felt a sensation of intense nausea. Then, as though he were standing right beside him, he watched Tadrin's father retch into a bucket.

The vision dissipated quickly as Rendiran opened his eyes and heaved his hearty breakfast over the railing, it was fish, bread and weak but thick ale. Crista was at his side a moment later, and he let her take his staff as he finished violently sending the contents of his stomach down river. "Are you all right?" she asked him.

"I'm farseeing, quite successfully, actually. Tadrin's father is horribly seasick, poor man," Rendiran replied quietly as he cleaned himself up with a rag. "I'm afraid I got a little too close to him. I'll try to see his mother from a little further back this time."

"All right, are you sure?" Crista asked, a little more amused that he thought she ought to be.

"Now that I've seen how easy this spell is to use on the unwarded, it'll be fine." He accepted his staff and closed his eyes. Concentration was easy to find, but he had difficulty dismissing expectations and preconceptions. After a few deep, slow breaths and taking a moment to remember Tadrin's mother, who he found very kind looking and sweet, another vision began to appear in his mind.

She was rubbing her husband's shoulders, a slender hand providing comfort, and looking at tall sails. He pulled away, as though he was a bird circling higher. There was a small group of dwarf and human paladins nearby, sorcerers manned the crows nests, and several of the soldiers aboard wore Forge Hin tabards. He recognized a few more as Merchant Guardsmen from deep within dwarf territory. They looked like professional soldiers in leather jerkins with a shield and a coin painted on them.

Rendiran circled higher still. They were aboard a large seafaring vessel with three masts. It was a dwarf ship called the Bearded Beauty. To the right he could see craggy shores made of black and dark brown stone. They were well past any shore he knew, any he'd seen. He felt like a spirit on the winds as he swept the shore northward, looking for major landmarks, and he found one almost immediately. A grand keep with four squat towers and a rich city around it. It sat upon a high cliff, and just down from the keep he could see a heavy system of pulleys transporting goods to and from a busy dockside. Surely someone would know exactly where that was, so he removed himself from his vision.

"Captain? Can I speak to you, Captain?" he asked as soon as he opened his eyes. Ollins was still nearby, looking at his book of small charts. "Aye, see something interesting?"

"A grand keep with large, broad towers and a bustling city. There were crane and pulley works leading to a dock below. The stones on those cliffs were black and dark brown, but mostly the former."

"You were looking at this from the sea? From the air?" the Captain asked.

"From above, mostly."

"Your vision rode the wind, that's useful, friend. As for what you're describing, that kind of shore must be south of Quarry Gate, well north of Worton."

"Pardon me, High Priest," a dwarf with a shaved head and long black beard said as he climbed the steps of the aft castle. "I think I know that keep. It's a Dwarven Stronghold, Galbarr. There are a few strongholds on that shore with pulley docks, but only one with the towers you're describing. My mother's father is from there. It's only seventy or so miles from Quarry Gate. Any chance you saw a bunch of dwarves with a crow flying left to right on their shoulders?"

"I didn't get that close, I'm sorry. It looked like the keep and town were prospering though."

"Good to hear, thank you," the dwarf said.

"What's your name, if you don't mind me asking?"

"Wyklow, looks like I'll be taking me and mine there if we can find a caravan."

Rendiran was surprised and reassured. Quarry Gate was the harbour closest to Forge Hin. By reputation there were massive docks and shipyards there, all controlled by the dwarves, owned by them, and all of the product of the northern mountains passed through there to Brightwill and other parts of the world. Tadrin's parents were close, perhaps a day away by sea.

The boy was still looking over the port side rail when Rendiran spotted him, and Tadrin looked back at him as though he knew he was being watched. "Come here," Rendiran motioned with a smile. He, Oria and a few of the younger dwarf children came to Rendiran, who sat down on a stool one of the crewmen put beside him. "I've found your parents," Rendiran said as the boy climbed into his lap. "Your mother and father are on a ship at sea, safe and close to Forge Hin."

"Really?" Tadrin exclaimed.

"I think they'll arrive there in..." he looked to Wyklow, who held up one then two fingers. "End of today, perhaps tomorrow."

"So I'll see my mom and dad tomorrow?" Tadrin asked.

"We're going to take a lot longer to get to Forge Hin," Rendiran said. "But they'll be waiting for us, safe as houses, so you don't have to worry."

"Oh," Tadrin said, looking as though he were half way between reassurance and disappointment.

"It's the best news, Tadrin," Rendiran said reassuringly. "They are eager to be reunited with you, even more than you want to see them. I'll get you there as soon as I can, but until then, you should take in everything around you so you can tell them stories for days, maybe for weeks."

"Stories for the winter," Heath said as he joined two of his children. One of them was Banna, who tugged on his hand, waited to be picked up, didn't get what she wanted quickly enough, and started to climb him. His thick arm was her line as she used her little feet to walk up his side. He stayed still as she slowly and quite successfully did so.

While Heath was being climbed, he explained the expression. "'Save your stories for winter,' my mother used to tell us when I was growing up in the north. You know, after we reached a certain age, not much older than you, we did, and the winters didn't seem quite as long after that. They have long winters in Forge Hin, so you should take it all in." By the time he finished talking, Banna had just reached his shoulder. He looked at her grinning little face; "yes?" She blew a puff of air up his nose as a response. He pretended to be irritated, picked her up and planted her on his shoulders.

Oria started to climb Marjay as soon as he joined her, and he stood still patiently. Rendiran's attention was mostly on Tadrin, whose mood seemed to be brightening a little. "So you'll have a lot of stories for them."

"Are you gonna leave us again?" Tadrin asked him quietly as he took Rendiran's undamaged hand.

"No," he said. "I will stay with you all the way to Forge Hin. I plan to live there too."

Tadrin gave him a long, squeezing hug, a surprise to Rendiran. "I'll tell Oria, she worries about you a lot," the boy whispered.

"Good, thank you, Tadrin," Rendiran replied. "Now, go watch the shore, I think we're about to come up on Hale Shire."

"Wale Shire," the Captain called over his shoulder as he descended the steps to the main deck. "We'll be loading apples and pears, kids. Watch quietly and you'll get one."

The gang of children followed as closely behind as they dared, which was only a few feet away from the heels of the Captain who constantly had his nose in his chart book. Marjay put Oria down only moments after she succeeded in climbing him and stetting on his shoulders. "I need to talk to Rendiran, you go watch the boat dock and keep the other kids out of the way, all right?"

She nodded, still not entirely happy at being put back down. Tadrin joined her and they followed the rest of the children. They were not absent supervision, many parents kept them close to the forward cabin doors so they were clear of the large boat's busy middle.

"I need to show you both something," Marjay said to Rendiran and Crista. He turned so only they could see a scabbard on his hip. It was covered in rough cloth and bound with a long strip of leather so no part of it was visible. It hung beside his short blade. He unraveled the leather band until the hilt was free and half drew the sword. Ancient Ondi-Ne and Dwarven writing was etched deeply down the middle of the blade, which was made of a metal that looked almost cloudy glass. "Haffor left the Sword of the Eventide on his horse."

Guilt and woe filled Rendiran, Crista was surprised and saddened at the sight of the blade. "Quick, cover it up," Rendiran said. "That sword must make it to Forge Hin."

"I was hoping you'd say that," Marjay said, re-binding the sword hilt in cloth and leather. "Half afraid you would tell me it had to go somewhere else, to be honest. Forge Hin isn't the traditional seat of our Paladin Order."

"It will be if I have anything to say about it," Rendiran said. "The Paladins have always been followers of the original laws given to us by Irenick and Viis. The Temple laws that have come in the last few decades have strayed from them, added too many details and barriers between Miradu and her people."

"Like celibacy and the fasting requirements for the High Priests and dedication costs to join the church as a devout," Crista added.

"Those are the two that always bothered me. It should cost the same thing to worship Miradu as it costs to worship her children: nothing," Rendiran said. "The dwarves of the north follow the old laws. I've always wanted to visit them, to see what that's like."

"You'll have your chance now," Marjay said. "Do you think you could use your sight to find Haffor?"

Rendiran thought for a moment, intimidated by the task. "If I can clear my mind well enough, I could do it. My worry is that he's with the enemy, and I may be found out. They'd immediately know our location."

"Is there no way to protect yourself?" Crista asked.

"There are ways, I don't know them well, but there are. Sorcery has never been my true focus, only a topic I read as much as I could in the temple."

"We must be far from anyone who would pursue us. Anyone launching from a river post would be days behind us, hours at least," Marjay said.

"Not if one of them was a nearby wind whisperer. There could be one only an hour up the river. They could receive word of our location from Highshield City and have a group of soldiers ready to meet us," Rendiran said. "It's dangerous, even the squire who was to take this journey with us is gone. We'll have to wait until we're in a safer place, perhaps find a sorcerer who is more practiced to use their sight instead."

"That makes sense, Rendiran," Marjay said. "I only want to know what to tell Haffor's father when I give him this sword."

"I don't envy you that, but I'll be standing beside you when you meet the King," Rendiran said.

"I'll be there as well, but only if we get to Forge Hin my way," Crista said. "The safest way."

It was unusual for Crista to seem so insistent. "If it's faster than going over land for a couple hundred miles, then I'll take it," Marjay said.

"It is, but it requires a promise of perfect secrecy," she said.

"You will have it," Marjay said.

"Absolutely," Rendiran reassured.

"There is a way into the Wandering Wood a half day's ride from where we're landing up river," she told them. "It's an outer branch of the forest, close to an ancient place where there are people who will want to help us. Friends of Miradu."

"I've only heard of the Wandering Wood in old crib side fables," Marjay said. "You're telling me it's real, and that we can use it?"

"Yes," Crista said. "I believe they will help us get to Forge Hin in a day instead of a few weeks. We can't take anyone but the children with us."

"Wait, I still don't understand. In the tales the Wandering Wood is a forest that exists in the deepest, darkest woodlands of our world. Its borders move and hide themselves. Treacherous beings lure people in, and when they come out they're either never the same, or they spend their entire lives trying to get back but never find a way."

"Some of that is true," Crista said. "I'll be your guide, so the nastier things there shouldn't be a problem. As for the nature of the Wandering Wood, well, a trained Weaver who knows travelling magic can see the borders, but they're invisible to everyone else. Most of it moves unseen, and parts of it do emerge, visible to everyone in sacred places that are filled with life. They're hard to find, the Wandering Wood has a will of its own and it only tells some Weavers where its borders will be next."

"You're one of them?" Rendiran asked.

"No, my Grand Aunt is, I'm too young, too inexperienced to know where the borders will be, the Wandering Wood doesn't trust me yet. She made me memorize a map though, it shows me where to look for the next few years."

"So it exists invisibly," Marjay said, struggling.

"Yes, like the High Heavens, or the Countless Hells and everything in-between. They're all just realms, some for the living, some for the dead and others can have both. They all exist at the same time, though only the Wandering Woods and a couple other realms cross over with our world on their own. The Wandering Woods are close enough right now."

"Is that where the Ondi hid?" Marjay asked in an excited, hushed whisper.

"Some of my people went there, yes, but I don't know where the rest went. Maybe the dwarves do, the people of Forge Hin were very close to my people. The entrance to the Wandering Wood is a couple days inland, maybe a day on horseback."

"We'll buy one of the horses in the hold. I don't want to get caught after we've left the river. After that, we should give whatever coin we have to Heath, so he can buy supplies and lead the refugees. When we get to Forge Hin, we'll see if we can send them aid. We'll take the children to the Hidden Path," Rendiran said He'd read a little about the Wandering Wood, and looked forward to seeing it for himself. Like Marjay, he thought it was nothing more than a myth.

---

32

*P*rince Norrich had seen death before, but never felt the loss of someone so close to him. Ofeur was his greatest friend, even though he played the part of servant extremely well, they had a history that threaded through his life all the way back to his childhood.

High Magician Irogen gently laid the black cloth back on the body, which had been stung by insects, beheaded and trampled. "Eye witnesses confirm that Haffor, Captain of the Eventide Paladins killed Ofeur. It was one clean, quick stroke, a mercy if it had to happen at all."

"Where is Haffor now?" Prince Norrich asked, turning away from the corpse. Through the window he could see the smoldering city, a ruin of heat blasted brick and burned out wood. The gated Miradu Temple, with its high reaching spires loomed in the distance at the other end of the ruins, in pristine condition.

"We've confirmed that Haffor has been taken by Lucents to Bright One High Priests at great expense. They've announced that he has been sacrificed to their God and are searching for the Sword of the Eventide. It went missing shortly before he was captured, if rumours are true."

"Dwarves know how to handle their treasures, I'm sure it's either far from here by now, or tucked under some stone where no one will find it," Prince Norrich said. "So revenge for Ofeur could be taken on the Eventide Paladins, perhaps the Miradu Faith itself, or the dwarves of Forge Hin." He knew Irogen was about to advise against it and held up a hand. "I know, punishing anyone at this point would only complicate matters." He sighed, wiped a tear from his eye and leaned on the window sill. "Would you blame me for wanting to make someone pay?"

"It is well understood that seeking revenge is a natural part of the grieving process, especially amongst the finer royal lines, such as yours," Irogen said. "I don't blame you at all. There will be a time for that, I believe. You only have to live long enough and prosper to your father's satisfaction. With time, an opportunity for revenge will present itself. Until then, may I suggest memorializing your old friend? Pour your grief into something beautiful for him, so everyone can see how deep it is, how important he was to you."

"Good advice, as always," the Prince told him. "Until then, can you have him properly embalmed and stored? I will build a memorial to him in the garden, and we'll put him to rest there when it's ready."

"Of course," Irogen said.

The pair walked into the hallway, where pillars made of smooth green and black stone held up the high vaulted ceiling. "Tell me, what's the worst thing that happened last night aside from the city burning to its foundations?" Prince Norrich asked through clenched teeth. He didn't want to hear anything about the world outside his castle. Every instinct told him to retreat to his private rooms and start sampling the wine stores, but he knew better. If he made no effort to rebuild, or reacted poorly to the situation he would be recalled to Brightwill, where he would have to face his father. That was the worst fate he could imagine.

"I'm afraid that's difficult to determine. There are several awful bits of news," Irogen said, tugging on a short, greying beard that curled awkwardly whenever it was allowed to grow too long. "Instead of testing your patience, I'll simply start with the docks. Everything made of stone survived, but everything made of wood was set ablaze by magical fire. The climate here, and the dry weeks leading up to last night created the worst kind of conditions for this kind of fire. It wasn't like the burning of Castin, when the fires lasted the better part of a week and a few things could be saved. No, the dry wood and magical influence has reduced the wooden buildings in the city to ash in less than a day, I'm afraid. So, when I say the wooden fixtures in the dockside burned, I don't mean pulley rigs and a few buildings. The walkways, offices with all their records, and so on were destroyed completely. The shipyard burned as well, leaving burnt half-built ships that will have to be removed before anything more can be done. Even the supplies we had in reserve to build new ships are ruined."

"I understand, no need for more detail, it's a disaster. How long to rebuild?"

"Rebuilding will take at least four months."

"Four months?" Prince Norrich asked, shocked.

"Yes, there are few craftsmen left in the city, most of them fled, so we'll have to depend on Tirus Embrow, our own head builder in the castle and anyone he can get together. Workers may also be hard to find, especially since we have nowhere to house them at the moment. Normally we could have rubble cleared, sunken ships broken up and new wooden structures built in less than two months, but we don't have the people."

"Gather everyone who can advise me on this, we need to find a way to ship goods to the rest of the Kingdom while we rebuild. That is even if Warton has to become the capitol for a year or two, even though Lord Idona's head will swell at the very notion."

"That brings me to our next problem, your Highness," Irogen said. "The warehouses are gone, and any leftover grain outside of the castle has been corrupted. Our next shipment of precious and channeling stones were also stolen along with the Quickamber."

The news was so dire that Prince Norrich stopped in front of the doors to the main hall. "Channeling stones and Quickamber gone? How? They were in the south tower!"

"Several of our own soldiers made off with three chests late last night. We only discovered this morning. The watchmen who let them through are in the dungeons now."

"Spread the story of the guards' negligence. They should be punished brutally, publically. Strike their feet off at the ankles tomorrow morning, then their hands the next day, and then put them in the square in the castle courtyard. When it seems they are near death, have them healed completely. Tell them they've served their sentence, and lead them to the headsman's block an hour later. I want the cost of letting Quickamber be stolen to be legendary. Meanwhile, I want you to scry for it, pay anyone you have to to find it, hunt it down, and bring the Quickamber back. There was enough there to pay for six castles this size, more than our entire provincial treasury in value."

"I know, your Highness. I'll have your instructions put into action immediately."

Prince Norrich's footfalls echoed throughout the grand hall. He ignored the statues in the corner, the embellishments on the floor and ceiling, the tall windows and columns as he strode through the empty space and took his seat on the provincial throne. "What else? I suppose Irenick and Viis' gifts are long gone?"

"Yes, but our eyes and ears report that they are safely travelling up river, well ahead of any pursuit. Do you want me to hire some men to give chase?"

"No," Prince Norrich said. "I'm finished with religious entanglements. I wish them the best, but I am going to extract myself and this province from religion, I think."

"I congratulate you on your wisdom, Prince," Irogen said with a half-bow. He straightened and cleared his throat.

"You're not leaving? There's something else?" Prince Norrich asked, near exasperation. He impatiently gestured for the older Magician to go on.

"I'm afraid our efforts in the city will have to wait at least a few days. The Miradu Temple Guards, over two thousand of them, have finally been ordered into our fair city, and they're chasing all impure elements out. While that includes Lucents, necromancers, unrecognized sorcerers, looters, and other irritants, we've also received reports of steadfast citizens being pushed out as well. Some have been put to the spear when they refused to leave their homes."

"Put to the spear?"

"When they refuse to kneel and praise Wydu, the Wise One."

"Religion is our undoing," Prince Norrich said to himself as he momentarily hid his face in his hands. He had never been so furious in his entire life.

"I'm afraid there's little we can do, your Highness," Irogen said. "At the moment, your Highness."

"Yes, there is!" Norrich said as the stood in front of the throne. "I'll take the example of my father. Whisper on the wind to King Sede, tell him I need the assistance of his army, and that I offer my friendship on this shore. Find every mercenary in the province and offer them twice the pay if they arrive at my castle within seven days. Offer craftsmen the same. I will raise an army and take the city, then I'll rebuild it in stone. Send word to the dwarves in the north that we will need them to ship everything bound for Brightwill here. They will send us their armies in support as well. We need their stone workers, and everyone else they can spare immediately. Wydu can have the temple, but the rest of the city will be mine, and I will manage the distribution and growth of our provinces personally so religion can't burn us out again."

"Your father, the King? He'll be expecting a large shipment soon."

"We tell him what fortune brings us after seven days. If he sees I have things in hand here, he may not send my brother, or come personally."

33

*L*onen thought Highshield City was the most beautiful place created by man or Ondi. When he saw it for the first time years before, he was a hazard, stopping in the street to stare at the construction, amazed by how the buildings seemed to lean and loom over everyone on the street. There were statues that seemed to be randomly strewn about the place. Some were new, human art, most were half destroyed or pockmarked Ondi statues of people he knew nothing about and creatures that he'd never seen. He loved the large landmarks the most. The Old Fort, the Royal Castle, and the Temple of Miradu seemed like towering examples of construction and artistry. The charred ruin that Highshield City had become was horrible.

The statues had been vandalized, historic buildings burned to the ground, the water that ran through the public system was grey, smoke still rolled out of the Old Fort's windows, and the outer walls of the Royal Castle were blackened. The Miradu Temple was the only jewel left, and the guards who were supposed to prevent such disasters finally marched forth from its gates, slaying everything that they didn't want in the city.

The worshippers of the Bright One were fugitives there, and he led a contingent charged with transporting Captain Haffor's body out of the Highshield. He volunteered with a plan in mind. He would not let Haffor's corpse become a necromancer's plaything. He found their kind disgusting, abominable. The thought that his High Priests, the people who guided his entire faith, would ally themselves with any necromancer was still unbelievable. What necromancer would be powerful or influential enough to be worth it? How could the Bright One accept that alliance?

The smell of charred flesh – a thick meat smell that was sickly sweet tinged with something rancid – brought his thoughts back to the present. They were passing through the secondary eastern gate. A bag containing all of Haffor's rings and his amulet was in one hand. Lonen kept his sword at the ready in the other. The last of the hold outs from the city, poor and rich citizens who didn't want to abandon the small square of land they had claim to, were rushing through the gate with them. Most of them were at least part Ondi, he could tell from their height and pointed ears. It occurred to him then: he hadn't seen any humans rushed from their homes or hiding places by the Temple Guards.

Somehow, Ondi were as much a pest to the Temple Guards as necromancers, looters and members of enemy religions were. It was a purge. The gatehouse was abandoned. Something had torn the heavy outer doors half off their hinges, leaving them open like a burnt wound. He led four acolytes and a pair of paladins through with Haffor's wrapped body in the middle of their formation. The open road lay ahead, and he began looking forward to reaching the bottom of the hill, where secondary townships would provide the cover he needed to execute his plan. He would turn on his fellow followers and behead the corpse of Haffor. Burning and crushing the head would be enough to prevent any work from being done on the body, so he only needed to escape with that.

He would present the ashes and Haffor's signet ring to someone in the Eventide Order, or the King, whoever he could get to, and offer himself to Viis, or Miradu herself through their priests. The gift Haffor sent him in his final moments of life was better than his moments in the sight of the Bright One. Lonen felt purified, his head was clear, and he no longer sought the light of the Bright One above all other things. "We must hurry, they could post archers on the wall at any moment," he said, urging the four acolytes that carried the Dwarf's body forward. Haffor's corpse was bundled tightly from head to toe, there was no way of seeing who it was, but to a Temple Guard, they would look like a group of Lucent soldiers running off with a corpse. More than enough reason for their archers to loose dozens of arrows their way.

"We're almost clear, brother," said Sir Berris, one of the paladins accompanying him. "Two hundred more steps and we'll be in Wattis, plenty of room for us, they don't care where the coin comes from, or who's buying the ale, and I have a shiny stack from this raid."

A raid, that's all this was to Berris. The greatest city on the continent was still smoldering, burned to the bricks and he called it a raid, celebrated a sack of coins he managed to collect from the pockets of the dead. He looked the man up and down quickly. He would be easy to kill, his pauldrons and his neck guard were loose, and his helmet was unstrapped.

They reached the bottom of the hill and passed through the tall stones that marked the edge of Highshield City limits far past the wall. When they turned the corner they all stopped. There was great violence under way in Wattis, a large town of newer buildings. There was a mill there, and many craftsmen and merchants were known to call it home because they were allowed to build larger houses. The looters and able bodied people who were displaced from Highshield City had moved on to ransack and demolish the outer towns, it seemed, and Wattis was a target. It was already beginning to burn.

"The Bright One has not sent his light here," said Sir Ondilen. He was a devout, and had given his nose and one ear as sacrifices to the Bright One. He may be more difficult to kill, his plate armour was still in good repair and he held his short sword at the ready.

"We must keep going, there's something more than what we're seeing going on here. There's some kind of magical power at work," said Berris.

Lonen felt it then, a powerful influence.

"We only have to get this sack of bones to Tiren Street," Ondilen said.

"How far is it?" Lonen asked as their group started running. The acolytes were as trustworthy as the High Priest predicted, keeping pace as they carried the body and tried to keep their eyes down.

"Less than a hundred fifty paces, four streets in," Ondilen replied. "Eager to leave this bastard behind?"

They passed the first row of houses, and Lonen felt the presence press in on his mind. It was like a siren's song that threatened to drown out all of his thoughts. 'Gather the gold, gather the gems, gather the eyes of all your victims,' it sang. It took power to invade the minds of others, power unlike he'd seen outside of the presence of the Bright One. There was no time, he had to act and escape.

Lonen pretended to stumble and guarded his hands from the others as he pulled Haffor's signet ring from the bag and swallowed it. If his plan failed, he may be able to escape. Maybe he wouldn't have the ashes of Haffor's head, but he'd have the ring to present at least.

"Ho, there, watch your step," Sir Ondilen said, stopping and offering his hand.

"She's in my mind! I feel I'm crushed under her song!" one of the acolytes cried, dropping to the ground, clutching his head.

Ondilen and Berris were distracted, so Lonen lashed out, driving his sword into Ondilen's chin and into his brain. The blade stuck, so he let the hilt go, picking up one of the paladin's swords. He charged Sir Berris, and he meant to slash at the man's throat, but found the tip of his short sword aimed at the man's eye instead. He drove it in deeply, quickly, and kicked his foot out from under him. Berris may have been crass, but he was always kind to him, so he made sure to dispatch the man quickly, ending him by leaning on the sword hilt and driving the blade deep into his head.

He rounded on the acolytes to find that they were already fleeing. Lonen raised his sword, preparing to strike Haffor's head from his shoulders, it would take several swings with the short sword, but it was sharp so it would still be quick.

With a roar he attempted to swing down, but his arms refused to move from where they were; over his head. The song that attempted to suppress everything else in his mind quieted only to be replaced with a powerful presence that sought to utterly overwhelm him.

"That is mine, Sir Lonen" said the beautiful voice of a woman. It was loud in his ears, but in his mind it was a symphony unto itself, howling. His hands failed to maintain their grip on the sword, and his arms dropped limply to his sides as he looked down the street.

A woman in long, blue and black robes with silver thread patterned in symbols of power, drifted up the street as she floated several feet above the ground. Over her shoulders were two stoles, one white, one black, and each had more symbols pinned to them made of precious metals and gems. She was human, of that he was sure, but more beautiful than any human he'd ever seen. A face that he was loathe to look away from with deep green eyes, framed by fine white and blonde hair. "You have seen the Bright One's glory and turned away. You have been cleansed by Viis and will swear to her," she said. "I would skin you alive and feed your flesh to my imps, but I can feel Viis' eyes. She watches you, and I would not enrage a Goddess more than I already have by taking the body of one of her favourite paladins."

He stared at her, trying to concentrate on keeping his own mind, refusing to let her presence mute his spirit. It struck him then, she was a Thanga, a master of powerful human magic that had been pried free of moral guidance. The power she drew upon was from forbidden sources, her methods were guided only by her desires, not by any code. She smiled at him, a joyous thing to behold, he wanted to take her into his arms on the spot, everything he was he would offer to her. He bit his cheek hard, drawing blood and giving him control over his own mind again. "You are right," she said, grinning like an eager carnivore. "I am Razthanga, the Light of Salcom and its ruiner."

With a gesture, his helmet broke in two and fell to the ground. She reached down with a soft, well-kept hand and caressed the open gash where his nose was before he sacrificed it to the bright one.

Razthanga grazed the scars on his cheeks where he'd woven metal bands through the outer flesh during Crimson Day. Tearing them free with his own hands during the Rite of Light several days later was spectacularly painful, and the cause of the Bright One's second visitation. Her soft palm cupped his chin, which had been slit so stones could be drawn out through the sides using wires pushed through his cheeks. He had suffered willingly, eagerly to show his dedication to the Bright One, to draw his euphoria causing gaze, and he had done worse to others. "Poor, deluded addict. You sacrificed more than most for your Bright One. I wonder, did Viis tell you his secret when she touched you?" Razthanga asked. She waited a moment, he didn't know what she was talking about. "I suppose she didn't. The Bright One was just a man, an Ava-Ondi man, who was powerful, greedy, jealous and perverse. He held two courts: one for those he needed to woo in order to get the support and love of their people, and another, secret court where he influenced innocent people to do savage things to each other and themselves. I would tell you his living name, but I don't give people that kind of power lightly. Viis is not as powerful as he is, but she is true. She states her beliefs and inspires people, living by the same code herself. I have seen her on the fields of battle in the High Heavens twice, fighting in defense of her mother's realm, and to rescue souls that would be captured by horrible beasts that could only exist in this world if it were consumed by complete darkness. You know none of this, but can feel that it's true, thanks to Haffor." Razthanga laid a hand on the dwarf's body. "Haffor who was true and wise. His spirit belongs with Her, with the ancestors who stand at Her side. I'm a little saddened to tell you that his essence is in the hands of the Bright One now, and that mad God is most likely having his way. I will take his body, you can't stop me, not even Viis can stop me. That is enough for me. His gift to you was far greater, calling Viis down not to save himself, because I'm sure your Priests made that impossible by binding him with silver, but to save you. I wonder, are you saved?"

"I..." he struggled. Her mental and physical touch were intense past any point of pleasure. "I am purified, forever grateful to Viis," he managed to say through blood tears.

"No, only promised to another deity. A better one, but I wonder if I can free you from your new faith?" The pressure in Lonen's mind doubled and redoubled until he was screaming and his vision turned red. Then, as quickly as it came, the sensation was gone. His ears still rang, blood trickled from his nose, and his head ached, but he was happy for the sudden relief. "I can't alter your mind," Razthanga said, surprised. "I could suggest anything, make you do what I like, except for harm yourself, but your beliefs can only be changed by your will, mine cannot influence you." She lowered her face to his. "With fortitude and dedication like that, you could be very powerful. You could someday defeat me," she whispered, in awe.

He had seen illusions before, and knew how to detect them. What he saw, watching her eyes, her lips, the subtle movements of her face as she spoke to him was no trick, she truly was the most beautiful creature he'd ever seen. "I could do anything to you and your will would remain unbroken. I've only met three men like you, two of them were great leaders. I had to kill those, but the third was an even greater man, and he was my master. I know you'll never serve me," she said, her lips so close they almost touched his. "But I will trade with you. You will tell King Nyder everything I have told you about his son, where his spirit is and that I have his body. Do you understand?"

"I understand, that is the price for my life," Lonen said. "I will tell him."

"No, I already told you, I'm not in the business of enraging Goddesses with so many followers, or with paragons among us. I have a sweeter gift for you." Her soft lips pressed against his gently. Her breath was sweet, as though she'd just eaten a cold peach. The delicious kiss lengthened as her hand stroked his cheek, and just as it felt as though she were about to lead him further into passion, she withdrew.

He was unable to move, and his mind felt muddied, but he was still in control of his thoughts. He was sure that if she wanted to,

Razthanga could suppress all but the most basic notions, as she did before. Imps whose skin was covered in red flame rushed past them. He could feel that they were her creatures, small beings that were enslaved by her and infused with the element of flame. They rushed towards the townsfolk and the people who were entering the town behind him, escaping Highshield City. The imps carried short, broad bladed daggers that dug at their victim's eyes, cut their purses, fingers and necklaces so they could be gathered. Humans and others who were enthralled by Razthanga were doing the same until the imps got to them, then they were stabbed, cut and slashed, their wealth taken.

Lonen's armour and clothing fell from him as though the straps, buckles and cloth were rotten through, and he realized that the scars on his thighs, chest and arms were gone. His arms were free to move then, and he touched his face. His nose was restored; the scars were healed. "I have given you new flesh, Lonen. I hope you enjoy it. If you ever oppose me, I will take it back." Razthanga drifted up several feet into the air and regarded him with a playful smile. "Now, run!"

Lonen found himself powerless to resist her command, and ran through the streets on bare feet. By the time he was through Wattis, it felt like the bottoms of his feet were bloody pulps, cut by sharp stones, glass, and burned by cinders. He still couldn't stop once he was past the town's limits, and followed the road onward, unable to change his course or to think of much else.

The sun began to set, his feet were ruined, every step was agony, and then his toes touched the water of the Hurien River and he fell in. Lonen emerged, sputtering. He was back in control of himself, but exhausted. The cool water stung on his ruined feet, but it was also an incredible relief. He wasn't strong enough to make an attempt at using healing magic, so he left his feet in the water as he sat back on the bank amongst the cattails. He fell asleep and dreamt of a kiss beyond any he'd experienced or imagined.

a day's ride away from the river took them through the edge of a tilled field so large that they never saw anyone who worked it. All the children saw for the better part of that day was an expanse of black and brown soil ready for planting. Tadrin fell asleep in the saddle where he sat in front of Rendiran, bored after hearing the explanation behind the featureless land. As soon as he heard that the land was being prepared for another planting, and his eyes couldn't find something new and interesting to focus on, his head began to loll back onto Rendiran's chest. It wasn't long before he was so deeply asleep that he would snore from time to time.

The ride gave Rendiran a lot of time to think. The boy was reserving questions, he was sure. Tadrin held Rendiran's incomplete hand even in his slumber. He was sure the boy would ask about it eventually, and he didn't know what to tell him. The real answer sounded mysterious and could be frightening; that he lost his fingers in an explosion, then couldn't regenerate them because his hand's new shape felt natural after using it to channel so much magic. The problem was that in his experience, the longer children with Tadrin's intelligence thought about a question, the more probing and difficult to answer it would be.

He could simplify the whole notion into a lesson. Magic came at a cost, especially when you tried to combine divine power with vulgar magic. Vulgar, or human magic as most people called it, was the easiest type of magic to use, but the most costly for the user. Combining it with divine magic made it even more difficult to balance, and he paid the price. Knowing how these things worked in theory and actually putting them into practice were completely different.

That was the new challenge before him. For years he was a young priest who healed people, studied the art of treating the wounded and in all his spare time he studied history, other types of magic and looked for answers to the deeper mysteries. That was the constant, even when his mentors changed, they still helped him pursue the same things. The nature of his progress rarely changed, and the amount of progress he made astonished many of his teachers.

A few trips outside the Temple and Highshield City provided a few breaks, and Crista's visits were disruptive in all the right ways. She was more knowledgeable about the world past Highshield wall in the north than most, and every time they had the opportunity to sit and talk over a meal he found new questions. Questions that led him to the library, to his teachers, or to a mentor. All along, none of them warned him that he would find new paths to power once he was out from under the protection of the Miradu Temple. It was true, he'd never been away from the wards, the controls and protections that the church offered, and it never occurred to him that they were a hindrance.

Outside of their protection he discovered the wealth of power that awaited him, and it wasn't as frightening as it ought to be. It was exciting. He could see the draw of the dark ways, the paths that led to incredible power but also corruption, the temptation to take life's essence to fuel acts of malice. When he twisted the flesh of others, it was in defense of children and those he felt were fighting for the light. He could already feel the guilt fading, but he would never forget how easy it was to kill things that didn't have protection against his power. He would find more responsible ways, less destructive ways to defeat beings who sought to interfere with him and anyone he protected. He would also find ways to passively protect himself, whether it was like the symbols tattooed on Marjay's arms and shoulders, or through a charm he could take off when necessary. Either way, he would find a way to protect himself without limiting his power. Rendiran knew he could accomplish so much good, learn so much more if he kept using his abilities. He needed to learn subtlety and balance, but Rendiran knew he already had the most important thing: a moral code that would keep him from the dark ways.

It was only when they topped the rise that Rendiran realized that the whole field they rode alongside was on a slight incline. When they did, the wall spanning the God Spine and Kol's Horn Mountains came into view. "Highshield," Marjay said, pointing the tall white and grey wall out to Oria. "Isn't that a sight?"

"How tall is it?" Tadrin asked sleepily.

"Most of its only thirty-five feet or so," Rendiran said. "If twelve children your height stood on each other's shoulders, then the last one could crawl on top." He pointed to the right, where it disappeared to the south. "It meets with the cliffs there, and there are a few blocked passes to the south where the mountains aren't dense enough to stop things from coming from the wild lands."

"How long is it?" Tadrin asked, his brow was furrowed, a sign that he was only beginning to understand what he needed to about the Highshield wall.

Rendiran mentally disposed of the complications surrounding that question, there were debates about how long it actually was. Should the measurement include the outer segments? Should keeps built into the wall be excluded from the total? There were other questions and sources of debates that not even he had patience for. "It's about seven hundred miles, and they're still working on it," he replied.

"That's big," Tadrin said. "I walked four miles with my dad once, it took a long time."

"You wouldn't want to walk the whole wall," Marjay said. "But there are people who do."

"Why?" Oria asked from where she stood in front of Marjay on his saddle. He provided stability by holding the back of her shirt.

"There's a lot of history behind the wall," Rendiran said. "Some of it is difficult to believe unless you see the places where memorable things took place."

"Like the Blackamber Keep, where evil wizards and monstrous things are kept in tiny cells," Marjay said. "It's built right into the wall, and the masters there keep their prisoners weak by drawing on their magic, creating blackened amber, a terrible ooze that only a few people touched by the light can purify."

"No," Oria said, shaking her head. "That's not real."

"It is," Rendiran said. He knew parts of the story Marjay didn't, or that he left out. There were the Narrow Cells, where Ava-Ondi and Ondi-Ne with great magical power were kept in spaces that were so small that they couldn't turn left or right, they were fed and watered from above, and they were bound in enchanted silver. None of them could access their power, and the space they were slotted into didn't allow them to sit, or even kneel, but to spend all their days standing or leaning. Madness was said to come quickly for many in the Narrow Cells, Rendiran had nightmares about them when he was a boy after seeing a drawing of them and reading a short description in a book. He blamed a persistent fear of dark, small spaces that followed him on those drawings. He decided not to tell the children about them. "It is true that there are terrible things kept in Black-amber Keep, but Marjay is being a little over dramatic. Nothing in that keep can use their power. The protections and practices keep everything inside, isolated from the rest of the world, unable to so much as cast their gaze in this direction. The people who take care of Blackamber Keep and what's inside know much more about magic and how to keep it under control than I do."

"That's a lot," Tadrin said, looking up at Rendiran. "Right?"

"Oh, so much. More than I could ever learn. Not only that, but all along the wall there are lords with keeps and castles built right in. They protect everyone to the west of the wall from anything from the wilds that would harm us, that includes Blackamber

Keep. They take their posts willingly because there are riches in the Eastern Wilds. The Lords of the Wall hire guides who take them on expeditions to undiscovered places where they hope to find riches."

"Crista's a guide?" Tadrin asked. He squirmed and got a foot under him, so he could stand in front of him. Rendiran looked at Marjay and how he was balancing Oria, and did the same.

"Yes she is," Rendiran answered.

"Where is she?"

"She'll be back soon."

"Irekirk spent most of his life in the wilds," Tadrin said. "He brought treasure and magic back from abandoned dragon hoards and found old temples to steal from."

"The best thing was the Jade Mother. There was a diamond inside that paid for most of the Temple's main hall," Oria added.

Marjay regarded Rendiran with an expression between interest and worry. "Have you two been dreaming about Irekirk?" Rendiran asked.

"Only a few nights. It's been boring mostly. He argued with King Jouris a lot, but made him agree to give his temple some land to control. I like when he goes treasure hunting though," Tadrin said.

"Did you know that King Jouris was the first to fully support the Miradu Temple? Without him, it wouldn't have been founded," Rendiran said.

Oria sputtered, rejecting the idea completely. "Sure it would. Irekirk was talking to Queen Izra and a lot of lords. Lots of people loved Miradu and her kids, they just weren't sure about Irekirk, and there some of them thought Wydu was still alive. They were afraid of him."

In everything he read, Rendiran had never seen anything that confirmed what the children were saying, but he found no reason to doubt them. He wondered how much was buried in the Origin Gospels or the other books that were forbidden to all but the highest members of the church.

"I like the dwarves, especially Princess Nussa," Oria said.

Tadrin nodded. "Jabnin is my favourite dwarf," he replied. "I like how he always wants to make her laugh."

"Have you seen them building the temple?" Marjay asked, a well pointed question since those dwarves were credited for building or at least guiding the construction of the oldest sections.

"Princess Nussa made a statue of Monder, making a copy of him out of stone just as he started laughing," Oria replied. Rendiran knew the statue, it was one of his favourites.

"That was funny," Tadrin agreed.

"They were friends with Irekirk, but he never let them come on any of his adventures, he told them their dad the King wouldn't like it. They spent a lot of his money though."

"Building the temple?" Rendiran asked.

"Well, yeah," Tadrin said. The children looked across the greener landscape ahead quietly for several moments. With the broad Hurien River far to the left, the mountain ranges ahead, Highshield Wall, and the thickening forest ahead there was plenty to see. "But they drank a lot too," Tadrin added.

"Oh, yeah, they were drunk a lot while everyone else worked," Oria said. "Princess Nussa spent a lot on dancing girls too."

"Well, that explains why she never married," Marjay said.

"Oh, she didn't like boys," Oria said. "Except for her cousins and Irekirk. She didn't like it when one tried to kiss her."

Tadrin shook his head emphatically agreeing. "Not at all."

"Did you know any of this stuff?" Marjay asked in a whisper.

"The basics, but not what we just heard," he replied. "I'm just wondering," he said to Tadrin. "How old is Irekirk in your latest dreams?"

"Grey hair old, and he uses magic a lot now," Tadrin replied.

"So Miradu has worshippers and the temple's almost finished?"

"Almost finished, there's only one tower though. A lot of the dwarves are leaving because they don't like how the humans are being treated while Irekirk is away. Most of them are slaves, it's bad."

"Humans didn't become truly free for centuries after that," Rendiran said. "Now only people who fall into debt become slaves."

"And Ondi people," Tadrin said.

"Not in this province, but, yes, in Brightwill there are a lot of Ondi slaves," Rendiran agreed.

Crista emerged from a thick stand of trees, smiling. Ander was close behind, after a stick in her hand. "We're close to the crossing," she said as she ran closer, teasing the dog then finally tossing the branch so Ander could fetch it. Rendiran couldn't help but notice how lovely the brown and red haired woman was. It wasn't the first time. He'd never seen someone so vibrant, adventurous or interesting. Her gaze met his and Rendiran looked away, but not before he noticed her glance at Marjay.

"Come down so you can get the stick back from Ander," she said to Oria and Tadrin. "He doesn't understand the second half of fetch yet, so you'll have to get it back from him so we can throw it." Ander watched everyone closely, his prized stick in his jaws, ready to dash away the moment anyone approached.

Marjay lowered Oria to the ground easily, but Rendiran was far more cautious and less experienced on horseback, so it took him a few moments to figure out a way where he lowered Tadrin without dismounting first himself. The former guardsman made it look so easy.

Rendiran didn't realize how sore he was until he dismounted, but walking around felt good.

A strange glimmer of light, as though the sunshine around Crista was bending and spinning nearly invisible rainbow colours around her, caught Rendiran's eye. Both the horses calmly approached her, and Haffor's mare lowered its head as though she was about to say something to her. "Are you sure? It's a long way," Crista said to her as she stroked the horse's cheek and fed it an apple. The aura around her faded as the brown steed Marjay rode there nuzzled her shoulder. Crista smiled at it and gave him an apple as well. "If you're sure, I can't blame you," she said. Turning to Rendiran, she smiled and told him; "The horses are going to make the journey home from here, they aren't going into the Wandering Wood with us. Do'lii has been there before with Haffor and she doesn't want to go back. She'll protect Blackhoof on the way to Forge Hin."

"All the way there?" Marjay asked.

"Do'lii isn't a normal horse, she was with Haffor for seventeen years, and needs time to grieve. She's found her way home across greater distances. Blackhoof is staying with her, which is pretty normal. He's young and likes her a lot more than his former masters. We should feed them while we break here for a while, then take our supplies and let them go."

"Unsaddle them as well?" Marjay asked as he started unloading Blackhoof. "I hope he makes it, he's a good horse."

"A paladin's horse carries blessings and enchantments that grow more powerful as they age," Crista said. "The same goes for their dogs, or their messenger birds if they have them. Most paladin companions die at an old age in their sleep, not in combat, but they carry a wealth of stories." Do'lii nuzzled Crista playfully, nearly knocking her over. She scratched under her chin before moving to untie the horse's feed bag.

Rendiran helped her, and they laid the large sack of feed on the ground. "They'll feed for a while, then start their journey to Forge Hin, grazing as they go," Crista said. "Once they pass the border into Tuur Hin they shouldn't run into many people. Chances are they'll be found by a dwarven Merchant Guardsman once they get closer to the major cities, and they'll recognize that Do'lii is an important horse so they'll bring it to Forge Hin for a reward."

"Isn't there a chance they'll be stolen?" Marjay asked low enough so the children, who were fighting with Ander for his stick, couldn't hear.

"I pity anyone who tries to steal her or Blackhoof. No, they'll be fine, don't worry," Crista said.

Rendiran watched as both horses rooted through their feed bags for the tastiest bits. The sun was setting as the children finished playing with Ander. They could tell something unusual was happening, since the horses were being unsaddled, freed of all tack and barding. "The horses are going home," Crista told them.

"We'll see them in a while, when we get to Forge Hin. Say goodbye."

Do'lii lowered her head so both children could pet her for a moment, then whinnied, took several steps back and reared up as though she was showing off, kicking the air with her great hooves. She was a beautiful white mare, Rendiran had rarely seen a finer horse, not that he was an expert. Her hooves came down, and she trotted away, Blackhoof following her. "They'll cross the river then run between towns until they reach Tuur Hin's border forest."

"Bye!" the children called after them.

Rendiran loaded a saddlebag over his shoulder and made sure he wasn't leaving anything important behind. "We have all this jerky and meal bread here," he said, looking through the last saddlebag.

"C'mon, kids, fill your pockets with jerky, then give a few pieces to Ander," Crista told them. They dug in, looting the large bags, filling their pockets with jerky and dried fruit. Crista topped her backpack up, and there was still a few days' worth of food left. Rendiran and Marjay took a meal's worth in their hands, starting their dinner early as the children took turns stuffing Ander with jerky. "Not too fast, or he'll cough it back up," Crista said.

There wasn't much left once they were all finished eating, but Crista left the bags open so nearby wildlife could take the rest. Once they were finished, she took Tadrin's hand. "Okay, we make a chain. Take Rendiran's hand," she told him. "Now, Oria, you'll take Rendiran and Marjay's hands, okay?"

The children were between them a moment later. "What about Ander?"

"He has a decision to make," Crista said, kneeling down and making a clicking noise once that caught the pup's attention immediately. He was nose to nose with her a moment later. Once again Rendiran saw a circle of warped air around her that caught the light in flecks of rainbow colour. "You could get lost or into trouble where we're going, Ander," she said to him. There was more going on, Rendiran could sense it. Ander was speaking to her in simple terms. He wanted to play, could smell the horses and was tempted to follow, was happy and full, and he wanted to keep filling his nose with the scents of the children – his fellow pups – and the adults around them.

Then, as a flash of thought, as though he was discovering a memory, a mental image appeared in his mind. A thick green forest with large leaves, the sounds of chittering, squawking creatures, and large things moving in the distant underbrush. The whole place was aggressively alive, growing at a rate that was menacing. There were scents and sights to discover everywhere, but just as much danger and nothing to eat for miles.

Ander whined and retreated a few steps, and Rendiran realized that he had in some way caught a mental image that Crista sent to the dog. She followed it up with another that outlined a journey where he followed the horses through fields, forests, running through towns, across two rivers, then to Forge Hin, where a great city with tall walls and a turreted stone gatehouse awaited. There wasn't much good food on this journey, but she left the distinct impression that he could find rabbits, mice, bugs, and other meals of opportunity along the way. Even still, Crista made it clear that there would be times of hunger too. To Rendiran's surprise, Ander ran to Marjay, the largest of them, and leapt at him.

Marjay caught him in his arm and laughed as the pup half crawled onto his shoulder so his weight could be better supported. "I guess he's going with us?" Marjay asked.

"If you think you can carry him, he's getting bigger by the day," Crista said.

"He's still a puppy to me," Marjay said as one side of his face was bathed by Ander's tongue.

35

---

*L*onen woke to the crackling of a modest campfire, and the smell of sizzling fish. He was wrapped in thick linens, laying on the ground with no recollection of how he'd gotten there. "I tried to bind your feet, but my healing powers are gone, I'm afraid," said a female voice he didn't recognize. He was upright and half out of his covers in a heartbeat.

She sat calmly in white and black robes that showed significant wear. It looked as though she'd seen as much fire and destruction as he had in the capitol city, but she was definitely better composed. A silver ring caught the moonlight as she ran a comb through her hair. The little firelight cast enough illumination for him to see that she was pretty, very pretty. "I've tested my luck too many times with beautiful women lately," he said, looking for something to wear.

"You think I'm beautiful? That's kind, thank you," she said. "There are some clothes there, but no shoes, sorry."

He snatched a tunic from a pile beside him. His feet stung, but seemed better than before. Lonen decided not to test them just yet. "Who did you steal these from, or did you strip a corpse?"

"I didn't expect one of the best young Lucent Paladins in service to the Bright One to be ungrateful or insulting," she said. "I bought them from a woman named Garicia in Lord Hill. I told her I was helping a knight who was nearly killed and she was happy to sell them to me."

"I apologize, it's been a difficult time, and my luck has been poor."

"I saw. You faced Razthanga and she let you go. Not without marking you forever, but she let you live, that's good luck, if you ask me. I almost lost myself in her song, and I was much further away."

"Were you caught there while fleeing from Highshield?"

"No, I was hoping to become Razthanga's apprentice. I renounced my God, now I only have the magic of my family."

"Which God?"

"Wydu, the Trickster. He had me convinced that I was one of his chosen, and I used every trick and spell I had to do his bidding. Now I count the death of one good man, another who is most likely dead, and I'm discarded by my own order as they take their places in the temple. Wydu's brat turned on me and now I'm cast out."

"So, Miradu, Viis and Irenick have no place in their own temple now?" Lonen asked.

"None, their shrines are covered with black sail cloth. Wydu will have a new shrine in the front of the temple. Only the Dwarven lands will praise those three, and I know their eyes won't turn my way. Regardless, I go north to put some distance between me and Highshield City, just in case that brat convinces someone that I should be hunted. You never know with that one."

"Which brat?"

"Nella, the Gift of Wydu. He saw that Irenick and Viis were about to bring their gifts into the world and, not to be left out, he sent me visions, pointed me to old prophecies that fit just enough, and sent me to go fetch a dead thing from the worst mountain hold I could have dreamt of. Who knows what I actually brought up? It could have been a thing he caught in the void that has no business in this world. I don't know, but now I have a story that the Dwarves may want to hear, since they praise Miradu in the old ways. They won't change, Wydu won't find a place to grow his power in Forge Hin. Maybe my story will earn me a meal, or a bed outside their walls. It's still safer than this province."

"Who are you?" Lonen asked, astonished by her story. He had seen a Thanga at work, been touched by a Goddess, and watched one of the greatest paladins in history die. If she was telling the truth, that she was the one who delivered Wydu's Gift to the Temple and began its corruption, he was next to yet another amazing and potentially dangerous person of significance. He was learning how mixed his fortune became as that sort of thing happened, and he wondered if he should throw himself into the river. Ending his journey by drowning may be mercy compared to what was ahead.

"I'm Lena, formerly of the Order of Wydu. My mother was Epheria, a Shadowsong."

"I'm sorry about what happened to your man, I wasn't there," Lonen said.

"I know, the Paladins didn't have anything to do with what happened at the Inn. Do you know if he survived?"

"He didn't. They finished him when they were sure he knew nothing," he replied.

"I wish I had handed that little girl over to your people. She would have twisted the Bright One's followers up until they didn't know light from dark," Lena said.

"They're not my people anymore," Lonen said as he started to put on the linen trousers. He was still amazed at how all the scars were gone from his chest, his arms, his and his legs. He was quietly eager to see his own reflection, but that could wait. He was starving. "I've been cleansed by Viis," he said. "So if you're here to trick me, to get revenge for your friend, I'm afraid I'm poor prey."

"No, I'm not here for revenge. I could tell you were Viis' creature when you confronted Razthanga. It was confusing, but unmistakable. I am here because I've seen you standing in front of the Dwarven King. In my vision you're presenting him with a ring, but I found none on you, or around you."

"I hid it very well," Lonen said. "It should make an appearance sometime tomorrow morning."

"Oh?" Lena asked. "Did you use some kind of magic or..." her inquisitive expression turned to one of realization then. "Oh! You..." she mimed the act of tossing a small object into her mouth and swallowing.

"I saw no other sure way," he said with a shrug.

"Good thing Viis was protecting you," Lena said, chuckling darkly. "Razthanga was in that town to collect wealth, she would have gutted you for that ring if she knew it was there."

"I didn't think of that," Lonen said.

"Well, your luck truly is enviable," Lena said. "Maybe I can curry enough favour with Viis to become a healer."

"How? You have my gratitude for this," Lonen said as he sat up and looked at his bound feet. The bandages looked fresh and clean, but he wanted to see what was underneath.

"You don't know my family's reputation, do you?" Lena asked.

Lonen shook his head as he gently started to pull at the bandages. The bottoms of his feet were still absolutely raw, he expected the skin was worn through.

"The women in my family have been seers for generations going back to the first age. My mother learned to shadow walk from Coriath when she was young, do you know what that is?"

"I've never heard of it, if I'm being honest," Lonen said, giving up on the bandages, deciding to eat first. There were two plump bass over the fire that looked ready to eat.

"I used to pretend that Wydu gave me the gift, so I didn't have to teach it to other people in the Order. He did help me when I did it, but I never needed Him to use the shadows to move here and there. I can move through any place absent light faster than any fish can through water. With concentration, I can take people with me."

"They call that shade walking where I came from, but I never met anyone who could do it."

"Now you have," Lena said. "Moments before dawn's arrival, I'll take you into the turning shadows that exist as light embraces this land, and in mere moments we'll be in Forge Hin. Travelling along the edge of morning or edge of night are the fastest ways to travel for people with my skill. There's only one problem, and I'm sure you can guess it."

"You can only go north or south?" he asked.

"Yes, exactly. You are smarter than you look," Lena said. "I'm starting to see why Viis chose you."

"She chose me because Haffor the Paladin directed her to. I'm sure that is the only reason why," Lonen corrected.

"Then why didn't she abandon you yesterday? Gods don't have infinite power. It may seem like it to us, but they only have so much to share. There are wars in the High Heavens, in the Many Hells, and everywhere in-between. Viis and her family are gods of goodness and justice, they draw followers to them, but those causes cost more than most. Perhaps Haffor brought Her attention to you, but She stays with you for Her own reasons now. If I didn't believe that, I wouldn't be here."

"I hope you're right," Lonen said. "I've done horrible things in the name of Her enemies, so I don't deserve Her gaze, but I hope you're right."

"Let's find out," Lena said. "Concentrate on making your feet whole again. Imagine them as they were yesterday, or whenever they were as they ought to be."

"I'm no healer," Lonen said, looking at his bandaged feet. "And I'm hungry."

"Forget that for a moment, and close your eyes. Think of how thankful you are to Viis, how you'll serve her in the future. She doesn't trade favours for favours, but it may get her attention anyway. Believe that it's possible for your feet to be whole again, and concentrate on what that looks like."

He closed his eyes and tried to imagine that his feet would magically grow skin back, and that he could walk on them again, but he found himself easily distracted. Sometimes the face of Razthanga would interfere with his attempts at concentration. The smell of the fish, the thought of eating said fish were also distractions, he'd rarely been so hungry! Then he recalled a half shattered statue of Viis along one of Highshield's city streets, and he began to imagine her. Viis was strong, a powerful warrior, but even he knew that She protected the weak, assisted those in need, and served justice. The ideals of a true paladin were Hers, and he remembered what it was like to dream of becoming one as a child. Lonen wanted more than anything to be the personification of the mighty warrior of light who protected the weak. That desire led him astray when he was too young and naive to know better. The Lucent Priests came and promised that he would bring light to the world with them and before he could change his mind, the Bright One looked upon him, filling his being with love and light. When it was gone, there was nothing he wouldn't do to experience it again – to himself or to others – and his ambition to be a paladin of the light was forgotten.

The influence of the Bright One's gaze was gone, Viis had cleansed him of the need to have it shine on him. The memory of the boy who wanted to help everyone, to protect everyone was clear, and Lonen embraced it. He would be Viis' warrior, learn Her ways, become that paragon of truth and justice. Instead of imagining himself surrounded by light, he pictured himself in armour covered in thin white leather, emitting pure white illumination against an oppressive darkness. There were places in the world that needed to be cleansed, and he would be Her instrument there. He heard the creak and grind of metal armour behind him for a moment, and when he turned to look, it was gone. He stood and looked around. "Was there someone here?" he asked. There was no sign that anyone had stood behind him.

Lena was staring at him, shocked. "No, but you brightened the riverside for a moment," she whispered.

He realized he was on his feet then, and there was no pain. With haste Lonen pulled and kicked his bandages off. He laughed and danced as he saw that his feet were perfectly healed. Lena joined him, and for several moments they danced and spun around the fire, on soft meadow soil.

"Praise Viis! True light and goodness are yours!" he cheered. Something pricked his heel then, and he pulled his foot up so he could see what it was.

"Oh, no," Lena said as she came to look.

"Only a pointy stone," Lonen said as he flicked the little rock into the river. "My Lady's miracle hasn't been undone."

"Our Lady's miracle," Lena said as she sat on the stone across from the rough linens she'd wrapped him in. "I think I'll only give to Viis' shrine from now on. I've never heard of her betraying anyone, and I've always liked her. Sometimes more than her Mother, at least from what I see in the stories."

"You know a lot about Her?"

"Perhaps more than most. I know a lot about the entire pantheon, really, I learned to read using the gospels and the histories."

"Can you tell me about Viis? I know so little," Lonen said, eying the fish. "While we eat?"

"Both good ideas. Where shall I begin?" She stood up and took one of the thick branches holding a bass off the fire and laid it on a flat stone.

"What drew people to Miradu in the beginning?" he asked. "Why did people start worshipping her?"

"You really don't know anything, do you?" Lena asked in surprise.

"I wouldn't have asked if I did," Lonen replied.

"I'm sorry, I've known these stories for so long, I'm surprised when I find people who don't know them." She cut a piece of steaming fish off and put it on a piece of cloth, skin down, then gave it to him. "Just after the Ava-Ondi landed on these shores a thousand years ago, there was an Ondi-Ne village called Drian-Vol. Loosely translated, it means All Are Welcome. That included the Ava-Ondi, who visited them in the late spring one year, bringing human slaves. After using Drian-Vol as a base camp for exploration, the Ava-Ondi offered to use their magic to ensure a wealthy crop. Seeing no reason to refuse the offer, the village leaders let Sambri Nore and his wizards cast spells over the fields and the shore."

"They left soon after to return to Brightwill," Lena continued between mouthfuls of hot white fish flesh. "The crops rotted instead of ripened, and the fisher folk found less in their nets as the season went on. Before anyone could do anything about it with their own magic, snows came, and the Ondi-Ne only had what they could hunt. Their hunters found very little in their own lands, and had to go deep into the forests for game and their people began to starve. The Sambri Nore had cursed them instead of blessed them, hoping that they would die during the winter so they could return and take the village of Drian-Vol for themselves in the spring."

"I never trusted Ava-Ondi," Lonen said. "But then, I'm no expert in who might be trustworthy."

"Can I go on?" Lena asked.

"Please, thank you for all this fish, and everything, by the way."

"My pleasure," Lena said. "Anyway, they managed to make it all the way into mid-winter without anyone dying, but then an elder named Whur Gilinig passed, and they say he was praying to the sky until his dying breath. The Ondi-Ne Gods were not with them, it seemed. Things began to look even more dire then, because villagers saw a giant black dragon circling overhead the next day. Its scales seemed to drink in the light, shimmering with rainbow colours like the scales of a darker fish do when it's under water. For fourteen days the dragon would come and go, always circling well above arrow range, not that any arrows were loosed at it."

"Why not? I'd be terrified if a dragon were circling over our heads, if all I had were arrows, and there was no point in running, I'd shoot even if it seemed pointless."

"Really? Seems foolish to me."

"A good shot could frighten it off," Lonen said.

"Or make it angry," Lena retorted.

"You have a point."

"Well, one boy, Vinit, did point an arrow up, but his mother stopped him before he could loose. She asked him; 'what would you like the dragon to do about your arrow?' and when he realized that he didn't know, he put his bow away. The Ondi-Ne of Drian-Vol weren't a violent people, they had good lives before that winter, had kin in the forests and on the waters who visited them often. Their militia was only large enough to fend off the occasional threat from the deep forest, the times of warring tribes were well behind them. As a

peaceful people, they decided not to interfere with the dragon overhead, in fact, a few of them began to draw it, one even began to sculpt
it, but she passed one cold night, the chisel freezing to her hand.
Without knowing what to do, they consulted the records they had
about dragons, which told them that some would leave if they had an
offering. Erizi, the sculptor who passed became that offering. They
lashed her to the half-finished statue and put it on a wagon that they
pulled to the outskirts of the village. Through windows and cracked
doors, the villagers watched the dragon descend several hours later.

Its wings sent a storm of snow in all directions as it landed, and
when the white settled, they watched as the dragon gently touched
the unfinished statue. It recoiled as it realized that there was a frozen
Ondi-Ne tied to it, and then it made unusual sounds. The villagers
didn't know whether to be afraid or not until they saw a tear roll from
its eye. It melted the snow around the cart and brought forth a font of
light for a moment. Erizi, the elderly carver climbed from the cart,
alive and warm all the way through, and she watched as the dragon
took flight once more. 'She is good!' Erizi shouted as she clapped and
ran after the dragon until she was waist deep in the snow."

"They say old dragons used to have powerful magic," Lonen said.
"I always wanted to see it for myself. What happened next?"

"Well, the dragon was not seen for an entire day," Lena said.
"Some of the villagers began to think that the way they lashed Erizi to
her statue and offered her to the dragon may have offended it, so
some blame was cast on a few elders. As night fell, they heard the
dragon's wings again. They watched as the great beast left five great
moose and nine deer around the cart at the edge of the village, and
there was no doubt in anyone's mind that it was a good dragon,
despite its dark scales and long claws. They feasted that night,
knowing that what remained would get them through several weeks,
long enough for their hunters to catch up. The next morning all the
meat they stored was rotten, infected by the curse. The dragon
returned, and Erizi was the first to approach it. 'I'm sorry,' she said,
'the Ava-Ondi cursed us, and all the food you brought us has been
destroyed.'

Unsure whether or not the dragon understood, the villagers brought one of the deer carcasses to see, and after smelling the rotten meat, it sneered towards the shore, as if she knew where the foul curse came from. For the next few days, the dragon brought enough food for the villagers to eat until, on the nineteenth day since the first saw her, she didn't come at all. On the morning of the twenty-first-day people were starving again, but they woke to discover their tables warped under the weight of fresh food, their larders were full, and their smoking huts were brimming. A mountain of food for man and beast awaited them at the wagon along with a dark haired woman who had wrapped herself in old linens from a clothesline that was allowed to freeze. 'I can't break the curse on your people without finding the wizard who cast it, so I have transformed my body into this bounty, all except for this form,' she told them. In transformation magic, a thing must shed extra matter if it becomes something smaller, like a duck into a frog. Normally that's a somewhat ugly process, with piles of flesh and bone being left behind. Miradu was a master of transformation, so much so that she could turn the dragon flesh she discarded when she became an Ondi-Ne woman into the kind of foods she'd seen their people eat. Becoming an Ondi-Ne woman was an incredible risk for her, because she didn't know the language very well, and she was far more fortified as a dragon. The food she created lasted well into summer, the curse was not able to touch it. Those are Miradu's first two miracles, the resurrection of Erizi, and the bounty. These stories are retold during Revelation, in the winter every year."

"What did she do when she had to turn back into a dragon?" Lonen asked, asked.

"She went into the mountains, where she used stone and earth to become a dragon once more. I know your next question; 'did the Ava-Ondi return?' They did, in mid-summer. The encounter between Sambri Nore and Miradu was disappointingly short. She brought Ondi-Ne warriors from her hills, dwarves from even further north, all of whom she armoured in ancient garb, and they attacked the ships once they anchored off shore. Miradu cracked Samri Nore's back in her teeth, then carried him deep into the water, where he drowned. This was to ensure that he could never be resurrected, she took his head to another shore that no man or Ondi has found. When she returned, the ships filled with human slaves were freed and the settling of the first humans in Highshield began. For a century there was no slavery here, and Miradu went on to have children who joined her in the quest to keep this shore, then called Inerese, free of slavery and darkness. Ava-Ondi came in that time, but they did so knowing that there could be no slavery or necromancy. That's how it began."

"But modern history teaches us that Miradu was only here for a short time, that the kings of Brightwill were able to force the settlement of other religions right away, during that century."

"Humans record the history they wish was true, I'm not saying that Ondi are any better, but they do live longer when you let them," Lena said. "I don't think anything a human touched from that age can be trusted, same with Ava-Ondi, now that I think of it."

"History is recorded politically," he said. "Now I think I understand what that means. You said you had stories about Viis?"

Lena smiled and cut another piece of fish for herself. "Enough to take us through the night, but I have to finish eating and get some rest, otherwise we could end up somewhere in the northern sea instead of Forge Hin."

36

"Now, every crossing is different at first, and this is an old doorway, so you might see some scary things," Crista said. The wording was for the children's benefit, but the warning was for everyone. "Whatever you do, don't let go of our hands," she told them.

Tadrin squeezed Rendiran's hand and looked to up at him to find him smiling back reassuringly. "Okay, I won't let go," Tadrin said.

"Me neither," Oria said, not to be outdone.

Crista led them several steps across the grass, they followed in a chain behind her until she stopped. "Sky, stone, and water were once all one in fire, in one place, at one time." Rendiran watched as the world around Crista began to twist and shift. "The world remembers that moment before creation, when all was one. From that holy fire, I summon a portal crossing of stone and air."

Rendiran felt the breath leave him as he was drawn into another place. The warmth of the evening was gone, the soft grass under his feet became hard crushed stone and the clear air filled with thick, cold fog that swirled around them. They were all still there, holding hands. All sound was muffled, as though someone stuffed moss in his ears. Crista gently pulled them across the gravel, kicking up dust that moved as though it was in water. The staff strapped the Rendiran's back felt heavy, and the large gemstone in the middle glowed with a pure white light.

A hand touched and pulled at his and Oria's from behind them, and when he turned it disappeared back into the darkness. Another yanked at his and Tadrin's, but they held fast. When Rendiran turned to see the assailant, he saw a creature that was gaunt, with pale skin stretched across too much bone, eyes that had many black-mirror like facets. The mouth was a thin slit that split the bottom half of its face. It opened revealing teeth that were more like claws that were made to to pierce and draw flesh in.

Before he could react, it withdrew, disappearing into the thick mist. They followed Crista, silently beginning to choke on the fine grit in the air. Tadrin and Oria were surprisingly brave, with worried expressions, and tight grips on Rendiran's hands, but they soldiered on without tears or panic. He missed the toes on his right foot, or his staff at the very least, but he was limping along fast enough to keep place.

They stopped suddenly, and after a moment, Rendiran saw why. Crista halted a few steps away from a cliff's edge. A strong wind moved through that crevasse that moved the mist like a river of smoke. Rendiran could see that the bottom was hundreds of feet down, and there was something, or many things, moving down there.

Crista turned and began to lead the group away from the edge. Tadrin and Oria were coughing, and Rendiran became aware that his eyes wanted to close as though he hadn't slept in days. A glimpse to the right revealed that Ander was already asleep, his head hanging down over Marjay's shoulder.

Tadrin fell next, his legs losing strength as his eyes closed, then Oria. Rendiran didn't let go of either of them. "What can I do?" Rendiran asked, the sound of his words seemed to die only a few feet from his face.

"Your magic will attract the hungry," Crista shouted back, her words barely audible. "I don't know how we got here." He could see fear in her expression, and that she was struggling to remain awake.

They both noticed a shape in the distance, too robust to be one of the hungry creatures he'd seen but still thin, and Crista smiled. "Guide, you are welcome. Guide you are needed!" she shouted.

A young man with a grim expression came into view. He was human, but short. Some of his shoulder length hair had been burned away, revealing ravaged and healed scalp. He was missing his right arm up to the elbow, and used a walking stick. His piercing blue eyes looked each of them over quickly and he nodded. With surprising grace he spun his walking stick, followed its momentum into a whirling dance, then etched a line in the loose stones at their feet, drew a circle above it, and stepped forward. Crista followed, dragging Tadrin, who was limp, behind her, then Rendiran, Oria who was also asleep and only held up by the grip of the adults on either side, and finally Marjay, who had lost Ander.

They emerged in a thick jungle exactly like the one Crista recalled for the dog earlier. Their Guide looked them over and, realizing that something was missing, then rushed back through the opening he'd made. A moment later he emerged, dragging Ander. "I'm sorry, I dropped him when I fell to my knees for a moment. I couldn't pick him up," Marjay said as the Guide laid the dog down in front of him. He checked to make sure the small blonde pup was still breathing and smiled, petting it gently before standing up. The smile disappeared as he regarded Crista and sighed.

In the golden light and heavy air of the jungle, Rendiran saw more of the Guide's ailments. He was losing sight in one eye, it looked like it had been scratched at one point, and his jaw was healed unevenly on one side. He looked to Tadrin and extended his senses into his body to find that the boy was generally fine, but there was something causing trouble in his lungs. Without delay, he picked him up and threw him over his shoulder, patting his back and forcing him to cough with a simple healing spell. "Do the same for Oria, Marjay," he told him.

After a moment the children were both coughing and retching yellow-grey dust laden spittle onto the ground. When Rendiran put Tadrin down, and Marjay did the same, the pair were wiping their eyes to clear the dust and involuntary tears, but they were fine. "I don't wanna go back there," Tadrin croaked.

"Maybe a little help here, too?" Marjay said, coughing.

Rendiran cast the same simple healing spell on him, and he leaned over coughing. He did the same for Ander, who retched more quietly, waking suddenly. A tug on his robe prompted him to face their Guide, who was smiling at him with interest. With his badly healed jaw, the grin seemed jagged. He coughed a little and ran his hand down his throat. "You want this too? It's a simple spell that clears the lungs, not pleasant but helpful."

The Guide nodded emphatically. "Me too," Crista said, raising her hand. "I still feel like I'm fighting a century sleep."

"All three of us then," he looked to Tadrin, who was wide awake and worried. "Don't worry, we're fine now, and we all just need to do a bit of dusting down there. It's..." Rendiran coughed, his chest rattling with a breath and another cough, "It's not pretty, but we'll all be fine."

"Okay," Tadrin said.

A moment later, under Rendiran's magical urging, he, their Guide and Crista were all coughing and spitting. The Guide had it the worst, as he doubled up and retched a bucket's worth of black into the thick bush beside the trail. When they were finished a few moments later, Rendiran put his hand on Tadrin's head and smiled at him. "Better now, see?"

"I know," he replied.

"Do we have to go back there again?" Oria asked.

"We weren't supposed to arrive in that place at all," Crista said. "I'm sorry, I thought the edge of the Wandering Wood was a lot closer."

The Guide patted her arm and shook his head. "The Wood moves fast now," he croaked. "A future found its way between, you didn't know how to avoid it."

"That was a future place? What do you mean?" Rendiran asked, alarmed. He didn't know much about portal travel, but there were more theoretical books on seeing through time and travelling to the future than he could have read in a lifetime, so he knew something about that. "Was that the future of that field? In the province we came from?"

The Guide nodded and held up one weathered finger. "Only one, but we see it more now."

"That's something to ponder," Rendiran said.

"Or forget as quickly as I can," Marjay retorted. "If we don't have to go back there, then I'd rather not dwell on it."

"We won't, don't worry," Crista said. "My Great Aunt will summon the next portal. She's been doing this for countless years. We'll be in dwarven lands by morning, most likely in Forge Hin. She'll be happy to offer you her hospitality," she said to the Guide. "I know she has spent some time as a Guide as well, you probably already know her."

"Master of the Amberstone?" he asked, struggling with the words.

"Yes, Mistress Erriyane, she's my Great Aunt."

He nodded happily and started to turn towards the narrow jungle path.

"One moment," Rendiran said, patting the man on the shoulder. He was definitely malnourished, in need of rest at the very least. "Do you mind if I take a good look at you? I think I can help."

The Guide looked to Rendiran, then to Crista. "He's one of the best healers I've ever met, Niomer. I was hoping we'd see you so he could check on you."

Niomer the Guide took Rendiran's half ruined hand in his and kissed the back of it.

"It's the least I could do," Rendiran said. "Just stand there a moment." He closed his eyes and expanded his senses, feeling Oria, Tadrin, Marjay, Crista, and Ander's forms. They were all in good condition, especially Ander, who had somehow bounced back with enthusiasm. Then he embraced Niomer with his senses and shuddered.

His heart barely beat, his stomach hadn't seen good food for months, and there were improperly healed breaks in one leg, the top of his skull, his jaw, and his remaining arm. Niomer the Guide was currently nursing two broken ribs, and hosting a few parasites that had no business in a human body. Much of the lasting damage was thanks to a bad healer. With only a little work, he discovered that Niomer himself had done most of the patching and mending, it was quick, untrained work. His slow heartbeat and overall low vitality was thanks to a self-inflicted enchantment. There was a lot Rendiran could do to correct the damage, but it would take great concentration. "I can correct all your ailments today, except for the arm. That would take more time if I can at all," Rendiran told him. "I am concerned about an enchantment you placed on yourself. Your heartbeat is dangerously low. I initially had the sense that you were near death." Tadrin and Oria looked at him, shocked and concerned. "But I was wrong, he's all right, he's all right," Rendiran said urgently.

"That's an enchantment a lot of Guides use to hide from nastier things in the other realms," Crista said. "It keeps them from being detected right away."

"Ah," Rendiran said. "Maybe you should take a break for a while, Niomer. Some sun and good food would do wonders for you once I've finished healing you."

Niomer only shrugged and gestured for them to follow him down the path. Rendiran met many craftspeople, warriors, and other dedicated folk who loved what they did so much, or saw its importance so clearly, that you could not stop them from working, even for a short, much needed rest. He got that sense from Niomer the Guide, and couldn't help but admire him for following his calling with such dedication.

37

*L*onen Kerd planted his feet on the grey stone walk in front of the gates of Forge Hin with relief. Lena was true to her word, transporting them across hundreds of miles in moments. In his disorientation during the journey he glimpsed sections of grasslands and shoreline, even the inside of someone's house while an old woman and man ate their porridge. Somehow, he could have sworn the land they passed over was curved, as though the world wasn't a flat plane, but a massive round ball. Looking at the second moon in the sky as it was fading, the notion made sense. If the moons were round, why not the world?

"Are you all right?" Lena asked.

He made sure that he had both his arms and his head was still correctly placed on his shoulders. "I'm well, thank you."

"Ho, there!" shouted a guard with an emblem on his chest that was half shield, and half coin. He wore leather armour with shining metal plates. The other guards, dressed in full plate holding pikes, watched with interest. There were ten of them, five powerfully built dwarves at either side of the broad gate leading into the city of Forge Hin.

Lena looked to the lesser armed guard as he approached. "Good morning, Merchant Guard, and three blessings to you."

"Three blessings to you, Miss. I hope you don't think me too direct in asking, but did you just appear out of thin air?" the dwarf asked.

"After a fashion," Lena said. "Are you available for hire today, Sir?"

"So happens I am, first one here, best one here. Barham's the name, Merchant Guard with a map in my head of this whole province."

"Good to meet you," Lena said, offering her hand. It wasn't empty, Lonen saw silver pieces in her palm. "I'm Lena, this is my friend, Lonen. We have come to request an audience with his Majesty the King."

"Well, I can't guarantee an audience, but I'm known by the Regent Council and the Seneschal so you have a fair chance of it with me. What's your business?" the dwarf didn't look at the coins directly, put dropped them into a pouch he kept tucked under his thick belt with an audible clink-clink-clink.

"I have news from Highshield City about his son, Haffor the Paladin," Lonen said. "And she has news from the Miradu Temple."

"Then I'm overpaid," Barham said. "I'm sure you'll be seen as soon as the throne room doors open. Come, stay close and let me do the talking unless you're addressed directly."

"Thank you, Barham," Lena said.

"Are there a lot of Merchant Guardsmen in Forge Hin?" Lonen asked Lena quietly. "And can we trust them?"

"It's an honorable profession across the dwarven lands," she replied. "They're some of the few people we can trust."

"Only one master at a time," Barham said over his shoulder. "And we protect our master as long as they're not acting against the crown or the innocent until we've earned our fee. Those are the rules that guide us. We're mercenaries, but with more honour than most."

"What if someone hires you after us and wants to know our business?" Lonen asked.

"I won't take offense to that, since you're foreign here, but any Merchant Guard worth a copper will keep your business private. That's not to say that we won't use what we know to help other folks, but when we tell them not to go to a place, or to avoid mentioning something because of a thing we heard in confidence, we won't tell them the details behind it. We won't tell them where it came from."

"I didn't mean to offend, it's just new to me. I heard of the dwarven Merchant Guard, but I've never met one."

"We're all across the province, I'm surprised you haven't run into us before," he said with a raised eyebrow.

Lonen hesitated to explain, and was relieved when Lena did. "I brought us here on celestial wings. We were near Highshield City only moments ago, so we haven't had the pleasure of seeing dwarven lands."

"I see," Barham said, looking a little surprised. "So you really did just appear there. Haven't seen that in many years."

"We did," Lena said with a warm smile.

"Right, then." Barham introduced Lonen and Lena to the gate guards then, and they were allowed to pass. What awaited them on the other side took Lonen's breath away.

The thick, banded iron plate gate opened a crack, just enough to allow them to pass. The doors did not creak as they moved, but caused a rumbling in the stone underfoot. On the other side of the entrance, he noticed that the hinges for the doors were on heavy tracks dug deeply into the stone sides. Smaller side doors were thick, and had a set of braces as well as a thick metal plate the same size as the opening beside them. "I've never seen such fortifications," he muttered. "And I've seen five great cities."

"That's an ancient dwarf gate. Doesn't matter what kind of ram you use, the door will absorb the impact. Our ancestors even charmed it against dragon's fire," The Merchant Guard said. "Forge Hin's never been invaded."

Once they were further inside, the smell of fresh bread and ham filled his nostrils. With a grumbling stomach, he looked up and beheld two statues that were taller than any he'd ever seen. A dwarf woman with a long beard crossed a large hammer with a male dwarf holding an equally heavy looking thick sword. They were both chiseled in incredible detail. So well that he didn't notice that there were windows built into the carvings at first, but then he saw guards in shining plate armour watching the gate and the broad stone street below from their posts inside the statues.

There was morning light from above, so much that he wasn't sure if they were entering the mountain, or if they were still partially outside somehow. "Is it magical? This dawn inside the mountain?"

"No, but it may as well be for all the ingenuity behind it," the Guardsman said. "There's a bunch of mirrors and glass set up in tunnels that bring light in from above. I suppose a lot of southerners think us dwarves dwell in dark, dusty vaults carved into the rock, but we love the sun as much as any taller or thinner race. You should see us on Hounfeast."

"Hounfeast?"

"It's the celebration of the arrival of the planting season. We celebrate the melting of lake ice with swimming, sunning, give gifts that we work on all winter, and eat red pie. Oh, it's something you'd never forget, especially if you bring a few things to give your favourite dwarves with you. It's not about gift giving, but it does show your dedication to the holiday."

"I'll remember that, thank you," Lonen looked up at the ceiling, so far above the street and the carved walls that he couldn't guess how tall the tunnel actually was. "I was sure I'd be hitting my head constantly if I ever saw the inside of a mountain city,"

"Not as often as you'd think," Barham said with a little smile. "Still, watch your head if you're invited to anyone's home. We still have to hang things within reach."

The floor of the cavern was smooth to a shine. In some places, especially going towards the gate, he could see where frequent walking had worn paths into the granite. The sides of the cavern were densely used, built as high as nine stories up, he could see balconies, stairways and windows across the entire face. Not an inch was wasted, and while he was amazed, he could understand how valuable space underground was, it made a great deal of sense to him. He caught the eye of a young dwarf woman with brown hair watering a planter filled with flowers on her balcony. She was beardless, like most young dwarf women. Instead of being startled at the sight of a tall human in her city, she smiled and nodded her acknowledgement of him before returning inside.

Their Merchant Guard led them to a carriage hitched to two short, stout ponies with long forelocks hitched to it was standing idle. "Oi, Shene," Barham said, addressing the driver who lounged on her bench behind the horses. "Just starting for the day?"

"Aye," she said, puffing at her well-groomed mustache and looking to Lonen and Lena. "Where are these ones off to?"

"The Stronghold, audience with the King," he replied.

"In you go, three coppers a head," she replied.

"That's robbery," Barham said.

"Best, cleanest carriage in the mountain, and one that's tall enough for your charges," Shene countered. "You're lucky I'm here."

"I'll pay it, don't worry," Lena said as she fished a silver and two coppers from her pouch and handed only the silver to the driver, who rolled her eyes. "What, you're not going with them? That's twelve coppers, or this silver and the two coppers still in your hand."

"Referral fee," Barham said, holding up the two coppers.

"Fine," Shene said, opening the carriage door. "But you ride up here with me, you beautiful man." She patted the bench beside her and winked at Barham.

"My pleasure, as usual," he said as he climbed up beside her.

Lonen waited for the door to close and the carriage to start moving before speaking. "This city is expensive. You've already spent more coin than I've seen in a few months."

The carriage lurched forward. The ride was surprisingly smooth and swift. "I'm not worried. I earned a great deal of coin. When this runs out, I will either find someone who needs quick travel, or visit one of my caches. I only hope that I'm still welcome here after I deliver the news about the Miradu Temple. If Vedon the Seer is still here, I will have to tell them everything. You may find that you face the King on your own after that."

"I don't know anything about this King or his reputation. I doubt your absence will change much, but I have to thank you for bringing me here so quickly. Even if he takes my head for being a part of his son's downfall, I'm grateful."

"If it comes to that, I'll try to take you with me when I leave, though I can't step into the shadows here. Wards are carved into the stone all around. All of them are out of sight, ancient and powerful, but I can feel them."

"Then we both face a fate-turning this morning," Lonen said.

"I only know you hand the King the ring you retrieved this morning," Lena said. It was obvious that she found its retrieval humorous. Every time she mentioned it, there was a hint of a smile on her face. Lonen was only happy he spent a great deal of time cleaning it in the stream, and hoped that he'd never have to hide anything that way again. "I wish I could see past that simple act to my own future, but no visions have come."

The sounds of the rapidly stepping hooves came to a slow halt. "We've arrived," Barham announced as the carriage doors opened. "Last chance to take a moment to wash the road dust off, so to speak. The public baths are down that way, the High Lord's Hall is up this stair."

"I would rather not wait to see the King if I can help it, but if you think it best if we wash before meeting him, then perhaps we should?" Lena asked.

"From what I've seen so far, I believe His Highness values cleanliness less than a quick messenger," he replied. "I'll speak to the Seneschal and see if he can introduce you."

Lonen and Lena watched their Guard disappear up a broad set of stone steps and only had to wait a few short moments before he came down with a man in silvered armour close behind. "This is Seneschal Orn," Barham said hurriedly. The dwarf he gestured to had a greying beard tied in three thick braids and carried two ornate swords, one on each hip. "He'll introduce you to His Royal Highness, King Nyder. I'll wait here until you sent for me or for the rest of the day."

"Thank you, Barham," Lena said. "Three blessings to you."

"Yes, thank you," Lonen said. "I'm sure I would have gotten lost as soon as I walked through the gates without you."

"Three blessings," Barham said, bowing. "And a little luck to you besides."

They followed Seneschal Orn up the long stairs. Along the walls in tall sconces were full sized statues of stately dwarven men and women. There were at least two dozen, from Lonen's rough count. "These were Kings and Queens?"

"Going back to this Great House's founding in Brightwill," Orn said. He voice was gravelly and weathered. "You come to the foot of His Majesty's throne during dark days. He is still learning the details of the Great Purge, or the Liberation War, as you humans have named it. When he began his slumber the Ava-Ondi were still ruling Brightwill and this dwarven province was still an independent kingdom. He may be quicker to anger than normal. Be sure to address him as 'Your Majesty' unless otherwise invited. Do not participate in any arguing. Only speak to myself or the King. If anyone else asks you a question, look to us first, especially if it's a member of the Regency Council. The Regents are all marked with a silver pin on their left shoulders. The pin will have a sword, a hammer and a symbol defining their responsibility – Jor has a coin beneath his hammer and sword, he's the Master of Coin, the others should be obvious as well – do you understand?"

"I do," Lonen replied.

"Yes, thank you," Lena acknowledged.

"Deliver your messages, and if there is a document or object you need to hand the King, you give it to me instead. I only have one more warning for you. There has been news from Highshield City. The Prince has made demands of our people, and we are awaiting His Majesty's decision. I normally don't peddle gossip, but a warning only seemed fair, since you both seem to come in good faith as messengers."

"We're also looking for a new home, perhaps just outside your walls, if you'll have us?" Lena said. "Though things may change after our messages are given."

Seneschal Orn stopped, looked them up and down and nodded. "There is room in the outer city. How should I introduce you?"

"Lonen Kerd, of no noble house," he told him. "Former Bright One Paladin."

"Former?" Orn asked, looking intrigued. "And you?" he asked Lena.

"Lena the Traveler," she said with a bow. "Formerly a follower of Wydu."

"Do either of you have an object to give him?"

"I'm afraid I do," Lonen said, handing the Seneschal Haffor's ring.

The old Seneschal's face turned pale as he looked at the gold and silver ring. "I see," he said quietly. "Then we won't delay. The other petitioners will have to wait."

They were quickly led up the stairway, and Lonen couldn't help but notice that there were as many empty alcoves for statues of future rulers as there were occupied spaces. The antechamber at the top of the stairs was filled with petitioners, most of whom were dwarves. They met the newcomers with expressions of disgust and irritation when the Seneschal led Lena and Lonen through the room, to the front of the line, then through the large polished steel doors leading into the throne room. It wasn't what Lonen imagined it would look like at all. Instead of a large, dim cavern, the throne room of Forge Hin was well lit by hanging crystal braziers where nets that were half emerged in clear liquid burned blue and white. The tall hall was lit as though as it was under a mid-day sun, and the polished white marble reflected it like fresh snow. The throne was the highest seat in the room by far, set in a shallow alcove that had enough room for another seat. The dais was high, with fourteen steps made to look like a serpent's coiled body. A dragon head sat above the King's seat, broad and powerful but black and beautiful. The space was also a shrine to Miradu, even Lonen could see it. Her wings were carved into the background of the alcove, spread wide.

In front of, and to the side of the base of the dais was a long table made of yellow and white marble. There were symbols in an old dwarven language set into the top using gold and jade. Six dwarves sat at it, and Lonen could see marks on the floor where the table had scraped its way from the middle of the hall to one side. The Seneschal didn't seem to care that he brought them into the middle of a vicious argument between the six dwarves at the table, some of whom were leaning part way across and shouting to make their point. An audience consisting of dozens of well-dressed dwarves filled the space between the thick marble pillars and the outer walls. Above them there were balconies, a gallery filled with onlookers. There were few whispers among them, as they paid rapt attention to the shouting that filled the hall.

"We can afford to fight! Our abundance has been plundered for too long!" shouted a dwarf with red braids who sat at a space marked by crossed swords. "This is an age that welcomes conquerors, and we have debts to settle that are more important than anything coin can repay! I say we take up our ancestor's trade as summer raiders down river and along the coast."

The King, a man with jet black hair and a long beard woven into two long braids, sat on his throne, watching the men argue with a deeply creased brow. His face, and his heavily muscled build reminded Lonen of Haffor, only younger. Instead of expensive silks, jewelry and furs, he wore simple leathers that had been dyed black. His sleeves were white, and where a number of sigils and marks of honour were embroidered from shoulder to cuff. He wore only two rings – a silver one on his right middle finger, and a platinum band on his left ring finger.

"We have had peace for decades, our cities grow and the people of the mountain know…"

"Your Majesty, and members of the Regency Council," announced the Seneschal in a booming voice. "I present Lonen Kerd, a former Bright One Paladin, and Lena the Traveler; a Formerly a follower of Wydu. They bring you messages and urgent news from Highshield City and were there only yesterday." The Seneschal stepped back and gestured for Lena to step forward first. The hall was massive, large enough for hundreds to feast there, and judging from stone tables that hung high against the ceiling by chains, that was one of the purposes of the space. Lena only crossed half way to the king before kneeling.

"Who do you follow now, Traveler?" asked King Nyder. He stood slowly, his gaze affixed on the woman before him, and began to descend the stairs. "Where is your allegiance?"

"I sought a just God, and have found Viis, but I am of Miradu and love her just as I do her daughter. As for my country, I am a woman of faith, and not a patriot. I go where my Gods are known and loved."

A round faced dwarf dressed in thick silk and fur robes emerged from a doorway hidden against the right wall, and nodded. "She speaks truth. The Traveler isn't as certain of her leaning within the Pantheon of Miradu – whether it is Viis or Irenick or Miradu Herself – but she is absolutely a follower. Her distaste of Wydu is as bitter as salted rhubarb."

The King found that worth smiling about, nodding at the gentleman. "Thank you Vedon." He returned his attention to Lena. "What news do you bring?"

"Your Royal Highness; Highshield City has fallen, and I am afraid I had a large part in it. By bringing Wydu's Gift – a girl named Nella – to the High Matron of Miradu, I gave Wydu the opportunity to take her into His thrall. He has done so, and the Matron is rededicating the Miradu Temple to Wydu as we speak. The High Matron withdrew all the guards from Highshield and in so doing she allowed the magical wards within to fall and the enemies of Highshield to loot and raze it. Now the towns surrounding Highshield city are falling victim to other raiders, looters and even Razthanga, who is murdering thousands and stealing their wealth."

The King ran up the stairs of his dais and snatched a piece of rolled parchment from the foot of his throne before facing Lena again. "So this message from the Prince is confirmed," Nyder said. "But how do you know all this? How did you see it?"

"I walk through shadow, and listen from the darkness," Lena said. "Though I owe my allegiance to no one as a spy or messenger."

"Then why bring your news here? Why to my Kingdom?"

"I know this is where Miradu and her God children are worshipped in the old ways, that you are Miradu's Gift, and I want to begin my atonement. My road was shown to me when I met my companion, and found that he had important news of his own to deliver. I am without a home, without a temple, and need time to contemplate my actions. I never wanted to see the Miradu Temple turn, only for Wydu to rise in prominence, to be as well-loved as His brother and sister; Irenick and Viis. He has overwhelmed the temple, brought about the deaths of tens of thousands and displaced so many more. If I had known His Gift would have brought such misery, I would never have retrieved her for Him. I thought she was as important as Viis and Irenick's Gifts, but Wydu's Gift was false. As soon as I heard that Miradu healed you and brought you out of your century sleep, I knew I had been fooled."

"So you were," King Nyder said. He seemed pensive, but a little irritated at the same time. "Any other news from you?"

"I bore witness to many significant events, Your Majesty, so I could help with details of Highshield City's fall, but I'm afraid all I really have to offer is advice. Perhaps you should consider removing any of Wydu's people from your great city, even from your province..."

"Kingdom! This will once more be a Kingdom, not some province owned by King Ormet!" King Nyder said. "And as for Wydu's people, I have already begun rounding them up and putting them on boats bound for the south. Miradu had many things to tell me while she brought me back into this world. I watched her weep as her son, Wydu, betrayed her, and will never forget her tearful warnings." He sat on the bottom step of his dais, looked at the rolled parchment in his hand for a long moment.

When King Nyder spoke, Lonen could barely hear him. Everyone in the hall was silent. "Do you know what we are deciding right now? My Regency Council and I?"

"No, your Majesty," Lena said.

"Nothing so significant, a simple thing, really. Only the way forward for my entire Kingdom. A Kingdom that has been called a province for decades now. A concession given to King Ormet the First when he finished overthrowing Queen Irissus the Ninth. An Ava-Ondi who I knew personally. Her mother held me as a babe, and I swam with her as a child in the spring pools here in this mountain, was nearly promised to her as a man. I wake to discover that King Ormet the First put her in a cage after taking her kingdom in Brightwill, killing thousands of her people. He watched her starve, hanging right beside his throne during the first twenty-eight days of his rule. Imagine, hanging in a cage, your kingdom fallen, your people dead or fleeing and you are starving to death. Not just that, no! He had her mother – the Queen Mother – killed in the middle of the throne room along with the rest of her family and every Ondi they could find, including several dwarves. Some were eaten by dogs and pigs who themselves were starved. Many were skinned alive or boiled at the request of the new ruler's young son – the man who now rules as King Ormet the Second. A child who knew about cruelty and torture and was himself twisted and evil enough to order a living person to be skinned then boiled. There were no slaves in that kingdom, human or otherwise. I know this for certain. There were in others, human slaves were so common in Brightwill that even I found it a horrific practice, but not in that kingdom during the reign of Queen Irissus. There was no cause for this savagery, Ormet only saw an opportunity brought on by revolution in Brightwill and used it to murder hundreds of thousands for their wealth. This council here," he gestured to the table at his right. "Were responsible for agreeing to join the Hullen Kingdom as a province so he wouldn't bring his armies to this mountain. Now, what am I supposed to do with them? I know if I were King Ormet I would have them eaten by dogs, or skinned alive, or boiled, or I would take some horrible pleasure in watching them starve." The King let his last comments hang in the air as he stared at the Regency Council, giving each one of them equal time with his harsh gaze.

One of them, a woman with blonde fuzz on her chin, cleared her throat. "Your Majesty, we..."

"We've been through it already," King Nyder said, waving her reply away. "You and your council are necessary. It's all established. I'm making sure our guest knows how to answer an important question, that she knows that it will factor into a decision that will affect a million lives." He looked to Lena then, holding the note in his hand up. "There are requests here from Prince Norrich. He wants our craftspeople, he wants the tithe we owe his father, King Ormet the Second which amounts to seven tenths of everything our Kingdom has produced in the last season, he wants workers and all three of our standing legions. You say you're a shadow, a spy for no one, but I'm going to ask you in the presence of my most powerful seer; one who can see lies like stains on fine linen. Did Prince Norrich try to prevent the burning of Highshield City? Did he do anything to save his people?"

"I cannot say for certain," Lena said, looking worried for the first time since Lonen met her. "But I did not see any guards from the castle, or any mercenaries acting as keepers of the peace in his name. Nor were there any knights bearing his mark. If he sent help from the castle, I am sure I would have witnessed some sign of it."

King Nyder let the roll of parchment fall from his fingers, then looked to the Regency Council. "Then my decision is final. I take my throne back, declare a separation from the Hullen Kingdom, and you will craft a response that makes that clear. While you ponder your wording, every banner and mark from the Hullen Kingdom in our lands will be burned or replaced. No longer will Ormet the Second be sent seven tenths of everything our lands produce, everything he claimed to own is now property of my Kingdom. We will pay our farmers, craftspeople, and everyone else who provides a service for the crown properly, and allow dwarves to purchase property of their own again. The tax will be reduced to one tenth for everyone and our borders will be shut to any soldier wearing a human device."

Nearly all the dwarves in the gallery and on the floor cheered and applauded, but the King didn't so much as crack a smile. Instead he waited a moment then raised a hand that signaled them to silence. "If this Princeling can't save his own city, and he is the offspring of a murderer king, then he doesn't deserve to employ our people. He'll be allowed to buy what we feel like sparing, but no dwarf will be allowed to work for him. Any dwarves currently in his employ will be paid to return to my lands then given a place in Forge Hin along with employment that suits their trade."

"Your Majesty," the Council Member standing in front of a coin symbol addressed. "There are already nine ships heavy with cargo on their way to Highshield bearing product from the mines. They have been at sea for three days."

"Send a message to them by wind whisperer: 'Return home at once. Give no wealth to King Ormet.'"

Applause filled the hall once more, and the Master of Coin showed his support by firmly knocking on his place at the table. "There will be war," said the Council Member sitting in front of crossed swords set into the table. "Ormet is a warmonger, worse than his father."

"Then let them come," King Nyder said. "I do not celebrate war, but this extortion must end. We have three legions, two companies of paladins in country, and five more across this land. When his army arrives on our shore, they will be sea weary. We will burn them in their ships, and we will crush them on the shore. Take inventory of our standing defences, whatever death machines we have and what has fallen into disrepair. We will rebuild them and fill gaps with more. Our Kingdom will have more wealth than it has in decades. It will only take a small portion of that to shore up our defences."

"About that wealth, Your Majesty," said the Master of Coin. "Keeping the seven tenth tithe that we were going to send to King Ormet the Second is good for our coffers, but much of that wealth is in the form of goods, like grain, preserves, metals, and other supplies that we will have to trade, otherwise they will rot in storage."

"First," the King said, holding up a finger. "Make certain that everyone in our Kingdom will eat better than they have in decades and that they are paid fairly for the last season's work. We need a census and to employ people to supply and guard every township's stores. As for trading the rest," he lowered his upraised finger to point at the Master of Coin. "You are an expert in trade, are you not?"

"Yes, My King," he replied.

"Then trade as greedily as if you were filling your own pockets, and quickly." They stared back at him as though he'd issued a challenge that was too great for any of them to surmount. "There is much more planning to be done. You council members will devise proposals today and present them to me tomorrow. Find the right solutions for our people while I see to the line of petitioners at my door." King Nyder returned his attention to the guest in the middle of the room. "Lena, do you have any other news for me?"

"No, Your Majesty," she said, curtseying low and remaining there.

"You will be watched while you are in our city," King Nyder said. "But you will be welcome in this gallery," he gestured to the space behind the pillars and the balconies above. "You may be called on for witness accounts, and I hope you give them. While you're here, I invite you to find a place amongst our people. Though most of our enemies are human now, I have never turned one of your kind away."

She rose. "Thank you, Your Majesty, you is most kind."

"Now, for the former Paladin of the Bright One," King Nyder said. "If you came bearing a sword, you would already be in the dungeon. Instead you come with nothing, and I'm intrigued. Approach."

Lonen did as he instructed, only when he reached the middle of the hall, he dropped to one knee and lowered his head. He made the decision to convey is message as quickly as possible. It seemed the King would respect nothing less. "Your Majesty, I am sorry to tell you that I witnessed the death of your son, Captain Haffor of the Eventide."

The Seneschal handed King Nyder Haffor's ring. Nyder turned it over in his hand, staring at it.

"I was able to escape, smuggling his signet ring, but I am afraid I was not able to stop Razthanga from taking his remains. I wanted to strike his head from his body, bless and burn it so his form could not be corrupted, but she was too powerful. I could barely control my own mind in her presence. I am sorry, Your Royal Highness."

"How did you become the keeper of his body?" King Nyder asked quietly.

"I witnessed his capture, during which he killed thirty-five fully trained Lucent Paladins, and was in the chamber when he was sacrificed," Lonen said as quickly and as clearly as he could. He wondered what a blade falling across his neck would feel like. Would he still be able to see after his head was off his shoulders? "He was not tortured long, and suffered far less than most of High Priest Datho's sacrifices. He died as a paragon of light, drawing the spirit of Viis down so she could cleanse me of the poison the Bright One left in my spirit. I follow Her now, and will until my dying day, even if it is this very day."

"Sacrificed to the Bright One?" King Nyder said. He stood and walked to Lonen, a long way across the hall.

Lonen kept his head down, kneeling low. If this was his final errand, he would do it in the fashion that offered the most respect to a grieving father. "I am afraid that is so, Your Highness," Lonen said. The King placed his broad hand on his shoulder, and Lonen saw a drop fall past his head to spatter against the white stone floor. "I would fight my way across the heavens to retrieve your son from the Bright One for you, for Viis, and to atone for my blind obedience to the Bright One."

"I am afraid every word that this man is saying is true," said Vedon the Seer. "Though there is something more, the shadow of an old enemy haunts him. This Razthanga is the pupil of Zishthanga, and she has power over him. What did she do to you?"

"She healed me of my scars, said she gave me new skin," Lonen said.

"Then she has power over it," Vedon said. "Not here, not while you are out of her sight, but in her presence, she can take it from you quite literally or cause great pain. You will never be able to face her, young Paladin."

"Then I will find my own vengeance when the time is right," King

Nyder said. "The Bright One has my son's soul, and Razthanga has his body." Another tear fell past Lonen's head to the floor, and then the King pulled on his arm, guiding him to his feet. "You could have written it down, put the paper inside this," he held the ring up to show him. "You could have sent the message rolled up, and sent it with someone else. Even if you left it with a Merchant Guard at the border of my Kingdom and given him a copper, the importance of the message would have seen it delivered in confidence. Instead you risk everything to bring it to me yourself, which tells me you are either an idiot, or more honorable than most. I will hold a feast for..." he closed his eyes tightly and turned back towards the throne. The King didn't speak until he was all the way up the fourteen serpent stairs of his dais. "You are my guest, Lonen. Consider your future." A door seamlessly built into the carving behind the throne opened and the King retreated through it.

38

*T*he outskirts of the Wandering Wood looked like the impassable jungles that Rendiran read about as a boy in adventure novels. Thick vines wrapped around ancient trees, luscious fruit dangled from low branches. The colourful fruit looked ripe and delicious, but Crista made sure to warn them that eating anything on the outskirts would mean certain death. The Wandering Wood defended its borders, but they were safe as long as they remained on the path and didn't allow temptation to get the best of them.

They walked with Marjay in the middle of the group. "The forest doesn't approve of his presence," Crista said. "Humans have done the Wandering Wood harm in the past, and it knows about the Liberation War, about the purge. Ondi-Ne have been nomads across the Wandering Wood for so long that its learned to trust us, and it defends us the same as any creature born here."

Marjay had been pricked by more than one thorn and his feet caught on roots that didn't bother anyone else. "Is there any way for me to convince it that I don't care about purging its people or cutting it down?"

A sudden deluge of rain undriven by wind drenched the entire party as if to answer. If it wasn't the first while they travelled, Rendiran would let superstition guide him at least a little, but it was the third such downpour they'd seen. Just as everyone found a broad leaf or branch to hide under, the rain stopped. Ander seemed energized by the thorough drenching, and shook the water from his fur with vigor. Before anyone could catch him, he ran directly off the narrow trail into the thick underbrush.

"Ander!" Tadrin cried, and Rendiran caught his arm before he could chase after him.

"He'll sniff his way back," Rendiran told him. "Even for a pup, he's..." to his surprise, the dog came running back onto the trail, leaping at him so urgently that he collided with his stomach, only barely missing a mark that would have been much more painful and embarrassing. He held the dog in one arm as it licked at him, whining as though he was grateful for being saved from something in the bush. "I think we should move on."

Following Crista, Tadrin, Oria, Marjay and Niomer the Guide, Rendiran walked as the heat and humidity settled back into the forest around them. The passage of time while they were on the winding path was uncertain. The sun was completely obscured by the tall trees, everything that sprung or clung to them and the things that dwelt in the higher branches.

The chirps of the birds, huffing and chattering of wild imps that were too shy to approach them, and other things that weren't so easy to identify filled their ears. It didn't escape Rendiran's notice that most of the din would go quiet from time to time. There was something greater than those small beings, and he tried not to wonder about what it was. The children seemed fairly oblivious, interested in every little thing. It was all new to them, and they didn't know enough about forests to be afraid. They thought the adults could protect them from whatever came calling, but Rendiran could imagine the trail closing in on them, or a creature too ferocious for them to handle landing right in the middle of their group. When he let his imagination run rampant, terrible things from the journals of explorers came to mind too often.

"Does anyone else feel that?" Marjay asked. A moment later, Rendiran knew what he was talking about. There was crisp air coming up the path absent the suppressive humidity.

"We're almost into the forest proper," Crista said. One more turn in the path brought them to an overlook, and everyone stopped. A valley so wide that the other side was barely visible lay before them. Rivers ran between several large lakes, and the thick forest was broken here and there by rocky golden meadows. To the right, they could see high, steep mountainsides. It was a surprise to Rendiran that there were no visible roads.

Near the center of the valley there were several mountains that looked like slivers of stone. Brown and green branches wrapped around them. The pillars were tall and jagged.

"There must be something important going on," Crista said, starting down a stone stair. "Normally we'd meet riders here."

The children gasped as the shapes of three dragons emerged from the forest. Rendiran had never seen a dragon, so he may not have gasped, but he was just as amazed by the sight of the great beasts taking wing and climbing up into the sky. "There they are," Crista said. "Showing off."

"There are riders on those?" Marjay asked.

"Yes, but they're not really dragon riders. Those creatures are dragon-kin, only drakes. They're an old species that have returned, a side effect of something else. Not many dragons allow themselves to be ridden, they find it demeaning."

"You know a lot of dragons?" Rendiran asked.

"A few," Crista said with a satisfied smile. "We're not far from the camp."

"I thought we were going to a city," Marjay said.

"There are cities in the Wandering Wood, but we're not going to see any of them," Crista replied. "My tribe doesn't live in cities if they can help it, not since they abandoned Ellaun." She pointed to the tall shards of stone standing in the middle. "That was a long time ago."

"That's a city?" Marjay asked. "What happened? Why'd you leave."

"It's a long story, maybe I'll find an elder to tell it if we're here long enough."

The drakes made flying look easy, flapping occasionally, gliding towards them. They looked like young dragons to Rendiran, large, but not house sized. They were mostly wing, and once they were close enough for him to see their horned heads, they looked every bit like the savage carnivores that roamed the skies well before he was born. There was something more though, something he should have expected but didn't. There was expression. Despite the sharp horns, great maws, and hard scales, these drakes looked like they were serine in their flight. The dark blue one actually looked elated to be aloft as it swept overhead. "I'm glad they're friendly," Marjay said.

"Only because you're with me," Crista said. "Humans and Ava-Ondi are not welcome here with only a few exceptions."

"I hope I make the list."

"You're Oria's guardian," Crista said. "These are Miradu's people, so they already know who you are."

"I suppose they would have a seer," Marjay said.

"Several, it's annoying sometimes. Every time I leave them I get warnings and advice for things that haven't happened yet. The funny thing is, following all their advice at the same time has gotten me into trouble before."

"Maybe too much advice is as bad as none at all?" Rendiran asked.

"Maybe, but it's there, so I take it into consideration anyway."

The rest of their journey didn't seem to take as long as the first leg. Stony steps and descending paths led to a flattened road that had little evidence of use. Trees closed in overhead, and weeds grew between the paving stones as moss threatened to cover and devour the flat rocks. "Someone settled here once," Rendiran said. "This road is a hundred years old, at least."

"They did," Crista replied. "The road is an age old, probably closer to three thousand years, we don't know who made it. There are cities outside this valley that are mostly ruins now. Some of them were built here, others are parts of cities that appeared here when the

Wandering Wood temporarily merged with other places, then took them when this realm moved on."

"So parts of the Wandering Wood just appear, collide with other places, then take chunks away when it moves on?" Marjay asked.

"There's a sort of trade. Parts of the Wandering Wood are left behind. That's why you need seers if you want to live here. It's the only way to know if the land you're standing on is about to cross with something else. People have been left behind before, when the Wandering Wood separates from another place. There are magically protected cities, but that can cause more problems than they're worth."

"It all looks so stable, so permanent," Rendiran said. "Is this where the Ondi who escaped are hiding?"

"No, not them, but a few other things are hiding from our world here," Crista said. "I honestly don't know where the Ondi who got away are. I wish I did. They won't tell me because I'm too young, so they say. I keep more secrets than most people five times my age have known though, so someday they'll tell me, or show me."

They walked along the road until the sun started descending below the mountains. The first moon began to rise, and Rendiran was not ready for what he beheld. It wasn't so much a moon, as another world with green and dark blue forests, rivers and blue-black oceans. Someone was once there too, as evidenced by tall, needle like towers that reached up from the surface.

"We're here," Crista said as they walked off the road. It was easy to pass between the trees, the vines and jungle vegetation were absent. The forest resembled the lush northern woods he was used to seeing. They reached the edge of a lake and he couldn't help but grin. Hundreds of Ondi-Ne had made camp along the bank.

Their hide and heavy cloth circular tents were a riot of colour and style. No two was alike. "Crista!" shouted a round faced young girl as she charged towards the newcomers. "You're back!"

"Sona!" Crista said as she picked her up. "Shouldn't you be getting ready for bed?"

"I saw you coming, and that you were bringing Oria and Tadrin with you. I couldn't miss it." Her brown hair was tied in a multitude of short braids that stuck straight out from her head.

Tadrin and Oria perked up at the mention of their names. Crista put Sona down. She was the shortest of the three, but she had the biggest smile. "I got these for you from the river, so you can put them at the shrines in Forge Hin," she said as she gave them each a blue-green river stone. "I think Viis and Irenick will like them."

"Thank you," Tadrin said. "Are you a seer?"

"The youngest ever, I think," Sona replied. "I see merge quakes before anyone else."

"Sona!" shouted a stout, half-smiling Ondi-Ne woman as she rushed towards them. "You're supposed to be in bed."

"I had to meet them, Mom," Sona explained. "So I could give them the stones."

"They'll still be here in the morning," her mother said as she picked her daughter up.

"No, not long enough for me to meet them, then it'll be years before we see each other."

"Well, say hello then," her mother said, putting her back down. "Hello, Crista," she said, embracing her.

"This is Panera, a friend," Crista said, properly introducing Sona's mother. She went around the group, greeting everyone with a warm embrace as she learned their names. Even though she seemed to be in a rush to get her daughter off to bed, there was nothing rushed about her greetings.

Rendiran was far more interested in the little seer meeting Tadrin and Oria. "I'm glad Viis brought you back, Oria," she said, hugging her.

"Thank you," Oria said, looking a little stunned. "I like your hair."

Sona moved on to Tadrin as though she were in a great hurry, nearly stumbling into him. "Hi Tadrin," she giggled. "Three blessings to you."

"Hello," he replied, accepting a hug from the girl.

"She does this sometimes," Panera whispered. "She has visions of people she never met, then she greets them like they have been friends for years."

"No, absolutely not," someone said harshly.

"Let's go, Mom," Sona said, taking her hand and guiding her away. "It's the Matron's turn to meet them now."

A Ondi-Ne woman in a long silk and silver fur dress marched towards Rendiran with a small crowd behind her that seemed far less urgent about their business than their leader. "You can't be here looking like that!" she said.

Rendiran realized the woman was looking directly at him.

"Slow down, please," Crista plead. "It's been a long day."

Rendiran didn't know whether to defend himself or run as this furious, much shorter woman approached at a near sprint. His indecision left him frozen to the spot as she grabbed him by the ear and chin. "I won't have you walking around this sacred place disfigured as you are. Someone has done this to you, and it was altogether wrong."

He felt an unfamiliar energy pass through his cheekbones, his ears, his jaw and his hands. It wasn't painful, in fact it felt as though splints and braces he didn't know he wore were being cut away, allowing parts of his body to take their proper shape. "Hold still for one more moment, and get this brat away from me," she said as she grasped Rendiran's face and tried to shove Ander away as he growled and pulled at the hem of her robe. "They reshaped you in terrible ways before you had a choice."

Oria picked Ander up, and everyone watched as whatever the woman was doing to Rendiran was being done. He felt a surge of energy through his entire body, and felt muscles grow larger, bones shift, and then it was all gone. "There, you're as nature intended. Ondi-Ne blood through and through, even though the humans probably told you you're only half, or a quarter, or whatever. Ondi-Ne blood always wins over human, so human you are not, no matter how much sculpting and flesh crafting someone did to you when you were a child. Welcome to your people."

Crista stared at him most of all, it seemed like she was pleasantly surprised. After a moment she looked to the elder woman. "He had nothing to do with what happened to him."

"I know," she replied.

"Then why are you angry at him for it?"

"I'm not angry at *him,* only that the ruse continued for so long. That he was disfigured at all was most likely to save some human's foolish pride."

"Well you could have introduced yourself first, Auntie, maybe told him what you wanted to do?"

"Who has the time? Besides, he looked ridiculous as a human. So stretched and narrow-faced and awkward," she said as she offered her hand to Rendiran. "I am Erriyane, Matron of this Band. Three blessings to you, Rendiran. I offer you and your people our hospitality, just make sure your human behaves."

"Auntie, that's Rude!" Crista said, exasperated.

39

That evening Matron Erriyane took charge of the events that would surround the arrival of her grand-niece and her party. Niomer was sent off with several healers who claimed to be lesser trained than Rendiran to be washed and prepared. A broad tent made of large grey and brown drake hides was erected in minutes. Furs, carpets and cushions were arranged inside, and a small fire was started.

Before he was finished inspecting his new middle finger, they had a place to sleep that night, and it was cozier than most homes he'd seen. To his surprise, he felt more like himself than ever before. He was still missing his toes, small finger and ring finger on his right hand, but the middle finger was back. His skin was less pale than before, but he hesitated to look at his reflection. "Am I shorter? I feel shorter," he asked Marjay as they stood outside the large tent. Crista was putting the children to bed, they were both so tired that they were becoming cranky.

"You're down to my height," he replied. "I'm a little short for a man, I've been told, but I've never strained to reach the high shelf. Don't worry, you're tall for an Ondi-Ne. By the way, is that thing ever going to stop?" he asked, pointing at the large crystal in Rendiran's staff. Soft white light emanated from it as strands of energy that were looking less like smoke all the time turned.

He touched the stone mentally, checking its activity and was surprised to find that it was gathering excess energy from somewhere beyond the realm they were in. The connection was fading, but he was sure it was made while they were moving between realms. From what he could tell, there was a reservoir of power there greater than he had seen, enough for anyone to destroy themselves if they expended it all at once. "There's a lot I have to learn about controlling the finer points of this. For now, I think I'll have to cover it at night."

"You don't know how to control it?"

"I know enough to keep from doing harm again," he replied. "I learned my lesson the first time." He held up his right hand. "If you draw too much power at once, you end up making some injuries permanent."

"I'll leave the magic to you and Crista," Marjay said.

A young man with a sword on each hip, wearing bleached leathers approached them as Crista emerged from the tent. "Your presence is required in the Elder Lodge," he said. "Please, follow me."

"Just me?" Crista asked. "Or all of us?"

"All of you, come," the young man said, glancing at Marjay's blades, which hung the same way on his belt.

"I'll stay with Oria and Tadrin," Marjay said. "I'm sure they're safe, but I'd rather not leave them alone in a new place."

"Good idea," Crista said.

They followed their guide to the Elder Lodge, a long building that was made of wooden half walls with heavy red hides above. It was long enough to have three holes for smoke to escape, and was the only building with a proper door. The wooden double doors were ornately carved with a long dragon encircling a pair of wolves in the middle.

The floor was covered with sturdy woven straw carpeting, and lit with small Quickamber lanterns that filled the space with yellow light. Most of the adults from the tribe sat along the sides of the large building, lounging on cushions that they'd brought. More Ondi-Ne than Rendiran had ever seen in one place at one time sat casually eating fruit, bowls of stew from the fire where large pots simmered along with yellow and brown flat bread. Rendiran and Crista were brought to the deepest part of the Lodge, where the elders sat in a semi-circle around Matron Erriyane.

"Please, sit and listen to Master Nauso," said one of the elders, a man with long black and white hair. Rendiran and Crista sat on plush cushions across from the Edlers.

A short Ondi-Ne man stood between them and the elders. Instead of leathers he wore layered wool clothing that looked like it had seen significant travel. "If I may continue?" he asked.

"Please, Master Nauso," Matron Erriyane said.

The din of conversation quieted, and everyone focused their attention on the Ondi-Ne standing before the Edlers. "The Thangas in Brightwill have begun to learn the secrets of weaving magic, and one of the first humans to use it has emerged. Charthanga has proven his power, holding demonstrations for royalty and the wealthy. He is drawing more interest to his order."

"You are certain that he's only human. No Ondi in his blood whatsoever?"

"I have spoken to two people who have been able to read his blood, trustworthy folk who confirm it. He is human, and he can use rudimentary weaving magic."

"Rudimentary? Are you saying he is weaving simply, harmlessly, or using elements?" asked Matron Erriyane.

"He has shown an affinity for fire and air. While no large feats have been performed to my knowledge, he can channel both into a source of power for human magic, or more weaving, start small fires, and his power is growing. There is nothing I can do."

"Yes, there is," said an elder who had several gemstones woven into the front of her hide tunic. "You can kill him while he sleeps. You have blade wielders in your tribe, send them up his walls, through his window. Slash his throat."

"I cannot risk the fate of the Woodland District and my people on an assassination plot," Master Nauso said. "Especially when we exist at the pleasure of our King. He could wipe us out on a whim."

"Master Nauso, I offer you our hospitality again. If our tribes merged, you would be safe, you would know peace," Matron Erriyane said.

"I will extend that offer to my people again, but most of us would rather remain in Brightwill. The very existence of our people there remind thousands of humans who are kind, who have always been friends to the Ondi, that their rulers are as cruel as the ones they overthrew in the Liberation War. If we leave, the resistance will stop growing, and it is growing."

"Then we invite you to enjoy our hospitality, and extend the three blessings of Miradu; health, wealth, and love," Matron Erriyane said.

Master Nauso bowed. "Thank you, and three blessings to you as well." He took a seat to the right of the Elders then, and they looked to Rendiran and Crista.

"You have come from Highshield City and have first-hand account of what happened there. We invite you to tell the story in front of everyone here," Matron Erriyane said, gesturing at Crista.

"If you don't mind, I'd rather Rendiran recounted it for you. He is a trained speaker, and saw much more than I did," she said. "I can fill in a few details here and there."

"A trained speaker?" the grey haired elder asked. She seemed pleased at the notion of a real orator performing.

"A Priest of Miradu," Rendiran replied with a bow. He used the opportunity to take a deep breath in, and release it, sending his gathering nervousness out with the air. When he straightened, he held his chin up high, his staff at his side, and spoke in a clear, expressive tone loud enough to fill the long building. "I'd be happy to tell you the story as I know it, though this is the retelling of how a city burned, how many people died, and how even more lost their homes."

"Please, I think I speak for everyone who has seen that great city when I ask you to tell us what happened, and to do so in detail," Matron Erriyane said.

At her invitation, Rendiran did just that. He used all his training as a preacher to present his story, calling on Crista when he thought she may have more detail, or when she signaled him with a nod. As a fox she saw the Eventide Paladins charge the old city graveyard. Her transformed eyes beheld the closing of the Temple Guard gates, and the barring of the castle after the small party were sent out to retrieve Oria and Tadrin.

Crista also told everyone there how a half dwarf and his family took Rendiran away after he fell unconscious and delivered him to the boat that took them up the Hurien River. Rendiran told the rest, and even though he was famished by the time he finished just past midnight, he only took a short break before healing Niomer the Guide on a bed of furs and cushions in front of the Elders.

When he was finished, Niomer's body was not only as it should be, but his missing arm was restored thanks to the power gathered in his staff. He would wake the next morning as a new man, much like Rendiran himself.

---

he Dwarven City of Forge Hin seemed endless. There were places where Lonen wasn't allowed to go – many of the common living areas, several of the town squares within the mountain were off limits as well, and anything that took him near a weapon or the city's defences – but he didn't feel very restricted.

He had no coin, but he couldn't resist visiting the Humber Market, where goods from across the continent, and from across the seas were sold by hawkers in booths. He could have spent an entire day there, watching street performances by strumming, singing minstrels, actors who reenacted the goings on of the throne room and performed scenes that detailed news from the realm. An epic multi-part play about the fall of Highshield was already under way, and each chapter was performed three times a day by actors who drew massive crowds.

From the room he was given adjacent to the Stronghold, he could see the entrance of the Miradu Temple. There was a grand chamber between his window and the entrance, which was shaped to resemble the open maw of a great black dragon. Around the entrance were dozens of shrines, all of them were much smaller than he was used to seeing. A person only had enough room for a donation bowl, a candle, a few small statuettes and a little painting of the person the shrine was for. They looked well-tended, and through all hours of the night and day dwarves quietly visited them. There were always guards and priests on hand, and Lonen was amazed at how often they would sit on the steps of the temple with people who came to pray to converse, and sometimes to bless.

He wished he had been found by the Miradu Order instead of the Bright One when he was younger. The people attached to Miradu's Pantheon didn't just seem kinder, but it seemed like people who went to the shrines to grieve felt much better when they left. Not only that, but even though he rarely saw the same person twice in the hours he watched through his window, the priests called out to dwarves by name. There was a community surrounding the temple, a kind of community he didn't know could exist thanks to a religion.

In the service of the Bright One, mourners were told that their deceased loved ones were in the service in His mighty halls. They were serving a high purpose, and that grief was for the weak, the Bright One looked away from such indulgences. People were told to be strong, to continue their service to Him so He may shine his light on them some day. The comfort most of the Bright One's worshippers sought was only offered in death, when they'd be in His presence, surrounded by His light. Meanwhile, most worshippers who had been given a glimpse of the Bright One's light during their lifetimes did anything to themselves and others in order to feel it again, to get their God's attention for an instant.

Lonen shuddered at the memory of that desperation. Every time he thought of the things he did as a Paladin in the Lucent Order to earn a moment in the Bright One's light, he felt remorseful and angry. He wanted to live in the way of the paladin, the true paladin, but the Bright One led him to practice a false version of that lifestyle.

When he saw an old dwarf with long silver braided hair and beard wearing the full regalia of a Miradu Paladin walking towards the temple, he ran from his room. Down the hall, down the stone steps, then through the foyer that lead into the grand chamber. He had to at least meet one, present himself, and see what the possibilities were.

Before he was half way across the grand chamber, the grey paladin turned to face him. His armour was polished, the white tabard was pristine, and he greeted him with an amused grin. Lonen dropped to one knee in front of him in such a rush that he slid a few feet. "I am Lonen Kerd, formerly of the Bright One's Paladins. I failed to help Haffor the Paladin, or to keep his body from corruption, and I put myself at your mercy."

"You've nothing to worry about. The temple here agrees with the King's sentence, boy, that you should live with us for as long as you like. A mixed sentence that may be at times. Careful, you might find yourself getting thick in the middle," the old dwarf said. His gravelly voice and thick accent were no surprise. He was the very picture and sound of what someone might expect a dwarf paladin to be.

"I," He stopped there, realizing that he hadn't thought of what to say next. Did he want to ask questions? Did he want to beg forgiveness for the few times he'd clashed with the Eventide? Did he want to become a paladin in the Miradu Order?

"I've been meaning to pay you a visit. Stand, my boy. I have no need for you to lower to my height."

Still at a loss for words, Lonen rose and fell in step beside the old paladin. They began walking at a casual pace around the cavernous space, past hall entrances that led in all directions within the mountain city.

"I'm Algus, Algus the Stone to some, but just call me Algus," he said, offering a thickly calloused hand. "I train paladins here."

Lonen took it, feeling like a beggar boy in his linen clothing and simple sandals beside the fully armoured paladin. "I'm glad to meet you," he replied. "I have questions."

Algus laughed and nodded. "I would be surprised if you didn't. I have some for you too, but those can wait."

"All right," Lonen said.

"Any question, I'll answer if I can."

"What kind of paladins are in the Eventide? What ideals do you practice by?"

"Starting with the real heart of the matter," Algus said. He started walking towards the entrance to the Miradu temple. "Mayhap it'll be of aid for you to know the oath all Eventide Paladins take when they enter into service. 'In service to Irenick and Viis, the son and daughter of our lady Miradu, I do pledge to protect those who cannot defend themselves, to speak no falsehood, to keep all promises given unless released, to combat corruption and unnatural darkness, to live in courtesy, honour, faith and to deliver justice when it is called for. Above all else, I pledge to serve the greater good for the rest of my days."

By the time Algus finished, they were inside the temple, standing at the entrance of a hallway. To the side was a table with small candles. Algus dropped two coppers into a bowl there, took a candle for himself and gave another to Lonen. "This is our memorial, where we mourn and celebrate paladins who gave their lives in service," he said. He lit his candle using a lamp at the entrance and walked inside.

Lonen lit his and followed, looking at all the alcoves, each less than one foot tall. There was a painting for every paladin who passed, the ones at the entrance looked old, but he could still make out details. A pair of dwarves painted new alcoves further in, and they stood back when they saw Algus approach. "Three blessings and thanks to you," Algus said to them before turning to face a freshly painted alcove. "Does it look like him?"

Lonen looked at the alcove and saw Haffor's face locked in a look of determination. He could recall the sounds of the man struggling under the High Priest's tool all over again, and a tear of regret rolled down his cheek. "It looks exactly like him," he said, putting his candle in the alcove.

Algus did the same. "He was an example to us all, and one of my worst students," he said with a chuckle. "He had a temper that made the summer sun seem cool and dull. At first, anyhow."

They left the hall quietly, proceeding through it instead of returning the way they came. There were thousands of alcoves, most of them vacant. The hall led deeper inside the temple, to the statues of Viis and Irenick, standing tall in heavy armour. Unlike many that he'd seen before, these stone representations were painted so well that they seemed life like, even though they were two storeys tall. "When I was a boy I would daydream about serving goodness and justice as a paladin. I didn't know anything about Viis, or the rest of the pantheon."

"I bet you had a little wooden sword and plank shield, defeated imaginary baddies with your friends in the fields," Algus said.

"I rescued a few maidens too," Lonen added. "Got rescued by a couple a few times, now that I think of it."

"I used to make hammers out of a stick and false rock," he said. "It's this stone they used to find in the mountain sometimes, so brittle you can crush it in your hands. I'd bash my friends over the head with that and send dust everywhere. They were pretending to be beasts from the pit, so it had to be done, you understand."

Lonen couldn't help but smile in response. There was something about the old dwarf that put him at ease. "If I could start over, I would have run from the Lucent priests. Run until I found a priest of Miradu."

"Let's strike a bargain," Algus said. "We'll talk about your time with your old order. You tell me everything, all your experiences with them from the very first day they found you, and I'll start training you. You want to start over, Lonen? Then do. Make a confession out of all your misspent days, and I'll forgive you, just because I can tell you need someone to. Then your new life can begin."

"When can we start?" Lonen asked.

"Today, my boy. Now, tell me where you've been, and what you've done so we can start fresh."

he Nomads of Amberstone seemed to do most things together. Meals, hunting, travelling and deciding when to rest and when to wake up especially. The cook fires in the middle of the camp were busy preparing breakfast when Rendiran woke, too soon for his taste. He was used to waking early, but the night before had been long, and it felt as though he hadn't slept at all.

Everyone else in his tent had risen and left already. He found Marjay and Crista by the large cook fire beside the lake. Tadrin and Oria were with them, each eating a bowl of some kind of porridge with vegetables and fruit. Rendiran joined them after washing his face, but didn't feel like sitting down. His legs wanted to wander, so he walked along the lake's edge until he reached another cook fire, but no one was breakfasting there. Instead, there was a large boiling pot that they were putting several types of eggs into.

Keeping his distance and minding his business, he worked at the large bowl in his hand, looking out over the serine lake. "One of the most beautiful things I've ever seen," Master Nause said as he joined him. He was peeling the shells from boiled robin's eggs and putting them into a small leather sack at his side. Niomer the Guide was close behind, healthy and grinning.

"Nature is an amazing force. It can create storms that change the world, or a place of serenity that we never want to leave," Rendiran said.

"I wish I could take my people here," Nauso said. "If they saw this they would never return to Brightwill."

"I wish you could too, but I understand. You can't let the momentum of a resistance fail," Rendiran said. "Many refugees have told me about the cleansings in Brightwill, how the Ondi suffer there." He wanted to go on. So many of the mourning people he comforted in his life spoke of how their families and friends were murdered by humans who didn't want to see Ondi magic rule over them again. It was senseless and cruel.

"You truly are a priest by practice, aren't you?" Master Nauso said. "When they explained who you were, I thought you were a traveler, another man pursuing knowledge and helping when it was convenient."

"I try to be more, but until only days ago I was a creature of the temple. I helped whoever I could, healed people every day, though I was still too young to be placed with one community. I saw people from the entire city and beyond, so I can't say I came to know anyone particularly well, not like a real priest with a congregation of their own. I suppose that was for the best though, I have a great interest in magic and the histories."

"I could see the struggle, between continuing study and settling in with one congregation. Do you think that's a choice you'll have to make in the future?"

"Not if I continue on the path of sorcery, which seems to be where my feet are pointing. If you asked what I was right now, I don't think I could tell you, if I'm being honest. A bit club-footed, limping around since the toes on my foot won't be returning. Maybe a little too conspicuous with this staff. A little afraid of this new power at times, but confident in the little I know. What else did they tell you about me?"

"You can use all three types of magic, divine, vulgar and the weaving way. It's extremely rare," Nauso said.

"I hate that term, vulgar magic, but I suppose it is. As for weaving, I've been seeing patterns, so I'm starting to get an understanding but I wouldn't call myself a practitioner."

"They seem to think you will be," Nauso said. He finished peeling the last of his robin's eggs and flicked the shells off his fingers. "I hope that when it comes time, I can enlist your help."

"I hope so too, I would like to see the Ondi return to Brightwill," Rendiran said.

"I sometimes wonder if it's worth the misery of that place. Whatever the Ava-Ondi didn't enslave or burn, it looks like the humans are set to crush or poison. Time will tell. Good luck, Rendiran. I have to get into position."

"Position for?" Rendiran asked.

"You'll see," Nauso said with a wink.

Niomer the Guide stepped in beside him then. After a moment's hesitation, the smaller man embraced Rendiran vigorously, squeezed then let go. "Thank you, Priest. You have given me life again. I was feeling like one of the dead, heart so slow and pieces so broken or missing."

"You're welcome," Rendiran said. "I didn't want to make a big presentation of the act, but the Edlers wanted to see my work, you understand."

"No, but it changes nothing," Niomer said. "I will see you someday, when you cross between worlds. Maybe you heal me then too."

"I hope I won't have to, but I will."

"Thank you again. I get ready to lead Master Nauso. Part of Wandering Wood will cross Brightwill soon, it'll be his only way back for a long time."

"You can't use a portal?" Rendiran asked.

"Nauso is about to receive a gift and can't bring it though portal. Good-bye Priest."

Before Rendiran could return to his friends at the cook fire, Oria and Tadrin ran to him, Marjay and Crista weren't far behind. They were joined by Matron Erriyane, who was carrying a pair of boiled chicken's eggs. "We're going to see a dragon today!" Oria said to Rendiran.

"Not some normal drake, a real dragon," Tadrin clarified.

"Drakes are normal now?" Rendiran asked, amused.

"Erriyane says that Lonilae only gives birth to one dragon out of a bunch of eggs, the rest are drakes, so the dragons are rare."

"Children," Matron Erriyane said, holding the boiled eggs out to them. "Each of you take one and stand over there with the others. Peel the shells off and offer it to Lonilae when she comes out of the water. Be careful, and be calm. Best behavior only, she's a very special dragon."

The children agreed, and Oria made sure to take Marjay with her by the hand when she joined the other children. "Apparently I'm going as a witness," he said. "I hope this dragon doesn't mind humans."

"The Ava-Ondi killed most of the dragons, humans are nearly blameless, boy," Matron Erriyane said without paying much attention to him. "You should be safe."

Crista gave Rendiran his staff and his bag. "They're taking the village down. Everyone is moving on after this."

"What's about to happen?" Rendiran asked.

"Lonilae is coming to give three young dragons to Masters who are returning to Brightwill, and to see us before she changes lakes. She was once called Xakshiss, a dragon of the wild, where she ranged from the great ocean to lands unseen by any man or ondi. She crossed realms over a century ago, and when she returned home, to the world you come from, she found that nearly all of her children and dragons she called friends had been killed by the Ava-Ondi and the humans murdered the rest. Instead of taking revenge, she decided to transform herself into a Quaso, a dragon that is both male and female that can spawn eggs several times a year. She uses dragon stones to resurrect old blood lines, even create new ones, so we search for them and the artefacts made from them and bring them to her."

"I thought dragon stones were only used to help a dragon navigate, like a compass," Rendiran said.

"They are that and much more. A dragon's essence can be summoned from them if they are used properly. Eventually all the dragon stones we bring her are exhausted of their essences, but she keeps most of them, others become gifts. Our smith has been given two."

"So one day these skies will be filled with dragons and drakes," Rendiran said, looking up.

"The Wandering Wood will not outlast your generation, I'm afraid," Erriyane said. "It is in its final days. Like us, all the dragons born here will have to return to your world. I'm going to travel with you to meet with the dwarves, our distant kin to see if I can begin finding a place for us there. The Weaving Masters are taking dragons back with them so they can learn about Brightwill and show humanity that they are not like the oppressors of old."

They were interrupted as several juvenile dragons, only as long as Rendiran was tall, leapt free of the water at the shoreline. They were swift, skimming along the water's edge as they looked at the people gathered. Matron Erriyane smiled and tossed a boiled and peeled egg into the air. It was snapped up by a glimmering silver dragon who circled her with a grin on his short maw before taking flight across the lake. "The eggs are most of her children's favourite treats. That one was called Grigna. He visits me on his own sometimes and I teach him about weaving magic."

A large, smooth white and light blue dragon with a friendly looking face emerged from the water. She was the size of a team of four horses, and several tiny dragons clung to a crown of silver horns on her head and down her short neck. "By the Goddess," Rendiran gasped quietly. "I've never seen a more beautiful creature."

Lonilae's eyes widened in surprise as she turned and looked at Rendiran. "Beautiful, he says, and he has a shiny," she said as she crawled on strong fore and hind legs in his direction, dragging her heavy belly across the grass.

He noticed she was looking at his staff and held it out to her. "A gift given to me by a great man, Haffor the Paladin," he said, offering her a little history.

The dragon's joyful expression faded a little as she neared him, her face so close that he could only focus on one of her big green eyes at a time. "Haffor who was brave and died?" she said sympathetically.

"You knew him?"

"I see his mark on you, how you remember him. You keep his gift." She nudged the staff with her nose. "Who are you, who walks with all magic?"

"I'm Rendiran, it's good to meet you, Lonilae," he said.

"How'd he know my name?" she asked Crista, who gently petted the front of her snout.

"We told him," she replied. "He's trustworthy."

Rendiran patted her just above the upper lip as well, catching a glimpse of the smallest dragons he'd ever seen. They lounged and yawned atop her head, protected by her crown of horns. Some of them were small enough to fit in the palm of his hand.

"You should visit with everyone else," Matron Erriyane said cordially, gesturing towards the people who gathered with boiled eggs in their hands. "They brought you the only gift you've ever asked for."

"Oh, treats from birds," she said with a smile.

"The masters came as well. They're prepared just as you requested."

"Masters? Oh, the Weaving Way Masters, yes. I forget things sometimes, especially when there are shinies," she said, taking a long, parting look at the head of Rendiran's staff before turning towards the rest of the crowd. The first one she approached was Oria, who was suddenly terrified, backing into Marjay. He held her free hand as she turned her head away from Lonilae, who smiled and approached her slowly.

"No, no-no-no-no, that's a dragon!" Oria whimpered, squeezing her eyes shut.

"Oh, you don't have to fear. I only eat plants and fish in the water," Lonilae soothed as she stopped within arm's reach of the girl.

"It's okay, Oria," Tadrin said, approaching Lonilae with a few of the smaller Ondi-Ne children. They all offered a hard-boiled egg which the dragon plucked from each of them using only her lips.

With Marjay's encouragement Oria finally opened her eyes and shyly offered the egg she held in her hand. Lonilae looked at the girl for a moment before gently taking it. "People see a little girl when they look at you, Oria, but I see a powerful paladin," she said. Oria's jaw dropped, and she watched as the dragon turned to Tadrin. "Another paladin who hides in a little boy. I see the hands of Miradu's children, and I knew her, I loved her when she was alive."

Lonilae turned back to the water so quickly that the tiny passengers in her crown rolled around and struggled to remain there. Without a moment's hesitation, she disappeared into the water. As the crowd was beginning to question her actions, she returned. With care she placed a heavy, misshapen but smooth glimmering black and grey stone at Tadrin's feet, then another in front of Oria. Despite the fact that the dragon had no problem carrying them, they looked heavy, perhaps almost as heavy as gold. "The stones of Miradu, from her body. Ask her dwarves to make you your armour and your swords when the boy and the girl are gone. I will see you again."

Marjay urged Oria to pick up the black, blue and white stone, and she couldn't lift it, neither could Tadrin. Lonilae laughed and slowly shook her head. "The little paladins will need help for a while before they can carry their armour." She turned to Master Nauso then, who had a Master to his right and left.

"I trust you will teach and protect my children," she said. Rendiran expected the adoption would be surrounded by ceremony and vows, but was surprised to see Lonilae pluck a tiny dragon from its home in her crown and give it to the first master, who handled it with more care than its mother. It began to cry, a familiar baby's wail that was much louder than he expected from a dragon so small. Lonilae gave it a kiss, which stopped the din for only a moment. "This one is called Mezia, my daughter."

Mezia began to cry again and the Master, a woman who looked half panicked, put a hard boiled robin's egg into the hatchling's mouth. It stopped and chewed, cooing at her after swallowing. "They are still fickle when they are this small, easily won with tasties and shinies."

"Why does she speak like that? It's a little..." Rendiran hesitated to finish his thought.

"Childish?" Matron Erriyane offered in a whisper. "Yes, when she took that form it was a transformation of the mind as well. It's not some weaver's trick, but a real change that she won't be able to undo for centuries. I have a theory that it simplified her mind a little, but she still sees more in people than anyone I've met. It's most likely a defensive measure, being able to see into a person's being as she does. Some of her children are already far more articulate though, which frustrates her from time to time."

Rendiran returned his attention to the adoptions as Lonilae finished giving the second child to a dwarven Master with no hair on his head, but a great beard bound by silver rings. The tiny blue dragon, named Sosala already seemed content in the dwarf's hand while he sloppily chomped on an egg.

Lonilae gave the smallest dragon of the three, tiny enough to fit into a chicken's eggshell, to Master Nauso. "This one is named Oroza, and he has been in my crown for years, watching and listening. It is the one you saw me hatch last time you came to this realm."

The Masters all knelt and lowered their heads. "We will treat them as if they are our own children."

Lonilae and the rest of her children returned to the lake then, her sleek body sliding into the water, barely making a wave. "I'll never forget this, nor will I speak of it," Rendiran said.

"Speak of it if you like," Maron Erriyane said. "There are thousands of lakes here, and Lonilae moves from one to another often. Her drakes are everywhere, hundreds are full grown now and all will answer her call above all others. Besides, the doorways to this realm are always changing, only the very best travelers can reach it now. That's why Crista's attempt resulted in a terrible misadventure. She is far from mastering the art of travelling from one realm to another."

"I've learned my lesson," Crista said.

"I'll continue to teach you, as I teach Rendiran the secrets of weaving," she replied. "He will be a Weaving Master."

"That is a generous offer, but I have to remain in Forge Hin, I can't travel back here with you," Rendiran said.

"I decided last night," the Matron said. "I've been Matron of this tribe long enough. I will go to Forge Hin, learn about and negotiate with the dwarves, teach you as you raise your little paladins. If you want to teach them to weave as well, I will help with that too. We need to do our best for all our children, so perhaps I'll teach a few young dwarves the art as well. I hear there are few weavers left among their people."

"Well, I would be happy to learn," Rendiran said. "You'll find I'm a dedicated student."

"Yes, I'm sure. We should go now, I've said my farewells," Erriyane said. "Diodan will carry one of Miradu's dragon stones, I'm sure Marjay can mule the other." She accepted her staff from a young Ondi-Ne man. It was a lovely piece of wood that twisted around several river stones.

"Be kind, Auntie," Crista warned. "Marjay's a good man."

"Yes, yes, but look at him. He's got more muscle than some horses, what is that for if not for lifting and carrying?"

"I don't know, guarding and fighting?" Crista countered.

"I must begin conjuring our portal, make sure everyone's ready. Rendiran, you will stay here and concentrate on watching how I channel the elements into this. You won't understand most of it, but you have to start watching for patterns sometime."

Rendiran watched as every colour of light began to focus into a circle in front of Erriyane, and for a moment, he could see what she promised: a pattern so simple that he was sure he'd be able to recall it. The rest was too intricate for his amateur eye to comprehend, but it was a promising start.

42

No legend, scroll or book prepared Rendiran for the secrets of Forge Hin. Erriyane's portal took them directly to what she called an Ondi Travelling Door. One moment they were in the Wandering Wood, the very next they were in a cavernous, dark chamber. It was as simple as moving through any doorway, and it took his mind several moments to adjust to the idea that they were in an entirely new place.

They hadn't emerged into the darkness of the latest hours of the evening, but the darkness of a place that had its doors shut long ago, an utter black. The still air tasted stale. "Give us some light, Rendiran," Erriyane said. "Use that gaudy staff of yours."

He realized then that the staff was barely visible, the intense glow it had while he was in the Wandering Wood was gone. With a thought he urged it to brighten, and the large room was so illuminated that it was as though someone turned on a white sun.

The cringing and complaining of his companions abated as he made adjustments so it wasn't quite so bright. The large room was entirely made of stone, and in every direction there were circular alcoves. In the middle of the room there were old desks with high stools, and rows of benches. "What was this place?"

"The Farland Room," Erriyane replied.

"Ondi who mastered travel across this world used to summon portals for people here," Crista said. "This is the largest portal room I've seen though."

"They didn't do it for free, mind you," Erriyane added. "The lesser portal mastery, the one that allowed you to transport people across only this world, used to be a respected profession. Few dwarves mastered it when this kind of travel was common, and the rest of the Ondi who were masters fled or were caught and murdered by nervous-brained humans."

The sound of a heavy door opening drew their attention to the far end of the room. A pair of young dwarves rushed in with lanterns in hand. "Travelers!" they looked Rendiran and his group over, then ran back the way they came before anyone could talk to them shouting; "Travelers! Travelers have come through the Farland Room!"

"Well, that wasn't the welcome I expected," Marjay muttered.

Erriyane marched towards the tall doors with the rest of the group close behind. Tadrin and Oria were wide eyed and open mouthed as they took the large space in, admiring the arches and artfully carved stone. They were met there by four dwarven guards at the entrance, who were taken aback when she faced the nearest one nose to nose. "I am Matron Erriyane Ossim, Keeper of the Amber-stone and Weaving Master. This is Rendiran, a Priest who has been charged with the delivery of Tadrin and Oria, who are gifts from Irenick and Viis. I am also accompanied by my Grand Niece; Crista and a human guard, Marway."

"Marjay," he corrected.

"Don't interrupt me, I'm getting us an audience with the King," Erriyane snapped.

A crowd was gathering, and Rendiran spotted Tadrin's father at the rear. "I think the only audience we should be interested in is Tadrin's parents." He took the boy's hand and nodded at Marjay, who followed him as Rendiran gracefully led the boy into the crowd. "Three blessings to you," he said to the curious people of the mountain as they parted for him. They quietly returned the sentiment, which was reassuring, since he wasn't entirely sure the people of Forge Hin still used it.

As soon as Tadrin saw his mother and father, who looked healthy, whole and well taken care of, he burst into a run. They knelt down and caught him in their arms. Ander was right behind, leaping from Marjay's arm, scampering across the stone floor and trying to get in between Tadrin and his parents, earning him a place there. Rendiran knew what should happen next, and knelt down to Oria, who watched the reunion with tears in her eyes. "I know Tadrin's parents would like to meet you too, would that be all right?"

Oria nodded as Marjay watched, smiling at her and Rendiran. He took one of her hands, while Marjay held the other. Tadrin's father was the first to notice them, then his mother, who wiped a shower of tears away. "This is Oria, a gift from Viis, and this is her guardian, Marjay," Rendiran introduced. Everyone was watching, he could only assume that word of their arrival in the world had spread to Forge Hin, and that they were expected. "Oria, this is Lesta and Nebrin, Tadrin's mother and father," Rendiran introduced.

Tadrin turned and wiped his tears away, offering Oria a hand. She took it, her lip quivering, and Lesta drew her closer, so she and her husband could encircle them both in a glad embrace.

THAT EVENING, shortly before the feast celebrating the lives of Haffor and his paladins was to begin, Rendiran, Marjay, Crista, Oria, Tadrin and his parents were invited to the private chambers of the King. The rooms where the King and his family lived were above the Great Hall, and the children's eyes darted from one tapestry to the next. Each told a story, but as they neared the middle of the private household, they became more interesting. At first there were generals and kings leading their armies against men, then Ava-Ondi. After the first half dozen there were depictions of great duels, paladin heroes, a beast that seemed to be made of darkness, a pair of dragons fighting each other, and finally a dwarf standing atop the head of a great dragon so large that only a horn and one corner of its eye fit on the tapestry.

"Dwarves kill dragons?" Oria asked.

"Only the bad ones," Nebrin said. "I think I know that story, my father used to tell it to me, I'll tell it later."

When they were led to the King's door, they found it open, and several servants were busy carrying gold plated lamps, and baubles from his room. The King, dressed as almost any working dwarf would be – in fine linen clothes and a leather vest – noticed them. "Oh! Come in, come in," he invited, showing them to a large room with several soft seats.

Another dwarf who was a little taller and much more well-muscled than the King entered the room carrying a wooden case filled with fine silverware. "I don't think this has ever been used," he said. "My wife would love to have this by the table." He stopped and looked to the visitors, smiling after a moment.

"This is my son, Kaffon. He is the master blade smith in Forge Hin," the King introduced proudly. "Kaffon, this is Tadrin and Oria," he gestured to the children in the wrong order.

"I'm Oria," she protested. "He's Tadrin."

"Well my sight must be going," the King said, making a show of rubbing his eyes and taking another look at the pair. "Ah, now I see it. Let's see if I can introduce the rest of you by the stories I've already heard." He went around the room, introducing everyone to his son, who offered a thickly calloused hand to each of them in turn.

"Pardon us, Your Highness, but would you like to sell any of the paintings or other wall hangings?" asked a servant after the introductions were complete.

"Only the gold sconces and that ram's head, the rest is family history," the King replied.

Paintings of his family going back many generations decorated the walls, and there were fine side tables that were quickly being emptied of gold and silver ornaments. "Actually, have a rest, we can continue this later," he told the busy servants. They bowed and took their leave. "I'm having some of my more unnecessarily gilded things sold. My family's coffers were mismanaged by my brother and then raided by the Regency Council. The only things left are baubles and gaudy gold things I have no care for, so I'm having them sold or melted down. I'm afraid I'm the poorest King I know," he said, in surprisingly good humour. "It's a good thing Miradu and I had long discussions about the true value of gold and silver. Please, sit, no kneeling, bowing or curtseying, please."

Kaffon closed the case and raised an eyebrow at his father, who noticed and nodded. "If you think that will gain me favour with your wife, then I can think of no better heirloom to gift to your house. Those dainty forks and knives weren't used in my time either. I'm also having a painting of your grandfather delivered."

"That grim one with him in a cave?" Kaffon asked.

"Aye," Nyder replied.

"Good thing I have the silverware then."

"Aye, do you think you'll need a second? I found two more sets squirrelled away this morning."

"Keep one, sell one," Kaffon said. "You'll might need a fancy setting someday."

"Good thinking," the King said. He turned to the group, who were taking their seats and smiled. "I'm sorry, selling off all the things my brother and our ancestors wasted their coin on while I was away is more complicated than I thought." He noticed that Marjay was not sitting, but stood with a sword in a fine scabbard.

Marjay took the opportunity to hold the King's attention, and knelt with reverence, offering the scabbarded blade. "I offer my deepest condolences for the loss of Haffor. I did not know him long, but he had a talent for making strangers into friends quickly, was a great fighter, and a great man."

King Nyder accepted the sword slowly as Kaffon put the silverware case down and went to his side. It was a little strange, Rendiran had to admit, Kaffon looked older than his father, his first grey hairs showing in his braided beard. The King drew the sword, revealing the magnificently crafted Sword of the Eventide. "Made using the dragon stones found in the skull of Xintaine the Terrible, the only ancient white dragon known to exist, slain by Eventide himself." He admired the fine blade, reading the old Ondi writing as he held tears back. "The sword given to my son on his proudest day."

"When they made him Captain," Kaffon said, putting a supporting hand on his father's shoulder. "Thank you for returning this to us, Marjay."

"How did you meet my son?" the King asked.

"He challenged me to a duel, Your Highness, to see if I was worthy to be Oria's guardian."

"What was the outcome?" Kaffon asked.

"He was the greatest fighter I've ever seen," Marjay replied quietly. He hesitated to continue for a moment. "When the duel was interrupted, we were tied: one to one."

"He must have seen you as worthy," King Nyder said.

"He did, Your Highness," Crista said. "He told me that he'd rarely seen a human fight like him, and that he wanted to offer a place in his company when he returned to Forge Hin."

"Do you want a place here in Forge Hin, Marjay?" the King asked.

"As long as I can remain Oria's guardian, then yes, I would be honoured to call your country home," Marjay replied.

"Then you will have a place here," King Nyder wiped a tear from his eye then brought the sword down, touching Marjay on one shoulder with the flat of the blade. "By the power vested in me by our Goddess, Miradu, I empower you to fight in her name as her children, Irenick and Viis did, and dub thee Sir Marjay, Knight of the Eventide," he said as he raised the sword and brought it down gently on the other shoulder. Kaffon held the scabbard as his father sheathed the sword.

Rendiran braced himself as he remembered the last step in all dwarven knighting ceremonies. Without warning, the King soundly punched Marjay, nearly sending him to the floor, then offered him a hand as he chuckled. "On your feet, Sir Marjay," he said.

Marjay shook his head and stood. "Never been that surprised in my life, thank you, Your Highness."

"My favourite part of the knighting ceremony," King Nyder said, patting the man on the back. "Have a seat."

"You know they don't knight people here anymore, right, Father?" Kaffon asked, his humour improving.

"Then that's another change I'll have to make," the King said. Then he knelt down before Oria and Tadrin, who sat on a small seat together. "Now, I've heard all about you two," he said. "You look like a fine young boy and girl, but not like great paladins."

Both children offered an explanation at the same time; "We're not trained," said Tadrin, while Oria said; "We need training."

King Nyder laughed and ran a hand down his braided beard. "Well, pardon me. Can I tell you a story, it's a short one, I promise." Both children nodded. "Well, a long time ago, before anyone here but me and my son were born, I was a young king. Someone came and threatened my land and my people, and I had to send my army to fight them. I won, but I was poisoned during the fighting. I thought I would die, but a wise man found a way to turn me to stone and make me sleep for a long time while he looked for a cure. What no one knew was that I was awake during that whole time, years and years and years. The poison burned, and I missed my family, my friends. I have a feeling you know what that's like, missing people you love. Well, it went on for so long that I thought I was going mad, and I may have, if Miradu didn't come down and coil around my spirit." He made a slow fluttering gesture and pushed Tadrin and Oria together a little, jostling them before letting them go.

"Miradu asked me if I would like the pain taken away, and I told her I would. She asked me if I wanted her to take my grief, because my brother and wife had already joined her in the High Heavens and I told her no, I would keep that, because it is healthy to grieve a loss. I did like hearing that they were safe with her, though, so I thanked her. It took some time, years, but she eventually purified my body, taking the poison away. While she did so we talked about life, about wealth, about what it was to be a good king, and how I could best serve my people. Then I watched her meet with you," he pointed at Tadrin. "And I thought, that's a good son, he's not prideful, or greedy, and he's kind. The world needs him."

He looked to Oria, who waited expectantly. "Then Miradu met

with you, and I thought that's a good daughter, she is honest, fair in her thinking, and brave. The world needs her, and they need each other."

He cleared his throat before going on. "Seeing that you both had been returned to this world, Miradu turned her attention back to me and said; 'they need you too, Nyder. Your people and your world needs you as well. We've spoken for fourteen years, the madness that was corrupting your mind is gone, and the poison that was ruining your body has become rich, red blood.' I heard a great knock all around me then, and my body became flesh and blood. I knew then that all three of us would be paladins together, so I will begin training at the same time you do. Not to make war, or to tell the world who to worship, but to serve the greater good."

ALSO BY RANDOLPH LALONDE

FANTASY

Brightwill

Highshield Book II

(Coming in 2018, available for preorder now)

SCIENCE FICTION

The Spinward Fringe Series

Spinward Fringe Broadcast 0: Origins

Spinward Fringe Broadcast 1: Resurrection

Spinward Fringe Broadcast 2: Awakening

Spinward Fringe Broadcast 3: Triton

Spinward Fringe Broadcast 4: Frontline

Spinward Fringe Broadcast 5: Fracture

Spinward Fringe Broadcast 6: Fragments

The Expendable Few: A Spinward Fringe Novel

(Also Known as Broadcast 6.5)

Spinward Fringe Broadcast 7: Framework

Spinward Fringe Broadcast 8: Renegades

Spinward Fringe Broadcast 9: Warpath

Spinward Fringe Broadcast 10: Freeground

Spinward Fringe Broadcast 11: Revenge

Spinward Fringe Broadcast 12: Invasion

(Coming in 2018)

The Chaos Core Series

Trapped (Chaos Core Book 1)

Cool Pursuit (Chaos Core Book 2)

HORROR

Dark Arts

And now, for a preview of Highshield Book II:

It was difficult for Rendiran to believe that it had been nine years since he first beheld the great halls of Forge Hin. The things he'd learned since could fill a small library. Oria and Tadrin took to their training and schooling with relish, craving capability and knowledge unlike anyone he'd seen.

There were times he wished he had the same seemingly endless reservoir of energy and interest, but Rendiran's education went well regardless of his less than tireless approach. He did one thing more than anyone else though; read. Anything he found, especially anything on the topic of history, was in his hands and being read within seconds of its discovery. When he finally got his hands on what seemed to be one of the forbidden histories of Miradu, he was more excited than he had been for years. Then he discovered that only five pages were filled. The rest was blank. He searched the rest of the abandoned library in Rigalta, deep in the wild lands beyond the Highshield wall, but found no evidence of a complete original copy. Two weeks later he had all the surviving books and scrolls rounded up, a portal open to Forge Hin where they would be transported to the library, but still no evidence that the book of forbidden Miradu histories he hand in his hand was anything but an introduction.

Some fool named Enos Latta went to the trouble of crafting an elaborate looking to me, writing an introduction that was so grand and flowery that Rendiran couldn't help but get his hopes up, and then stop. He used every magical and alchemical method of checking the blank pages for hidden text that he knew and a few that he learned for the purpose of discovering something – anything – in that tome. Still, nothing but blank pages.

Marjay provided security for the long excursion to the ancient library. He enjoyed his hard earned reading skills and was curious about ancient books. To his disappointment, most of them were in languages that were rarely spoken, impossible for him to read without one of Rendiran's code books, so he helped the Dwarves move rubble and made sure they weren't about to be jumped by beast or man while the work was under way.

When he saw a task he could undertake to help Rendiran with his mysterious book after returning to Forge Hin, Sir Marjay was the picture of curiosity and support. He even went to the lengths of travelling to Zaranoba's Alchemy several days' ride away and asking the master of that shop if he had another way of detecting hidden writing. The solutions he brought back were effective when tested on well-hidden scribbles, but when applied to the book, they revealed nothing.

Then the thought struck Rendiran: who was Enos Latta? The name was absolutely unfamiliar to Rendiran and everyone in Forge Hin. Finally, after inquiring with every learned person he knew, he resorted to asking the wandering spirits. He waited until the darkest hours of the night, when no one would interrupt him before setting all his protections and wards. When he was certain he would be in full control of whatever may visit him, Rendiran sat in the middle of the room with a smoky mirror he chose as a spirit glass. "I call to the near wanderers, the spirits who share this evening with me, and have not moved on to another life or another realm. I ask that you appear to me in this glass, and answer my questions." He waited, staring into the spirit glass, feeling more foolish by the moment. It was a child's game, calling spirits to the glass, used with old poor quality mirrors when boredom set in with the middle of winter. He dropped several old gold coins into a dish of water, a symbolic offering that was meant to lure spirits there, then waited until he nearly nodded off.

"Perhaps I should be more specific," he said, clearing his throat. "I call on any knowledgeable spirits, I am in search of information the living don't have," he sat for a few moments longer. "Please?"

He was beginning to take comfort in the fact that he never trained as a spirit channeler, or as an oracle, so there really was no disgrace in failure when he started yawning. It was during one of these late-night, past bedtime, wide open yawns that he heard a gruff voice from the mirror say; "What ya want?"

Startled, he was on his feet before his mouth was finished closing. Looking down at the mirror, he saw the ghostly face of an old dwarf smoking a pipe. He puffed deeply, smoke issued forth from his nose, and from beneath his beard. "Sorry, I was sure this wasn't working."

"Well, working now, isn't it? What you call me for, elfling?" replied the gruff dwarf.

"I was wondering if you know anything about Enos Latta. I found this book," Rendiran fetched and held up the over decorated tome, "and it's almost completely empty. The introduction talks about the great glory of Miradu, about how the secrets of Wydu will be revealed, and how only the faithful will discover anything."

"Enos Latta? An author? Places can't write books, idiot," the spirit replied with a chuckle. "Enos Latta is an old place, a dead place, a place Miradu would weep to see. Go there with paladins, or not at all, foolish Ondi whelp."

"I don't know the name," Rendiran said, sensing that his time with the spirit was growing short. "Where is it? Is it known by another name in another language?"

"Scale Crest," the spectral dwarf in the mirror said, shaking his head and puffing smoke. "Goin' now, good luck, idiot Ondi."

"Scale Crest?" Rendiran repeated quietly. Then he remembered something. "Thank you, spirit, would you leave me your name so I can make an offering to Miradu for you?"

"Off with you, elfling, and piss on your offering," the dwarf said. "See you soon."

"Farewell, then," Rendiran said with a bow, remembering to be respectful even though the dwarf spirit was anything but. "Go in peace."

Rendiran pulled book after book off his shelves, consulting notes and references to places, people and histories he'd learned over the years. When Marjay found him late that morning he was surrounded by old scrolls, journals and tomes, some of which was from the disused library they just raided. "I'm just triple-verifying something here, but I'm sure. I'm certain we've found our weapon in this upcoming war." He looked to the knight and said; "I know where

Wydu's body fell. We have to go there, it must be done in secret, and it must be done immediately."

Thank you for purchasing and reading Highshield. For the most up to date information and more work by Randolph Lalonde, visit www.patreon.com/randolphlalonde

AN ABRIDGED GUIDE TO NEMORI

This guide is included to assist the reader in their understanding of the broader world of Nemori and the events that shaped the social, political, and religious environment that applies to the historical text it is attached to, Highshield Book I. Brightwill and the New Lands are the main subject matter of the selections taken from the Unabridged Guide of Nemori, but you will find no maps or other illustrations because the New Lands are largely unmapped and artists were difficult to find in Nemori at the time of writing.

While many of the entries here are simple, only including basic facts about people in this world, you will find that several entries go into great historical detail. This is a reflection of when this Guide was written: in the middle of a century that is most well characterized by the sweeping changes that affect everyone and every place.

***Use this guide** as a companion to reading the historical text it is attached to, Highshield Book I, or you can read it afterwards as a selection of stories.*

***One more thing** to consider when reading this guide is that all the entries were written to reflect the status of each character and place as they were at the beginning of the historical text. The changes these things undergo are not reflected.*

A

Aldum: Considered one of the most beautiful cities in the world, it is currently inhabited by humans. The Ondi-Ne are solely responsible for its creation and lived there for hundreds of years before they disappeared. King Hobart, a human ruler that attempted to take the Eastern Provinces in the New Lands for himself during the Liberation War, marched on the city only to find that all the Ondi-Ne and Ava-Ondi inhabitants were gone. He left a garrison there and marched on for less than a year, dying mysteriously in his bed.

Amerano Square: Located in the Shale District of Highshield City. The centre of the poorest area of the City, it is visited daily by acolytes of the Miradu Temple so they can heal people, clean the shrines, hear their woes, and pass out bread as an orator gives a sermon and presents daily news. Festivals are also held there, though guards are not as common as in other parts of the city, so there are many cutpurses and kidnappers.

Ander: A blonde puppy given to Tadrin and Oria by Haffor before he met them. His Sergeant brought them the gift in the morning of his arrival in Highshield City, it was only eleven weeks old, but after two years will grow into a heavy Ondi Riding Dog.

Ava-Ondi: For ages the Ava-Ondi were considered the most intelligent beings on two legs. No one believed it more than the Ava-Ondi themselves. It is widely believed that they were the first to develop written language, mathematics and Weaving Magic. They also practiced vulgar magic, an easier to learn form of spell casting that comes at a much higher cost. Through the majority of recorded history they have been the rulers.

Only in recent history, since the Liberation War, has Brightwill been absent Ava-Ondi Kings or Queens. In some other parts of Nemori Ava-Ondi are still in power, and the humans who hold Brightwill still fear their return.

Ava-Ondi are normally between three and a half to five feet tall, are thin, pale skinned, and have light coloured hair.

B

Barham the Merchant Guard: The guard who showed Lena and Lonen to the King for three silver. He has often overheard telling visitors that he is "The greatest Merchant Guard in Forge Hin."

Blackamber Keep: A famous structure in Brightwill and the New Lands for its function. It only exists for imprisoning magical beings. It is the only effective prison for magical practitioners and horrific creations when they are not killed instead. Built before the wall by three Master Stone Weavers who have never been named in any historical record.

The caretakers accept any being who is considered evil, has done irreparable harm on a large scale, or who has a powerful sponsor who wants to see them imprisoned. While few people have studied the prison in the last century, so a great amount of detail is not available, some things are well known. The Keep is built into the middle of the southern half of the Highshield Wall. Many Ava-Ondi magicians were brought there during and after the Liberation War. Oxodix the Dragon is imprisoned there in a black orb. The magicians who guard and control the prison draw power from the inmates, focusing it into an ancient porous stone so they can create Blackamber, a substance that is pure magic and pure evil. The Blackamber is then purified using a secret process, and it becomes Quickamber, which they sell to pay for the continued operation of the prison and for profit.

The prison is also famous for The Slots. Most Ondi and human magicians who are imprisoned are placed in channels made from solid granite. The slots are nine feet tall, up to thirty feet wide, with a width that is adjustable thanks to an ingenious system of gears. Each prisoner is chained by the wrists using enchanted silver and given only enough space to stand, breathe but not to kneel or sit or turn. The slots are always less thick than the smallest occupants' shoulders, so no prisoner can sit or turn. Water is poured down on the prisoners once a day, and food is delivered with a long ladle from above. A heavy iron grate is all they have to stand on, and refuse passes through the bars. Once a week the prisoners and the slots are cleaned by quick, thorough flooding.

Of all the styles of imprisonment available in the Blackamber Keep, the slots are the most commonly used since they are considered cost effective, highly secure, easy to maintain, and an appropriate punishment for most of the inmates.

Bounty Day: A day celebrated by farmers and villagers at the end of the last harvest in a year.

Bright One, The: A God who promises His light to any who make pain or blood sacrifices to him. Sacrifices of wealth are also accepted. Whereas most Gods have pantheons that include at least a few lesser Gods that are also revered and sometimes almost equal, the Bright One does not allow this. His pantheon is filled with much lesser beings who were his servants in life, called "Lucents" or "Light Seekers" and they are not to be worshipped.

Shrines to one's loved or admired dead are allowed, but only so the living can pray that the subject of the shrine is in the Bright One's light, not so they can return to life or be communicated with.

It is said that the followers of the Bright One who sees His light will forever seek its illumination for the rest of their lives. They will do almost anything to be in His light again. The ideal sacrifice to the Bright One includes the removal of all features of vanity (ears, nose, fingernails, toenails, sexual organs), then the plunging of a knife in the heart of an enemy. In lieu of that, many of the most dedicated followers scar their faces and the rest of their bodies to draw His attention.

Lucents wear masks when they are in areas that do not approve of, or are not held by the Order of the Bright One. These masks serve two purposes: to hide the scars of the person wearing it, and to mirror the faces of the ignorant, or non-followers around them. This is a method of mocking and dehumanizing people who don't follow the Bright One.

The most common praise and response is: "We clear the way so the Bright One may shine on us." To which the respondent says; "May He shine eternal."

C

Challen: A half Ava-Ondi, half Ondi-Ne High Priestess of the Wood. Many believe that she is still alive, hundreds of years after she betrayed Irekirk and Doro the Dwarf, living somewhere in the wild lands.

Celestial Houses, The: In the High Heavens and all the spirit realms between, Gods and Goddesses fight for territory as their priests and priestesses in the living world compete for the devotion of followers. Divine magic is said to wax and wane depending on the success or failure of the Gods and their representatives on both battlefields. The Celestial Houses is a term for the many Pantheons and Ancient Beings that each have their own realms in the High Heavens.

Chirana, Caves Of: The caves of Chirana were originally a natural formation in the northernmost tip of the Shores of the Small Sea, or New Lands. The dwarves who settled nearby were attacked by Ubnacron, a powerful necromancer after they began exploring them. Irenick, Viis and their knights heard of their trouble, and aided them in rooting out the necromancer. Cerkan Eventide, one of the most formidable knights with Irenick and Viis dealt the killing blow. Shortly after Ubnacron's death, they discovered that the necromancer was defending the caves because there were extensive gemstone deposits there. Further down they discovered large seams of iron and more precious metals. The Knights took no payment from the dwarves, but the incident is one of the reasons why the city of Forge Hin and the province surrounding it worship Miradu. It is the Second Miracle of Plenty.

Creeping Woods: The woodland border stretching from north to south beyond the Highshield Wall. Named centuries ago by a returning expedition east. The moniker held as the woods seem to grow back after being cleared quickly. Regardless of that characteristic, more of the territory is harvested for lumber and cleared for farmland every year. No one on record has ventured all the way through the woods and reached the other side.

Crista Vasto: An Ondi-Ne who is friend to Rendiran, and a wildling raised in the Lower Timber, a forest to the southeast of Highshield City. She is a servant of Miradu, but not inside the order. A hireling who seeks out ancient artefacts and secrets for the the Miradu Temple, she is trusted, but one of a few wildlings that are welcome in any Miradu Temple.

D

Dark Leaf Tea: Dwarven tea that is brewed for longer than most, has a bitter flavor but a soothing aftertaste. It is enjoyed during times of relaxation and in a much more concentrated form to relieve high anxiety. It is also an important export.

Datho Umbra, High Priest: The Justice, the Diviner for the Bright One.

Deri-Sen Training: A specific style of two bladed fighting that originates with the Ondi-Ne. It is an ancient style that employs a straight blade with two edges and a second blade with deep teeth on one side and a sharp blade on the other. It takes years to master the initial forms used to defend and disarm, then the more aggressive forms are easier to learn. The Ava-Ondi embraced Deri-Sen fighting, as did humans to a lesser extent. Thanks to the the culling of the Ondi during the Liberation War, the fighting style has become rare.

Dim Fort, The: The main fortification outside Forge Hin, built by humans centuries ago. Named thusly because it spends half the day in the shadow of the mountains.

Do'lii: Captain Haffor's trusted steed, a stout, heavily muscled white mare. She was enchanted at birth and comes from a long line of horses bred for paladins. Her mother was Proud Maiden and her father was named Iron Clash.

Doro Ofhin: A friend to the Miradu family, but especially Irekirk. He was seen in the High Heavens within Miradu's Valley in the present day. His adjacency during many of the Miradu children's adventures have firmly established him as a lasting legend.

Drikson, Combat Priest, High Priest: A legendary combat priest for the Eventide Guard. The first human to rise to the position of High Combat Priest of Forge Hin and a well-known battle commander.

Duhin: Tadrin's Ondi-Ne Grandfather on his mother's side. He was a wanderer, trader and adventurer.

E

Elise Wirin: Original name of the Grand Matron. Before she surrendered her title as Duchess, she was a daughter of House Wirin, the founders of Worton and holders of the Gronoth Crown, a significant kingdom with lands in Brightwill and on other shores.

Ellaun: An abandoned Ondi city in the Wandering Wood that is set atop and within the Rippe Shards. In ancient times, it existed in Inerese, well into the interior of the continent. It was a peaceful city that all the Ondi called home, including Ava-Ondi, Ondi-Ne, Ondi-Un and the now extinct Ru-Ondi. It was a centre of trade, travel, and the largest focal point for the Weaving Way anywhere for centuries.

A travelling and weaving master named Onru-Kun and his disciples opened three forbidden portals while searching for a place of great power and brought a terrible enemy into the world. Some say they were devourer dragons, other experts maintain that parasitical spirits were brought across, while another tome records several species of demon that assailed the city. Regardless of the foe, they could not be defeated. The portals were closed and the city as well as the mountains were sealed then sent to the Wandering Wood. The hope was that the evil inside would wither over time in the Wandering Wood, which smothers such contamination.

No one has broken the seals that hold the doors of Ellaun closed since its arrival in the Wandering Wood.

Erriyane Ossim, Matron, Keeper of the Amberstone and Weaving Master: Crista Vasto's Great Aunt.

Eventide Guard (Order of the Eventide): The Miradu Pantheon Order of Paladins. Named after the first Knight who was a close friend to Irekirk, the founder of the Miradu Faith, and Eventide's daughter, who founded the order of Paladins in his name.

F

Farland Room: A large space in Forge Hin and some other old major cities dedicated to portal transportation. They were largely abandoned and sealed off after the Liberation War since most of the masters who summoned portals for a living in such places were hunted down and murdered or escaped.

Forge Hin: The first city of the dwarves in the New Lands, located in the northern most mountains on the west coast. Hin translates literally into "the solid, level place where a forge should be built."

G

Gachin Province: A province of the Hullen Kingdom in the New Lands east of Brightwill. The capitol is Highshield City and part of its success as an agricultural centre is thanks to the Hurien River, which passes through it, eventually letting out to the sea. This prominent Eastern Province was first established over nine centuries ago by the Lords of the Ardes Kingdom and the Miradu Faith.

Great Carn: The neighboring mountain to Hin.

The Great Key: A mountain beyond Highshield Wall. Stones near the top are roughly shaped like a key.

Gold Wine: Not actually a wine, but a potion that uses a tiny amount of Quickamber and many ingredients that enhance its effects, increasing the subject's focus, power to twist reality and give the immersing the imbiber in a euphoric state.

Gomal: a slightly portly human who wears blue and brown rough robes in the new tradition of a Miradu Temple Healer. He spends little time healing in the temple. Instead he performs the role of Master Interrogator and disciplinarian for the Temple Guard.

H

Haffor Entin: Captain of the Miradu Paladins, the Eventide Guard. He is a ninety-six-year-old Dwarf who hails from Forge Hin, a great city where many paladins are trained. It is also his ancestral home. His brother is the Master Blade Smith in Forge Hin and for the Miradu Temple, named Kaffon. Haffor surrendered his right to rule after his uncle died, leaving the Regency Council of Forge Hin to continue running the dwarven province.

Hidel of Lightcliff (Commonly known as **Hidel Lightcliff**): A divine sorcerer who was Rendiran's last trainer before he departed the **High Miradu Temple.** He is a rare Ava-Ondi and Ondi-Ne half-breed who is partial to smoking many different substances in his pipe, and prone to sudden bouts of restlessness after long periods of study.

Hinsha River: The deepest and second longest river known in the Eastern Provinces. It passes through Eimlar Province, a part of the Shenda Kingdom and is largely used for the transport of goods to the sea, then to Brightwill. It is also the most polluted river in the Eastern Provinces.

King Hobart: A human ruler that attempted to take the Eastern Provinces for himself during the Liberation War. He marched on the city only to find that all the Ondi-Ne and Ava-Ondi inhabitants were gone without a trace. He left a garrison there and marched on for less than a year, dying mysteriously in his bed.

Horoli "The Bear" Mire: A famous friend of Irenick's who was an unusually large half Ondi-Ne who was well known for turning into a vicious bear during combat, or a large, furry comical version of the same during celebrations. It was considered luck to bring him an ale while he was in that form during solstice celebrations. He was last seen after the funeral ceremony for Miradu, Irenick and Viis, but some say he still wanders the woods beyond the Highshield Wall.

Hounfeast - the celebration of the arrival of the planting season. Dwarves of Forge Hin celebrate the melting of lake ice with swimming, sunning, and the giving of gifts that are typically made during the coldest weeks of the winter. The occasion is also marked with the eating of red pie, which is made from sweet pale tubers that turn red when baked. The celebration is said to be "something you'd never forget, especially if you bring a few things to give your favourite dwarves."

The Hullen Kingdom: Device for the Hullen Kingdom a ram and a horse head facing right, as though the two beasts were running together. The Hullen Kingdom is only two generations old, founded by King Ormet I of House Hullen, the first land to be captured belonged to an Ava-Ondi, Queen Irissus IX. It was called the Kingdom of Ardes then, and was one of the few prospering Kingdoms in Brightwill that allowed humans to be free. All slavery except the enslaving of debtors was outlawed for every race. King Ormet I took advantage of this, and stoked the hysteria that existed at the time surrounding Ava-Ondi rulers, inciting a revolt against her. He tortured and murdered everyone with a claim to the Ardes throne publicly, often in his own throne room and in front of his then young son, Ormet II, an endeavor that took months. After his first year on the throne he renamed the Ardes Kingdom to Hullen, claiming that his ancient ancestor ruled over the land when it was known by that name. All evidence points to Ormet I and his ancestors living as peasants and slaves on the border of the Ardes Kingdom and there is no proof that there was ever a royal line attached to Ormet I that was not recently manufactured.

The modern Hullen Kingdom encompasses one ninth of Brightwill, two thirds of the New Lands to the east (including Highshield City and half of the wall), and is ruled by Ormet II, who is known first and foremost as a warlord.

The Hullen Kingdom and Forge Hin: At the conclusion of the Liberation War, the Regent Council of Forge Hin attempted to enter trade talks with King Ormet I with hopes of continuing a lucrative trade deal they had with the Ava-Ondi Queen, Irissus IX. Instead of penning a new deal, King Ormet I threatened to invade Forge Hin and the surrounding lands unless they become a province of the Hullen Kingdom and submit seven tenths of everything their province produces, just like the other Miradu Faith provinces in the New Lands. After much consideration, the Regency Council saw no other option than to agree. Since then, seven tenths of everything Forge Hin and the surrounding northern province produces has gone to the Hullen Kingdom in Brightwill, and the dwarves have survived on the remainder.

I

Imartine Pantheon: A fallen pantheon with only a few remaining temples in the east. The Bright One's followers, the Lucents, and the King that supports them – King Tividus – are largely responsible for its downfall. Some Wydu followers are aware that their Trickster God manipulated King Tividus using well placed agents and by sending his oracle dreams to convince him and the Lucents to destroy that Pantheon.

Imp: A scrawny, large-eyed, pointy eared, short creature that can be found well past the Highshield wall. They are not unnatural creatures, but a diversion of the root race that evolved into every type of Ondi. They are normally between one and a half and three feet tall, and curious by nature. The imp found in nature is also sometimes shy, only engaging their curiosity when they thing no one is looking or after they've determined that there is little chance of harm. They build nests half way up tall trees using any found materials, and can sense magic more easily than any creature known, so an imp nest that has existed for several years almost always has a naturally or hand crafted enchanted item inside. Natural imps click and blow puffs of air at each other, as their main form of communication, reserving whistling for more urgent messages. They don't have their own written language, but know how to use basic tools and understand trading. They have been known to sneak into villages to steal food and baubles, and if they are not caught for long enough, they can become so bold that they steal during the light of day.

Imp, Enchanted: Imps are highly susceptible to magical enchantment, enhancement and manipulation. Wizards will commonly capture or pay for a natural imp and cast a binding spell on it so they must serve them or maintain a home. Some kinder wizards have been known to befriend imps instead after rescuing them from captivity. After an imp is prepared to serve a wizard, they are normally enchanted. Sometimes they are enchanted with an element such as fire and sent into a village or town with flaming skin. The imp is unharmed, but often runs from home to home in a panic, setting the settlement ablaze. One famous imp, Oyolo, was enchanted permanently with the element of air so thoroughly that he can leap hundreds of feet and glide for miles with the assistance of two large fans he was given by his master, Kirta the Artificer, who uses him as her messenger. Unfortunately, Oyolo and Kirta's example, in which the two are good friends, is rare.

Most imps are trained to steal, enchanted as bombs and sent to difficult to reach enemies, or kept as highly agile but disposable soldiers. A captive imp is normally driven by fear, so as long as they are afraid of their master more than anything else, they will follow through with whatever order they're given. If they are magically bound to their master as well, they will not be able to disobey until the bond is broken.

Inerese: The old name of the Eastern Shores, New Lands, or New Provinces. Often used when Ondi or (even dwarves) refer to the whole continent, not just the settled areas and the known wild lands.

Irenick the Guardian: A God within the Miradu Pantheon. In life, Irenick was Miradu's half Ondi-Ne first son. He was extremely large for a half Ondi-Ne, taller than most humans. In death, he is the God of Justice, and is often worshipped by the poor because it is believed that He has sympathy for them the most. He sits at Miradu's left side. Some believe that He grants miracles to followers who are fair and good to others. A smooth river stone at a shrine that is built by his followers is a perfectly acceptable substitute for a few coins, especially since His Laws demand that the poor bring no metal or precious things to his donation plate. All his donations are collected by the Temple of Miradu. The river stones are often used in the construction of new temples. His father was named Rin, an Ondi-Ne.

Irenick and Viis Ceremony: A Call For Justice: This is a special ceremony that can be performed at a shrine to Irenick or Viis where the petitioner demands justice for themselves, a family member or a friend be visited upon a person who has wronged them. The person must be clean, have atoned for their own wrong doings already, and have a broken iron dagger or sword. They approach the shrine with only their broken weapon and a bag with an offering that is a significant portion of their wealth. When they place these things before the shrine they must say; "Irenick, Viis, my blade has failed me, the laws of this world have failed me. I petition thee to deliver your justice upon those that have wronged us. I will not seek it myself, leaving the burden of the matter to you so I may lighten my heart and go forth."

Irekirk: Irenick's older brother, the founder of the Miradu Faith and builder of the First Temple in Highshield City. After the death of his mother Miradu, brother Irenick and sister Viis, Irekirk began to build a temple and a following for them as an act of mourning that lasted the rest of his life. It is believed that Irekirk lived over ninety years, successfully calling enough followers to the Miradu Faith to draw the attention of Kings and Queens who wished to become allies so the faith could manage land in their stead. While he didn't complete the actions required to see that done himself, the work was completed by charismatic followers he recruited. He set the original laws of the church according to his mother Miradu's philosophies, and let people he eventually placed at the head of his organization select teachings to support them, creating gospels and an extended set of laws for servants of the faith.

He was friends with a famous knight named Cerkan Eventide and they went on several expeditions into the wilds which were recorded but sealed since his death. Only the highest ranking members of the Miradu Faith have ever seen the records of his later travels, when he was more magician than swordsman.

Irekirk was Ondi-Ne of dragon blood, meaning that his father was Ondi-Ne, and his mother, Miradu was a dragon who transformed into an Ondi-Ne woman to couple with her consort. These are rare conditions that many believe create an offspring that is part dragon in some way that is not visible.

The fate of Irekirk is unknown. The most common story about his final appearance is that he attended a great celebration for his lost mother and siblings, slept in a hastily made bed at the foot of his mother's shrine, then left, making a promise to return to a guard named Trin Ume near the entrance of the Miradu Temple in Highshield. Cerkan Eventide departed with him, and disappeared his well. His daughter, Gillian Eventide, found his sword in her scabbard seven weeks later. She became the first Paladin of Miradu, and founded the Eventide Guard.

Irogen: High Magician to Prince Norrich while he watches over Highshield.

J-K

Kaffon Entin – The Master Blade smith for the Miradu Temple and Forge Hin. By the time his uncle, the Regent of Forge Hin, died, he was already an established weapon crafter. When his brother, Haffor, allowed the Regency Council to continue ruling the dwarven provinces, he had an opportunity to take the position of Regent for himself. He took a place at the table of the Regency Council as the Master of Craft instead, providing a voice for all craftspeople in the province.

Kena: A young, promising female dwarf paladin who is a member of the Eventide Guard and follows Haffor.

Knights of Amru: Worshippers of Xanis, a God that believes nature should not be manipulated, especially by Ondi.

L

Lena of Castle Nightbreak: An earth priestess of Wydu who leads two mercenaries to save Wydu's Gift. She is following signs from the Drowned Maid Prophecy given to her in visions had while under the influence of gold wine, and in dreams.

Liberation War: After Coriath trained several humans to use magic he left. Most of his students began training others, and human magic became key to the revolution against Ava-Ondi rule. The Ava-Ondi used their own magic to rule over humanity, and millions of humans were kept as slaves. The Ava-Ondi also kept some of their own and Ondi-Ne as slaves for finer work in their homes. Slaves of impure or mixed blood Ondi were highly prized for fine work, while humans were kept for hard labour or dirtier work.

Less than twenty years after Coriath left, the human uprising successfully overthrew the worst of the Ava-Ondi leaders, and a slaughter of Ava-Ondi and Ondi-Ne that lasted years began. Some Ondi-Ne did work for and were related to Ava-Ondi, but the majority were against all slavery, and stayed away from Ava-Ondi. Even so, the new human rulers didn't spare them because all Ondi use a similar form of magic called weaving. The only Ondi that were spared completely were the Dwarves (Ondi-Un), who were allies with humans and Ondi-Ne, but also too well armed to conquer without incurring incredible casualties. The majority of dwarves did not participate in the war.

Light Seeker: A follower of the Bright One.

Lonen Kerd: A Paladin of the Bright One, in His Lucent Guard, He joined the Lucent Guard after dreaming of becoming a heroic paladin for his entire life. He comes from a farm near the Highshield wall, where the nearest village, Hopbur, is several days away on foot. Little is known about his family.

Lucent: A follower of the Bright One.

M

Marjay: A senior guardsman of the Miradu Temple who escorted Tadrin to Viis' shrine in the middle of the night and then stood watch as Oria was resurrected. He was named Oria's Guardian by Viis during Her appearance after she apologized for not being able to resurrect his daughter, who he lost along with his wife at the end of the Liberation War. While Marjay only looks like he's near mid-life for a human, he is actually nearly sixty. When he discovered his wife and daughter were murdered by Ava-Ondi Nux Assassins, he dedicated his life to hunting the last of them down and killing them. He became a member of a group called the Black Vassals, who hunted escaping Ava-Ondi magicians down and killed them or placed them in Blackamber Keep. While it is not known how many Nux Assassins or Ava-Ondi magicians Marjay killed during his time with the group, it is clear that he rose high in their ranks and lived in Blackamber Keep for a time as a resident guard. At one point he was bested in combat, by what or whom is not known, but when he was resurrected in Blackamber Keep days later and he appeared over twenty years younger.

Something he experienced during his resurrection prompted him to leave the Black Vassals, journey to Highshield City and join the Miradu Temple Guard there.

Mirac Alta: A set of books written by Shene Mirac, a High Priest known for preaching forgiveness and kindness. Mirac was a hermaphrodite seer whose lasting legacy exists in recorded visions that came to be called 'Cold Portents.' Mirac allowed Gods and spirits poses them during many writing sessions. Mirac disappeared mysteriously after writing for the cause for fourteen years, producing twenty-one large tomes that are only available to the record keepers, translators (not all of the spirits wrote in the same language), and highest ranking members of the temple. The arrival of Tadrin, Oria and Nella are foretold in some of the translated text. It is said that their arrival marks the Time of Return.

Miracles of Plenty: These are miracles that occurred during Miradu's lifetime that involve her or her children and the dwarves (Ondi Un). In the first, she prevented the starvation of the first dwarven settlement on the Northern Small Sea Shore by bringing enough food to last them the winter.

The second came years later when Her son and daughter, Irenick and Viis, helped the dwarves liberate the caves of Chirana. The caves led to the first successful dwarven mines on the continent. The third came after the deaths of Miradu, Irenick and Viis.

Only a few years after the founding of Forge Hin, an Ava-Ondi named Sarizix and his white dragon led their armies against the city so they could enslave the dwarves and take everything they had. When they were almost beaten, the first King of Forge Hin, Gannus, had a dream of an old Ondi-Ne city in the mountains. When he woke, he led his people there and discovered the city of Sembado (a name which translates to Tower Garden). The Ondi-Ne said that Miradu came to them and asked that they help King Gannus and his people. With their aid, they defeated Sarizix, and the leader of the Ondi-Ne, Pumin Oxot, tamed the white dragon, who was then named Arexnok. Even tame, the dragon had an evil nature, so the Patron of the Ondi-Ne guided him away from the kingdom, and was never seen again.

There are other Miracles of Plenty, but the aforementioned are the three most popular, and are retold seasonally during ceremonies.

Miradu: The Matriarch of the Pantheon of the same name. Best offerings include gemstones of different quality depending on the suppliant's wealth, tulips of any colour and red roses. At the end of a wedding ceremony in front of her shrine it is traditional for the bride and groom to simultaneously feed each other a piece of traditional Ondi-Ne sweet flat bread, which reflects the Goddess' hedonistic joy and celebration of the union. This tradition has been modified by the modern Miradu faith, where only the groom must feed his wife a piece of sweetened pork instead, which is from an ancient human faith called Field Worship.

In life Miradu was a hedonist who admired beauty, enjoyed comfort, and used magic to grant wealth to herself and others. Her time in civilization became interesting when lords looked to her for advice, and she was given responsibility by the people who loved her. Her lessons came hard as she found herself tricked into using her power for their ends. After being deceived by nine lords and ladies, she retreated to the wilderness.

Twenty-one years later she emerged with children and a new purpose: to provide justice for the low born and anyone else who would join her cause. She still brought a plentiful bounty with her, but she watched for the greedy and careless this time, and anyone who partook too much found their meals rotting in their bellies, and their hands unable to grasp any more of her gifts. During her lifetime, Miradu sought to make the world a place of justice, peace, beauty and happiness. She believed everyone had a right to good health, an opportunity for wealth, and love unless they wanted to hamper the opportunities for others to quest for them.

Miradu Priests: The guiding principal at the core of the priesthood Is as follows: Love calls us, love guides us and in love we serve. This was given to the first healers Miradu took as apprentices during her lifetime.

N

Nauso: An Ondi-Ne weaving master who comes from the city of Ankon in Brightwill. See the novel: **Brightwill** for more information.

Nebrin: Tadrin's father, one eighth dwarf, seven tenths human. He was an apprentice stone mason without a master in Highshield City and was often failed to find employment in his field due to an oversaturation in stone workers while he lived there.

Niami: The Sky Goddess, a woman who is at once maid, woman and crone. Playful but wise, both participant and onlooker. A force for good, but never a judge. She is an Ondi Goddess from ancient times.

Nidela: A master realm traveler who is an Ondi-Ne. She recruits many Ondi-Ne into her coven and tries to teach them the arts of travelling magic. Even though she is a master, and can travel further in a shorter time than most, she still requires a guide to most places. It is believed that she was one of the few Ondi-Ne who know where thousands of their people escaped during the Second Purge (Liberation War).

Nella (Originally named **Shani** after her resurrection) – Wydu's Gift. She was brought into the world by Wydu after he found her spirit wandering in the void. During her first life she was sacrificed by imps to their Goddess and her body was left in a narrow but deep pool.

Nightbreak Castle: The home of the Worshippers of Wydu, those who practice Wydu's Way.

Niomer the Guide – A Guide of the Realms. He is a human magician who learned from the disciples of Coriath and then uncovered the secrets to travelling through realms. He eventually learned that he was part Dwarf, which allowed him to use weaving magic. For reasons he has never revealed, he has dedicated himself to guiding people who are lost between, and in realms to their destinations. Niomer is well known amongst the Ondi, who he helped during the Liberation War in their escape.

Prince Norrich: The representative of the King Ormet II and the Hullen Kingdom. They own the most land in the outer provinces, or New Lands, as they're commonly called. He is closely connected to Miradu's Order and a devout follower of Viis.

Nux Assassins: An order of Ava-Ondi assassins that served the Kings and Queens of Brightwill during Ava-Ondi rule. After the Liberation War they formed a new leadership from the most experienced members. They began to assassinate humans who were responsible for overthrowing their rulers and the new royal families. Before they were eventually hunted down and killed, two new human royal families – the Denylus and the Korden Houses – were murdered along with many other new royals. The Nux Assassins were all trained fighters and many of them used the Weaving Way as well.

King Nyder: A dwarven king who spent ninety-one years in a stone sleep after losing in single combat against an Ava-Ondi Queen named Vishen. Realizing that it was only a distraction, Vishen fled and has not been seen since. During his life he was the ruler of Forge Hin, the greatest dwarven territory on the continent. He has two sons: Haffor and Kaffon his wife was captured and killed by humans while she was visiting King Tuzen, an Ava-Ondi ruler.

O

Odilexa: Great green dragon. Deceased and ascended as the Goddess of the Wild Lands. Seen as an evil Goddess of decay and rot by most Pantheons.

Ofeur Nemon, Esquire: The official Advisor to His Highness, Prince Norrich and longtime friend.

Ondi-Ne: The earliest recorded Ondi-Ne, dating back five ages or over eleven thousand years ago, were savage nature dwellers. They were territorial in nature, short in stature, and highly agile in trees and on the ground. As their ability to write and record history sharpened, and they learned to use the Weaving Way, an appreciation for nature calmed their savage ways, eventually leading to the development of Ondi-Ne philosophy and a highly evolved version of their magic, the Weaving Way.

Most modern Ondi-Ne love peace, many are still nomadic, even though they began building a few cities during the last age. Ondi-Ne warriors are deadly, quick, and have a blade wielding style all their own that compliments the Weaving Way, but allows for a level of violence that reminds many witnesses that they were once savages.

The Ondi-Ne are typically as short as three feet tall, or as tall as five feet, have pointed ears, skin that ranges from tanned to dark, and are rarely fat.

Ondi-Un: A long discarded racial name for Dwarves. They abandoned it in the first age, when they went to war with the Ava-Ondi and lost. They were banished to the mountains, and made their homes there instead of rallying and fighting the Ava-Ondi again. The Ava-Ondi learned to regret sentencing their distant cousins to live in the mountains, since they became masters of mining and metal within a century. Ondi-Un have always been characterized by their overabundance of hair, shorter build and thick bones. After their banishment to the mountains ages ago, the typical dwarf became shorter and shorter, but also more muscular. They are still identified as Ondi because they kept their pointed ears, though they are seldom visible thanks to full heads of hair and their love of broad hats when venturing out from the mountains.

Onhin Mountain – One of the lesser mountains near the Highshield wall. Former home to the Munixen Kingdom which was destroyed by disease when Shani (later named Nella), emerged into her second life. It had become corrupted to the point where most of their people where goblin kind.

Oria Ofshea: Viis' Gift, a born guardian. Her emblem is a blood red right hand on white. She is also right handed. She originally died with her parents in a fire set by Odilexa's followers. Since her parent's souls passed into another life, Viis found a guardian for her named

Marjay, who had lost his daughter and wife at the end of the Liberation War.

King Ormet II – Ruler of the Hullen Kingdom.

P

Pantheon: A group of Gods and Goddesses arranged in a hierarchy. Pantheons can be any size, and can include other types of entities as well.

Pantheon House: A sub-group of a pantheon that can have its own (but normally similar) laws that is led by a deity within the parent pantheon. For example: Irenick is the male God of Justice and Honour, and his House is directly beneath his mother's, Miradu, who is the Grand Matron Goddess and has her own House.

Paulo: Tadrin's best friend in Shaletown, Highshield City. Tadrin was running across the street to see Paulo when the carriage killed him. Paulo was only made aware of it later, when Tadrin was resurrected.

Lake Pirem: One of the largest known lakes on the continent. It is connected at both ends by the Hinsha River, the second largest and deepest river known. Samlen occupies one of its banks.

Q

Quarry Gate: A port city owned and governed by the dwarves of Forge Hin. It is also the closest port to the great dwarven city, only three miles away. Most humans in the area settle there instead of inside Forge Hin.

R

Razthanga, The Light of Salcom (and its ruiner) – A master wizard known for her power, knowledge of human magic, and for her Guardians, who are re-ensouled dead. She is also known for her stunning beauty. She enjoys controlling small populations using stolen power from living sorcerers she captures. Commands an army of imps that are imbued with fire magic. She also collects the bodies of important, powerful figures to use as vessels for spirits she anchors in them. Mother of Damma who was fathered by the Dwarven King. He betrayed her, killed her master Zishthanga the Dark Star. Damma is a student of the Thanga Practice and in hiding.

Rendiran: A Priest of Miradu who specializes in healing. His long face is also often seen in libraries and at social events where mystics are encouraged to exchange knowledge. He has had several mentors who guide him in his quest for arcane knowledge.

He was surrendered to a Miradu Orphanage as a baby and was raised as a healer in the faith, first taken under the wing of Master Healer Jungen Post at the age of nine. He was curing disease and healing people in the Miradu Temple of Highshield City at the age of fourteen.

Rijen: A taller half dwarf, half Ava-Ondi who knew King Nyder well before the stone sleep, and became life-long friends with his son, Haffor. He is a paladin of the Eventide Guard, and has served Miradu for the better part of a century.

S

Samlen: A walled city that is often considered competition to High-shield City located in Eimlar Province, a part of the Shenda Kingdom. The Lucent, followers of the Bright One rule it for King Tividus. All buildings are white washed so the city has a celestial appearance from afar, and a clean appearance up close. It is on the bank of Lake Pirem, one of the largest known lakes on the continent. It is connected at both ends by the Hinsha River, the second largest and deepest river known.

Saserin Temple: One of the oldest Miradu Temples. It was originally a castle owned by Duchess Te'lisne, an Ava-Ondi who was saved by Priestess Caleno, a healer who was travelling through the Duchess' lands at the time of the Lady's illness. What she suffered from is unclear, but afterwards she donated her castle and the lands surrounding it to the Miradu Church. It has been a stronghold where a library of forbidden tomes, scrolls, and etchings are kept along with many artefacts in the centuries since. While many have theories about what is in its vaults, only a few Miradu High Priests and Priestesses actually know.

Seneschal Orn Makil: An older dwarf who can be easily recognized by three greying braids and his silvered breastplate. He is a former paladin and trained in Ondi Blade work. One of the greatest fighters in the land, but retired. He was pressed into service as Seneschal by King Nyder only two days after His Highness awakened from his stone sleep. The sigil of his house is a heavy hoof drawn in a circle with a green background.

Shenda Kingdom: The realm of King Tividus.

Silverport: One of the main port cities on the eastern coast of Brightwill. Within King Ormet II's territory.

Storo: A mercenary hired by Lena to help her retrieve Wydu's Gift.

Surwood: A village northeast of Highshield. It was there that Oria Ofshea and her parents burned to death when they were trapped inside the long house during a raid by Odilexa and Challen's followers.

T

Tadrin: A boy who was killed in a tragic carriage accident at the age of seven. Nebrin and Lesta are his father and mother. His sigil is the crimson hand – a blood red hand on white, the left. He is left handed.

Telin City: Quarry Gate is the name of the harbour that Telin dominates. Behind Telin is Forge Hin. Forge Hin owns both.

Titan Chain, The: The range of mountains running north to south well beyond the Highshield Wall. Magicians and seers believe that there are stones in those mountains that prevent them from far-seeing past them.

King Tividus: Ruler of the Shenda Kingdom in Brightwill with small provinces in the New Lands. Follower and patron of the Bright One and enemy to King Ormet II.

Toriz: One of the many hell realms. A place where magic is wild, twisting and corrupting everything that enters.

Tuur Hin: The old name for the North Eastern Kingdom of the Dwarves, it pays homage to the capitol city and central mountain of their territory: Forge Hin, and the Hin Mountain. Translates from Unso into "Foundation North."

U

Ulleyo The Paladin: Once the greatest of Paladins in the Eventide Guard, he was tasked with being the Grand Matron's protector, always at her side, and she eventually took him as her consort. He failed to save her from an attack by Odilexa's follower that left her severely deformed. After a few months of trying to find her a remedy, he left in disgrace, unable to take the shame of failure. It is a well-kept secret that he is currently imprisoned in Blackamber Keep.

Umner the Dawn Shaper: A High Priest of Miradu who wears the white and black cloaks indicating that he is also a worshipper of her son, Wydu. He was inside the carriage that killed Tadrin. He was on the way to see the Master of Artefacts of the Miradu Order who was arriving in Highshield Harbor after a long stay in Brightwill.

Unso: The ancient language of the Ondi-Un, rarely used by dwarves even in ceremony. It is an ill-remembered language because it dates back to the days before the Ava-Ondi banished the first dwarves to the mountains.

V

Vedon the Seer: A cousin to King Nyder who is extremely talented at seeing what is on the surface of a person's mind and determining whether or not they are telling the truth. He has been an essential member of the court for nearly two centuries, serving three kings and the Regency Council.

Viis: The little sister to Irenick and Irekirk by one year. During her life she merged Ondi-Ne style blade fighting with heavy shield combat, creating the foundation for the fighting style all Eventide Guard are trained in. Most shield bearing paladins from other orders borrow most of their technique from her style as well. Aside from being one of the greatest fighters in history, she protected the weak and served the cause of common morality based on equal justice for all people.

Her life as a paladin was challenged by many knights who believed that champions should always serve a King or Queen. She was also challenged because she was a woman, and only lost three times to a man in her younger years. She only took revenge for one of the losses, Sir Giblin, who gloated and insulted her family when she conceded. A year later he challenged her to another duel, and he demanded they use sharpened blades. Viis allowed it, blocked his opening attack, then put one of his eyes out. He refused to concede, so she struck his helmet off and knocked him unconscious.

The record of Viis' life is required reading for all Eventide Paladins, because she is considered to be the ultimate model of a just paladin. That is not to say that she didn't make many mistakes during her life like any mortal, but they are used as lessons. During her life, she preferred to fight as an equal beside her brother, Irenick, who she could coordinate with instinctively. No matter what obstacle or enemy they faced, they were never defeated when they were together. Her father was named Olm and was Ondi-Ne.

As a Goddess she is looked to as a champion of the weak, prayed to by mothers who want a guardian for their children, by the destitute who wish to rally, and the lost who are seeking a guide. She is referred to as a Guardian, and a paragon of justice alongside her brother, Irenick. Unlike her mother, she had no recorded lovers, though she did fall in love more than once. Thanks to this known history, people who need to be chaste for any reason or length of time tend to pray to her when they face temptation.

Her preferred shrine offerings are quartz of any colour but especially blue, silk (though that is a recent development of the last forty years), and white roses or iris preferably but any white flower is acceptable from the poor.

W-Z

Wandering Woods: A mysterious land that a few travelers over the last three centuries claim to have seen. Everyone who comes back states that they knew that they crossed into it because the plants, the animals, sometimes the weather, and even the sky was different. A few travelers claim they were hunted by strange natives, others have said that they were saved, healed by masked dwellers in the wood. All accounts end with the travelers leaving the forest and being unable to find its boundary again. Many search for it deep in the Wild Lands, past the Highshield Wall.

Well Stone: A specially cut and treated stone of high purity that is imbued with the ability to gather magical power. This power can come from certain types of environments, magical places, but it most often comes from the user channeling vulgar magic into it. Most well stones work best with one or two types of power, the most common of them being life energy.

Wydu: The dragon offspring of Miradu. He became a God in the

Miradu Pantheon and represents wisdom and cunning, which most followers of Miradu or her children reinterpret as trickery.

Most of the details of his life are either lost or hidden by the Miradu Faith or his own following. Of the Miradu Pantheon Gods, he is the least popular and the mere mention of his name is disallowed in many villages.

Yimere: Personal servant, guard and decades long friend to Hidel of Lightcliff, a master divine sorcerer. He is a master blade wielder and in possession of an unknown level of magic. It is rumored that he serves Hidel Lightcliff as a sort of penance for something he did to the wizard a long time ago.

Yut: The Imp Goddess, also the Matron of Fools. When children are lost or a person fears that someone they care about is going to do something foolish, it is common for uncultured people to pray that this Goddess sends her imps to save their loved one. The expression; "Yut-Yut" is still used by mountain people and free folk who don't hold to one Pantheon but pick and choose from the old Gods to create their own. It is an invocation that is meant to protect the stupid or innocent.

For as long as the world has known imps, the symbol of Yut, a beaked woman's head, has been drawn by them. This is their version of the Goddess, depicting a woman who can fly and protect them from being kidnapped, killed or enchanted.